PORTRAIT OF A GIRL

PORTRAIT OF A GIRL

Dörthe Binkert

Translated by Margot Bettauer Dembo

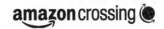

Published by AmazonCrossing, Seattle
www.apub.com

ISBN-13: 9781477823446
ISBN-10: 1477823441
Library of Congress Control Number: 2013923611

Cover design by: Lindsay Heider Diamond

Look at me so that I may exist.
—*Old Egyptian saying*

PORTRAIT OF A GIRL

Maloja, 1898

"Her name was Nika, and she was here for only one summer." Achille Robustelli gazed thoughtfully at the painting hanging on his office wall; tomorrow it would belong to the man standing next to him. "Then she moved on. God knows where she finally ended up."

The painting showed a green landscape and a nude young woman with long strawberry blonde hair gazing at her reflection in a pool of water.

"You mean the woman who posed for Segantini in this painting?" asked the man who had purchased the picture for fifteen thousand gulden. He was a Viennese collector who considered Giovanni Segantini one of the most exciting painters of the era. He took a step closer to the canvas. The painting wasn't very large, about thirty-nine inches high and forty-nine inches wide. It had been completed the previous year, and was dated 1897.

"And how is it that this painting is hanging here in your establishment?" he asked with a note of puzzlement in his voice. "In a hotel, without protection? After all, Segantini doesn't give away his pictures just like that."

"It's a long story," Achille Robustelli replied, his voice suddenly hoarse with emotion. He cleared his throat and asked hesitantly, "Would you like to hear it?"

The collector nodded. "Of course. Every art lover likes to know the provenance of the artwork he acquires." He sat down in one of the easy chairs arranged below the painting.

Achille Robustelli took the seat next to his guest and began his story.

"I met her for the first time two years ago, in 1896. It was toward the end of May, or perhaps it was already early June, and I realized much too late that I had fallen in love with her . . ."

Maloja, May 1896

Gian blinked in the bright light as he looked up. "The sun makes you half-blind," he mumbled, holding up one hand to shade his eyes and pointing skyward with the other. With one finger, he traced the circles a bird of prey was making overhead. Such birds were not uncommon in this rocky part of the Swiss Alps, but remarkable to Gian all the same.

"Come on, let's go," said his brother, Luca. Gian reluctantly lowered his hand, and for the first time noticed a person lying crumpled, motionless, a stone's throw from the path they were on.

It was a young woman. Her eyes were closed. Her bare feet protruded from a long black woolen skirt. One of her ankles was badly swollen. Her shoes lay nearby.

"How did she get here?" Luca asked in surprise.

Gian looked up again into the cloudless sky. "She's beautiful," he said. "She's not from around here."

He looked at the girl's face, reddened by the sun and by sleep, then turned away, as if it wasn't proper to be watching. But Luca continued to stare at her, undeterred. Some blades of grass had gotten caught in her thick hair—slivers of bright green intertwined with her unruly strawberry blonde locks. That seemed odd, since there wasn't a lot of new grass yet, especially not at this high altitude. Even though it was May, and they stood in the noonday sun, the air felt cool.

"Let's wake her up," Luca said. Just then, Gian saw the young woman's eyelids twitch. She was awake, even though she hadn't opened her eyes. Luca tugged gently at the shawl the stranger had wrapped around herself. Cautiously she opened her eyes, blinking in the bright light, just as Gian had done moments before. Then she closed them again.

"She's exhausted," Gian said, "and that ankle of hers doesn't look good."

"You sound like quite the expert," Luca retorted. Then he raised his voice and asked the young woman, "Are you sick? Where are you going?"

She didn't answer.

"Maybe you know where she's headed," Luca said to his brother, "since you seem to know so much about her."

Gian knelt down next to the girl, touching her swollen ankle with a knowing hand. It wasn't unusual for someone in the village or an animal to sprain an ankle. The young woman winced at his touch.

"She's in pain," he announced. "She can't walk. But we'll get her down the mountain to Maloja somehow or other."

"You think we can?"

"Yes," his brother said.

"She's a strange one," Luca said, and kicked away a rock.

But Gian was happy. Finally something had happened, something quite unexpected. He'd heard about meteorites that suddenly fell to earth from space and created deep craters. It felt a little like that with this girl—her appearance had interrupted the eternal sameness of their days.

Luca and Gian were coming down the path from Grevasalvas, where the farmers from Soglio summered their animals. Now that the weather was warmer, they were going to bring the cows up. That morning they'd begun putting the hut in order and building a fence around the pasture.

Luca pulled Gian off to one side. "What now?" he asked impatiently. "What are we going to do with her? Should we just sling her over our shoulders and carry her down?"

"She isn't a ewe," Gian said.

Meanwhile, the young woman was sitting up, leaning against a rock, and watching them. She had picked up her shoes and was holding them.

They could see she was wearing a white blouse under the rough woolen shawl still wrapped tightly around her. The topmost buttons were unbuttoned, so that you could see the hollow at the base of her neck. Luca pushed his black hat back and scratched his forehead. The girl was wearing a chain with a golden locket that glinted in the sunlight. In the center of the locket, a small gem-stone glowed in the sunlight like a drop of red blood. It confused Luca. People who were so shabbily dressed never had any jewelry, or at most, they wore a little cross. It struck him as strange; there was something suspicious about it. He nudged Gian in the side, but his brother just smiled idiotically.

Luca put the stranger's shoes into his rucksack. Then the two boys helped the young woman get up. They held her between them. She grimaced with pain.

"Put your arms around our necks," Gian urged her gently. "You're not heavy; we'll carry you."

She looks like a bird with a broken wing, he thought. It wouldn't have surprised him if she really had wings. Broken wings. Because otherwise she certainly wouldn't have ended up in this place.

Benedetta pulled the soup pot over to the edge of the stove, where it was less hot, deciding not to add any more wood to the fire. Where could Gian and Luca be? Gian always found something to distract him, to make him dawdle. Hard to believe that he was her oldest. Maybe it was because the birth had taken too long; neither the midwife nor the doctor had wanted to undertake the long, difficult journey to their house. Gian was a winter child, born in snow and ice, lucky that he had survived a birth that could have gone terribly wrong. Not like Luca. Luca was strong and would get along, as her husband, Aldo, liked to say. Aldo made sure that his favorite son didn't miss out on anything. But Gian . . . It was just as well if he spent the summer up in Grevasalvas with the cows. The quiet life was good for him, and he had fewer attacks up there. Besides, there really wasn't much else he was able to do.

Benedetta stepped outside the front door and turned her face to the sun and the transparent blue sky of spring. The sky always seemed lower in the summertime. She glanced up to Lagrev. Then she blinked in disbelief. Luca and Gian were coming down the slope, but who was it were they dragging with them?

"There's no room in the house for her," Benedetta said firmly as soon as she saw the stranger.

"But we have to take a look at her ankle," Gian said.

They let the young woman slide down onto a chair, and even Luca nodded in agreement. "Her ankle looks really bad. Is lunch still warm? We're hungry. I'm sure she is too."

Benedetta pointed to the soup pot and the bowls they used for everything—coffee, milk, soup, and polenta.

Then she bent down to the girl and said without much sympathy in her voice, "Let me take a look at your foot. Let's see if it's broken." Carefully, she touched the swelling. The young woman winced.

"Where were you going?" Benedetta asked, thinking a question might distract the girl from the painful examination. But there was no reply.

"She doesn't talk," Gian said.

Benedetta straightened up and, putting her hands behind her back, turned to the young woman whose sea-green eyes were fixed on her. "The ankle is just sprained. But it'll be a few days before you can really put any weight on your foot. I'll make a compress. Gian, bring me the arnica tincture from the night table." Benedetta put a bowl of soup in front of the girl. The whitish barley was thick and had soaked up almost all the liquid. "Here, first have something to eat," she said. Her tone was kinder now, and she even fished a piece of sausage out of the pot.

The stranger hungrily ate the soup. Benedetta gave her a slice of bread as well. Then, while she was bandaging the sprained ankle, she returned to the subject that was on her mind.

"There's no room here in the house." Benedetta looked meaningfully around the room that served as both kitchen and living room. "For years we've wanted to go back to Stampa in the Bregaglia Valley." She moved her head vaguely in the direction of the mountain pass. "But the way things turned out . . . We got stuck here because there's always work at the hotel. Aldo, my husband, does carpentry. He works everywhere, that is, except here in the house, where there's so much that needs to be done." She checked the compress she'd placed on the young woman's ankle.

"But if you like, you can sleep in the barn until you feel better. Where are you from? And you probably have a name too . . ."

"*La straniera non parla,*" Luca said. He was annoyed by the girl's silence.

"But she can hear," his mother insisted. As if to prove her point, she asked, "Are you tired? Do you want to lie down in the hay?"

The girl nodded gratefully.

"All right then. Luca, take the stranger to the barn. Here," she turned to the young woman, "here's a blanket so you won't be cold."

A Palace at the
End of the World

The Spa Hotel Maloja was preparing for the 1896 summer season. Waiters, cooks, porters, chambermaids, and laundresses were arriving from all the villages of the Engadine and the surrounding valleys of Bregaglia and Valtellina, as well as nearby areas of the newly founded Kingdom of Italy. Achille Robustelli, the assistant director, who was in charge of the personnel, directed the proceedings as if he were conducting a difficult symphony. He swept through the hallways in his black suit and seemed to be everywhere at once.

Salaries had been arranged a long time ago, and food and lodging were free. But not all the employees received as princely a wage as the chef de cuisine, Signor Battaglia, whose pay was set at nearly four hundred Swiss francs per month, roughly twice as much as a schoolteacher. The waiters would get fifty francs per month.

On the other hand, Andrina, as a chambermaid, would have to be satisfied with twenty francs per month. This was what Signor Robustelli informed her when he received her in his office. Perhaps the black dress, white apron, and little starched cap—the uniform provided by the hotel—was supposed to be a consolation.

"But since we have a well-to-do clientele," Signor Robustelli added quickly, smiling and turning his signet ring as if to conjure up some magic, "you can count on an additional thirty francs in tips each month. So it doesn't look bad at all."

Better yet, Andrina was informed that she would be sharing an attic room in the hotel with another chambermaid. That was a triumph! She wouldn't have to sleep in a narrow room with Gian and Luca any longer. Luca was always ordering her around, asking her about everything she did, and in general treating her like a little girl, even though she was already eighteen and only two years younger than him. Before that, she'd slept in her parents' bedroom, which hadn't been good at all. At the end of each day, her father would try to wait until he thought she was asleep to lie down on her mother again. But Andrina hadn't fallen asleep easily since kindergarten. She hated having to listen to her mother's soft sighs floating up to the low wooden ceiling and hanging there.

And now it was going to be Andrina, of all people, the youngest—whose birth was followed only by miscarriages—who would live at the most elegant hotel in the Alps, perhaps in the whole world. She'd be living high up in that immense palace with the cupola on top of the ballroom, far above the three hundred guest rooms, the dining halls, and the elegant lobby. She would live higher up than anyone else she knew, even Signor Robustelli, whom she'd just met.

Count de Renesse had built the hotel near the Maloja Pass summit, at an altitude of almost two thousand meters. He went bankrupt, and afterward many nasty rumors circulated about the hotel, but none of them were true. In nearby St. Moritz, they claimed that the huge structure had sunk three feet into the swampy subsoil near the lake; that the fabulous heating plant, fed by giant coal-fired boilers, had exploded; and that the completely unique and innovative ozonizer, which ventilated the hotel, was circulating poisonous fumes to the guest rooms. What a lot of stories they told! But Andrina knew better, because her father had told her so. He'd been working at the hotel for years, doing repairs and carpentry.

Once, rumors spread in nearby towns that the hotel had been hit by a fever; at another point, it was alleged to be a gambling den. Nonsense, all of it. Twelve years after its opening, the Spa Hotel Maloja was still the most beautiful place one could imagine. Here, you were close to heaven. Yes, Andrina thought, the Spa Hotel Maloja was like a precious jewel sparkling in the clear light of the mountains, a heavenly Jerusalem that opened its gates only to the richest and most elegant—and to her, Andrina, the loveliest chambermaid of them all. She sensed a great future ahead of her.

Achille Robustelli took a sip of coffee and with a grimace pushed it aside. Lukewarm coffee was an insult to the palate! Then he glanced at the door Andrina had just vigorously closed behind her.

The carpenter, Aldo, had sent Andrina, his daughter, to see him. She was looking for work and Aldo had thought the signore might have a job for her. Well, he certainly did. First of all, he still needed to fill some additional staff positions, and secondly, Andrina was quite good-looking.

Achille Robustelli loved his profession. He'd gotten quite far— even if sometimes via detours. He came from a well-off middle-class family and had grown up in northern Italy, in Bergamo. For his father, who had fought valiantly at the Battle of Solferino and would have given his life for the Risorgimento, there had been no question about whether his only son Achille, born in 1865, would also take up a military career. For his part, Achille had never dared oppose his father's will. Nevertheless, a few years later, when his only sister died, and shortly thereafter his father also passed, he was not unhappy to be able to honorably give up military service in order to take care of family affairs.

Constantly handling weapons did not suit his temperament. And although his talent for leadership had led to his speedy ascent to officer rank, his sensitive nature was not the type usually appreciated in the army. In addition to his talent for organization, his interest in technical matters, and his gift for thinking strategically, he also had one totally unreasonable passion: he loved playing cards for money. This was another reason he felt happy to get away from his army comrades.

It wasn't long before Achille decided that a career in the hotel business would make the best use of his many talents. To his mother's dismay, he went to try his luck in Milan, a city that offered more possibilities than Bergamo.

He worked his way up rapidly in Milan. He was adept at spotting problems and always kept a cool head. He knew how to deal with the staff and had a knack for handling the guests. He didn't suck up to people, but he was willing to listen to what was on their minds, no matter what their status. He was discreet, and people respected him for that. Meanwhile, his own needs fell by the wayside, at least as far as his love life was concerned.

His mother, having lost both husband and daughter, was glad of this. She had done everything in her power to allow her son, who was named after the Greek hero, Achilles, to go through life brilliantly and unhurt. His sole vulnerability, she thought, was falling under the influence of a woman besides herself.

Then Robustelli met a hotel director from the high-altitude Engadine valley, known for its beautiful chain of lakes, who convinced him that he had a great future up in the Swiss mountains. The valley had superb hotels both in St. Moritz and nearby Maloja, which attracted the aristocracy, not to mention rich and powerful people from all over the world. And so Achille Robustelli, without any guilty feelings whatsoever, skipped a visit to his mother in Bergamo in order to meet with the hotel director in the Engadine. There, he was told that the Spa Hotel Maloja, which had been shaken by scandals surrounding its founder, needed a reliable man to act as right hand to the hotel director.

Robustelli accepted the position. In the spring of 1888—he was all of twenty-three years old—he kissed his loudly protesting mother good-bye, despite her premonition that terrible things would befall him in a foreign country. Promising to return and visit her during the winter months when the hotel closed for the season, he moved to Maloja.

This year, like those that had come before, Robustelli would indeed spend the winter months in Bergamo. His mother, meanwhile, had gradually come to realize that a young woman in her son's life could have its advantages. Perhaps falling in love might make him return to Bergamo, for example. But for that to happen, the woman had to be from Bergamo or its surroundings, and pass the test of her maternal scrutiny. The problem was that her son's taste did not coincide with hers. Not one of the young women she introduced him to interested him, and she hadn't approved of any of the women he had met and introduced to her.

Such were the thoughts going through Robustelli's head as the pretty Andrina left his office. But it was time to get back to work. In his position, he couldn't afford to daydream.

Segantini's Dream

The day felt strange from the moment he opened his eyes. It wasn't out of the ordinary for him to wake up from dreams that left him soaked in sweat, but today they'd been especially vivid . . .

Giovanni Segantini reached across the bed. Yes, Bice was there. She lay turned toward him. Only half-awake from his touch on her shoulder, she moved closer to him without opening her eyes. It was still early. Dawn was just breaking. Segantini didn't like the half-light, especially not after waking from a nightmare. He took a deep breath. Gradually he began to make out the shadowy outlines of the bedroom furniture. Then, as morning came and the first rays of sunshine illuminated the Moorish-style carvings, his dream faded.

As a painter, Giovanni Segantini worked slowly and without making preliminary sketches. Moreover, he often repeated the same subjects. He even sometimes made drawings that replicated the final versions of his paintings. In his dream, though, one of his pictures had changed without any help from him. How dare a dream touch one of his paintings?

The canvas he'd dreamed of was one that depicted a purgatory of bluish ice surrounding lustful women. They were bad mothers, women whose breasts had remained dry, women who didn't want to be mothers as destiny decreed. A poem by Luigi Illica, which he'd read and reread, had inspired him to create the painting. It was said to be a translation of an Indian text. The poet's vision of an icy cold in which the depraved women, with naked breasts and frozen blue lips, were doing penance for their own coldness, had seized him. He'd been unable to let it go until he had transferred it to canvas—to the displeasure of his friend, patron, and dealer Vittore Grubicy, who did not like mythical figures. In fact, the two men had almost had a falling-out over it.

During the night, the painting had come alive in his dream. Its dead and barren winter landscape had turned verdant and green, and the cold skin of the women had come to life, rosy warm and pulsating. Voluptuously they had stretched, awaking from their icy rigidity. At that point, Segantini had woken up in horror.

His hand again wandered toward Bice lying next to him in bed. Of course she was there, at his side, the covers drawn up to her chin. She had given him four children, dedicated her life to him ever since she had been seventeen. How blonde and dainty she had been then, still half child herself. She was the sister of his friend Bugatti, who had allowed her to pose for *The Falconess*, which he'd painted in 1881. By then, Segantini was already twenty-three years old. It had been easy to fall in love with Luigia Bugatti. He'd asked her if she would like to stay with him. She'd said yes. He'd called her Bice, after the heroine in a novel he had liked.

He closed his eyes and rolled over, remembering. She had left behind everything when they set out from Milan together. Even her name. Soon no one knew anymore what her real name was.

She had followed him all the way here into the high mountains, to Maloja. Her "Segante," as she affectionately called him, who was drawn ever higher and farther away from the depressing lowlands. His wife and companion, how well she knew him, and how unreservedly she accepted him.

His mother, on the other hand, had hardly known him; she had died young. Yet, even though he had been only a little boy back then, he would recognize her if she stood before him today. She had been beautiful, not like the sunrise, or midday, but like a sunset in spring. That's exactly how he would express it in his autobiography, like a sunset in spring. A tall figure, but always sickly after he'd been born. Not only did he almost die when she gave birth—there had to be an emergency baptism—but his mother had never really recovered. The treatments she'd received in Trient didn't work. He had been five, if his memory was correct, when he'd lost her. She'd died, leaving him behind.

He imagined *The Falconess* would have appealed to his mother, given her descent from landed gentry of the Middle Ages who had produced and sent forth warlike soldiers of fortune. A long time ago.

Segantini rolled over again, back toward his wife, but Bice had already gotten up. The sheet next to him was cool, as if she had never lain there.

The lake lay calm and still in the afternoon light. So still that the young woman knelt down on the boat dock and, holding back her long hair, leaned far out over the mirrorlike surface to gaze at her face reflected in the unmoving water.

There were pebbles, fish. Light turquoise at first. Then the blue quickly became more intense, and she could no longer see the bottom. Nika had never seen water like this. The gurgling, bubbling mountain brooks; the roaring waterfalls, whose sound swelled in the spring; the small Alpine lakes that beckoned like clear blue eyes—they were different. This lake drew one's gaze downward to the depths. It kept its silence, as did she.

Nika fell into such a deep sleep after Luca led her to the barn, that Gian, coming later that evening to ask her whether she was hungry, found her still unmoving and left quietly. When she woke up around noon the next day, she found a piece of bread and a bowl of milk next to her. Her bandaged foot still hurt, but the sharp stabbing pain had lessened; it was more like a dull thumping. With a sudden fear, Nika put a hand to her throat—ah, her necklace was still there. And with her fingertips she could feel the soft engraving on the locket: a rose in full bloom. She had gazed at it so often she could have drawn it with her eyes closed.

She hadn't been careful. Gian and Luca, and the woman, too, had probably seen the locket. She mustn't be that careless ever again. Carefully she buttoned the top buttons of her high-collared blouse. In Mulegns, where she had come from, she had had a hiding place, but here it would be smarter to wear the necklace concealed on her body.

For a long time Nika hadn't known about the locket, not until the postmistress at the inn in Mulegns told her about it. Nika must have been around eight or nine then.

"I was the one who found you, seconds after the horses had been changed and the post coach had driven on," the postmistress said. "The coach was going up over the Julier Pass to the

Engadine. And they abandoned you, an infant, wrapped in a blanket with the locket and an envelope of money, right here at the Post Coach Inn, where all the travelers get out for a midday stopover and a bowl of soup."

"What kind of locket?" Nika had asked, "I don't have any locket."

"I'm not surprised they didn't give it to you," the postmistress replied. "A foundling wearing jewelry—who ever heard of such a thing?" she laughed. "The farmer was raising a girl to work for her keep, not an elegant lady who'd spit on his head." And with that she went inside, still laughing.

But Nika had waited patiently until, one day, the farmer and his family had all been invited to a wedding in the neighboring village. They had hardly left when she sneaked into the house and began to search. The farmer was poor. A table, a couple of chairs, a chest, a few beds that many had to share—there wasn't much furniture. If the locket wasn't in the chest, it could only have been hidden in the bedroom under the mattress.

Quickly she searched through the chest, and there indeed, under the shirts, socks, and woolen hats, she found a crushed box, and in it a golden chain with the locket. Tears welled up in Nika's eyes as she held it in her hand. This was the only thing her parents had left her as a reminder of them. But still, they had left it with her. And that meant that she, Nika, had meant something to them.

The locket belonged to her, not to anyone else in the world, even if the farmer had taken it away from her. She slid the necklace into her apron pocket, put the empty box back, and neatly arranged everything in the chest.

During the winter, she slept in the house under the stairs; now in the summer she had a corner partitioned off from the animal stalls—neither of them a good place to hide her treasure. And so she wrapped the necklace in a rag and buried it behind the barn, marking the spot with a stone.

Nika trembled with fear whenever she thought that someone might have noticed that the necklace had disappeared, and yet from that moment on, she found consolation in the locket. Soon she no longer understood how she could have withstood the farmer's heartless treatment of her without this comfort. Whenever she was beaten, whenever she was hungry, she thought of her secret jewel.

Now and then, when nobody was around on the farm, she would take the necklace from its hiding place, look at it, and carefully open the locket, eternally expecting a new miracle that might explain things. But each time, to her disappointment, she found inside only a small, folded piece of paper with something written on it. Nika did not go to school. But she vowed she would learn to read and write one day, so that she could find out what was written there.

She had first discovered the locket ten years ago. She'd been a little girl then; now she was a young woman. And even though she was stuck here in Maloja, she was grateful to Gian and Luca for having shown her some kindness. Carefully Nika hobbled out of the barn and across to the house, relieved not to encounter anyone, either inside or out.

She had had no choice but to accept the offer to stay a few days longer. She had no money for the post coach, and with her injured ankle she wouldn't get very far walking. Yet the journey that lay before her was a long one. Italy—it was nearby and yet reaching it seemed like an unattainable dream.

Someone had attached a shelf above the sink where she washed. On it lay an old, hard piece of soap and a shard of a mirror. She propped the triangular fragment against the wall and ran her fingers through her thick hair. She didn't dare use the comb lying next to the soap. Carefully she looked at herself. She was thin. Her chin jutted out prominently, and in spite of an early summer tan, you could tell she was fair skinned. Nika held a finger under the ice-cold water and wet her lips, watching herself like a stranger. A tongue, cautious and soft, appeared from between the stranger's lips and licked off the drops of water. The face was her face. She hadn't often seen her reflection in a mirror. Where she had grown up, people had other things to think about than what they looked like; they used their money for more important things than buying a mirror. She put her face so close to the mirror fragment that her features blurred and she could no longer recognize herself. The glass became fogged over from her breath. Her bluish-green eyes gleamed back at her as if out of a mist.

She started when someone entered the kitchen; quickly she stepped back from the sink. But it was only Gian, who came toward her slowly, his hand reaching out reassuringly, as if she were a frightened animal.

"Good thing you're up," he said. "You'll have to stay here a while. The ankle won't heal all that quickly, but I see you can already get about a bit. Come, I'll show you the lake."

She hobbled along beside him, out of the house and into the light of the afternoon. Gian guided her across the road and past the majestic hotel, which obstructed the view of the valley's chain of lakes. Nika took Gian's arm for support, and he, surprised and proud, supported her. No girl in Maloja had ever taken his arm or held his hand because he wasn't "quite right," sometimes falling to the ground with foam on his lips and jerking limbs. He knew that people talked, said the oldest of the Biancotti boys was possessed. But the Protestant minister kept explaining that it had nothing to do with possession, that it was just an illness, and that doctors couldn't yet heal all illnesses.

When they arrived at the lake, Nika let go of Gian's arm, and he realized that she wanted to be by herself.

"There's a boat dock there," he said. "You can put your hand in the water, and then you'll feel how cold and clear it is. Will you find the way back by yourself?"

Nika nodded and knelt down on the dock.

When she got up again, she saw that an elegant carriage drawn by four horses was just driving into Maloja. A man leaned out of the open carriage window and turned around to look at her.

The one thing she noticed was his dark, thick, curly hair. Then the carriage was gone.

Segantini was returning from St. Moritz. Regardless of his financial situation, he liked certain luxuries. So today he'd ordered a carriage drawn by four horses to take him from Maloja, where he lived, to St. Moritz, a bigger town that was not much more than a half hour away. He'd met with Dr. Bernhard to tell him about an idea he'd been mulling over for quite a while already. The conversation had started at the bakery of Fritz Hanselmann, whose pastries they both loved, and then continued at the doctor's house.

Segantini had a project in mind that he couldn't put into effect by himself. At the next world's fair, he wanted to exhibit a monumental panoramic painting that would show the world the incomparable beauty of the Engadine, the most beautiful valley in the Swiss Alps, in his opinion. But that wasn't all; the painting was to be exhibited in a huge pavilion that he had envisioned. Visitors would climb up an artificial mountain peak, stroll along streams, hear the sound of cowbells, and be surrounded by paintings of the landscape. The fair was scheduled to take place in Paris in 1900.

Oscar Bernhard had listened to his friend's idea closely, taking the time to grasp the extent of the concept and the amount of money that would be required to make something like this happen.

"You know how highly I think of you, Segantini," he'd said after a few minutes, "and the longer I think about it, the more rewarding your idea seems, even though, you must admit, there's something unrealistic about it."

He'd paused to think some more. "Actually such a project would create a good deal of publicity in Paris for the Engadine. Hundreds of thousands of people will be attending the fair, indeed, millions from all over Europe and from overseas . . . You'd have to stir up enthusiasm among the big hotel owners here and get their support. But I can't think of a better way of attracting visitors and hotel guests to the valley." He'd poured Segantini another cup of tea and looked at him in admiration.

"This shows that not only are you a great painter, but that you have very close ties and loyalty to the Engadine . . ."

Segantini's dark eyes had flashed, and with a proud, self-conscious gesture, he'd passed his right hand through his splendid hair. "You're right. I love the mountains. In my panorama I'd like to paint a picture of nature that will make people fall silent in reverent awe." The fire in his eyes was contagious.

Bernhard had nodded. Yes, indeed, this was the Segantini he knew. But he, himself, also had a vision, and his friend's disclosures had inspired him to reveal something he had been thinking about for a long time.

"My dear Segantini, now it's my turn to tell you about an idea I've been considering. I'm a physician, and I not only see a lot of patients in the summer, but all year long, since we now also have a winter season here in St. Moritz. Badrutt was right; there's hardly another place that has as many days of sunshine in the winter as we do." He laughed. "That fox. He vowed he'd reimburse traveling costs to guests at his hotel if his promises of winter sunshine were not fulfilled. Since that time, he's been making twice as much as before!" He'd cleared his throat before continuing to confide his innermost thoughts to his friend.

"Hear me out. The sun is an enormous asset because it draws visitors, but it's also important to medical science. The sun has the power to heal. That's even truer here at this high elevation, where the air is clean. I have observed that wounds exposed to solar rays heal better. The tissues are regenerated more rapidly, and the wound dries more quickly." He'd again cleared his throat.

Segantini had looked at him in surprise. This was a side of the doctor he didn't know. Usually, he got to the point immediately.

"Don't laugh, dear friend, if I use our superb dried meat as an example. It was this technique of drying beef in the sun long enough to turn it into our delicious *Bündnerfleisch* that inspired me. In the sun, the raw meat dries without rotting or spoiling. And so I started to think about something I call 'heliotherapy.' Wound healing through sun radiation. For instance, if you expose wounded individuals, or rather their wounds, to as much fresh air and sunshine as possible, then—according to my theory—the patients will recover more quickly and in a completely natural way. I suspect that, above all, tuberculosis would respond well to such a treatment. I'd like to show—" He'd interrupted himself. "You're not a doctor, and I don't want to bore you. But since you told me about your idea, I also wanted to tell you about mine."

Segantini had assured him that he was interested. He had a curious mind, and as a self-taught man, he was anxious to fill any gaps in his knowledge. He had always planned for his children to grow up differently than he had and receive a better education. From the beginning, he had insisted on hiring a tutor who came to the house to teach them, even when he could hardly afford it.

"What you're saying makes sense to me, Oscar. In your own way, you'll be competing with the high-altitude clinics in Davos. I hope our dreams will bring us closer together. What else is there to sustain us if not our dreams, and what should we strive for if not for their realization?"

A New, Unfamiliar World

"Nothing will come of it, anyway," Benedetta said, in the negative tone of voice that her daughter hated so much.

"And why not?" Andrina said, bristling. "Will there ever be a plan or idea that you agree with or approve of? Could you ever simply say, 'Oh, that's nice, what a good idea!'" Angrily, she pushed her polenta away. "You always make everything so difficult that it feels as if one's apron pockets were filled with rocks. It *is* a good idea, and we'll all benefit from it."

Andrina looked at her father and Luca. Gian didn't count, and neither did the girl they'd taken in.

"Say something, Father. I've been slaving away for you here without anyone really noticing."

Old Biancotti just kept spooning up his polenta, his eyes hidden beneath the brim of his hat. He wore his hat even when he ate. It gave him a feeling of security and dignity.

He knew his wife, who was always against everything day in and day out, and he also knew his ambitious daughter Andrina.

"I just want to eat in peace and quiet," was all he said. Luca took Andrina's side.

"She's right. Her idea will help us all. The stranger might just as well work while she's here and eating our bread. It doesn't look as if she had a lot of money hidden in her clothes, unless there were some jewels in that locket."

Nika was frightened and instinctively held her hand over the locket hidden under her blouse. But to her relief, no one dwelt on it, and Luca went on, saying, "How is she ever going to go anywhere? In the hotel, they need laundresses. She'd earn something, could give us some of it, and save the rest until she can take the post coach back to where she came from or some other place."

"And I would be making a good impression on Signor Robustelli," Andrina added, "by finding him a worker." She raised her bowl of cold milk to Luca in a toast.

"Who is Signor Robustelli?" Benedetta asked suspiciously.

"He's the assistant director of the hotel, in charge of all the employees." And he likes me, Andrina thought, not saying it aloud, and without having the slightest proof of it so far.

Gian looked over at Nika. "Would you like that? To work at the hotel and earn some money?"

"Why wouldn't she like it?" Luca joined in, but Nika looked only at Gian and nodded.

No. There weren't any gemstones hidden in her locket. In it was only a small, folded-up piece of paper with some writing on it, and she couldn't read. The symbols were still strange to her, even though the postmistress had finally given in to Nika's pleas and agreed to teach the girl the alphabet and some basic things about reading during secret visits, using the Bible she otherwise rarely took out of the drawer.

The postmistress had tapped each letter on the page with her finger, teaching them to her until Nika slowly and doggedly learned the sound of each one. The postmistress herself read only haltingly and tried to keep the lessons short, but Nika was an eager pupil who pushed her teacher mercilessly, soon wanting to go beyond the woman's capabilities. "That's enough!" the postmistress said one day, annoyed, and closed the pigskin-bound Bible. Nika would have loved to have taken the book so that she could work through it from beginning to end on her own. The stories seemed very exciting and suspenseful. But the Bible had disappeared into its resting place, the postmistress pushing the drawer shut with a relieved bang. And that had been the end of it.

At the table, after one more glance at Gian, Nika nodded again in agreement.

"So there you are," Andrina said to her mother. "You'll get used to it. And then later on you'll be quite satisfied with the arrangement."

In everyday matters, that might be true, Aldo thought. Yes, that's what she was like, Benedetta. Without saying anything, he pushed his plate toward her, and with the wooden spoon she gave him more of the *bramata*. He liked cornmeal best when it was coarse grained. She really could cook well. This he'd never deny, although he never said thank you. He did carpentry; she cooked. After all, she never thanked him either for doing his work, year in and year out. On the contrary, again and again she would bring up the subject of wanting to go back to Stampa, to the milder climate of the Bregaglia Valley. Up here, the winters were too severe, she complained. What else Benedetta thought or felt, no one really knew. Just as she never showed any enthusiasm, she also never expressed any strong feelings of anger, sadness, or exasperation.

"All right, then," Aldo said and got up. "Andrina will mention the matter at the hotel. And then we'll see what comes of it."

Nika had never before had such a good life. She now ate at the table with the Biancottis as if she were a member of the family. She was going to be working in the hotel laundry, and for the first time in her life, she would be paid for her work. She'd have to give part of her pay to the farmer, but the rest she could put away, and one day she would have enough to buy a ticket for the post coach or the train. Small smoke clouds would rise from the locomotive steam stack and its shrill whistle would slice through the air just as the steel rails sliced through the landscape. And the world would be divided into the world that lay behind her and the world that lay before her.

One day, Nika thought, I'll stand facing my mother. There is a place where I belong. Everybody belongs somewhere. The day will come when someone will recognize the rose on my locket and understand the message hidden inside.

Nika touched her ankle and gently moved her foot back and forth. Carefully in the dim light of the kerosene lamp, she rubbed it with the tincture Benedetta had wordlessly pressed into her hand.

In Mulegns she'd had to eat standing up. The food was passed out at the head of the table by those who were sitting down, and what was left was then passed down to the foot of the table, to her. Here, on the other hand, one could relax at mealtimes. Benedetta had even given her a brief inquiring look at dinner to see if she'd wanted some more. But she hadn't dared to nod yes.

The farmer in Mulegns had been unpredictable, especially during mealtimes. Sometimes he would take off his belt. That meant something was bothering him or had made him angry. And she was always the first one he struck. The others would just sit there as if turned to stone. As if rooted to their chairs. If he wasn't content with beating her, he would have a go at his own children. Reto, who was the same age she was, would wail and scream, "Why? What did I do?" and try to hide under the massive wooden table. That was stupid because then he got it even worse. Nika never asked, "Why me?" She didn't even give the farmer the pleasure of whining, and she certainly didn't scream or cry. When the old man beat all eleven of his children, then his hand would grow weary by the time he came to the last ones. But not with her, the foreign brat. He always started with her, while he was still full of anger and his arm wasn't tired yet.

Then a few days would pass before he was again in a bad mood and full of anger. The beatings were a ritual for him the way going to church was for other people. It freed him for a moment of the week's hardships and the relentless everyday existence that engulfed him. Once the storm had broken, a smile would come to his lips, which, in that gaunt face of his, seemed almost indecent, and he would order Hans, the eldest, to fetch him a beer.

Nika stroked the cows Gian had tied up in the barn. They were brown and dainty, the fur in their ears was as white as milk; their horns, gracefully curved. All four animals stood quietly, looking at her with their dark eyes. Steamy gusts of breath came from their nostrils. The heat of their bodies warmed the stable. Feeling safe in the familiar smell, Nika put out the lamp. The darkness would bring forth a new day. More than that, in fact: it would bring a new job and an unfamiliar world.

St. Moritz,
Early June 1896

The morning was as fresh as a clean, unworn starched-and-ironed white shirt that you've just taken out of a dark closet. Edward Holbroke opened a window and breathed in the cold air until he felt a chill. The façade of the Pension Veraguth, where they were staying, was still in the shade. And St. Moritz was a sleepy nest that had yet to be cleaned out for the new season. Soon it would become a brilliant backdrop for the illustrious company arriving in the coming days and weeks from England, France, Germany, and Italy—the wealthy guests who, with their servants, would fill all the nearby grand hotels and villas.

The exotic attractions of a stay in this part of the Swiss Alps included the especially rousing effect champagne had at high altitude and the mountain tours led by native guides, during which you could look directly into the face of nature, confronting its power and its precipitous abysses without any worry of falling prey to it. And those who were too afraid to explore, even with a mountain guide, could play golf or tennis, or shoot clay pigeons. The alpine air was healthy. The sun shone more often here than elsewhere, and the St. Moritz mineral springs helped relieve nervous weakness, anemia, and—so it was whispered—even barrenness. Milk cures and goat's milk would make you as healthy as the local peasants, who supposedly had indestructible constitutions.

Edward yawned contentedly. He wasn't concerned with any of that.

"Good morning, my dear fellow!"

His travel companion burst into the room without knocking, a sign of great familiarity, which also showed a certain lack of consideration.

"Well, how do you like the view from your window, Eddie? Last night right after our arrival, I was too tired to think much about the place." The young man went over to where his friend stood by the wide-open window and gestured broadly, as if he wanted to describe the entire landscape and at the same time dismiss it. "But now I see where you've brought me. You don't seriously think that I'd want to spend several weeks here?"

"The lake, the mountains, the fresh air—isn't all that enough for you?"

James Danby gave his friend a contemptuous glance but said nothing. Instead, he dropped into the flowered easy chair next to the window and lit a cigarette.

"If I had told you that I wanted to study the high-altitude plants of the Engadine, you wouldn't have come with me," Edward said.

"You'd have been right about that. But you're pulling my leg! Do you really intend to set forth with your collecting box? Tell me, will our stay feel like a children's birthday party where we're playing blindman's bluff?"

"Come on, Jamie." Edward closed the window and put on his jacket. "At least, let's go and have breakfast before you leave. In any case, Marcel Proust liked this pension. And you might regret not staying on to play blindman's bluff. In a couple of weeks, the most beautiful ladies of European society are going to arrive here. I heard that an English princess is coming for the opening of Badrutt's Palace Hotel. She might enjoy meeting you. Haven't you always been on the lookout for a good catch? 'Too bad you couldn't meet him,' I'll say then . . ."

Edward pulled his friend up out of the easy chair, took him by the arm, and opened the door. The aroma of café au lait came up from the ground floor of the pension and coaxed an almost agreeable smile to James's lips, even though he always drank tea in the morning.

James Danby did not leave, although it wasn't quite clear whether the thing that prevented it was the pleasures Edward promised or a sense of duty that, although not strongly developed, did make itself felt from time to time. Besides, he had to earn some money, and he'd promised the English newspaper he worked for that he'd write a story about Giovanni Segantini. The artist was famous all over Europe, with the exception of France, where they chose to ignore him. Since 1893, his painting *The Punishment of Lust* had been hanging in the Walker Art Gallery in Liverpool.

James had been impressed when he saw the painting. Except that he couldn't forgive the title, for he definitely did not think that women should be punished for their lust. Most of Segantini's paintings, however, featured simple peasant women or mothers holding children in their arms—much like Madonnas, James thought. Those he was less intrigued by, since he saw them as having little use in his life or in art. Yet the painting *Ave Maria*

Crossing the Lake, which James viewed as yet another of Segantini's Madonna pictures, had been awarded a gold medal at the world's fair in Amsterdam. It was the foundation for Segantini's international reputation.

Who was this man? James had heard the man's childhood had been difficult. Supposedly, he had even been put into a reform school in Milan after the police picked him up off the streets several times. One thing James knew: he and Segantini didn't have much in common, not only because of their views on women but also because the painter had left a large, exciting city like Milan and withdrawn to the Alps. These mountains which James found so incredibly dreary were obviously Segantini's favorite subject.

Edward was delighted at the idea of meeting Segantini. True, he had recently been occupied primarily with garden architecture and plants, but his field was actually art history. He was interested in divisionism, a new direction being explored in Italian painting, and Segantini was definitely its most important exponent and practitioner. Edward was less concerned with how Segantini painted women than with the painter's exciting modern techniques—methods of painting that Segantini had developed all on his own. He admired Segantini's ability to catch the clear and almost painfully strong mountain light with his paintbrush. But he wasn't surprised that James was less excited to meet the painter because of his attitude toward the opposite sex. James was always moved by women, even if they were just in paintings.

"Let's first go and explore the village," Edward suggested. "Have you already unpacked your photography equipment? The weather is marvelous. You could take a picture of the pension . . ."

"Absolutely not," James replied.

Making Plans in Zurich to Go for a Health Cure

"Betsy? Why Betsy of all people?"

"Because I like her. Because I can talk to her. Because she understands me! Because we enjoy each other's company . . ."

"That's exactly why I'm against it. You're ill, child, remember that. And you must get well again as quickly as possible, not 'amuse' yourself."

"But I'll get well again faster if I can have fun, Mama!" Mathilde looked at her mother defiantly.

"You went to the wrong boarding school. Or rather, you went around with the wrong sort of girls there. I told your father a thousand times that your girlfriends weren't the right sort for you. But your father is interested only in his work."

Emma Schobinger shook her head disapprovingly, but more at Mathilde's inappropriate desires than at her husband's indifference. In all honesty, Franz wasn't the worst husband, and he acquiesced to her in most things. Every now and then, however, he felt he had to set an example and would insist on having his way in domestic matters as well. Those moments didn't happen predictably, so one couldn't prevent them, not even with the most careful planning. Sometimes it helped to point out that she had contributed a considerable sum of money to their marriage. But that argument came to weigh less with time, for—with his wife's family's startup help—Franz had become quite a successful building contractor and developer. And once men have their own money, Emma thought not for the first time, they become unpredictable.

"All right then," she continued, handing Mathilde a brochure, "you're going to the New Stahlbad Surpunt in St. Moritz, together with my cousin Frieda. That way the poor dear will get out a bit too. She can't afford to go anywhere or do anything. Remember, Mathilde, marriage is a good thing, but being widowed is terrible. Sure, Frieda doesn't have to work in a factory to earn a living like other widows, and because her children are big boys already, the authorities haven't taken them away from her. But she doesn't take anything for granted. Frieda will take her assignment seriously. Besides, Betsy is already having enough fun on her own."

After this long lecture, she rang vigorously for the servant girl to keep Mathilde from having her say. But Mathilde threw herself into her mother's arms. She had been educated at a girls' secondary school in Lugano, with the primary purpose of learning to run her own household and staff in the near future; that is to say, right after her wedding.

"Not to Stahlbad! What an awful-sounding name! Never!" Her protest sounded both anguished and rebellious. And more softly but still with a firmness she probably inherited from her mother, she added, "and not with Aunt Frieda."

Just then, the servant girl's head appeared at the parlor door, "Madam, you rang?"

"Never mind, Irma, it's all right. Not right now, in a while . . . Please close the door; we're not finished here yet."

The girl disappeared, and Emma Schobinger made another attempt. Mathilde was merely being obstinate, that's all.

"Just take a look at the brochure," she said. She took back the brochure she'd just pressed into Mathilde's hand, turned it over, saying, "Look, here on the back it's printed in French: 'Grand Hôtel des Nouveaux Bains.' Doesn't that sound absolutely elegant? In addition, the hotel has mineral springs and is considered one of the most magnificent places in the town."

"And why can't I stay at the Hotel Victoria? It has more charm . . ."

"Because it doesn't have its own therapeutic baths. And for the last time, you're not going to St. Moritz for pleasure, but because of the springs. Because you're anemic and are suffering from a nervous disorder."

"If I have to go to the Stahlbad, then I'll only go with Aunt Betsy."

Mathilde was not as naïve as she seemed, Emma knew. She smoothed her rustling black taffeta skirt and tugged at her white cuffs; she knew that Mathilde would run to her father and pester him until he gave in. That had to be prevented. If that happened too often, it would weaken her own position in the family and with the servants.

"And what about poor Aunt Frieda?"

Mathilde sensed a sudden shift of opinion, and was instantly silent as a lamb. Her eyes really were very blue. She lowered her eyelids as her mother continued.

"First of all, your behavior toward me is not appropriate—after all, I'm your mother—and even less so toward Frieda. Do you think she's just there to be pushed around all the time? What happened to her could happen to you one day too. But young people just don't want to think about such things! That still doesn't justify such behavior on your part."

Mathilde sat there, gentle and peaceful. Her curly blonde hair was pinned up, but small ringlets escaped from the pins like tiny springs. They reminded Emma of her sister, Elizabeth. Betsy had looked exactly like that when she was nineteen, except that Betsy had dark hair and perhaps even bluer eyes than her niece. If Mathilde took after her—and it seemed that might be the case—then, as the girl's mother Emma knew, she would have a lot to cope with.

"Mama, it's really simple," Mathilde said, with gentle emphasis. "First, you talk with Aunt Betsy and ask her if she'd like to accompany me. After all, she's a widow, too, like Aunt Frieda . . ."

"But she has more money."

"Yes. If she agrees, then you can tell Aunt Frieda that Aunt Betsy insists on going with me. Everyone in the family knows what Aunt Betsy's like. Nobody can change that. There isn't anybody who can stand up to her when there's something she wants."

"And Frieda?"

"You invite Frieda to join you when you come to St. Moritz. You'll surely want to visit me sometime. When you do, you can come up for a couple of days with Aunt Frieda."

Mathilde could tell from her mother's sigh that she'd won. She looked at her mother—dressed in black as usual, even though her husband was in the best of health—and pressed a kiss on her small hand.

"Thank you, Mama!"

Emma glanced out the window at Lake Zurich and then back to the large pendulum clock in the parlor. At last she said, still sounding cross with her daughter, "It's six o'clock. I certainly won't tell your father about this. You can tell him yourself. You know how he feels—young girls with nervous disorders actually have other problems. He doesn't understand the need for you to go for a cure anyway. Either with Frieda or without her."

❧

Mathilde was Betsy's favorite niece. She herself had never been much of a family animal. She'd always tried to avoid the kind of interference that some of the older family members—even if sometimes with good intentions—often felt called upon to exert.

And Betsy knew that Mathilde liked her, perhaps just because they were so much alike. She would accompany her niece to the Engadine. However, she had no intention of staying at the Stahlbad. She preferred to stay in a place as far away from the usual St. Moritz bustle as possible. She didn't have the slightest desire to stay among the ailing, hysterical, anemic, or barren people who went to the mineral springs to be "saved." Emma, her older sister, refused to understand this, and so Betsy decided to discuss the question of lodgings with her brother-in-law Franz, who enjoyed life, loved his daughter, and in the end could always put his foot down.

For quite a while already Betsy had wanted to spend some time at the Spa Hotel Maloja, which was supposed to be quite sensational. So that was where she felt determined to go. After all, Mathilde wasn't going to be confined to bed. And they would be only a half hour away by horse-drawn carriage from the healing mineral springs of St. Moritz. And while Mathilde was taking therapeutic baths, she could explore the surroundings. She was fit and loved the mountains, and there were guides who could take one safely to any of the various peaks. Betsy had a soft spot for strong men.

She had married young, at the age of twenty, and had experienced both good and bad times during her ten-year marriage. Several of her illusions had fallen by the wayside, but on the whole, she couldn't complain. Walter, her husband, had died three years earlier of a heart attack, quite unexpectedly, for he was not overweight and there were no signs that he'd found life especially burdensome. And so suddenly, even before she turned thirty-two, she was a widow.

Her family hoped she would remarry. There was no shortage of candidates, for Betsy was young, attractive, and had money. Once remarried, everything would be back in order, and they wouldn't have to worry about Betsy stepping out of line every now and then.

But Elizabeth Huber, "née Wohlwend," as she liked to add because the name Huber sounded too ordinary to her, was busy exploiting the new role suddenly thrust upon her.

She had been married. Now she was a widow, and in her view, remaining one had some advantages. The freedom it gave her—especially because she was well off—was quite exhilarating.

Her sister Emma saw this desire for independence with some misgivings. The topic came up when Betsy came by the house to discuss possible plans for traveling to the mountains with Mathilde. "Oh, Betsy," Emma said, "there are already enough lonely widows whom nobody wants anymore . . ."

" . . . and who," Besty continued, "not only have no place in society but also have become miserably poor. These women have no protection whatsoever, yet they must try to bring up and feed their children by hiring themselves out as laundresses or factory workers. Provided, of course, their children aren't taken away from them and put into orphanages or state homes by officials who say that mothers like them can't take care of their children properly at home or bring them up to be good members of society."

Betsy's temper had a tendency to flare up, and Emma found it particularly uncomfortable when her sister, as she had recently been doing, voiced her social, even socialist, ideas.

But Betsy was not about to cede her point.

"Emmy, dear, being a widow has a very big advantage. I am the one in charge of handling my money. Walter and I had a decent marriage. He died young, and I mourned. But things are what they are. And this will probably surprise you—I am absolutely not going to marry again and give up control of my money. On the contrary! I will use my money to fight for the financial and social betterment of widows here in Zurich and in the rest of our country. They have the right to get insurance coverage and receive a widow's and orphans' pension. Because then their children won't be taken from them after they've already lost their husbands and they are forced to take over his role totally unprepared. The role—would you believe it?—of breadwinner, caretaker, and head of the family."

Betsy had talked herself into a passionate rage. Her eyes flashed at her poor sister, who, lips pressed together, sat with her hands meekly folded on top of her black skirt.

"And you know what? Nobody objects when—after the death of their husbands—these women who've been considered incapable of doing almost everything, not only raise their children and manage the household as they're supposed to, but also run the farm, the vegetable store, the coal company, the carpentry shop, or the textile factory with its umpteen workers. Then, suddenly, they can do it, these women. And everybody considers it a matter of course. Yes, after all, who else is supposed to do it if the son is still too young to take over?"

Betsy, fired up by her own ideas and full of energy, rose from the sofa and stretched. She bent down to sniff the slightly dusty dried blossoms in the potpourri bowl on Emma's coffee table, and concluded her monologue. "I'm going with Mathilde to St. Moritz, Emma. But your daughter is going to be exposed to somewhat different viewpoints in my company than she's used to from her home and girls' boarding school. I hope you're aware of that."

Oh yes, Emma was fully aware of it. That was why Frieda had been her first choice as Mathilde's companion rather than her youngest sister. But it was too late now. Franz liked his vivacious sister-in-law and had already approved the plan.

So she simply said, "Yes, Betsy, I'm fully aware of it. I only hope you won't inadvertently sow any anxiety in Mathilde's mind. We don't need that at this point in time, as you well know. Not at all."

"And, Emma," Betsy said, ending the discussion without reacting to Emma's last remark or mentioning her plan to discuss the choice of a hotel with Franz, "I think, quite apart from all this, you could really dress more colorfully. I think Franz would really like that. After all, I'm the widow, not you."

The Season Can Begin

The women ironing in the Spa Hotel Maloja's overly warm laundry room looked up only briefly from their work when Nika was brought in. They were busy slamming heavy irons, filled with glowing charcoal, down onto wrinkled napkins and tablecloths with a dull bang. The orders were that Signor Battaglia's culinary creations were to be served only on the most perfectly ironed, flowered white damask to delight the fussiest eyes and palates.

After the table linens could come the bed linens, which had been in storage over the winter and smelled of mildew and needed to be washed again—and ironed—before being used. In the first week of the season, 150 guests were expected; two or three weeks after that, all 400 guest beds would be occupied. So far, due to the enormous cost of heating the hotel, the Maloja had not been open for the winter season.

"She can hear but she doesn't speak," said the head house-keeper, Signora Capadrutt, as she pushed Nika toward a plump, older woman. "Giuseppina, can you show her what to do? She's living with the Biancottis in the village. They call her '*la straniera*,' because she's an outsider and no one knows where she's from. She can help with the ironing too, if you're in urgent need there." The head housekeeper pressed a large pinafore into Nika's hands and hurried off.

Steam hung in the laundry, condensing on the high windows and the walls.

"Come," Giuseppina said pleasantly. "Let's see where you're needed most." Nika nodded and followed Giuseppina, who seemed to be in charge of the laundry staff and assigning people to jobs.

"The tablecloths and bed linens are handled separately, but thank God, they're all white. That simplifies things. Look here, the laundry is first soaked in this tin-lined tub. The rule of thumb is for every hundred quarts of water, use one pound of soft soap, half a pound of soda, four to six tablespoons of ammonia, and four spoonfuls of turpentine. Then you put the dirty laundry into the tub. Lake water would be the best water to soak it in, but we use tap water because it's simpler. The soaking water should be lukewarm, and the laundry stays in it ten to twelve hours. Mina," she interrupted her lecture, waving to a young girl, "put the cover on the tub! Who forgot to do that again? If the cover's not on, the laundry will get cold, and then you'll have problems rinsing it out!"

She turned back to Nika. "It's much nicer to handle the laundry if it hasn't gotten completely cold in the soaking water, because after that it has to be rubbed on the washboard and wrung out. If some spots remain, soap them again. So now," Giuseppina continued, leading the new girl onward, "here is the laundry stove, and on top of it are the steaming kettles. The white laundry is boiled here for at least one hour in a new soaking solution of brown soap and soda, but you know all that. Look over there. Giovanna, Ursina, and Selma are just about to take the boiled laundry out with wooden tongs. Then it's rinsed, wrung out, and put back into the emptied soaking kettle. And over there is Maria," she said, pointing to an older woman. "She's the one who prepares the weak soap solution which is then poured over it. Maria, please use the borax sparingly. You don't need to use that much of it!"

Giuseppina's sharp eyes saw everything, and Nika swallowed nervously, wondering if she'd do the job right, even though she knew all about laundry days from working on the farm.

"And that's it. After a few hours more of soaking, the laundry is rinsed in cold water, and then it goes into the bluing water to make it look whiter. Do you know how laundry bluing is prepared?"

Nika shook her head.

"Well, I always say the best thing for bluing is a good pulverized ultramarine. You put it into a little flannel bag, tie the bag closed, and draw it through the water until the water gets to the right color. And after the bluing, you wring out the laundry and hang it up to dry, right over there," she pointed toward the place where the clotheslines were strung.

"And so, that's all there is to it." She saw Nika's skeptical look and added kindly, "In a couple of days you'll be as familiar with it all as I am. Oh, there's one thing I forgot to tell you. The kitchen things are soaked in a special basin, with a stronger bleach solution. Before they're boiled, they have to be well rinsed and soaped. And look here. We have a wringer machine. It squeezes out twice as much water as all of us can manage together by hand." She smiled. "The laundry dries faster and it's easier on the linens." She laughed. "Just think how much we pull and tear at these linens when we wring them out by hand! My husband always says men have to be respectful of washerwomen's arms, or they'll be the losers."

Nika gazed at her, taken aback.

"Don't look at me like that, child. We don't beat each other up at home. I'm much too tired for that in the evening. Even with strong arms, after eleven hours working, you're bushed in the evening."

Giuseppina looked around to find the best place for Nika to start.

"Still and all, an eleven-hour day is progress. After all, my Fausto wants me to have something left over for him too. Do you have a sweetheart?" But Giuseppina shook her head and put her hand up to her forehead. "What a stupid question! If you had one, you wouldn't have left the place you came from. And you don't answer questions anyway."

It would feel good to work with Giuseppina. Nika knew that after only a few minutes.

Giuseppina signaled her to follow.

"By the way, Saturdays we work only nine hours. Did the head housekeeper tell you that? You have to watch the clock like a hawk, my Fausto always says." Nika nodded repeatedly.

"Then come along, I think they could use you at the soaking tubs. Once the season is fully under way and the table and kitchen linens really pile up, I'll explain how to remove wine, fruit, and fat stains. But for now just get started; you won't remember everything, even if you're very smart."

As she was leaving the hotel that first day, Nika felt proud. She would be earning fifteen francs a month, she would keep five and give the Biancottis ten, as Andrina had suggested, and for that she could eat with the family.

Just as she was wearily turning into the street that led from the hotel to the village, a man came toward her. She was startled because he was walking directly toward her, as if he had been looking for her. But the next moment she recognized him. He was the one who had stuck his head out of the carriage that afternoon as she was looking at her reflection in the lake. The same dark, curly hair. Nika stepped aside to let him pass. The man was no longer young; he must have been close to forty. He had almost reached her when he slowed down. He wouldn't just stop in front of her, she thought. But that's exactly what he seemed to be doing. He was wearing a vest and a suit of coarse wool. His full black beard left only his lower lip visible. She dropped her eyes as his dark gaze fell on her. The man gave her a penetrating look as if he knew her and was trying to remember where he had seen her before. When she looked up again, he was still looking at her inquiringly. She was confused and looked aside. He was so different from the other men she knew. He carried himself with a kind of self-assurance she had never before seen. He wasn't like the Mulegns farmers or the village people here in Maloja. He was from another world. He was a stranger, like her. The man nodded at her. It wasn't until after he had passed her with a brief greeting that her heart started to pound.

In confusion, Nika patted down her unruly hair, tucking in a strand that had come loose from her bun, but nothing could soothe her bewilderment. The man's dark eyes had made her dizzy; the pounding in her ears was almost enough to make her feel ill. She wasn't used to having people look at her like that. In fact, she wasn't used to having people look at her at all.

Contract children were nobodies. And she'd grown up as a contract child living with a foster family—the farmer's family. Children like her didn't even have names. They were referred to as "the boy" or "the girl," no matter what their real name had been. People didn't look at them—especially not in the penetrating way the dark-eyed man had looked at her. Contract children weren't allowed to play with others, and except inside their yard, they weren't allowed to speak with anyone unless it was absolutely necessary. They never became part of the village community where they lived. That's what it had been like for her, growing up; that's how it was for all of them. That was why she'd trained her heart from the time she was little to be as obedient as a dog on a chain.

And now her heart was pounding in a totally uncontrollable wild beat of its own. Someone had looked at her. Suddenly she felt she wasn't just anyone or anything. She was a woman. And he was a man. And her heart told her that this man with the dark gaze had seen deep into her soul.

Nika forced herself to walk on and not look back. He was a stranger. Yet she suspected he knew loneliness, the terrors of the darkness, the kind of longing that nobody can assuage. Like her. With that thought, she did turn around to look. And at that same moment, he stopped to look at her again. They had recognized each other, in the blink of an eye.

Segantini continued walking but restlessness pursued him. It had taken him a moment, but he'd finally remembered where he'd seen that face with the unusual features before—the strange blue-green eyes, the strawberry blonde hair. She was the woman he'd seen on the dock bending over to look at herself in the lake when he'd been traveling back from St. Moritz and his visit with Oscar Bernhard.

For days, he'd been haunted by the way she'd held the long hair out of her face. He had drawn her in his head, again and again. She was so familiar he felt certain he recognized her from some earlier part of his life; but he couldn't say to which period she belonged, or whether he'd seen her before in Milan or Brianza or during his days in Savognin.

She was beautiful, beautiful in a way different from Bice. He pushed these thoughts out of his mind and continued on his stroll. But whenever he reflected about his idea for the panorama painting, the thought of the girl gazing at her reflection in the water intruded. Slender and naked.

☙☙

James Danby was bored to death. Without a big city and women, life was meaningless for him. He'd never developed a taste for the Alps, no matter how enthusiastically many of his fellow countrymen spoke about their sunrise mountain treks. He liked to sleep late and loved having a hearty breakfast with good old English Breakfast tea—the right blend which, naturally, they didn't have here—while immersing himself in the Paris edition of the *New York Herald*, which arrived miserably late in St. Moritz. All this was enough to spoil his morning.

He couldn't understand what had gotten into Edward to make him such an avid nature lover and collector of flowers. Weren't men the hunters and women the gatherers?

He had agreed to spend one more week at Pension Veraguth, for Segantini hadn't yet replied to the letter he had sent him. And he didn't want to leave without a story. But once he got his story, a hundred horses wouldn't be able to keep him from returning to London.

Still, he had to admit that the longer he thought about it, the more curious he was to meet with Segantini. The painter's fame was quite phenomenal, especially considering that he didn't make the rounds in the salons or artistic circles. He didn't even have the advantage of being famous in his Italian homeland—there he wasn't held in high esteem at all. Yet in other countries, people obviously saw something in him. His landscapes were especially admired, probably because they satisfied a longing for an ideal world, for harmony with nature even as mechanization was advancing throughout the world.

Yet one couldn't help but see that Segantini's paintings radiated a profound melancholy. The silence of his sunsets made one shiver with loneliness and isolation. The shepherdesses and farmhands in his pictures did not live idyllic lives; you sensed that their existence was hard and that, like their cattle and work-horses, they carried a yoke. James shook his head a little to let go such thoughts, which seemed to bring with them an invisible burden; such musings didn't fit in with his current view of life.

The feeling didn't lift, however, and suddenly he was gripped by the memory of the loneliness that had so heavily weighed him down during his days at boarding school, especially during the first few years. He had become friends with Edward back then, probably because Edward had a German mother and spoke German. James's real name was Jakob Scheffner, he was from Berlin, and owed the opportunity for his good British education to a distant uncle, Albert Danby. His parents didn't have much money, and this much older relative of his mother's who lived in England and was well off kindly took on the cost for the boy's education. And so Jakob became James, and James eventually also adopted the name Danby, even though he inherited nothing else from his uncle.

Thus, for a moment, thinking of Segantini's pictures, James again felt the loneliness he had felt when the other boys went home on weekends. When the halls and bedrooms of the boarding school emptied out, and the polished stairs no longer clattered with the lively sound of boys' hurrying feet. Sometimes Edward was allowed to take James home with him, which solidified their friendship. But James Danby did not like being reminded of those days, which perhaps contributed to the feeling of unease that overcame him whenever he thought of Segantini and his pictures.

Happily, there were other distractions at hand. The first vacation and spa guests were gradually beginning to arrive, and James Danby had already seen several pretty women among them. Unlike his friend, he would try to spend this last week there as a hunter. He figured the tan he'd gotten from playing tennis was becoming, and he resolved to court the prettiest woman he could find at the St. Moritz mineral springs while Edward went in pursuit of spring flora.

He smiled at the thought, and selected an elegant suit instead of knickerbockers and tweed to stir up some interest on his day's adventures.

❧❧

"Madam?" James got up politely from the park bench and indicated his seat. "Such a beautiful day! You looked as if you might like to sit down for a moment . . . May I offer you my seat on this bench?"

If he was at all concerned about embarrassing the lady, he was certainly in error. After turning around with a sort of bored disgruntlement, her expression sprang to life, and she reacted to his question as if she'd been waiting for exactly this kind of exchange.

"Is that all you have to offer? A seat on a bench that's available to anyone?" she asked with a scornful smile even as she sat down and pulled back the veil on her hat.

James gazed into her willful blue eyes with delight. But she looked away, waving to a man in a dark suit, probably her husband, who was deep in conversation with another man.

"I'll follow you right away, Robert darling, just go on ahead," she said.

Then she turned back to James with a radiant smile, "Well, kind sir, what else do you have to offer me?"

James Danby didn't easily lose his composure, but she was a real provocation.

"Well, I could invite you for an ice cream at some time of your choice," he said, stroking his smooth-shaven chin.

"Oh no," she said, laughing. "It's still too cold for that. What else?"

He watched spellbound as she adjusted her vine-embroidered gloves, slowly pushing with the fingers of one hand between the fingers of the other. She spoke English with an American accent, and he wondered whether she had ever lowered her eyes in modesty.

When he didn't answer her right away, she continued in a conciliatory tone, "Perhaps you'll have a better idea tomorrow. I have to go now; my husband is waiting for me." She lowered the small veil on her hat over her blue eyes and straightened the skirt of her white dress. Just as her husband turned and looked back at her to ask, "Kate, are you coming?" she gave a gesture that clearly indicated that she'd be at his side in a moment.

She didn't say good-bye to James, but then, she hadn't suggested that he speak to her in the first place.

ʘ

Segantini laid the letter aside in annoyance; he was unable to make it out. A person named James Danby had written something to him that neither Bice nor anyone else in the family could make sense of because it was in English. Segantini himself spoke only Italian and rarely considered the fact a drawback because the people around here were all familiar with his native tongue. Of course they were. After all, the wine came from Valtellina, the polenta from northern Italy, the farmers were from the Bregaglia Valley, and people spoke Romansh, which was related to Italian anyway. Segantini decided not to answer the letter, to continue with his normal schedule. But for some inexplicable reason, he didn't throw it away. Every time his eye fell on it, he felt a little pang. Finally, he had a sudden inspiration; grabbing the letter, he hurried over to the Hotel Maloja.

"How nice to see you, Signor Segantini," Achille Robustelli said, getting up from behind his desk. "Please sit. What can I do for you?"

Segantini sat down awkwardly and handed Signor Robustelli the letter. "I'd be grateful to you if you could translate this for me. I don't know English, and there might be something important in it . . . you never know."

Achille Robustelli nodded and scanned the piece of paper. "Good news," he said. Someone wants to write an article about you for an English newspaper, and the gentleman asks for an appointment with you."

Segantini frowned, "And do you think this is on the up-and-up, Achille? Is the man trustworthy?"

"Absolutely," Robustelli replied. "It will be perfectly all right for you to agree to talk to him. Mr. Danby is a journalist; he would also like to take a few photographs. He is staying at the Pension

Veraguth in St. Moritz." He noticed Segantini's hesitation, "If you like, I can send him an answer on your behalf."

Segantini nodded but still seemed to have some doubts, and so Robustelli said, "I'm sure I can find an interpreter who would be suitable for the interview. It's an opportunity you shouldn't turn down."

Segantini agreed, but did not stand up to leave, even after he had thought it over and told Robustelli just when such a meeting would be possible.

And so Robustelli said, "I think you'll probably be interested in the concerts we're planning for the summer season. You have been in previous years. I know how much you like music. But I can't give you any details yet since the season has just begun, and the dates haven't yet been set. However, I'll keep you informed."

Segantini still didn't get up, but seemed to be getting ready to say something.

"Robustelli," he began, then paused as if gathering his thoughts one more time. "There's something else I wanted to talk to you about. I heard that you've hired the young woman the Biancotti sons found on the mountain path that leads from Grevasalvas to Maloja. They say the girl doesn't speak, and people in the village are saying all sorts of things about her. She's living with the Biancottis, no one knows who she is, and everyone is making guesses about where she might come from."

Robustelli waited politely, for it seemed that Segantini had not finished yet.

"Well, Robustelli, I saw her at the lake, and ever since I've been mulling over where I'd seen her before." Segantini crossed his arms over his chest, then uncrossed them again as if he had just thought of the answer.

"She's from Mulegns! From the other side of the Julier. Did you know that I lived in Savognin until 1894? We lived there from 1886 on, and Savognin isn't far from Mulegns, only two post coach stops."

He paused, but Robustelli just nodded; he still didn't want to interrupt him.

"I saw her at one of the village celebrations in Mulegns, about three years ago, at any rate, it was shortly before we moved to Maloja in 1894. She was fifteen, maybe sixteen years old back then. I noticed her because of the unusual color of her eyes and her beautiful hair. But she was shy and just stood at the edge of the fairground. And no one invited her to dance. I asked the proprietor of the Lowen Inn about her, and he told me a strange story. The girl had been abandoned as a baby; it was his wife who had found the child. A woman who was traveling through had left the baby there when the coach made its midday stop at the inn."

Segantini cleared his throat, and Robustelli pushed a glass of water across the table to him. He had heard that Segantini had been abandoned by his father as a boy and had, so it was said, never seen him again. The story of the girl had obviously moved the painter and brought back old, unhappy memories. Achille Robustelli cleared his throat in empathy, but still said nothing.

"The mother also left an envelope of money with the child, which they gave to the farmer who took the child in. After that, the child was treated the way they treat *Verdingkinder*, contract children; she was put into service. Even when they are very young, these children are treated as workers who have to toil as if they were adult servants or farmhands."

Segantini took a sip of water; his voice revealed sympathy as well as some anger. "The proprietor of the inn just shrugged his shoulders. The girl, he said, doesn't talk, which isn't unusual since nobody listens to these creatures anyway. Worse, he said that such children—usually orphans, illegitimate children, or the offspring of impoverished families—are often forbidden to talk at all. Because frequently their quarters and care are worse than that of the farm animals, and the farmers don't want them complaining to anyone."

Segantini had gotten up meanwhile and was agitatedly pacing back and forth in Robustelli's office.

Robustelli said, "Yes, the young woman works here. Andrina Biancotti asked me if we could use her at the hotel. And since she doesn't speak, which is a certain disadvantage, I sent her to work in the laundry. There she uses her hands, not her mouth."

"Well, I would like to look after her," Segantini explained. "I know from the innkeeper in Mulegns that she can speak, and if she can speak, then perhaps she could do some better sort of work."

Robustelli, beginning to feel a bit tense, started turning the ring on his little finger. And even though this suggested some act of magic, he was fully aware that he could not perform any magic and might even have to disappoint Segantini.

"What do you think should be done about the girl, Segantini?" he asked cautiously.

Segantini answered him with sudden fierceness, "I've become what I am because, after many years of tribulation, somebody finally believed in me and encouraged me. And here, in the case of this girl, I think I can help. Indeed, I feel that I have to help! You can lend me a hand. Give the girl a job in a place where I can see her. I want to get her to speak. And after that we'll see."

Robustelli suppressed a sigh.

"I'll do whatever I can," he said. "But I can't promise you anything. First, let's answer this photographer or journalist. I'll explain the situation to him."

Robustelli got up, a bit exhausted at the thought of all these tasks Segantini had put on his shoulders.

Segantini fixed him with a penetrating, hypnotizing look. "I believe in destiny, Robustelli, and that nothing happens without a higher power. Thank you. I knew that I could turn to you in confidence."

❧

Robustelli pondered the things they had discussed. Segantini was a famous man, and it was inadvisable to refuse his request outright. On the other hand, he didn't even rightly remember who the young woman Segantini had been talking about really was. The hotel had 150 employees, and although he had at some time or other hired them all, he couldn't remember the face that belonged to each name. But he did remember quite well that the lovely Andrina Biancotti had once asked him to hire a dumb but otherwise healthy girl to work in the hotel laundry because she had heard that they needed additional help there.

And then Andrina had actually brought the young woman to see him, and he had immediately hired her. But his eyes at the time were fixed on Andrina; she was such a pretty thing, firm and fresh as a chestnut bursting out of its shiny shell. Brown hair, dark lively eyes, and full lips. And he felt she was looking at him in a certain way, too, even though he was quite a bit older than she was.

Robustelli took a silver cigarette case from the top drawer of his massive desk and opened it. He didn't take out a cigarette but rather looked at himself briefly in the reflective interior of the cover, passing a hand over his dark hair, which, unlike Segantini's, was simply combed back.

On the whole, he thought, compared with Segantini, he was rather unimpressive. The fact that his mother thought he was very good-looking left him rather skeptical. All right, he had nice brown eyes, but not Segantini's penetrating, mesmerizing gaze. And although he agreed with his mother's proud appraisal to the extent that he did admit to having a masculine, well-proportioned, even Roman profile and a pleasant brownish skin tone, the gray at his temples made him look older than his thirty-one years.

But why compare himself with the painter? He had an important position and was doing well financially. More and more frequently, he thought the time had come to start a family. Up to now, the right woman just hadn't crossed his path, or perhaps he just hadn't taken the time to look around closely. And yet he thoroughly enjoyed life and was enthusiastic about railroads and playing bridge as well as dancing, something quite rare for a man. In fact, he could take some pride in the fact that there were quite a few women who raved about his abilities as a dancer.

Once a week he played bridge with friends in St. Moritz, a sacrosanct date, and whenever he could, he sought opportunities to go dancing. He loved the polka, and at that very moment, envisioned himself zipping diagonally across the dancehall floor with a flushed Andrina, her skirts gathered up.

With that last image in mind, he closed the cigarette case engraved with the initials A and R, and put it carefully back in the drawer. Then he had someone fetch from the laundry the girl who didn't talk.

"Well . . ." Robustelli said, drawing out the word and then pausing. He wasn't quite sure how to address a person who didn't speak and from whom he couldn't expect to get an answer. He started with a silly question—and was instantly ashamed. "What is your name?" he said, but then added, "Excuse me, I know you don't talk . . ."

Looking at Nika standing before him, calmly waiting, he tried to imagine what about her fascinated Segantini so much. It couldn't be just her sad story that made Segantini want to help her at any cost. There were contract children all over Switzerland whose situation was presumably no less awful than hers.

Very well, thought Robustelli, who wanted to be fair to the painter and not jump to any conclusions. Segantini had noticed her before he did. And perhaps understandably, considering that both had been abandoned by their parents. Achille's own life was perhaps too protected for him to be able to imagine the wounds that such a situation might leave on a young soul. And still . . . Anyway, he liked Andrina better. The new girl was too thin for him. Although she did have remarkable eyes; that was true. He couldn't see her hair—which Segantini had singled out—because it was concealed under the cap that all the in-house laundresses wore.

Robustelli gazed at Nika thoughtfully. Where could he put a girl who didn't talk?

He reached for the newspaper on his desk and held it under Nika's nose. "Can you read what it says here?" he asked.

Nika squinted slightly, seeming to think hard. But whatever the result, she just shook her head. This was quite a task Segantini had taken on. If she worked as a helper in the kitchen, he wouldn't see her any more often than in the laundry, and without any education and silent as a fish, she was unsuited for dealing with the hotel guests.

Nika was still standing there, waiting. And it dawned on Robustelli that she had no idea what this was all about.

"Someone has approached me on your behalf and asked that you be assigned a different job in the hotel," he said pleasantly, "and I'm trying to figure out what sort of work you would be suited for."

Nika was at first surprised, then she smiled, and her smile made Robustelli change his mind about her . . . for it was enchanting, both shy and radiant. It was as if the sun had suddenly come out from behind the clouds, shedding light and creating gentle, colorful shadows where before everything had been gray.

An inspiration came to him: she could work outside! Gaetano, the gardener, could use a helper, and at the same time, he could train her. After all, the old man wouldn't be able to go on forever. And then the painter could see the girl whenever he wished.

"Well," he said with satisfaction, "I think we've found a solution. Go tell Giuseppina that we need you elsewhere and that she should talk with the head housekeeper about finding a new laundress. No, never mind; I'll talk to her. Tomorrow, early in the morning, go immediately to see Gaetano, the gardener. I'll speak to him today, as well as the head housekeeper. You're in good health and can do garden work, can't you?"

Again Nika's face was lit by a brief smile before the radiance once more went into hiding. He couldn't possibly know how much she loved nature. She observed animals and plants so closely that she could draw them from memory, that is, if she could find a scrap of paper and some time before going to sleep.

Nika looked at Achille Robustelli as if he were a saint sent from heaven or a hero who had just dismounted from his horse and who, after proposing this elegant solution, would be spurred on instantly to put the next plan into action.

"All right, you may go now," he said, turning his ring again as if he really could occasionally perform magic with it.

"Two things, Andrina. The girl you brought to work in the laundry—I need her for another job. She'll be helping Gaetano, our gardener. Second—" He saw how she stood there, pursing her full lips, in expectation, and he enjoyed the moment. "Second, I spoke with the head housekeeper. She praised your work. Even though you're still young and don't yet have a lot of experience"—he thought a moment—"you apparently handle things skillfully and deal with the guests courteously. Signora Capadrutt thinks you're ambitious enough to work your way up in the hotel. This takes time, of course; and Signora Capadrutt is a strict supervisor. But you'll probably be pleased to hear that we're aware of your contribution, and I intend to promote you if you keep it up. When we reassign rooms next season, you have a good prospect of getting a single. As well as a job with more responsibilities." He looked up at Andrina, "That is, as I said, if you keep working hard."

Andrina opened her cherry red lips and said, more softly than was her wont, "Thank you, Signor Robustelli. That's very kind of you. I won't disappoint you."

Games and Game Rules

James Danby was an excellent tennis player. And if he was right about the intrepid lady he had met in the park, a brisk exchange of balls with those in her own social set would intrigue her more than exploring the unique features of the local landscape. Besides, her husband seemed to be quite a bit older and there was the hope that he would be occupied with handling business affairs by phone or telegraph while his wife filled her day playing golf or tennis with the other guests.

He was in luck. She had signed up for a lesson and was flirting with the tennis pro, but she discovered James sooner than he had expected. He felt flattered when she interrupted her game and, cupping her hands around her mouth, called over to him: "In ten minutes I can try out what I've just learned on you! But a lemonade before we match our skills would be marvelous!"

He got the hint. Spurred on by the prospect of beating her in a few rounds, he came back just minutes later with a large glass of lemonade.

She took the cool, frosted glass, sipped at the lemonade, and said, beaming, "Thanks! You've saved me from dying of thirst!

Though an orangeade might have been even nicer." Before he had the chance to think about what he'd done wrong, she gaily took his arm and said, "Come on. I'd like to beat you. Right this moment. The tennis instructor was quite pleased with me."

The game was brief. James was more athletic than he looked. He couldn't tell from his partner's eyes whether his speed and intelligent game had impressed her. The lady—he'd learned her name was Kate Simpson—wiped her brow.

"You're no gentleman, sir. Didn't you know that a gentleman always lets the lady win? And in such a way that no one can tell?"

But she was already laughing gaily, and James only nodded as she went on, "I'm hungry as a bear. Won't you come with me to the restaurant? I have a date with my husband and a couple of friends for lunch, and I'd like to introduce you to them. A good-looking man isn't such a bad trophy . . ."

She took his arm and pulled him toward the changing rooms.

"I'll see you in ten minutes in front of the entrance, all right?" She cast him a look with her blue eyes that was like blowing a kiss, and she was gone.

She's quick and witty—not at all bad company, James thought. And she was exactly what he needed to make St. Moritz bearable, even if she was a bit spoiled. But spoiled in an amusing way. And she was pretty.

He looked at his pocket watch. Where was she? He'd already been cooling his heels there twenty minutes; the noonday sun was burning hot, and sweat was collecting under the rim of his straw hat. He couldn't go into the ladies' dressing rooms, and it would have been rude just to leave.

She came out just as he had finally had enough and was turning to go.

"It's not nice to sneak away like that," Mrs. Simpson called out in a good-humored way.

This time James couldn't suppress a trace of annoyance, "I've been waiting for you for quite a while already."

"Oh, I was looking for something; it's all right now. Let's go. But we have a short ride there first." She took his arm and dragged him along. "My husband and I are staying at the Hotel Maloja, and the others are waiting for me there. We'll take a carriage and be there in half an hour. Come on!"

James was no longer quite certain that he wanted to have lunch with her. But it was too late to back out.

❧

"Are you in love with him?" Betsy asked her niece and fanned herself with the telegram the waiter had just brought to their table. Mathilde made a grab for it, but her aunt held on to the envelope. "First, answer my question, are you in love with . . ."

"Adrian?" Mathilde finished the question.

"Yes, with Adrian," Betsy nodded. "In any case, he wrote to you even before we arrived here . . . and now this . . ." she handed Mathilde the telegram, "even though, you called home to tell them, but you completely forgot to tell your fiancé."

Sometimes Betsy really is impossible, Mathilde thought. Mama, who hated indiscretions when she wasn't committing one herself, was right about that. Why did her aunt have to be so observant! Under her aunt's gaze Mathilde felt herself blushing as if she'd been caught doing something forbidden.

"It's all right, Tilda," Betsy said with a smile. "I was just kidding!"

Betsy really liked the Hotel Maloja. It had a reputation for measuring up to the best hotels in the world, and it more than lived up to that. It hadn't been all that difficult to convince Franz that, since his daughter had to go for a cure, it made sense to make her stay as pleasant as possible. He cared a lot more about luxury than his wife and would have made a similar choice for himself.

Betsy's eyes swept the sparsely occupied dining room. She was happy here. The room was elegant and airy; the stucco ceiling and white columns gave it a Mediterranean feel, almost as if she had landed on the Côte d'Azur. And indeed, sunlight was streaming through the windows; it was a glorious day.

A small, cheerful group of English and American guests were sitting around a table nearby. A slender young man with blond hair caught her attention. He stood out because he was clean-shaven and thus seemed younger than the other men, who had respectable beards. He had just turned to the lady on his right, a petite, pretty blonde who was animatedly whispering something that caused him to look in Betsy and Mathilde's direction. Catching his glance, Mathilde lowered her eyes.

Betsy noticed it. "He's quite good-looking," she said, all the while calmly looking him up and down. She was aware of the effect she had on people, and in spite of being in semi-mourning, always dressed with a certain flamboyance. She loved large hats and fine fabrics, and slender as she was, it was not particularly difficult to display her small waist. Still, it wasn't only her wasp waist that attracted the attention of men. There were also her intensely blue eyes, which contrasted so dramatically with her dark hair.

Betsy had always taken this attention for granted. She herself was the youngest in her family, almost an afterthought, and she had been treated as the family pet much like her niece had been.

Aside from her widowhood, she had been largely protected from trouble. Where she and Mathilde differed was in age and experience. Her niece had the advantage of the soft bloom of youth and a somewhat more affectionate nature. Her eyes, in a face framed by blonde curls, were open and inquisitive rather than shrewd and worldly. But Betsy smiled; it would be a mistake to underestimate her niece, she thought. Mathilde knew exactly what she wanted. And it was one of the reasons Betsy liked her so much.

Kate was the one to draw James's attention to the two women, after she had introduced her new conquest to her circle of friends.

"My dear James," she said, "let me explain something. I would rather you look around at the other tables than here among my friends. You see I'm already keeping a jealous eye on you." She briefly laid her hand on his arm. "Even though I have no right to you." She smiled at her husband sitting at the other end of the table, who had just directed a searching look toward James, and tilted her head toward the table where Betsy and Mathilde were sitting. "Have you noticed the two ladies over there? They arrived last night. I wonder whether they're sisters. The older one is a little too young to be the mother of the other, yet I wouldn't describe her as untouched by life." She examined the two women thoroughly and concluded that the older one might prove to be her equal if not superior in appeal, and for that reason she said, "She is trying a little bit too hard to compensate for a lack of youth by her extravagance." And smiling broadly at James she went on, "It isn't easy to admit to yourself that after a while, to go on pleasing men, you need a great many other qualities to compete against youth."

As she had expected, James picked up on that.

"What are you talking about, Kate! You know full well how pretty and young you are!" He took her hand in his as if to kiss it. "Don't act so modest. Because you're not, and you know it."

But Kate lifted her chin indicating the other table and said, "No really. I feel old next to an enchanting young girl like that one over there. Doesn't she have everything to warm your unattached heart: loveliness, youth, energy, and sufficient inexperience for you to shine as a seducer?"

James sighed. "What can I say? Didn't I wait patiently for you after our tennis game and follow you like a puppy to this place? Am I not exposing myself to your husband's suspicious looks, just to be with you, at this very moment? What else would you like me to say, beautiful Kate?" While he was speaking, he looked over as she had ordered him to at the two ladies and thought it charming the way the younger one lowered her eyes as he looked at her. Of course, she was well brought up, but it wasn't just good manners that made her avoid his eyes. She liked him, of that there was no doubt.

Kate, who had been watching James, asked, "What else would I like to hear? Well, naturally, that you find me irresistible, and that you'll think of me tonight."

James smiled. "I'd certainly be doing that if I didn't know that by then you'll be lying next to another man."

"Oh, then have some flowers sent," she said, without hesitation. "Their fragrance will make me think of you whether I want to or not! We'll be together in a most innocent way."

He flushed hearing these words because he couldn't imagine anything innocent in connection with her.

"Will you promise to think only of me tonight?" Kate's voice was insistent. "And not of the pretty girl over there? Look, you really have confused her."

He laughed and nodded obediently. Kate got up, and while James was saying good-bye to her friends, he managed to look unobtrusively at the other table, and received a furtive glance in return.

꧁꧂

Dear Mr. Danby,

Signor Giovanni Segantini has asked me to reply to your kind letter of June 12, 1896. He is prepared to meet with you to discuss his work. If the date is convenient for you, the meeting can take place on June 20th at 4 o'clock in the Spa Hotel Maloja. Signor Segantini speaks only Italian. If you need an interpreter, please let me know. I'm sure that I can be of assistance in that case. I would appreciate your confirming the appointment.

With best regards,
in the name of Sig. Giovanni Segantini
Yours faithfully,
Achille Robustelli
Assistant Director, Spa Hotel Maloja

James Danby examined the letter from all angles and then went to find his friend.

"Eddie, things are getting serious. But not now, not till an eternity from now, not until June twentieth. Didn't I plan to be back in London long before then?"

Even though it was only a rhetorical question, Edward, lying on his bed reading, mumbled, "I thought you had met an interesting woman and were staying for an indefinite time."

"Whatever," James said, dropping into the flowered easy chair. "Segantini wants to meet with me June twentieth. At the Spa Hotel Maloja. The same place the lady I've been seeing recently is staying. And you're coming along."

"Oh." Edward lowered his book.

"Yes. Because being an art historian you know Italian. Segantini speaks only Italian. Someone from the hotel had to write the letter in English for him. And besides, you wanted to meet Segantini too."

Edward sat up and closed his book.

"I can read Italian pretty well, but I can't speak it."

"Oh, you'll be able to manage. Don't let me down. Besides, you've been neglecting me, Edward."

Edward gave his friend an amused look. "I didn't think we were married yet, Jamie. Actually, you care as little for my presence as most married couples who have been acquainted as long as we have. Habit. It's all just habit, my man."

They'd been friends since their days in school, and even though both of them were only around thirty, that was a long time.

"Nonsense," James continued. "It's like this. If you leave me alone too long, I get involved in difficult situations."

"That's news to me," Edward said.

"You dragged me here even though you know that I'm not much interested in nature. So I've been looking around for beautiful women. Not without success . . ."

"I'm aware of that. Nice for you. And so where's the problem?" Edward asked. A skirt-chaser like James could apparently never get enough.

"Well, the lady is married . . ."

"But, you're not bringing her here to share a room with me! And I still don't know what you're getting at," Edward said.

"You'll understand in a minute. I would like you to meet Kate. After all, you're my friend. And that's not all. There are two other ladies staying at the same place, this Spa Hotel Maloja where Segantini wants to meet. The other two ladies, so I am told, are an aunt and her niece."

"Well, and so?"

"Don't be so unimaginative."

James pointed directly at Edward's heart.

"The niece is very pretty. She has blue eyes, and she's shy . . . well, actually not shy, just young . . ."

Edward was on the verge of saying something, but held back.

"Anyway, they're both blonde and blue-eyed. Kate is older, maybe twenty-five, and to put it bluntly, pretty shrewd. She monopolizes me as if I were her slave. We play tennis and golf and eat with her friends. She's constantly provoking me, even in front of her husband, and—well, it's quite titillating, and I think she isn't prudish."

James paused. "I think I'll soon be at a point with her . . ."

"And you need an official blessing that I'm supposed to give you," said Edward, whose dealings with women were much more reserved.

"That, yes, in any case. No, it's only that Kate keeps pushing me toward the younger one, and I don't know what it's supposed to mean. It's as if she wants me to keep proving to her that I prefer her, Kate, above anyone else. And I think she likes to play with fire. She can see that the young girl is falling in love with me. Yet the aunt sticks to her like a postage stamp."

Edward sensed that he was supposed to perform additional blessings.

"But if you have just the slightest spark of decency, Kate is the only one you can have an affair with."

"You know that I have no sense of decency," James said.

Love and Desire

Segantini dressed with great care. He chose a white shirt, he combed his hair, he checked to see if his shoes were polished, something he often forgot to do. Then he stood at the mirror and looked deeply into his own eyes where the melancholy of his childhood could never be erased.

"I won't need you today, Baba," he said to the servant girl as he stepped into the kitchen. "I won't be painting today."

Bice was standing by the window with her back to him. He turned her around to face him. Her light eyes did not reveal what she was thinking, even less what she was feeling. Then he kissed her forehead. She asked no questions; briefly, gratefully, he stroked her cheek and left the house.

Signor Robustelli had kept his word. Segantini knew the Spa Hotel Maloja's gardener. He had talked with him now and then when he walked past the hotel. Now he could see him from afar. The girl was with him, her reddish-blonde hair escaping from under the headscarf she had knotted at the back of her neck. She was nodding at the gardener's words. He seemed to be explaining something to her.

Segantini reached the two, but the gardener unhurriedly finished his explanation. "The stone pines are also called Swiss pines. This is the time they bloom, now, in June and July. And as you can see stone pines like to grow near larches . . . "

Nika showed no sign of the shock she felt when Segantini came up to them. She had learned his identity not long after their first memorable run-in on the street; this man with the black curls and dark eyes was the famous painter Segantini. She had run into him occasionally in the village.

Once, in the laundry, Giuseppina talked about him. "He is a gentleman. Different from us. He came up here from Savognin with his family. They say he had a pile of debts back there and wanted to get away from them and his creditors. He lives in the Chalet Kuoni. Baba, their housekeeper, brought them to the village here because she knew that the house was for rent. The signore comes to the hotel sometimes—he loves the music. He also loves his wife, Signora Bice, and he has four children with her. Baba follows after him like a dog, carrying his paint supplies. They say she reads to him while he paints."

In spite of learning these details, Nika couldn't get Segantini out of her mind. It was as if his gaze had buried itself so deep inside her that she couldn't escape it. In the mornings she hoped to run into him; in the evenings, she feared such encounters. It was frightening to feel that another person could have this much sway over her thoughts and her innermost being.

She looked down at the ground. Putting her hands into the pockets of her gardener's apron, she dug her fingernails into her palms to get a grip on herself.

"Good morning, Gaetano," Segantini said to the gardener, "I see you've got help." Then he looked at Nika and asked, "Do you like working outside better than in the laundry? I'm Giovanni Segantini, but I'm sure you already know that since we've seen each other before. I heard that you'd been working in the laundry and were living with the Biancottis. You've got a good teacher in Gaetano."

So he was behind it. He was the one who had asked Signor Robustelli to take her out of the laundry, give her a different job. Nika raised her eyes and looked straight into his. She wasn't going to try evading him. What was he thinking? That he could treat her like a little girl? She hadn't run away from Mulegns just so that another man could order her around according to his whims, the way the farmer used to!

Not a good beginning, Segantini sensed. But Gaetano, who was in a good mood, engaged him in conversation.

"Will you be going to hunt eagles again this summer, Signor Segantini? I saw the photograph of you coming down the mountain with an eagle. You climb like a native; no one would think you're from Milan."

Segantini shook his head. "I'm not sure, Gaetano. Maybe. But I have too many ideas for projects in my head. Pictures that I want to paint in the next few months." He sat down on a bench a few steps away and gestured for Nika to sit down next to him.

"I'd like to speak with the signorina for a moment, all right?" he said to Gaetano. "There's something I want to talk to her about. She'll rejoin you shortly. Just go on with your work."

Nika sat down next to him. Her heart was jumping as irregularly as a goat let out to pasture. She inhaled his scent. So that's what he smelled like. Woody. And like a fresh breeze. Different from other men she knew.

He was as shy as she was. It had been easy for him to court and win over Bice, and after that, it had never occurred to him to do it again. When he realized how little practice he had in such things, he laughed. He was amused at his own timidity.

"I've forgotten your name," he said, "but I did know it. Someone told me a while back."

Nika was silent and looked off into the distance. She had to concentrate hard to hear what he said.

"I recall," he went on, "that when I asked about you, they told me that you don't speak. Back then, you were fifteen, perhaps sixteen. You had the same eyes then and were already cocooned in your own world. It was the same for me long ago."

Segantini watched her attentively. He saw her expression change now, become softer.

She felt confused. He said he knew her? That he'd seen her before? But she had never met any strangers. And if she really had seen his face before, how could she ever have been able to forget it? Impossible!

"Wouldn't you like to ask me where I saw you?"

She looked aside, uncomfortable, but made no attempt to speak.

"I know you can speak," Segantini said, as stubborn as she. "Or at least that you could, once. Some other time I'll tell you where I know you from. But perhaps you'll want to ask me yourself some day."

He paused and frowned.

"I saw you a couple of days ago at the lake. You were leaning over the water and looking down into it at your reflection as if it were a mirror. You were holding the hair back from your face." He imitated the gesture. "Like this."

Nika nodded, smiling at him for the first time.

"I keep thinking about it," he went on. "I can't get the image or your gesture out of my mind. I'd like to paint this picture that's in my head. You gave me the inspiration. Do you understand? You're the model I see for it."

Yes, she understood. He wanted to touch her with his eyes. She nodded. She wanted it too.

Segantini got up from the bench. A cloud had floated in front of the sun. It soaked up the light like a huge ball of cotton, and for a moment, the spot where they were sitting was immersed in semishadow. He stood up suddenly in front of Nika—an imposing figure in black, like the statue of a hero looking prophetically into the distance.

Segantini thought for a while. Finally he said, "Go back to Gaetano. Now I know where I can find you. I have to search for the right place for my picture. A spring, it has to be a spring over which you are bending."

When he smiled again, she quickly put her hand on her chest as if to defend herself against his smile. He laughed when he saw the gesture, took the hand, and held it for a moment in both of his.

"Thank you for being willing to do this for me," he said. The look in her eyes was really as unfathomable as he had seen it in his imagination. "I'll come again soon. And please write your name on this piece of paper. Then you won't have to say it aloud. But I'd like to know what it is."

Nika continued to sit there, not moving. She felt as if what had just happened might dissolve into the nothingness of a dream if she dared to move the slightest bit. It was no coincidence that Segantini had come by. He had been looking for her. And he would come again.

"Well now, has the signore turned you into a pillar of stone? Does that explain why you're still sitting here, glued to the spot?" Gaetano said pleasantly. "I have to admit it's an honor that he came to look for you here, while the elegant ladies and gentlemen at the hotel are all hoping to meet him. That's something to be proud of! But come now, we still have a lot of work to do."

Nika loved working in the hotel gardens. When she noticed Andrina start keeping a notebook at the Biancottis, into which she wrote all sorts of numbers, Nika had indicated to Andrina that she would like to have a notebook too. And Andrina had actually bought her one, along with colored pencils. The girl had rounded off the price in her own favor, telling Nika that buying it had taken a lot of time. And anyway, Nika had no idea what paper supplies actually cost. Nika paid her with the first money she had ever had in her life. She regretted only that Gian wasn't there. She would have loved to show him her treasures. But he had returned to Grevasalvas with the cows a few days before. He, more than anyone else, would understand how much a notebook and colored pencils meant to her. She planned to go back up to Grevasalvas with him the following Sunday after the church service. He came down to Maloja for the occasion each week, and he'd expressed a wish for her to go back up with him afterward. It would be a chance to draw. By then, she would have already drawn the first flowers and plants in her new notebook. The intensely blue gentian was already in bloom, and soon red alpine roses would be dotting the landscape.

But delighted as she was with the new notebook and the happiness she'd felt ever since Segantini had approached her, something bothered her. He'd asked for her name. But if she had tried to write it for him, it would have been a scribble. The postmistress had stopped the lessons too soon, had put the lesson book along with its instructions for a God-fearing life back into the musty dark of her drawer. Nika wanted to work on her penmanship. She would write his name a hundred times, and master her own; he must never be allowed to forget her name.

There was a school in Savognin, but in the winter it was too difficult for the children to get there, and in the summer they were all needed at home to work. Yet, a few had somehow learned to write, read, and do arithmetic. Of course, the contract children who were taken on to do farm- and housework had no spare time for lessons, even self-taught ones. The best Nika could expect was to have shoes in the winter like the farmer's other children, even if the shoes she had were practically coming apart and had to be patched with cardboard because so many feet had already walked in them and outgrown them.

Nonetheless, Nika had often dreamed of going to school. There, she probably would have learned something about Italy. The Mulegns postmistress and innkeeper who'd told Nika the story of how she was abandoned swore up and down that the lady who'd left her as an infant on the front step of the inn had been speaking Italian with her female companion.

Working the hotel gardens gave Nika the chance to think back over the conversations she'd had with the postmistress. Now she remembered one in particular.

"Nika," the woman had said one day when Nika had come for a secret visit. "Nika, I swear that the woman who left you was your mother. She was a beautiful lady, an elegant lady. I saw her, after all. She climbed out of the coach with her companion while the horses were being changed. She'd asked for hot soup in the restaurant like the other passengers. I tell you, she was a lady of the best social circles, and she was speaking Italian. I could hear it distinctly. She had dark, full hair and dark eyes, like Italian women have."

Nika had listened with bated breath.

"And the woman with her looked like her servant, well dressed, but less elegant than your mother. She was older, and she was hunchbacked."

"She was what?" Nika had interrupted her again.

"Well, she had a hump. But she wasn't a cretin."

"A what?" Nika had broken in again.

"Just let me finish. It was only a little hump. She wasn't dim-witted and malformed, like cretins or idiots often are. But I did notice it."

"You mean like Lorenz? Is he a cretin?"

"Yes, Lorenz is one. Poor Serafina. To have a son like that; nobody would have wished that on her. But did you want to hear about your mother, or didn't you?"

The postmistress had set a glass of milk down for Nika; she poured herself some apple cider. The guest dining room was usually deserted around this hour. It was a while still before the next coach would stop, and the servants knew what they had to do. The postmistress always gave them clear instructions. A fly was buzzing around the table and then settled on her cider glass, crawling around the rim until it finally fell into the murky liquid.

"If she *is* my mother . . . ," Nika had answered thoughtfully.

"Of course she's your mother. After the mail coach drove on, there was this bundle left behind, and that was you. She just laid you down when no one was looking and got back on the coach. You were wrapped in a blanket; the locket and an envelope with money were lying next to the bundle. Quite a bit of money." She said this with a certain degree of resentment, for such a dowry was a rare thing, and she herself would have bestowed somewhat more care on the foundling than Nika had received. "And on the piece of paper it said that your name was Nika. But nobody here knows whether you've been baptized."

The postmistress had sighed. What a day that had been. As usual, she had been the one to deal with everything. One hundred forty people lived in the village, and sometimes there were as many as eighty to a hundred horses in the stables for the mail and passenger coach transport. That day, the coach had needed fresh horses to cross the Julier, and so she'd had to take charge of harnessing them up. Then there were all the other things that needed taking care of at the hotel, the restaurant, and the post stop station; managing the children, the stable hands, and servant girls was a whole other issue. Somebody had to keep track of it all, and her husband, for sure, wasn't capable. But she, always pregnant, was supposed to be able to handle everything. There was a plan to construct a railroad over the Albula Pass to the Engadine. It would have taken some of the burden off the Julier Pass—off her. But until that actually happened, she'd have to cope with it all.

She sighed again. She could have used the money that came with the child, but the little one had still been an infant and had needed a wet nurse . . . Nika nudged her to make her go on. The postmistress cleared her throat and gathered her thoughts:

"I would have kept you, but I had no milk left, I had just weaned my last child. And I didn't want you to die from cow's milk and gastroenteritis, and I had no time to try to feed you with goat's milk. That's why I went to the minister to discuss the matter. 'Ursina,' he said, 'you know better than I do who in the village would be able to nurse a second infant. Those are women's things. But show me the money; I'll make a note how much it is so that there will be no question whatsoever about how much the foster family was actually paid.'"

The postmistress, first fishing out the dead fly, took a sip of her cider. Nika didn't interrupt her this time.

"Well, then I thought of the farmer whom you know only too well by now. His second wife had just had a child. She still had plenty of milk because this was only her second child. The farmer's first wife had died in childbirth with the ninth child. She didn't have any strength left in her body—and no wonder."

The stout woman sighed again and crossed her hands below her bosom, which despite all her drudgery wasn't flabby, but round and expansive like a pillow filled to bursting with goose feathers.

Nika was still silent. She wanted to hear everything the postmistress had to say, didn't want to interrupt the flow of words with a remark at the wrong moment.

"And so that's where they took you, that same evening. By then you were crying pitifully with hunger. Such a little, abandoned creature. The farmer took the money, and Hanni, his wife, took you under her wing. Reto and you, you grew up together at her breast, and so the farmer now had twelve children. But in spite of the money, he always treated you like a contract child. Actually he didn't treat the nine children from his first marriage any better or worse than the ones from his second marriage, and none of them were treated much better than you."

Up to now, Nika had listened without moving. "So you're certain the lady on the post coach was really my mother?" she asked.

"I'm absolutely convinced she was," the postmistress replied.

"Then I'll go and look for her," Nika said resolutely.

The woman scratched her head. "Nonsense! That's what comes from having told you. I shouldn't have told you any part of the story. I only let myself be persuaded because you pestered me so. You won't be able to find your mother. First of all, you're too young, only twelve, and you have to stay with the farmer and work for him. And secondly, you'll never find your mother."

"And why not?" Nika asked angrily.

"Because you don't even know her name, you don't know where in Italy she lives, and you have no idea if she's even still alive. Where do you intend to look for her? And with what money?" The woman shook her head at so much foolishness.

"There are things," she went on, "you can't change. You have to accept them. You're a child without a mother or a father. That's the way things stand. So it's better if you don't ask any more questions. Be glad that you didn't die a miserable death. And now clear out."

Nika looked sullenly at the floor.

"I'll find her," she said so calmly and with such conviction that the postmistress looked at her in surprise.

☙❧

Signor Robustelli closed his office window. He rarely missed anything that happened in the hotel or its immediate surroundings. Segantini, it seemed, had not delayed in coming to meet with the strange young woman. He obviously couldn't wait to see her again. Perhaps he'd stop by to see him in his office . . . Robustelli went over to his desk and arranged the correspondence into new little piles. Segantini might come to say thank you, he thought. But the day passed without the painter making another appearance at the hotel.

A Purposeful Picnic

Dr. Bernhard shook his head. His new patient, Miss Mathilde Schobinger, had shown him a report from her family doctor in Zurich, which didn't quite coincide with his own diagnosis. He had no reason to mistrust his far-off colleague but had his own ideas nonetheless. The regimen he had prescribed for Miss Schobinger, who actually looked in blooming health, was not a very strenuous one—taking the therapeutic baths and drinking the mineral waters. This would give her time to enjoy the summer that was just starting. If she really had been suffering from exhaustion and anemia back in Zurich, then the famous healing waters of St. Moritz would do her good. Besides, he would be seeing her again, quite often.

"And please don't try to restrain your appetite for vanity's sake," Dr. Bernhard said to Mathilde as he was leaving. "Breathing the pure air up here, and bathing in the mineral springs stimulates the appetite, and this is a good thing. It is an inherent part of the therapy. You won't gain any weight in spite of that," he said, smiling. "And best of all, your cure program should allow you sufficient time to have fun."

Betsy used the afternoon in St. Moritz to buy some clothes suitable for the mountains from a dressmaker who had been recommended to her. The stay here was exactly the right moment to put aside her mourning. Walter would not have objected; he had never been narrow-minded. If he had been, he'd never have married her. At this point, she was sick and tired of the eternal black, even though she'd recently been brightening it up some by wearing a little white.

A bit of color was good for the soul after three years of drab outfits! She knew that many widows stayed in half mourning for the rest of their lives. She could already imagine how her sisters would reproach her when she returned home. But she had such a great longing for a change. A person deserves that now and then, she thought, and decided to get a velvety moss-green outfit and a dark, raspberry-red dress, nothing too showy. For the evenings, she chose an elegant silvery-gray dress of exquisite silk. She would wear her pearls with that. Wasn't the eternal black actually intended to minimize the fact that widowhood also entailed some freedom? She didn't have to put up with that.

She was advised to buy some high leggings in case she decided to go on mountain hikes. It made sense to protect her long skirt on the upward climb. There was an elastic strap below the hips that would allow her to tuck in the ends of her skirt. This gave her more freedom in walking. The dressmaker said she would deliver all the items she had chosen to the hotel.

Betsy felt happy as she lingered in the shop. Holding the dark-red fabric to her face, she looked at herself in the mirror. A trace of color was flattering. The chance to enjoy the fresh air, mountain climbing, and meeting new people . . . all of it felt like life getting back to normal. Betsy left the store. The sunlight felt warm on the back of her neck. She squinted up at the sun, which was much more intense up here than on the plain below, and opened her parasol.

It's spring, she thought. My God, it's *spring*! How beautiful it is.

❦

James Danby wasn't sure he would have noticed Mathilde if Kate Simpson hadn't pointed her out to him. But now he couldn't get her out of his mind, in much the same way as he could not stop thinking of Kate. Kate had aroused in him the love of conquest. It was clever of her to fan the flames of his desire this way. For if he had fully accepted that she was, after all, a married woman who was only available for a superficial affair, the flame of desire inside him would perhaps have subsided by itself. But by confusing him, giving him hope, then pushing him in Mathilde's direction, only to remind him that her erotic experience trumped anything the young girl might offer, she had captured his imagination more strongly than she could have without this confusing, ambiguous game.

As for Mathilde, she was falling in love with him, that much was obvious. With each meeting that Kate orchestrated, her happy bewilderment grew and her defenses diminished. The young girl's face was an open book, and James felt flattered to find himself on every page. Yet it was Kate who was in charge of the game. It annoyed him, but also spurred on his desire for conquest. The tortures she arranged for him were sweet and risqué enough to keep his interest in her alive.

He'd allowed Kate to persuade him to come along on a hike from St. Moritz to Pontresina. The party, in addition to a few friends of Kate's, would also include Mathilde and her aunt. Not a strenuous expedition. The plan was to picnic at Lake Staz. The

Simpsons' servants were sent ahead with checkered tablecloths, folding chairs, picnic baskets, and an assignment to find a suitable spot. Afterward, they planned to have tea in Pontresina at the Kronenhof and then return by horse and carriage.

James described the excursion to his friend in the most attractive terms, and then he added, "Eddie, I need you. You'll come along, yes? Please, as a favor . . ."

Edward could sense that he had been chosen to play a special role that afternoon. "It's nice that you need me, Jamie. But what's my assignment?"

He wasn't enthusiastic about going for a walk in the surroundings with other people. They'd all be talking incessantly, probably about themselves, exchanging a lot of vain and stupid remarks, paying no heed to nature. In the end, they'd hardly know what landscape they'd walked through.

"I'm sure you'll like the route we're taking," James cajoled. "The birds there fly right into your hand if you hold out some food for them. And you like birds, after all . . ." Edward tried to hurry his friend's recital with an impatient gesture of his hand. "And it would simply be wonderful if you could spend time with Mathilde's aunt, you know," he continued.

"So that's it—I'm supposed to clear the path for you by keeping Mathilde's chaperone at a distance."

"Exactly," James said, relieved that his friend had understood what it was all about.

"And you want to shoot your prey right in front of the wicked Kate's eyes and lay the trophy at her feet."

"She won't keep playing the cat in this cat-and-mouse game," James said, contradicting him. "She'll die of envy when she realizes that the lovely Mathilde is surrendering while you're distracting her aunt, and she'll agree to meet me by herself! I'll have her with me tonight, I swear!"

"Which one?" Edward asked.

"Well, Kate, of course!" James cried, surprised at his friend's obtuseness.

Edward was silent. Then he said, "And if I won't do it?"

James wasn't surprised. He had expected him to balk. Edward was simply too staid.

"Then you'll deprive yourself and Madame Betsy Huber, née Wohlwend, of a lovely afternoon. You could converse in German and finally have a chance to show off your language facility. Besides, she's quite attractive. Remember, I pointed out the two of them to you at the dairy farm recently. You have to admit that the lady, if she didn't have to take care of her niece, would be getting a lot of attention and sympathy. She's exceptionally good-looking, I think. She's elegant and has—well—I think she's a woman with spirit."

Edward hated hearing James talk about women as if they were horses.

"What you'd like to say is that you really like her quite a lot, except unfortunately you're too busy to acquire her as well?"

James laughed. He'd won the round. Edward wasn't thrilled about it, but he'd come along. Otherwise, he would have turned mute, the way he sometimes did when he really had determined not to do something.

"Maybe she'll come to occupy a special place in your affections. I'm sure you'll enjoy her company, Eddie. But now get a move on. We're meeting in an hour at the Waldhaus Restaurant by the lake. The excursion starts from there. Just think, today you may find happiness."

Some find happiness and others lose it, thought Edward, but didn't say it aloud, because the sentiment wasn't quite apt—only something you already have can be taken away from you. No recognizable happiness had come Edward's way in a long time. And he'd forgotten how to be that kind of happy person who reached out for joy with determination. Of course he'd forgotten! Emily had been his great love. Yet his unhappiness didn't even have the tragic dimension that might, in the end, have permitted him to draw some satisfying sense of melodrama from his dismal fate. Love had simply been distributed unevenly. Emily had loved him less than he had loved her, with the result that one day she had dissolved their engagement and married another man with whom—as far as he knew—she was actually happy.

No, his story wasn't exceptional, but it was enough to make him rather hesitant to approach women. However, instead of worrying about the situation, he found new interests. His father, a wealthy businessman, was certain that his oldest son, Anthony, would follow in his footsteps and succeed at the family business of manufacturing bathtubs and bathroom appliances; this was especially true since more and more private households and hotels were being equipped with them. With this in mind, he had allowed his younger son, Edward, considerable freedom in choosing a career. And since the father had always dreamed of having some intellectual professionals in the family, thereby increasing its social position, Edward had studied history and art history. Soon afterward, he had gotten an extraordinarily well-paid and pleasant position with an art institute in London that left him a great deal of freedom.

At first, after Emily left him—without really giving him any solid reasons—he went for a while to Paris and Rome, but no matter how hard he tried, he couldn't regain his inner peace.

And so he returned to London and withdrew to the small manor house and lands in the southwest of England that his father had bought from an impoverished lord. As the artistic member of the family, he had been assigned to plan the much-needed renovation of the estate. In the process, he had discovered his love for garden architecture and the innocent beauty of plants. He designed and planted new gardens, became absorbed in botany, and was proud of his experimental garden in which he tested plants from distant regions to see which ones might also take root and thrive in English soil. He found a happiness in this new activity which differed from the happiness he'd had with Emily.

He realized that he would have preferred to become a biologist—a scientist—even though he loved the arts and excelled in his knowledge of music. His real purpose in coming to the Engadine was to study the Alpine flora and take back plants to England, even though his friend James shook his head over this passionate involvement with botany. James didn't mind old men finding joy in their gardens. After all, the ancient Romans had suggested that it was one way of finding happiness. But Edward was still young, as James kept pointing out to him, even younger than he was, and he needed a woman.

"Don't tell me you don't have any fantasies!" he would often say. "That's impossible. I don't care if they're unusual, but you must have some. Absolutely. And you probably have some very bad ones. After all, people want . . ." James didn't know how vulgar he could be in Edward's presence, and so he didn't finish the sentence.

Edward was disgruntled. Why was it so easy for James to have a good time? Why was he able to enjoy himself without any feelings of guilt, certain in the belief that he could make any woman happy without ever asking himself if it was really so? Why did he, Edward, so rarely come across a woman he really liked, while Jamie found something in every woman he ever met—enough at any rate—to make her desirable?

Deep down he was envious of his friend—he couldn't deny it—a little bit anyway. And it was only because he didn't want to admit it that he was allowing James to use him to play an obsequious Leporello to his own Don Juan.

Glumly, he put on his shoes, as always meticulously tying a double knot—because that was the kind of person he was.

"Mr. Holbroke, how nice of you to join us," Kate said, smiling radiantly at him. "James keeps you away from us too much; keeping a jealous guard on you, always making excuses, saying you had other plans. One might think he was afraid his best friend might compete with him. Otherwise, I would have to assume that you've been avoiding me, and that would make me sad. In any case, you look in fine shape today. Don't you agree, James?" She turned to James, but he was already greeting Mathilde and Betsy. Just then, he called over to Edward, who left Kate with an apologetic smile, and thus avoided having to answer her.

It was warm. A few clouds swimming in the sky were reflected in the blue of the lake. At that moment, a cloud covered the sun, casting a subtle shadow over the small group of people and the shore of Lake St. Moritz. Betsy extended a hand to Edward, who took it. His mother was German and shaking hands was familiar to him. He made a slight bow and in German said, "I'm so happy to meet you, Madam."

Betsy smiled at him. She was wearing her moss-green suit and a hat that would have shaded her face even without the parasol. Edward thought of Jamie's remark about Mathilde's aunt's predilection for extravagant hats. He returned her smile. Her narrow face was framed by dark hair, as much as her hat allowed him to see of it, but it was the dark-blue eyes that he found utterly amazing.

"Mathilde!" Betsy called, turning toward her niece.

Mathilde, a few steps away, was watching James being impatiently pulled away by Kate. Mathilde's face was radiant with delight at the thought that he would be near her for hours.

"Can you come here for a moment, Mathilde?" Betsy called again.

Mathilde's face still bore the happy if somewhat absent expression it had exhibited when she'd been watching James. But when the sun suddenly came out again from behind the cloud and flooded her face with light, it seemed as if her smile deepened at the sight of Edward. In any event, that's how Edward interpreted it.

Up to now, he hadn't really looked at the girl, he thought. It was as if the sun had just lifted a veil from before Mathilde's, no, from before *his* eyes. Mathilde was as tall as her aunt and resembled her in many ways. She seemed a bit softer, as if not all the baby fat had melted away yet. On the whole, there were fewer sharp contrasts. Her hair was blonde and curly and suited her blue eyes. Betsy's nose was prominent and gave her a bold air, but Mathilde's was small and discreet. Her cheeks, he noticed, were almost feverishly flushed, and Edward felt a pang at the thought that James had won her over so easily, even though he was only toying with her affections. Edward was almost ashamed for his friend. But this feeling was balanced by the thought that it was the woman's fault if she was taken in by a man like James.

The Simpsons' servants had found an ideal spot for the picnic at the edge of the forest, near the enchantingly situated Lake Staz. A few charcoal-colored wading birds, alarmed at the party's arrival, swam away across the calm water. After briefly admiring the surroundings, the group, laughing and talking, settled on blankets and beach chairs. The servants withdrew discreetly to a place where they would not be disturbing the ladies and gentlemen, yet near enough so they could quickly return when summoned.

Suddenly, before they'd really settled down, Kate's closest friend, Myriam Shuttleworth, attracted everyone's attention. She was waving her arms wildly and emitting sharp cries. Of course, under the circumstances, that was the worst thing she could have done. For it induced the bee attracted by her flowery perfume to actually sting her. Myriam had a hard time recovering from the scare, the painful sting, and the fact that her husband hadn't even been capable of chasing away a bee. For him, it signified the end of a carefree outing. He suggested to his wife that he could take her back to St. Moritz and from there to Maloja. She angrily turned him down since they were already halfway to their goal.

Next a photograph was taken for which they all arranged themselves ceremoniously. James made funny faces and found it difficult to stand still, especially because the photographer was Kate's husband, a total amateur at this art who was taking himself very seriously. James regretted that, with development of these easy-to-use cameras by the American company Eastman Kodak, every Tom, Dick, and Harry could take photographs. Like this philistine, for instance. It was quite another matter when an expert like James used one of the new cameras on his travels.

"We should have invited Segantini to come on the picnic with us," James said, after the photo-taking seemed to have been going on forever. "He would have made a painting of us in the same amount of time this is taking."

"Who is Segantini?" Robert Simpson snapped. His feelings had been hurt, James saw with satisfaction.

"Oh, just a neighbor in Maloja," he mumbled, at which Myriam Shuttleworth's husband burst out laughing.

"Robert, do you mean to say you've never heard of Segantini?" Mr. Shuttleworth continued, ensuring that every last person at the picnic became aware of the gap in Kate's husband's cultural knowledge.

"But he's represented in every important exhibition. The Japanese pay huge sums of money for one of his paintings," Mr. Shuttleworth said, still laughing.

"Well, it's not quite like that," Myriam said, correcting her husband. He enjoyed showing off in front of other people, but in their married life, he wasn't such a smashing success. "You don't hear much about the man in France, or in Italy. Do any important art critics write about him? Come on, leave poor Robert alone." She patted Robert's arm, but then took another swipe at her husband, which might have had something to do with the bee sting he had not defended her against. "Yes, there's a lot being written about him. But it's more about him as a person. People are simply fascinated by him. The way he looks, his lifestyle, his enormous strength . . . some people could take a leaf out of his book."

No one failed to get her meaning. To move the conversation in a different direction, the gentlemen decided to uncork the champagne.

In the course of the picnic, Robert Simpson proved to be especially skillful at that. Kate played hostess and dished out the food packed by the hotel, which included cold meat pastries, *Bündnerfleisch*, and *Speck*, a type of pork, for the very hungry. As she went around distributing the plates, she added her own comments to each of the conversations she heard.

Edward, for his part, involved Betsy in conversation when he saw James sitting down on the grass next to Mathilde. He was surprised how easily Betsy was won over by his considerate behavior. She was not only lively and interested in almost everything, she was bubbling with energy. It took some effort, but he managed to keep his eye on James, who seemed to be furthering his cause with some success. In any case, he had been holding Mathilde's hand for quite a while already—this was only possible because Edward had placed himself so that Betsy had her back to them as she and Edward talked. She seemed to be enjoying herself, finding the conversation with Edward most stimulating.

"Have you ever gone on a real trek in the mountains here?" she was just asking him.

Edward shook his head, but said he thought it was a wonderful idea.

"Many of the locals offer themselves as guides," Betsy went on, "and I've decided to make the climb from Maloja up to Lej Lunghin, the source of the Inn River. Nearby there's a beautiful trail to the Muottas Muragl. There's supposed to be a fantastic view from up there—across the entire valley and all the lakes. I just have to make sure that Mathilde won't be left alone. She has been prescribed several medical treatments at the mineral springs in St. Moritz, but," and here she turned around to look, "someone has to keep an eye on her. I have to bring her back home to her parents and fiancé safe and sound."

"And she's probably just fallen for our dear James," said Kate, who had come to offer them some cheese and fruit. "You can't begrudge her that. But maybe it's the effect of the champagne. I had no idea she was already engaged." She laughed brightly. "But complicated stories are far more interesting than simple ones." She turned suddenly serious and put a small consoling hand on Betsy's shoulder. "You mustn't worry, Betsy, I'll still be here. If you want to climb the mountains, you can do it at any time."

She turned briefly to Edward. "Wouldn't you like to accompany Betsy? I couldn't imagine any more pleasant company for a hike in the mountains." And beaming cheerfully, she added, "I'll gladly offer my services as chaperone for Mathilde. I certainly don't intend to scrabble up any mountains. My athletic ambitions lie elsewhere. I promise you, Betsy, I'll guard your niece with my life."

Andrina was sulking. Wasn't a luxury hotel like this supposed to see to it that its guests were satisfied and content? To fulfill every wish of theirs before they'd even uttered it aloud? And now she'd been told that she would not be permitted to go with Mrs. Simpson's servants to the picnic at Lake Staz—when Mrs. Simpson herself had suggested it! She'd told Andrina she was a nice girl and knew the local area better than her own servants. And she told her to ask if she might be excused from her job for that one day. But the head housekeeper, Signora Capadrutt, had raised her barely visible blonde eyebrows and given her a penetrating look.

"Even if it were your day off, Andrina," she said at last, "even then I would forbid it. And remember this for the future, hotel employees are not to speak to the servants of the guests, and they certainly may not accompany them on excursions. I thought you knew the regulations. Apparently I shall have to explain this matter to Mrs. Simpson too."

Andrina knew full well that Signor Robustelli would not change the rules governing hotel personnel for her sake, no matter how much he liked her. If she didn't want to let herself be ordered around, she couldn't remain a chambermaid in this hotel. It had once seemed like a heavenly Jerusalem to her, but that feeling had worn off a bit. In any event, it seemed advisable for her to concentrate on the here and now, and to depend on her own common sense rather than some divine Providence.

Alpenstich, Pneumonia

Sunday came, but Gian wasn't in church. Nika waited for him in vain. And Segantini didn't come either. It worried her that Gian hadn't come; that Segantini wasn't there surprised no one. He didn't go to church, even though the Protestant minister, Camille Hoffmann, was his friend.

Nika's mind wasn't on the sermon. She understood as little about the righteousness of God as about his mercy. Afterward, she returned to the house with Benedetta and the family. She hoped she might have the chance to go up to Grevasalvas on her own that afternoon to see how Gian was doing.

"I wonder if something is the matter with Gian," Benedetta said, spooning up some rabbit stew. Her voice sounded worried but none of the other family members appeared to be upset. Aldo was picking his teeth—using the pointed end of a little twig that he'd pulled off the bushes in front of the house, having first removed its leaves. He pushed his black hat back off his forehead, and held his plate out for another helping of rabbit stew, which was so thoroughly overcooked that the meat fibers got stuck in one's teeth.

"He probably just didn't feel like going to church," he said, "and up there you can always find an excuse. Sometimes the cows get away; that's just how it is. I'm sure he'll come down when he starts to miss us."

Andrina and Luca laughed.

"That's just like Gian, always a little different from the others. Let him be. He does his own thing, and he likes it that way," Luca added. "Besides, there's something I want to say. Gian herds the cows and he isn't much use for anything else. But I want to earn some money and not be stuck here forever. Signor Robustelli from the hotel has already gotten Andrina a job, and he's going to help me too."

Andrina smiled proudly.

The whole village knew that Signor Robustelli was passionately interested in the construction of the railroad and knew everything about it. But she, Andrina, had plucked up the courage to ask him whether he would be willing to talk to her brother who wanted to find a job as a railroad worker and was eager to get Signor Robustelli's personal advice. Achille Robustelli had said, "Very well, Andrina, have him come to see me. I'll see what I can do."

She looked at Luca and nodded her encouragement.

"In any case," said Luca, picking up the thread again, "they're just building the stretch between Reichenau and Thusis, and with Signor Robustelli's help, I'll probably be able to get a job as a construction worker with the railroad company. The work is hard; they can't use weaklings, but," and he showed them his muscles, "they've got the right man in me."

His father was pleased and smiled so broadly that one could see where the teeth were missing in the back of his mouth. Yes, indeed. This was his son! But Benedetta's expression, as always, indicated to everyone her thoughts that good beginnings usually come to bad ends. Everyone looked at her in amazement as she now not only made her usual face but actually spoke. "Then just be careful that your muscles aren't bigger than your brain. This sort of work is not just hard labor, but a lot of the workers die. Almost two hundred were killed during the construction of the Gotthard Tunnel."

"That was more than ten years ago," Aldo said.

"And besides, that was a tunnel," Andrina added. She didn't want to see her efforts to get Luca a job wasted because of Benedetta's eternal objections.

"All this sounds like a silly idea put into his head by Robustelli," Benedetta replied emphatically. "And I know you're involved. The two of you gave Luca the idea!"

Andrina jumped up from the table in anger.

"What are you saying? Signor Robustelli offered to help Luca because I asked him to, what's the problem with that? Don't you understand that Luca doesn't want to stagnate in this dump where the winter snow suffocates everything? The rich people come here to enjoy themselves in the summer, they squander their money, and we don't get anything out of it! Absolutely nothing. How far did you get with all your work and drudgery? Look at yourself, always wearing the same black skirt. You don't even have a mirror. And look at the pot standing there with the skinny little rabbit. Do you have any idea what the guests in the hotel eat? Things you haven't even heard of."

Benedetta got up and slapped her daughter in the face.

"Sit down, the both of you," Aldo said in a loud voice, "and stop talking. I'm proud to have Luca taking part in building the future of this country. And that's that."

Andrina grimaced, but was silent. Only Benedetta refused to be silenced.

"The future. The future? He'll be working on someone else's future, not his own. His life will be as miserable as ever. It'll get worse. They'll work him to the bone, till he's burned out. The workers will never ride on the railroad they build."

"You can talk as much as you want," Luca shouted. "I'm going to do what I want. The future belongs to the workers, to industry! Not to the farmers. In Italy, the workers are on strike fighting for their rights. But here," he swept his spoon off the table, "children will keep going barefoot, hungry, and miserable for a long time. They'll be peddling bunches of alpine roses to the ladies and gentlemen being carried on mule-back up the mountains in exchange for pennies."

"So, go, do what you want," Benedetta said. "But now somebody has to go up to Grevasalvas to check on Gian."

Nika nodded to indicate that she'd go. After Benedetta filled the tin canister that Aldo usually took to work with rabbit stew and polenta for Gian, Nika slipped out to make the journey.

Nika could have picked a different way to go. But she chose this one. It led up to the Hotel Belvedere past Segantini's house. You could also climb up to Grevasalvas from the Chalet Kuoni. The coziness radiated by the big wooden house gave Nika a pang. Segantini must feel comfortable here, in the circle of his family. They said he owned porcelain dishes and silver cutlery with the monogram *GS* engraved on it. The family was probably still sitting at the table eating, he, his wife, and the four children. If he saw her passing by his window now, he would not let on in any way that that he had gone to see her in the hotel gardens. So why didn't she try to avoid him? After all, he had taken her out of the laundry because he needed a model for a painting that had nothing to do with her. How was he any different from the farmer who used her to work on his land?

The door of the house swung open. Three laughing boys came out: Gottardo, Alberto, Mario. Giuseppina had told her their names; gradually, Nika was getting to know the people who lived in Maloja. There weren't that many, all in all. She waited for Bianca, Segantini's youngest child, but she didn't come out. Nika could have kicked herself. Obviously, she'd been hoping to cross paths with him, but instead of him, she saw all the things he had that she didn't have: a family, a house, a sense of belonging. And he also had a homeland.

She felt for the locket hidden under her blouse. It reminded her that she was determined to find her own place—her homeland, her family. Each day was just a part of the journey, part of the long road she would have to travel. But it was a beginning.

Carrying the lukewarm metal canister with Gian's Sunday dinner, she walked quickly past the house. The boys called out a greeting. Nika didn't turn around at first because there were tears in her eyes. But then, she did turn around, and saw Segantini standing in the doorway of his house. He raised his hand; for a moment it hovered motionless in the air, then he let it drop. He looked massive in his dark suit.

Dumb *straniera*, she thought, you're a foreigner.

In his life as well.

It was hot. Nika felt the sun warming her thick hair right down to the roots. Tiny drops of sweat formed on her forehead and at the back of her neck. The path led upward, and there was no shade. The light was dazzlingly bright, and the mountain peaks on the other side of the lake were sharply silhouetted against the sky: Piz Roseg, Piz Corvatsch, and Piz da la Margna . . .

How lonely Gian must feel up here.

As she climbed higher, she saw the few huts of Grevasalvas silent in the sun. Occasionally the sound of a cowbell reached her, as unreal as if in a dream. Up here, there were no trees; everything was rock and grass. A brook ran through a meadow with glowing yellow buttercups, a sea of sky-blue forget-me-nots, gentian, houseleek, Alpine pinks, and some scattered rose-colored orchids. Farther on, nearer the huts, she spotted blue monk's hood.

The Biancottis' four light-brown cows were in the overnight pasture near the hut, which Gian had fenced in with wooden posts and wire. So he hadn't driven them anywhere that morning.

Nika found him on the cot inside the hut in a feverish sleep. The hay-stuffed sack that served as a mattress had slipped halfway off the bed frame, and the matted wool blanket was on the floor. His limbs were shivering in the cold, and the light-brown hair that grew in whorls, which she often wanted to mess up with her fingers, clung damply to his forehead. Nika sat down on the stool next to the cot and took his hot hand. He woke suddenly from his restless sleep, but didn't immediately recognize her, even seemed afraid. Nika brushed the hair from his forehead, covered him again with the blanket, and went to get a pitcher of water.

Gian closed his eyes and let her sit by his bedside. As she washed his face like a little child's, he seemed to recognize her. His face was so hot that the towel she dipped in cold water and placed on his forehead warmed up even as she was holding it there.

His fever was dangerously high—you didn't have to be a doctor to know that. But Nika could never have managed to take him down to Maloja by herself. She rinsed two rags, and wrapped them, still damp, around his legs to draw out the fever, and gave him water to drink. From his confused words, she gathered that he had had a dream, but in his feverish mind, the dream and reality were all jumbled together. He had seen Segantini and Nika together, he mumbled. He seemed very distressed about what he'd seen, but his thoughts were confused and made no sense.

Tears came to Nika's eyes, for she didn't know how she could help him. Then, with his hand still in hers, he fell asleep. His face softened, and his lips, slightly parted, trembled every time he exhaled with a sighing sound. Nika wept because she had never seen him so exhausted and confused and because she was so very fond of him. At that moment, it seemed as if Gian was a piece of her homeland, Gian, now so fragile and sick. Just knowing him had made the risk she'd taken in leaving the place where she'd grown up worthwhile.

She turned around with a start as the wooden door of the hut opened with a creaking, grating noise and Luca and Aldo entered the room. Nika, accustomed to making room for others and becoming invisible, got up so that the two could get close to Gian's cot.

So they really were worried, although it was probably only because of Benedetta's persistent urging that they'd made their way up to the hut. Whatever complicated emotions they had about each other, they were a family, each inextricably part of it and responsible for the others.

Quietly, Nika left the hut and sat down on the bench outside. The two men would bring Gian down to the village. Not a good day for her. Either you're part of a family or you're not.

"It's *Alpenstich*, pneumonia," Benedetta said. "We don't need to call the doctor. That would cost more money than we have and will be of no use anyway. Either Gian will make it, or he won't.

Torriani, who also has cows up on the mountain, and whose milk Gian used to bring down, stopped by here a while ago. He told us that Gian had pains in his chest and was coughing. So Aldo and Luca finally decided to climb up."

Benedetta was sitting at the kitchen table, brushing away some imaginary crumbs. She pushed a bowl of milky coffee toward Nika.

"Rabbit stew is not the right thing for him now." She looked at the canister Nika had brought back, unopened, and then to the closed door behind which they had laid Gian on his old bed.

"Torriani is going to take care of the cows now. Who else is supposed to do it now that Luca is leaving?"

Nika nodded in a daze. *Alpenstich* was a matter of life or death. How were they going to help him get better? There had to be something they could do to fight the fever! How could Benedetta sit there so unmoved?

As if she'd read Nika's mind, Benedetta went on, "You know, I've lost a lot of children already, two girls, Arietta and Mirta, right after they were born, and one boy, Elio. He was a treasure, a ray of sunshine for three beautiful years. Then came Gian, Luca, and Andrina. After that, only miscarriages. One day you may know what that's like. Nothing's ever going to make you forget that. It changes you. So, no, I'm not going to let my Gian just lie there like that—which is what you may have been thinking. There's an old woman in Stampa who knows a lot about plants. She makes a medicine from monk's hood that works against fevers. She sells the stuff around here. But you have to be careful with it. Monk's hood is poisonous. It's not something to play around with. Not just anyone can brew a medicine like that."

Nika nodded. The cure was something they knew about in Mulegns too.

"I've already given Gian some silver thistle tea. When he wakes up, I'll give him soup made of borage and some other herbs, which is the same brew you give to sick cows. But for now, we'll let him sleep." Benedetta shook her head. "The men gave him schnapps mixed with an egg and some honey, the same stuff you give a woman who's just had a baby." She was silent, probably thinking of all her deliveries.

Then, seeming to notice that Nika was very worried and uneasy, she added, "You like Gian, I know. It will be all right if you go and sleep for a while. I'll take care of him."

Another Sort of Fever

More often than he liked, Segantini's legs were taking him in the direction of the hotel, in spite of the commands from his head to the contrary.

He usually got up very early, at sunrise, and Baba adapted to his rhythm. Sometimes he was already at his easel by five a.m.

The paintings he was working on were in various spots outdoors. He locked them up each night in heavy wooden boxes specifically made to protect them, so they could safely stay outside no matter what the weather.

Baba would follow him each morning to whatever canvas he had in mind to work on, and crouch at his feet, patient as a dog. As she handed him paints, he would put down color on the canvas with short, strong strokes. First, he'd begin with the colors that would determine the tone of the painting.

He worked on canvases he'd already primed with turpentine and terra rossa. The dark rust-red surface grounded him and lent the brightness of his colors a deep undertone that ran like a bass note in his symphony of light. Over the years, his palette had become lighter, brighter, and he now used only a few pure unmixed colors: zinc white and silver white, black, cobalt green and emerald, cobalt blue and darker ultramarine, four shades of yellow, and vermilion. Between the brush strokes, he left spaces of almost the same width as his brush strokes. Later, he usually filled these spaces with complementary colors, putting red next to green, for example. The colors would blend in the eyes of the viewer.

Usually, before beginning work outdoors, he would have already roughly sketched the composition he saw in his mind onto the canvas in simple white strokes and planes of color. During that phase, he would also search for the locations that would provide details for the picture: a church steeple, a depression in a meadow, a mountain. For most of his paintings, he used several locations. When he reached the last stage, he'd select just one place to work where he could capture the harmony of light that would give his painting its atmospheric mood.

He usually worked on several paintings at once. And, practiced and tireless mountain hiker that he was, he traveled long distances each day to find the different light conditions he wanted.

As he settled down to paint, he'd often say, "Read to me, Baba." And listening to Baba's voice, enveloped by its murmuring flow, he'd put paint to canvas almost as if in a trance—in any case, without thinking.

Each day, Segantini went home for lunch, and ever more frequently he sought out the route that led past the hotel. He would scan the garden. Her strawberry blonde hair could be seen from a distance, and its abundance drove him crazy: it was a carpet he wanted to spread out, or better yet, be enveloped within. He wanted to wrap himself in its fragrance, which he already knew was half-flower and half-animal. But he did not allow himself to go near Nika after spotting her. Instead, he would greet her from afar.

He also felt drawn to walk past the hotel in the evening. And it was only then, once his work was done, that he would occasionally say a few words to her—that much he allowed himself. At that time of day, she seemed to be on the lookout for him.

Although her eyes never revealed anything as he came closer, he saw how blood rushed to her small face at the sight of him. She had soft, light skin, even though it was tanned from being exposed to the sun. Like Bice. No, quite different from Bice's. That was, of course, the crux of it. Had she been like Bice, his imagination wouldn't have tormented him, for Bice gave him everything that a woman like her had to give. From Bice he got everything he needed. This half-tamed girl had all the things he didn't need. She made him feel restless; she disrupted his work, which Bice had so wholly subordinated herself to. It made him feel oddly weak. For he *was* his work. His work was what held him together. It was the framework on which his life was built. He had constructed a world for himself in which darkness and fear could not overpower him. Thanks to his work, to his ceaseless striving, thanks to nature and the alpine light, he could live and even love. The girl belonged to the other side of his life, the side he had tried to hide, to forget about.

Yet in spite of that, he was driven to seek her as if he were looking for his own shadow. His life now had only the one side, the bright side; he had achieved this with great effort. Yet deep down, he knew that the dark side persisted, just as death is a part of every life.

Nika had a problem. How could she tell people that she wanted to learn to write and to draw without speaking? She showed her notebook to Gaetano, pointed to the plants she had drawn and then to the empty space next to the drawing. But Gaetano was even less able to write than she was.

"Show your notebook to Signor Segantini, to whom you've become so indispensable," he said, hoping to distract her from his own shortcomings.

"Every time he comes to see you, he's actually stealing time from your work. But I can't complain because he's a friend of the hotel director's. Ah yes, that's how the world turns," he mumbled. Yet he spoke without any real anger, like someone who long ago had reconciled himself to such things. And then, to encourage her, for he liked Nika, he added, "Go ahead, show him the notebook. Look there, he's already on his way here. Pretty soon you'll be able to set your watch by him."

"I'd like you to talk," Segantini said, after he'd beckoned to her and she'd walked away from Gaetano.

Together they'd strolled to the shore of the lake, where they stood side by side, looking into its clear depths. Stones, bits of root, lake grass barely trembling with the tiny movement of the water. Segantini bent down and, picking up a flat pebble, tossed it at a wide angle over the surface of the water. It touched the surface, causing a ring-shaped wave to spread out across the water; it skipped, once, twice, and then sank.

He stood up and looked into the girl's face. He reached out a hand and touched her hair; it was only loosely and casually pulled together to form a knot at the back of her neck. Taking a strand of hair, he wrapped it around his finger.

His first contact was with her hair; *her* first contact with his hand. It was a broad hand, fleshy, almost ungainly, yet also gentle. Nika took hold of his hand, pulling it down so that the strand of hair slipped out, and looked at it, while shyly stroking his wide fingers with the fingertips of her left hand.

"I . . . want . . . to . . . learn . . . to write!" Nika suddenly said haltingly, not looking at him. "I want to learn to draw!"

Segantini lifted her chin so that she had to look at him. He gazed carefully at her face. Said nothing. Nodded.

Lost in thought, Nika stroked her skirt and ran her fingers through her hair, imagining her hand was his; when she slid her tongue over her lips, she had the sensation of feeling his lips. She practically felt the texture of his beard on her skin.

She watched as he flipped open her notebook and paged through it, looking at her drawings with his lips slightly pursed. Then, he fixed his dark, penetrating gaze on her and said, "You've done well. I'll take the notebook with me."

She didn't dare contradict him, even though she was worried about losing it, the only treasure she had besides the locket.

Later that night, she found she couldn't sleep. After putting out the lamp and lying down, she stared into the dark. She missed the warmth of the little brown cows; they were all up in Grevasalvas now. She stood up again, wrapped her woolen shawl around her, and stepped outside the door. Looked up at the sky. The stars were out, and the Milky Way formed a diagonal trail across the heavens as if the milk pail had slipped out of a heavenly Gian's hand. The stars were very far away. There was a slight, scarcely perceptible breeze, as though the night were breathing softly.

Nika spread her arms as if to embrace the night. Now, because there was an ear ready to listen, it was worthwhile talking again.

Nika had stopped talking years before because it didn't make any difference whether she talked or was silent. She had grown up with the same milk and the same language as the other children in Mulegns, and yet the others understood Nika as little as Nika understood them. She didn't even know if anyone noticed when she suddenly stopped talking.

The farmer had forbidden her to speak with the people in the village. And then there was the affair with the cave.

The farmer's older sons had promised to give her an apple if she would go with them. It was late summer; the farmer was gone for the day. Otherwise, they couldn't have sneaked away from the farm that easily. A couple of children from the village came along too.

Nika had a bad feeling about it. You didn't simply get an apple for nothing. She worried that the boys might have discovered her buried locket, or been alerted to the fact that it had disappeared from the chest. She *had* to go with them. Because she had to find out. She absolutely had to make sure.

"Well, come on, you coward!" Hans called to her, holding out the apple. He was the oldest. Almost imperceptibly, Reto shook his head. Maybe he'd found out what his older brothers had planned, even though they usually didn't include him, the youngest, when they were hatching some mischief. He was sometimes the target of the coarse pranks in which even the old farmhands, whose lot had made them merciless and rough, often took part.

The big boys had already encircled Nika like a pack of yowling dogs and were chasing her out to the edge of the village and beyond. From time to time, Hans held the apple up triumphantly, and then, with the others laughing, he would let it vanish into his pants pocket. There were girls in the group too, Maria and Elsa. That gave Nika some hope that Hans wouldn't pounce on her as he had threatened to do.

Nika felt even more anxious when she realized where they were heading. She knew that not far from the village, set far back from the road, was a well-concealed cave, which the young people used as a meeting place. It was also a place they could hide things they didn't want to show anyone at home or hand over to their parents.

That's where they took Nika. She started to tremble with fear and said, with her teeth chattering, as firmly as she could, "Let me go. I've got to work."

Hans made a face. "Don't be afraid. I like Elsa better than you. I'm not going to kiss you."

Elsa laughed and took the apple out of Hans's pants pocket, not without brushing her hand along his leg, and smiling at him. "Well, go on. You'll get your apple inside." Elsa ducked and went into the cave.

Hans gave Nika a push that made her stumble in after Elsa. Reto let out a muffled scream, and when Nika turned around to look at him, she saw that Hans was holding his mouth shut, hissing, "Shut your trap. Otherwise you're in for it."

Elsa held Nika by the arm, and Hans followed them inside and blocked the entrance.

The prank had been prepared beforehand. When Hans gave the sign, the others with joint effort began to shove a big chunk of rock in front of the entrance. Outside, Maria was holding Reto's mouth shut; he was whimpering with fear. "If you don't keep quiet, we'll put you in there too," she told him.

When the rock almost completely blocked the entrance, Elsa let go of Nika.

Hans nodded to Elsa and said, "You get out now."

"And you," he said to Nika, "you'll get your apple, you really will. You didn't think you would, did you?" He laughed.

It had gotten so dark inside the cave that Nika couldn't make out his features. Elsa, squeezing out of the cave through the narrow opening, protested, "Hey, I want the apple."

Hans pressed the apple into Nika's hand. "Elsa is really an awful person. Here, you can take it."

Then he pushed Nika even farther back into the cave.

"Why are you doing this to me?" Nika asked. "Why are you locking me up in here?"

"Just because," Hans said, and he too squeezed out through the narrow opening.

Then they pushed the rock so as to block the entrance all the way, and it was totally dark inside.

They hadn't found the locket, or noticed that it wasn't in the chest anymore. They had no reason for what they were doing to her.

The cave was damp and chilly. All sorts of junk and garbage had collected there, but it was too dark to know what anything was. Nika knelt on the ground near the entrance. No sound could be heard inside the cave.

She lost all sense of time. At some point, it would be getting dark outside too.

When the farmer's wife asked them about Nika at supper, Hans gave Reto a threatening look.

"No idea where she is," he said and shrugged.

"She'll be in for it when she gets back," the farmer said.

"Maybe she ran away," Hans said.

The next morning, in spite of being afraid, Reto couldn't hold it in any longer, and he told the farmer's wife where Nika was.

She sent the boys off. "Bring her back here. And make it quick," she said. But she kept Reto at home, so he wouldn't be beaten to a pulp.

They were all silent as they pushed the rock away from the cave entrance and Hans pulled Nika out.

Then Hans said to the others, "She was so scared she made a mess in her pants."

But nobody laughed. They took Nika, who was shivering with cold, back to the farm.

The farmer's wife didn't say anything; just sent Nika off to work with a gesture of her hand. The farmer waited till Sunday. Then he took off his belt and said, "You filthy brat, if you disappear again you'll get a good hiding."

From that day on Nika stopped talking.

Walking a Tightrope

Achille Robustelli was at his desk. He felt vaguely uneasy. His attention was entirely focused on seeing to it that the hotel operated smoothly, but he also had a well-developed sixth sense that alerted him when something was not quite right in his surroundings. And there seemed to be several things amiss.

Andrina was apparently upset about the *straniera*'s being transferred from the laundry to the garden. As a chambermaid, she got to see the insides of the hotel guests' rooms, yet she, herself, was practically invisible. And when she did enter their rooms, it was usually after the illustrious guests had left, leaving her only the thankless task of cleaning up after them. On the other hand, the *straniera*, in Andrina's eyes, could almost take part in their social life, or at the least observe it. This put Andrina in a bad mood, Robustelli saw.

In addition, he knew, Andrina's family had problems at home, much more serious ones. Gian was still fighting for his life. Robustelli would gladly have helped the family, for the pretty Andrina's sake, but the girl's mother held it against him that he had smoothed the way for Luca to get a job with the railway.

Besides, she would have been too proud to accept money from a stranger to pay a doctor—and she didn't even believe that the doctor could help her son.

Meanwhile, Luca was gone, but that seemed fine to Robustelli. Many young men were leaving the rural areas for the cities to work in factories, or taking jobs with the railroad. It was the march of time. Robustelli saw these developments matter-of-factly. There was no going back, not even in the Engadine, where foreign visitors were now the largest source of income. Not all the locals profited from this, and the difference between the poor and the rich was enormous, even among the natives; the difference in means between the vacationing visitors and the valley residents was nearly incomprehensible. Yet the visitors provided work for the residents, even if they weren't prepared to share their affluence directly with the poorer locals.

The truth was, Achille had gotten to know his wealthy clientele better than he would have liked. He was a careful observer, and what he saw—although it didn't turn him into a misanthrope—did quash any idealistic notions he might have had. He was too middle class to get anything out of class-war slogans, but he saw the situation quite clearly, and as a consequence, he never admired rich people just because of their money.

On the other hand, he had thought a lot about what Segantini had told him about the strange young woman. He had also been brooding about Segantini himself. In contrast to those two, who'd been abandoned as children, he had grown up in loving and sheltered circumstances. Not that his mother's affection had always been problem-free. Sometimes he felt as if he were suffocating under her love. But that same love, especially while his father was still alive, had nurtured him and made him strong enough to see himself with sympathetic and appreciative eyes, and to defend himself against unjust demands or attacks.

Segantini's story about the girl's origins made him aware for the first time that not all people grew up with the warm and secure kind of upbringing that seemed so natural to him because he'd had such a home. He wondered about the development of a person who is deprived of love at the beginning of his life. He'd contemplated it, but felt he really couldn't quite imagine what being abandoned felt like. Yet he could tell that Segantini, in contrast to him, was able to empathize with Nika's story, probably because he'd had a similar experience early in his life.

It was obvious that Nika and Segantini felt magnetically drawn to each other, because of the unspoken bond that this common experience created. Since the young woman had started working in the garden, Segantini passed by much more often than before, seeking her out. Segantini had fallen in love with Nika; Robustelli had no doubt of that. But he didn't know where this could lead in a village like Maloja, where everybody knew everyone else, and everything came out into the open sooner or later. Segantini was respected and had a family. And the thought that by helping and encouraging Nika—with the best and noblest intentions—the painter was thereby also causing her new difficulties and possible harm saddened Robustelli. For in the end, any relationship that ensued would be blamed on Nika, not on Segantini.

Isn't it bad women who lead men astray?

This train of thought made Achille feel uncomfortable. Not because he adhered to a narrow moral standard, and not because he knew the stories of these two people who were so close to him. Rather, watching a situation develop for which he could see no practical solution was hard for him. His ability to find solutions for almost all the problems he encountered was what had made him so successful and content in his profession. But a resolution to what he saw coming between Segantini and the girl eluded his pragmatic mind. The dark, confusing field of human emotion and passion was a strange and mysterious landscape for him. Achille Robustelli liked common sense, clarity, and order, and for that reason, he now switched his focus from musing to finishing his correspondence.

❦

Finding a guide for their mountain hike wasn't hard. The locals were all familiar with the area, and many of them hired out as guides, easily identifiable by the hemp glacier rope slung over their shoulders. They sat on the benches in front of the big hotels, with gray felt hats on their heads, waiting for customers, smoking, talking among themselves, and all the while unobtrusively studying the tourists. Betsy approached one man and began the negotiations, and proved to be a good businesswoman.

"Let me do it," she'd told Edward. "I know these people better. Tourism has spoiled most of them. You can read about it in the guide books on Switzerland."

Preparations for the mountain hike took some time. With his friend looking on in disbelief, Edward acquired an alpenstock, a spiked wooden walking pole nearly as tall as he was, and sporty leggings. He even had his most sturdy pair of shoes resoled with nails to assure safe footing on the mountain. Of course he would wear a white shirt, necktie, and vest, but wasn't quite sure whether he should also buy a hiking jacket. James flatly vetoed that idea.

Betsy picked her moss-green suit to wear, thinking she would take the jacket off if it got too hot. She liked its practical features, like the elastic band that could be used to hitch up the skirt while climbing. She also bought a walking stick. But she didn't opt to have nails put on her shoes, for she felt sure on her feet. And for that same reason, she gave their good-looking, tanned guide, Caviezel, a contemptuous look when he recommended that she let herself be carried up to the source of the Inn River in a sedan chair. Still, she did agree with his suggestion that they take a mule along. The creature could carry the picnic in its rather ridiculously decorated saddlebags.

Their handsome mountain guide had said nothing. The lady would perhaps be glad at some point for the mule, he thought. They arranged that on the chosen day they would all meet at the horse-drawn omnibus station at the Hotel Maloja at nine in the morning. From there they would begin their climb.

The morning was clear, and the air smelled of fresh hay. As she was waiting for Edward, Betsy wondered, just for an instant, whether as a widow she should really allow herself to be this adventurous, and if it was all right to have some carefree pleasure—and with a man she hardly knew. Then there was Mathilde, whom she was leaving behind. In general, though, since she didn't tend to have feelings of guilt, the happy sensation of being alive soon prevailed again and even pushed her worries about her niece to the back of her mind.

Edward was also surprised to find himself in such a good mood as the horses drew his carriage from St. Moritz to Maloja. He felt as if a strong wind had swept away all his caution and misgivings. He was looking forward to the day with Betsy. To his left were the lakes, all in a row like a pearl necklace—after Lake St. Moritz came Lake Champfer, Lake Silvaplana, and Lake Sils.

He gazed out the window as they went through Sils-Maria, a sleepy village off the main road. The place practically belonged to the Germans and wasn't on the high-society circuit—perhaps the international set found the village too quiet and consequently boring. At most, an amusement-seeking group might be lured to the place for an afternoon excursion—if they wanted to have their tea in the high mountains just as they might have back in the salons of London, Paris, Rome, or Saint Petersburg. In any case, for several years now Nietzsche, who had made Sils familiar in intellectual circles, no longer spent his summers there.

Edward was pleased when moments later the carriage approached Maloja and the grand hotel that dominated the small village came into sight.

The climb took longer than Betsy thought it would. Although the path wasn't dangerous, it was steep and strenuous. After only a few meters, they left behind the timberline and the shade cast by the last of the stone pines—but, stubborn as she was, Betsy didn't easily give up. Feeling warm, she took off her suit jacket, silently cursing the long skirt. The material was heavy and impeded her climbing. She envied the men, even though Edward now and then loosened his shirt collar and took off his hat. The guide was smart enough not to mention the mule anymore. Betsy cast a longing look at the saddled animal trotting calmly up the mountain. There was little conversation. Breathing became labored.

Now and then, they stopped to rest, take a sip of tea, marvel at the view. No sooner would they make a halt, than peasant girls appeared out of nowhere, holding out small bouquets of edelweiss and alpine roses, begging for pennies. Edward gave the first girl a coin and gallantly handed the little bunch of flowers to Betsy. Beaming, she pinned them to her belt. She hadn't been given flowers by a man in a long time, certainly not red roses, even though these were only alpine roses.

"The tourists have shot all the ibex, the mountain goats," their guide explained, as if to compensate for the fact that the natives were picking all the most beautiful Alpine flowers.

The grass became sparser as they climbed. Ahead of them, silvery green granite glinted in the sunshine, with cliffs oxidized to a reddish brown. Blooms of gentian were visible here and there, glowing with an intense blue that demanded to be admired.

Betsy felt let down when she saw Lej dal Lunghin, the lake into which all the gravel springs from above collected. The water was wonderfully clear and blue, but it reflected nothing except the surrounding bare cliffs. She had liked the Inn River, babbling down the mountain in light, foamy cascades, better than this lonely spring-fed lake. She missed the grass and trees and asked Edward if they could have the picnic farther down the mountain.

The guide was disappointed. Not going up to the Piz Lunghin was like giving up just before reaching your final destination. Hoping to inspire them, he explained to them that one drop of water from the lake could be carried from that point into any one of three seas, depending on the direction in which it flowed downward—into the Black Sea by way of the Inn River, into the Adriatic from Lake Como and the Po River, or northward into the North Sea via the Rhine. This explanation was the high point of his guided tour. He was counting on Edward's resolute ambition to carry the day.

But Edward felt much closer at that moment to Betsy. He loved the plant world—and here, nature was barren and unfriendly. The surroundings made him think of how insignificant he'd sometimes felt after his disappointment with Emily. Of course, in this powerful landscape, any human being appeared insignificant. But like Betsy, he did not feel at home; he wanted to get down as quickly as possible to a place where you could stretch out in the grass.

Their guide emphasized that even if they returned early, he was to be paid the full amount agreed upon. Then he gave the mule a brusque slap on the back and initiated the climb back down.

Betsy smiled at Edward. They understood each other, even without a lot of words.

Actually, Betsy was a bit surprised at herself. She'd thought herself more adventurous and bold. Down in the valley, looking up, no peak had seemed too high. But now she was quite content to sit down on one of the folding chairs the mule had been carrying and enjoy some cold roast beef with pickles while Edward stretched out on the picnic blanket with his hat pulled down over his face.

"There's Segantini, the painter," the guide said, his voice intruding on the sleepy midday mood. He pointed at a man and a young woman coming quickly nearer; it was Segantini and Baba returning home for lunch. Edward jumped up as if electrified when he heard the name.

"May we say hello to the master?" he asked Caviezel, who nodded and called out, "Good day, Signor Segantini!"

Segantini stopped. "Were you up on Piz Lunghin with the lady and gentleman? Such a beautiful day today!" He nodded appreciatively at Betsy and Edward.

"It's an honor," Edward said, and introduced Betsy and himself. But Segantini, who spoke only Italian, asked Betsy to repeat it all for him. He was a friend of James Danby, Edward had her translate, a reporter living in England who had already been introduced to Segantini. Segantini remembered. Yes, he had agreed to make an appointment to meet with the gentleman at the Hotel Maloja.

"I paint almost exclusively outdoors, not in my studio," Segantini said. "Perhaps your friend should come with me some day when I go to work on my paintings. In fact, why don't you and your friend come for a modest supper at my house in the next few days," he suggested, adding, "I would be happy, of course, if you would also come along, Signora."

Betsy hesitated a moment. Could her niece come along too? She didn't want to be presumptuous, but she thought this would be a marvelous opportunity for Mathilde . . .

Segantini agreed. Then he and Baba continued on their way, as the mountain guide watched in admiration.

"The whole world wants to meet him, to visit him. It's become fashionable to make a pilgrimage to Maloja just to see the master. And they say he generously receives and feeds all these people."

"Well, then, we'll be following the fashion," Betsy said. "But thank God, we won't need a mountain guide for that pilgrimage," she whispered to Edward, for she was somehow disappointed in the handsome Caviezel.

⁂

Mathilde had an appointment with Dr. Bernhard. Today, of all days, when she could have seen James for the whole day without the presence of her aunt, who was clambering around in the mountains. It turned out the cure was taking up much of her time. This entire morning would be taken up with it.

"Dear Miss Schobinger, I don't like the way your lungs sound," Dr. Bernhard said. "You must continue with your treatments. I'd like to see you again soon for a more thorough examination."

"But except for my cough, I feel wonderful!" Mathilde said. "I just have a cold. It's always so cool in the mornings, and then during the day the sun is so hot . . ."

"Nevertheless, you are running a temperature. If you take a look in the mirror, you'll see that your cheeks are quite flushed." Dr. Bernhard did not say that he'd had his doubts about the family doctor's report right from the first visit.

"But I . . ." Mathilde knew what Dr. Bernhard was trying to tell her. "I'm just a little excited today."

Dr. Bernhard said, "If you're looking forward to a pleasant rendezvous today, I'm happy for you. But I must repeat, it is important that I examine your lungs more thoroughly, and it would be good if your aunt came along next time. Please have the nurse make an appointment right now for you to come back, either tomorrow or the day after tomorrow. All right?"

Dr. Bernhard accompanied Mathilde to the door. He did not like worrying his patients without reason, but he felt in this case, he needed to emphasize his point.

Mathilde pushed Dr. Bernhard's words as far to the back of her mind as she could. She took a carriage back to the hotel. There, she took all her dresses out of the closet because she didn't know which one to choose. After a long back and forth, she chose the white one, and a light-blue wool shawl. She rang for the chambermaid to bring fresh water.

James would be waiting for her in front of the hotel and would take her somewhere for lunch. They didn't want to eat at the Spa Hotel Maloja, for then Kate would immediately attach herself to them, and Mathilde didn't like the idea of that at all. They wanted to be by themselves, just the two of them. James had whispered in her ear last time they'd talked: "You'll see. We'll get away from them all, even if I have to kidnap you."

That was, of course, highly improper and for that very reason especially attractive. Aunt Betsy would surely have a screaming fit if she found out that Mathilde was planning to be alone with James. But she wouldn't find out, because Edward, who might have noticed had he been in St. Moritz as usual, was on the climb with Aunt Betsy. And Mathilde was sure she could find some excuse to explain to Kate why she hadn't been at the hotel for lunch. As she hurried down the great stairway to meet James, she was in high spirits, tapping every step with her parasol and almost tripping over it.

James stood waiting discreetly near their agreed meeting place, the hotel entrance. He'd told Kate a little white lie.

"James," she'd said two days earlier, taking his arm, "I have arranged for you to have a day with Mathilde while Aunt Betsy and your friend are away from the hotel. In fact, I've arranged for the two of them to attack the mountains together this coming Wednesday. Now, what's my reward for that? You owe me!"

James had kissed her hand. "I would be deeply indebted to you if you hadn't done this with an ulterior motive. But I know you too well to think otherwise. So, tell me, what is it you get?" For just a moment, he looked past Kate, which was one mark against him. "What do you get out of my spending the day alone with Mathilde?"

"Dear James. I shall be Mathilde's chaperone and not let you and that curly-haired lamb out of my sight. I take my assignment seriously, you know."

She beamed that radiant smile at him, which, on first meeting her, had seemed so spontaneous and innocuous. "I'll enjoy Mathilde's infatuation. Isn't it beautiful to witness the awakening desire in a pair of lovers? Do you know of anything more enchanting than the sprouting of young love?"

"And that's enough for you? You don't want anything for yourself? Is it perhaps that because your husband satisfies all your longings so well you only want to see others as happy as yourself?"

They had been walking in the gardens at the Spa Hotel Maloja and had stopped outside the front doors. Kate had shaken her head in pretended despair.

"You really don't know me well at all, James. I'm ready to give you a private lesson. Let's say Wednesday evening, after Mathilde's aunt has come back from her excursion? My husband is going to be working in Chur that Wednesday. It's a difficult trip, and he will start in the morning and be back, at the earliest, three days later. So you may choose when you'd like to have your private lesson. I'd suggest we have it here. The Pension Veraguth is perhaps a little too small. And anyway, it's proper to make it as convenient as possible for the lady."

With a quick movement she'd shut her parasol, and the porter had noticed, and opened the hotel door. But James, holding on to Kate's arm, had pulled her close and whispered in her ear, "Are you serious?"

"Of course," she'd replied coolly and freed herself. "You really don't know me, James. It's time we remedy that."

With that, she had vanished into the hotel.

And now Wednesday had arrived. Betsy had arranged with Kate that Mathilde was to report to her after returning from her doctor's appointment in St. Moritz. Kate had said she would be glad to spend the afternoon with the girl, and make sure that James did not make inappropriate advances. To James, she had suggested that the three of them have lunch together at the Spa Hotel Maloja and then play a round of golf or watch the target shooting in Isola and have blueberry cake with whipped cream at the restaurant there. James told Kate that he would like to come for lunch, but that he could not make a definite date.

"It all depends on how my tennis match goes," he said, pleasantly vague. "But I'll try my best. Don't wait for me to eat. In any case, we'll see each other at the golf course, right?"

"And what if Mathilde and I decide after lunch that we'd rather go to Isola?"

"If I don't find you both at the golf course, I'll take a carriage and get to Isola as quickly as possible."

"And if we decide to take a carriage ride to the Roseg Glacier?" Kate asked rather sharply.

"Then you'll be depriving yourself of the pleasure of my company," James said with a charming smile that perfectly matched hers.

He had won the duel, but she passed over it, saying, "Oh, James, my newspaper wasn't delivered this morning. Even the best hotel isn't perfect. Would you be kind enough to get me one? You know how unhappy I am without my paper. You'd make me very happy with this little favor."

And there was her radiant smile again and the casual demand on his time that was hard to object to. But he could sense an underlying touch of fury in her request.

This time James didn't bring her the newspaper, nor did he regret even for a moment his little white lie. Mathilde was going to sneak out of the hotel before Kate could notice. And there she was, already coming down the staircase—she was such an enchanting young bird that James felt for an instant quite like a cat. It was a good thing the serious-minded Edward wasn't nearby.

Life was so exciting! Mathilde gazed at him with such hot cheeks, such childish expectation, that James was almost overcome by a feeling of anxiety. But he suppressed it as quickly as Mathilde had suppressed her unease at Dr. Bernhard's words. Instead, he picked up the shawl that had slid off her shoulders, carefully draping the blue cloth over her shoulders, and said quite casually, "So that the blue of your eyes will shine with even more intensity." And without waiting for a reaction to his compliment, he went on, "I'd like to make a suggestion. The Kulm Hotel at the top of the mountain in St. Moritz, which you wanted to go to, is absolutely huge. It would take forever to get something to eat there, and it's a place that we could go anytime with your aunt. We'd have to behave properly there, as is expected of the guests of a grand hotel."

He took Mathilde's hand and pulled her away. "I know something we could do that would be much more entertaining, if you don't object to being a little daring."

Of course she didn't object. She was curious. She wanted to do something daring, something her family had not permitted so far, and at that moment, she felt flattered that so experienced a man should be interested in her.

"And what would that be?" she asked, eager to know, pulling her hand out of his.

"I bought a splendid picnic and took everything up to Pension Veraguth. Food will taste as good there as at the Kulm Hotel. I even got some champagne . . ."

Mathilde was taken aback. This was too risky, simply too daring. After all, the Pension Veraguth was where he was staying. His plan was far more compromising than anything she had imagined. She stopped in her tracks and shook her head.

"But nothing is going to happen that you don't want to happen!" James said. "What do you imagine I could do to you? Or should I be worrying about what you are thinking? If I were sensitive, I might really feel hurt now."

He brushed a strand of blond hair out of his face. Mathilde shook her head again.

"No, no. And you know very well that you've suggested something improper."

And yet, the prospect of lunch at the Hotel Kulm had lost its glamour and thrill. He was right. It was a boring idea, even though it had at first seemed so terrific to her. She looked at James, not at all sure, and said nothing. Within moments, James had called for a carriage, and in no time, the two of them disembarked in St. Moritz.

They'd strolled for several blocks when James suddenly said, "There's the streetcar. Have you ever ridden up to the village on an electric streetcar?"

Mathilde shook her head.

"No? You haven't gone for a ride on the just-opened tramline that all of St. Moritz is so proud of? You've just ignored it up to now? Then come on, we'll take the tram up to the village, and then you can decide whether you want to go on to the top of the mountain or come with me to my castle," he laughed, "by which I mean Pension Veraguth. The decision is all yours. You just have to promise me that if you feel queasy on the tram, you won't jump off while it's in motion. If you do feel queasy, it will be better if you just reach for my hand—promise?"

His laughter was contagious. It seemed to indicate that he thought the idea of Mathilde's being afraid was ridiculous.

The streetcar conductor in his open driver's stand rang the bell.

"All right, then," she said.

James reached for Mathilde's hand. Her resistance was minimal, no more than a slight tug. Then her hand surrendered and came to rest softly in his.

"We'll be there soon," James said. "The post-office square is the terminal. And now there's no escape: You have to make a decision."

With a boyish smile he leaned toward her; his smooth hair almost touching her cheek, his expression looking as if they were about to hatch some conspiratorial plot. There had never been anything quite this exciting in Mathilde's small, cloistered life.

"We're nearing my castle,'" he said. "Yes, Pension Veraguth is right there at the Postplatz. Oh, you'll see," he added soothingly, "I'm just showing off. It's actually just a decent middle-class house. It's not intimidating, nothing to be afraid of." He pointed to the right and said, "The Hotel Kulm is a bit farther on up there. A few minutes' walk," he sighed. "We'd of course lose precious time with that. We can't make Kate wait forever."

The hand he was holding was hot, even though the day wasn't very warm; clouds covered the sun every now and then, creating cooling slate-blue shade.

Mathilde said nothing. That was it then . . . everything was up to her.

His hand was firm and self-assured. The smell of his aftershave confused her, and his body was nearly touching hers. And she was wearing these stupid white crocheted gloves through which he must be able to feel her hot hand.

I'm engaged, she kept telling herself, but Adrian was infinitely far away, practically vanished from the face of the earth. The cosmopolitan scent emanating from James made her quite disloyal— the strand of hair falling across his forehead cast a slight shadow over his dark eyelashes. She felt overwhelmed by his eyes, the hand that held hers, his nonchalant voice. She must think of her parents, of Betsy—but what power did they still have over her? After all, she was really a grown-up now. James had recognized that; he had taken her seriously. He had left the decision up to her because he understood that she was capable of making her own decisions.

The electric streetcar stopped with a jolt.

"Come, we have to get off here," James said, helping her down. How lovely she was in her confusion, how touching in her naïveté. A blind man could have seen the inner struggle with conventional virtue on her unhappy face.

"Don't look so unhappy, Mathilde," he whispered, pressing her arm, "people will think I'm leading you to the scaffold. But all I want is to have lunch with you."

He was just a few years older than she, and those few years were decisive—and in his favor. He knew it, of course.

Mathilde smiled gratefully at him. What a fuss she was making! It really was all just about having lunch together, and after that she'd take a carriage and hurry back to Kate, giving the excuse that she had been held up because of Dr. Bernhard's examination. She and Kate would then go to the golf course, and James would come upon them and ask them innocently, "How are the ladies doing today?"

"Here is the Pension Veragouth," James said, breaking into her thoughts and pointing to a large old Engadine house. "And again there are various possibilities open to us, in case you agree that we shouldn't waste time strolling up the mountain to the Kulm Hotel. There's a shady terrace here where they serve meals à la carte, and on the second floor there's a *Stüva*, a Swiss pine-paneled room, where we can probably eat quite undisturbed because most of the pension's guests don't stay at the hotel for lunch. But we could also"—he let go of her arm in order to let her know she was free to make her own decision—"sneak up to my room like two adventurers. The champagne is chilling in cold water in the sink. You'll laugh when you see my improvised arrangement . . ."

Mathilde nodded, undecided.

James took that to mean she agreed to his last suggestion. He stepped into the pension's hallway, looked around, and then pulled her up the stairs.

A moment later Mathilde was standing in his room. A rustic double bed almost completely filled it. Involuntarily she took a step back, leaning with her back against the door.

"Unfortunately I don't have a suite like yours," James said, "but don't look at the bed, just look at the view, our picnic, and perhaps at me?"

He almost felt sorry for her, standing there like that. Her lower lip trembled as if she were about to break into tears, but then she merely said, "I left my parasol on the streetcar."

Then she was silent.

James spread a white towel on top of the little table near the window and took the bread, small pastries, and cheese out of a basket. Then he moved an armchair next to the table for her and invited her to sit down. From a drawer in the bureau he took two plates and two champagne glasses. He opened the bottle of champagne without letting the cork pop.

Once she'd had a glass, she would probably loosen up a bit. My God, he would actually have to wake up this Sleeping Beauty with a kiss. And yet in the presence of her aunt she hadn't been at all shy. James almost came to regret that he hadn't simply sat her down on the terrace below and then in a little while brought her back to Kate at the hotel.

But she was here now; she already had the champagne glass in her hand, had taken off her straw hat, and was smiling shyly at him. Her eyes sparkled. Kate's eyes didn't sparkle when she looked at him, he thought suddenly; they mocked, and flashed provocatively, but they didn't sparkle. It was remarkable, he thought, the feelings, the emotions that sparkling eyes could inspire. But Mathilde was just a nice young girl, no more and no less. Nothing earthshaking.

"Would you like to take your gloves off for the picnic?" he asked, to his surprise sounding almost affectionate, with only a hint of mockery in his voice.

She remained silent, but didn't refuse when he took her glass and said, "Wait, may I . . .?"

❦

Kate was angry. Mathilde had not shown up for lunch. Nor had James. She'd waited for quite a while, which wasn't like her, but her other friends had gone to Pontresina; there was no one else, and so she finally had to eat by herself. Robert had left early in the morning for Chur; it was an incredibly long journey with the post coach—thirteen hours. Lord knew when the train tracks would be extended to St. Moritz.

She was sitting with her coffee when Mathilde finally turned up. The girl was breathless.

"Excuse me, Kate," Mathilde burst out as she sat down. "I'm really sorry, but I was detained. The examination with Dr. Bernhard took a long time. I hope you didn't wait for me too long with lunch."

Mathilde looked absolutely distraught. She must have been rushing to get here.

"Don't worry, dear, I didn't. I really don't mind at all eating by myself. But I hate lack of punctuality."

She didn't ask whether Mathilde had eaten anything, but got up before the waiter could even ask Mathilde if she wanted something.

"Then let's go now. What did we decide? Were we going to play golf? Actually, I don't feel much like playing . . ."

Mathilde swallowed. James would be coming to the golf course; that's what had been agreed. "Yes," she said, "we agreed that we would play golf. As far as I know, James was going to meet us there . . ."

"Oh, James," Kate broke in, "you can't depend on him. We'll enjoy ourselves without him, won't we? I feel like going to Isola. We could take a carriage or walk there if you'd like. What do you think?"

Mathilde felt awful. And what about James? Maybe it was better after all if they didn't see each other this afternoon. Actually, it would be best if they never saw each other again. From now on, she really had to do whatever she could to avoid him. Best of all would be to leave Maloja immediately. Only, how could she survive if she didn't see him again today?

"Oh, I had no idea this would be such a difficult decision for you," Kate remarked. "I didn't know you cared so much about James. You probably don't want to disappoint him, to stand him up; how—" She interrupted herself and laughed. "Oh well, forget it. But you could at least do me this one favor."

She waved to a lady she apparently knew. Then, not waiting any longer for an answer from Mathilde, who actually didn't know what she should say, she turned to the doorman, "A carriage, please."

Once she was sitting in the carriage with Mathilde silent beside her, Kate's mood improved. James would come to Isola if he didn't find them at the golf course, thank heavens. With just Mathilde for company, even something fun like shooting clay pigeons would be the most boring thing in the world. In any case, the weather was decent and the ride to Isola was lovely.

The restaurant in Isola was open, and the two ladies hadn't been sitting long on the wooden veranda with hot chocolate and blueberry cake when James joined them. Mathilde blushed when she saw him, which prompted Kate to say that James should beware of seducing frivolous, young girls who were engaged.

"You do know that Mathilde is engaged, don't you?"

"How was I supposed to know that?" James replied while Mathilde's face turned an even darker red.

"Well, I'm telling you now. That is probably what Betsy would have done too. And I'm taking her place this afternoon, so to speak." Kate put on a severe expression. "But tell us what you did this afternoon, since you didn't come for lunch." She took his arm in a familiar gesture, just as he was about to sit down next to Mathilde, and directed him to a chair next to her. "Stay right here. And now tell us what you did."

James looked around him for a long time, saying nothing, but Mathilde's heart was pounding as if it were about to explode.

"It's really beautiful here," he said and smiled at Mathilde. Then he turned to Kate.

"There's not much to tell. I lost a tennis match, even though I'm an excellent player—as you know."

Mathilde heaved a sigh of relief and concentrated on her blueberry cake topped with a billow of whipped cream.

"But who could possibly beat you? It would be a first, since I've known you," Kate replied.

"And would you believe it, it was a woman who beat me. I think the best thing for me is not to say anymore."

Kate darted a sharp glance toward Mathilde. But she had just turned to the hostess to ask for a glass of water. Then Mathilde looked at Kate inquiringly as if she'd missed part of the conversation.

"Did you hear that, Mathilde?" Kate said. "James lost a match, and not only that, he lost to a woman. I really don't know how I'm supposed to take that!"

The entire situation seemed highly suspicious to Kate.

Mathilde didn't answer her, sending instead a prayer to heaven that Kate wouldn't pursue the matter. Her prayer was answered. For Kate never revealed all her trump cards—at any rate not prematurely and not in situations that brought her no rewards. She suggested, instead, that they go and watch the sharpshooters before engaging in some shooting as well.

James pushed his sports cap lower on his forehead and said, "I can watch, yes, but I can't shoot today. I've had enough strenuous activity for one day." He laughed, bending over and holding his back like an old man.

James seemed unaffected by what had happened between him and Mathilde. He seemed both relaxed and inaccessible. Mathilde was disappointed. She'd obviously not been able to rattle his composure, and that really hurt. What she felt was a violent stab of pain that made her heart contract. Made worse by her shame at being dumb enough to want him even more now after the game was already long over for him. At least so it seemed.

Mathilde didn't know which was worse, her shame, her guilty conscience, or her longing, which seemed to grow minute by minute, for a tender look of understanding from him.

That prayer was not answered.

Kate was the only one enjoying herself, effusively applauding the victorious shooter.

Mathilde spent a restless night, coughing more than usual and waking up repeatedly after crazy dreams that she couldn't remember. For some time already there had been nights when she perspired excessively. She would get up and change her nightgown as quietly as possible so as not to awaken Betsy sleeping in the adjoining room. She was running a fever and couldn't pretend otherwise anymore, even though she would have liked to. And at breakfast she told her aunt—who was still talking enthusiastically about the hike with Edward—that Dr. Bernhard wanted to examine her more thoroughly today after the earlier routine examination and that he wanted to talk with both of them. Betsy was taken aback, but she reluctantly agreed when Mathilde implored her not to involve her mother, at least for the time being, but to wait until after they had seen the doctor.

"Now tell me honestly whether you have pain in your chest here and here when you cough," Dr. Bernhard inquired after he had carefully listened to Mathilde's chest and back with his stethoscope. "And no evasions like yesterday."

Mathilde nodded. Yes, there was pain when she coughed, but it was normal for one's chest to hurt when . . .

"And you never feel a shortness of breath?"

"No," she answered, with some trepidation, for she was getting worried. "No . . . not every time. The cough isn't always the same . . ."

"But you know what I mean. And you probably also feel feverish in the evenings? You are actually running a fever now." Dr. Bernhard blew his nose with a white handkerchief, then wiped it once to the left and once to the right across his bristly mustache before putting it back into the pocket of his white coat.

"So now I shall tell you and your aunt what I think. You ought to stop the bath treatment immediately; it is much too strenuous for you. You have tuberculosis. But I think it is still at a relatively early stage."

Tears came to Mathilde's eyes. Betsy took her hand, shocked. Tuberculosis. It was almost as if, out of the blue, a judge had pronounced a death sentence on an innocent.

"I am sorry to cause alarm. I know this isn't good news."

"Good Lord, no! But what does it mean?" Betsy cried.

But Dr. Bernhard, a burly man with a kind soul, seeing the hectic red in Mathilde's cheeks, decided not to give them a long exhaustive explanation right then, but to make sure first that Mathilde was put to bed.

"Madam, I'll explain in greater detail what we know, medically, in the next few days. Right now, we should first consider what to do. The lucky thing in this situation is that up here you are in one of the best possible places for treatment and healing. The high-altitude air and sun are exactly what your niece needs now."

Mathilde felt as if she were living in a bad dream. Still, she didn't have to leave, to leave James. Was that what the doctor was saying?

"But," and now he turned to Mathilde, "you must go to bed as soon as possible! The first thing we have to do is to bring your temperature down. Only then can you even think of taking some short walks which can gradually be extended."

He smiled at Mathilde. "After a while you'll even be able to take real walks in the mountains, never fear. I could recommend the fresh air sanatorium in Görbersdorf in Germany, or refer you to one in Davos, where there are several sanatoriums for lung diseases."

Mathilde flinched and clasped Betsy's hand more tightly. Under no circumstances did she want to do that!

"I myself treat patients using heliotherapy, taking advantage of the healing power of the sun," Dr. Bernhard continued. "I first used this method on slow-to-heal surgical wounds, but I also treat clinical tuberculosis and various other forms of the disease, such as skin, bone, or joint tuberculosis with this method. So, if you wish, you could remain here, and I would place you in my clinic in St. Moritz. The air here is just as good as in Davos."

Mathilde nodded emphatically, and Betsy said, "Yes, of course, I'm sure that would be best. We'll need a certain amount of time anyway before we can quite understand what it all means . . . and naturally we have to discuss how to proceed with Mathilde's parents. You understand, I'm sure, that your diagnosis has hit us like a bolt out of the blue."

"Very well, then. I shall have them prepare a room in the clinic," Dr. Bernhard replied briefly. "Your niece can move in tomorrow." He got up, and taking Mathilde's hot hand in both of his, pressed it encouragingly. Before showing the two women out of his office, he said, "You'll see, Miss Schobinger, we'll get you on your feet again. We'll start with six meals a day, a glass of red wine or two, preferably our local red, which is especially good for you, and lots and lots of fresh air taken on the balcony of your room. The rest cure will soon make you well once more, I'm quite sure."

"What did Dr. Bernhard mean, Mathilde, when he said you were evasive yesterday?" Betsy took Mathilde in her arms. "You have to tell me everything, you hear? Otherwise I can't help you. And I have a vague feeling that something is bothering you."

The midday light flooded the sitting room of their hotel suite, making Betsy's raspberry-red dress glow. Mathilde, suddenly emotionally overwhelmed, sobbed, and throwing herself in the direction of the raspberry fabric, buried her head in Betsy's lap. She was shaken by a fit of crying, little sobs escaping every now and then. Betsy had to smile at the staccato and bitterly sad melody. Softly she stroked the blonde curls.

"Come now," she murmured. "I'm sure it can't be as bad as it sounds right at this moment. With Dr. Bernhard we're in the best of hands, and we'll find a solution for whatever else is troubling you."

But Mathilde's sobbing was getting worse as if old, long-repressed misery were now breaking free, and piling on top of this new one.

"I can't marry Adrian," Mathilde said in a halting voice without lifting her head from Betsy's lap.

"No one would ask that of you right now."

Then, raising her head, Mathilde said quite distinctly, "I love James."

Then her face disappeared again in Betsy's lap.

After this declaration, the room was quiet. The sobbing ebbed away, and Betsy digested what she had just heard.

Suddenly she said, "Mathilde, I'm hungry. Let's go eat, what do you think?"

From under the curls came a muffled "No way. I can't go into the dining room. My eyes are all red from crying."

Betsy was relieved to hear her say something sensible. It sounded as if Mathilde had reached safe harbor after a stormy sea voyage.

"Let's have a look." She raised the young woman up and wiped the tears from her face. "Hmm." The poor child's face really was all red and puffy. "Maybe we can have something sent up to the room, all right? You should be lying down anyway, Dr. Bernhard said so."

"Aunt Betsy, did you hear what I just said?"

"I did. But when I'm hungry, I can't think. And there's a lot to think about here."

"And you don't know everything yet," Mathilde added.

"I was afraid of that."

"I . . ."

"Stop, don't go on. I'll ask the chambermaid to bring some water. Then you can wash your face and lie down on the couch. I'll cover you. The room service waiter will bring you something to eat. Then I might excuse myself to get a glass of wine, or maybe even two—because it isn't as simple as I thought it was. And then we'll see."

Betsy sighed. All at once, she sympathized with her sister Emma, instead of just her niece. She admired all these women who were mothers. My God, you had to be devilishly careful not to say the wrong thing.

She went to the door and rang for the chambermaid.

Did it have to come to this? Betsy shook her head. Of all people, James. That ladies' man, that Don Juan. A journalist and, she suspected, a man without much money. That was too bad, because if he'd had a fortune, that might have made up for his being a newspaperman. A man she herself liked. Of all things.

She was thirty-five, experienced, financially independent. She could afford to take on a man like James, if she cared to, even if nobody—nobody!—would have approved. James had many qualities that a more mature woman could appreciate. But Mathilde! Not only would her parents naturally forbid this relationship, but the girl had clearly gotten caught up in feelings that James surely did not reciprocate. After all, she, Betsy, had seen how inseparable he and Kate had been all this time. How could he possibly fall in love with this naïve child, to say nothing of having a serious or faithful relationship with her? Betsy had one marriage behind her, with all its illusions and disillusions. Given this experience, her expectations of love were totally and fundamentally different from Mathilde's imaginings.

But what right had she to judge? Love was a big word. Each person supplied it with his or her own ideas. Betsy excused herself to go to the bathroom, where she paused to look in the mirror. She scanned her own dark-blue eyes, adjusted her pretty horn comb, and checked to see that her pinned-up hair was in place. With both hands, she touched the nostrils of her prominent narrow nose. Then she returned to the sitting room. She took a deep breath, ready to listen to whatever else Mathilde was about to tell her.

"And why did you get engaged to Adrian if you don't want to marry him?" Betsy asked.

"Because back then I didn't know what love is," Mathilde said.

"Aha, and what do you think love is?"

"What I feel for James, that's love."

"But, even before we met James, you weren't at all eager to thank Adrian for his letters and telegrams, or to call him on the phone. Am I right?"

Mathilde was silent. Finally, she said, "He's nice. He's good-looking. He loves me. He'll inherit the bank."

"But?"

"He's boring."

Betsy bit her tongue. She had been on the point of saying that, on the whole, these were pretty good grounds for a marriage. "Hmm. And James, I take it, isn't boring."

Mathilde, brightening, sat up on the sofa.

"James is incredibly exciting. He is charming, witty, experienced . . ."

" . . . and full of secrets. Who knows what else he does," Betsy said, completing her statement.

"He knows how to treat a woman . . ."

"But you're still a very young woman."

Mathilde blushed. "Aunt Betsy," she said, "I feel awfully tired."

"Very good. Take a little nap. But at some point, you'll tell me where you lost your parasol, yes?" And with that, Betsy left her niece alone in the room.

⊗⊗

Kate had called the chambermaid and asked her to prepare her bath. The girl, whose name was Andrina, was quick and efficient and Kate always asked for her because she preferred bossing around pretty girls rather than ugly ones.

"Are you aware of how pretty you are?" she asked Andrina when the girl told her the bath was ready. "I'm sure you'll have an easy time in life. Beauty smoothes quite a few paths. That's why I like to tip the ugly ones; they have to work so hard, the poor girls." And with that, she dismissed the chambermaid without giving her even a small coin, but with an encouraging smile.

The warm water, the bath salts, the soft, fragrant towels relaxed and energized Kate. She had let James know that she would be having supper at the hotel with Betsy and Mathilde and that she expected him afterward in her room. James had remained vague. Edward, he said, would probably want to tell him about his mountain hike and he didn't know how the evening would turn out. To that she had replied, slightly annoyed, "Nobody's talking about the evening, dear."

He would come. She felt sure a man like James wouldn't forego a night with an attractive woman. And certainly not if she was available without consequences: no emotional outbursts, no clinging, no future expectations, and no forever—in short, no handcuffs and not even the risk of syphilis.

The evening with Betsy and Mathilde was brief. Descriptions of the mountain landscape Betsy had seen, the mule, and the alpine roses bored her; and the name Segantini still didn't mean any more to her now than the little she had found out about him during the picnic at Lake Staz.

After dinner, Kate returned to her room. She contemplated her body. It was small and supple, always ready, like her head, and looking for opportunities to win. Like her heart and her mind, her body did not surrender, and it fascinated men to find out how smoothly and directly it sought satisfaction. Kate dusted herself with the powder puff, coughing as she breathed in some of the fine particles. The perfumed powder filled the bathroom with its fragrance. She slipped into her housecoat and the little velvet slippers that showed off her small feet. Then she returned to the sitting room and rang for the room-service waiter. He just stared wide-eyed. Yes, she knew the housecoat was captivating with its showy, velvet flowers in pale pink, salmon, and gold on the silky, soft-flowing background. Her husband, who used to call her "my little hussy," liked things a bit more vulgar, but actually that had nothing to do with her essence. Pleasure for her came from getting her own way, not in the physical, sensual sense, but in exerting control over others—and in never forgetting herself or losing at anything.

The waiter was still standing there expectantly.

"Please bring up some foie gras and champagne along with two plates and two glasses. And stop looking at me like that. The second glass isn't for you."

Suddenly she was angry that James was not yet there. And all at once, even as she was placing the order, she saw herself left sitting alone with the champagne. What a humiliating experience it would be if the waiter were to ask, "Shall I open the champagne now for Madame, or would you like to wait a bit longer?"

When there was a knock on the door, she was relieved to find that it was James.

"You certainly weren't in a hurry," she said in greeting instead of hello. She pulled him into the room.

"You look enchanting, Kate," James countered, sitting down on the sofa. He stretched both arms out across the sofa back and gazed at her with a smile.

"Well, take off your hat, James," she said, returning his smile. "Or would you like to remain quite formal?" Leaning affectionately toward him, she took the hat off his head.

Kate's perfume was seductive; James took her by the waist and pulled her down into his lap. The silk housecoat with the delicate flower appliqués slipped off her shoulders, and James kissed her neck, the flawless shoulders, and placed a finger on the delicate spot between her breasts.

Kate didn't wait for him to kiss her on the lips. With a small, involuntary sound of triumph, she placed her mouth over his and with her tongue carefully parted his lips.

The room service waiter spoiled this good beginning. He was standing outside the door with the champagne, and Kate had to open it for him. James sat up properly again after having slipped dangerously into the horizontal with Kate in his arms.

He made no special effort to take up where they had left off before the interruption, but instead poured them each a glass of champagne. Then he lifted his glass and said, "To you, Kate."

What was the matter with him, she wondered. Why was he acting so lukewarm?

"Well, what do you think of our young Mathilde, James? The girl is very much in love with you."

"Yes, she is indeed," James said, showing no emotion.

"And do you still feel flattered, or is it already beginning to get on your nerves?"

He turned away from Kate, answering her almost peevishly, "I don't know yet."

"How unresponsive you are today, James. Really, quite uncommunicative. I have to admit I was suspicious when the girl didn't meet me after her health treatment. And you didn't turn up at lunch either . . ."

"But I told you, I had a tennis match."

"Excuses are nothing unusual in the business of seduction. That's no proof that you weren't with her during the time I was waiting for both of you in vain."

Kate could see from his expression that this conversation was in danger of veering off in an unexpected direction.

"But why talk about the girl," she said, "when we can indulge in grown-up pleasures."

She took a bit of foie gras, refilled his glass, and began to undress him. He didn't help her much, and she tried to convince herself that it was because of the pleasure it gave him to play the passive role of desired object and not a growing disinterest in her.

She was skillful and experienced. And he did gradually surrender to her, sliding off the sofa onto the rug, pulling her down with him. Her housecoat opened wide, and she lay there naked on the golden silk with its pale pink and salmon-colored flowers. She took pleasure in the looks he gave her, seeing him as a voyeur reining in his lust even as she became aroused.

Supporting himself on one elbow, he gazed at her, at the same time spreading her legs with the other hand, still coolly, almost dispassionately, but Kate didn't give in to him at once. Then finally, he threw himself on her. He'd forgotten Mathilde now. Kate had won again.

Uncertainties

Nika was talking. But only with Segantini and Gian. It was hard for her to find her tongue again after the many years of silence, and words were too treacherous and too valuable to waste.

Nika waited impatiently for Segantini's visits when she worked in the hotel garden, but they weren't as frequent as she would have liked. He had many appointments, and Baba always went with him when he was painting. But sometimes he sent Baba home, saying he would follow shortly.

He still had Nika's sketchbook. She had talent. He'd seen it immediately. She should be encouraged. She wanted to learn how to write properly and to draw, like him. He knew it well, this hunger for the education that has been kept from you, the urge to express yourself, the longing to be seen and acknowledged—to see the appreciative look in the eyes of others, and to realize: I am, and it is good that I exist.

"I've been thinking how it could be arranged," Segantini said to her one day, when he'd found her at work outside. He didn't want to have her join his children, who were taught by a private tutor. She didn't belong to that part of his life, and he didn't want to mix up the two worlds.

"Perhaps I can talk with the priest; I'll see what can be done." He didn't want to admit to her that when it came to writing he wasn't very sure of himself.

"You still have my notebook," she reminded him. "I can't go on sketching because I don't have another one."

"Right," he said. "I looked at it very carefully. You have a good eye. Your hand is still hesitant, you don't trust yourself, but that's just a matter of practice. You see what's important, the essential, and that's what matters. If you don't see the essential of what you are drawing, then no amount of technique is of any use. Moreover, if you can't express the essence of what you're drawing, then the picture will be boring and uninteresting."

Segantini was silent for a moment, looking at her hair glowing in the evening light. A warm golden tone like that of the gold leaf that as the last step he rubbed into the barely visible grooves produced by his way of painting—placing one stroke of color next to another in the divisionist style. The technique gave his paintings a singular shimmer and a magic that viewers could not account for. It was much the same magical effect that Nika's hair had on him. And the blue-green of her eyes, wasn't that the exact color that was dominant in his painting *The Spring*? Wasn't she the beautiful nude, lying next to the bubbling waters?

Nika lightly touched the sleeve of his black jacket, looking at him questioningly.

"Call me Segante," he said, almost indignantly, because she had interrupted his thoughts, "that's what my friends call me."

"But we're not friends," Nika said. "Even if you come to see me here."

He looked at her in surprise. "Well, as you wish. In any case, I thought that I might teach you to draw. If you like, I'll bring your notebook with me next time. I'll give you an assignment, and when we see each other again, we'll discuss how you could improve it."

She stood there transfixed, as if he'd said something terrible. Then her eyes filled with tears. "You would do that? For me?"

"Why not. We could give it a try."

He looked away in embarrassment. Did she have to cry? And because he wasn't looking at her, he couldn't prevent her from taking his hand, pressing it to her wet face, and kissing it.

"Don't," he said.

"Oh yes," she said, her voice choking with tears.

As Segantini was walking past the hotel, Robustelli, who had just stepped outside, raised a hand in greeting. Segantini returned the greeting and quickly walked on. He didn't care to get involved in a conversation just then.

His fear was unfounded. Robustelli saw lots of things without feeling the need to talk about them.

❦

Betsy telephoned her sister Emma. Despite being so far away, she tried as much as she could to cushion the panic that would probably break out in Zurich in the Schobinger family.

"Emma, we've done everything we can do right now. The doctor she has is good. I wonder why your family doctor didn't see the signs before. But be that as it may, Dr. Bernhard thinks that she hasn't had the illness for long. The private clinic in St. Moritz is new, well managed, and comfortable. Mathilde has a lovely room with a balcony where she can lie with a view of the lake. She is glad she can stay there and not have to go to a sanatorium in Davos or elsewhere."

She stopped just long enough to take a breath, because she didn't want to let her sister get a word in before she had told her the most important thing.

"And look, it just so happens that I have nothing else planned right now and can extend my stay here so as to be with Mathilde. First, you should gently break the news to Franz. And then you or the two of you together can come for a visit as soon as you can arrange it."

Betsy sighed and held the receiver out at arm's length as a torrent of words assaulted her ear. It wasn't surprising that Emma wasn't taking this unexpected and alarming news calmly.

"We have to tell the Zollers, too," Emma was just saying. "It's really terrible. What will they say! We were supposed to start on the wedding preparations right after your return from St. Moritz. And now a blow like this. Has Mathilde spoken with Adrian yet?"

"No, Emma. I think at the moment it really would be better if you could do that. And don't send him up here for a visit right away, you hear? First Mathilde herself has to digest this diagnosis. Her mood is very changeable at the moment. We really don't want to create an unintentional misunderstanding with Adrian, just because she's still very upset right now."

One thing at a time, Betsy thought. She didn't want her sister to have a heart attack on top of everything else.

"You're right, Elizabeth."

Thank God, the trick had worked.

"All right," Betsy said. "So you'll keep everyone away until Mathilde has calmed down a little and gotten used to the clinic routine. Then—and you've got to prepare yourself for this, unfortunately—she'll have to stay here for a while, you know. You'll have lots of time in which to come and visit."

While Mathilde, under Dr. Bernhard's care, still had a long road with an uncertain end to travel in the fight against consumption, Gian lay between life and death—without the care of a doctor. Benedetta couldn't bear the thought of losing him and looked after her oldest child night and day. True, the veterinarian had stopped by and given Benedetta hope. The herbs from the old woman from Stampa were having some effect, and the vet felt that anything that was good for cows wouldn't hurt people either. Not everybody died of *Alpenstich*. Gian was young and strong and could make it. And so it was.

In the evenings, Nika sat with him, holding his hand. At first, he was aware of it only hazily as a distant hallucinatory echo, but as the fever slowly left him, it touched his soul profoundly: Nika had said his name! She was speaking! Then he sank back into semiconsciousness. But gradually, in the course of a few weeks he returned to the world of other people.

Luca didn't come home often. Like the other tracklayers, he lived in improvised quarters near the construction site. Most of the laborers came from Italy. Luca got along well with them. They were self-assured, held strong, aggressive viewpoints, and stuck together.

Aldo missed his son more than Benedetta did, but he didn't talk about it. He was proud that his son was participating in a great project that would change the world. Luca would come back one day with lots of money and more experiences than any other member of the family had ever had. Luca would amaze the villagers. He would tell them what it was like to blast apart cliffs, to build bridges and tunnels.

He didn't know that Luca would also be able to tell them how quickly—as quickly as one could snap one's fingers—a life could come to an end in a landslide or a fall from a bridge substructure, and that they kept having to bury comrades. Comrades who were young and had wives and families. They worked, advancing through the mountain; with simple pickaxes they attacked rocks that were tricky, and sometimes only loosely in place and would crumble. It was hot inside, and the sweat ran down their dirty faces. The petroleum lamps often went out, and the darkness of the mountain scared even these brave men.

Aldo knew nothing about that aspect of the work. His thoughts remained focused on the day when Luca would come back, and Aldo's reputation among the villagers would rise. He remembered that Count Camille de Renesse had also planned a rail project for Maloja. But in the end, that one had come to nothing. Who knew, maybe Luca would become an important man and would one day turn the count's idea of making Maloja accessible by train into a reality.

Benedetta, on the other hand, spent more of her time wondering what they would do about Gian. Could they keep sending him up to the high pasture by himself? She would have preferred to keep him closer to home. But Aldo said if he couldn't take care of the cows then he was totally useless, and he had to make some contribution, like Andrina and Luca.

Andrina didn't spend much time at home, and when she was there, she bragged a lot about her experiences at the hotel.

"You should see the wardrobes of the ladies there," she would boast. "When I clean their rooms, I look at their dresses, their jewelry, and believe me, those things would look just as good on me. And they not only keep changing their dresses, they also change men . . ."

"Andrina!" Benedetta would say, when all the talk got on her nerves, "Don't keep babbling such a lot of nonsense."

"But you have no idea," Andrina would reply. "Life in other places isn't like it is here for you at home. I saw with my own eyes Signora Simpson—who wants only me to wait on her—having men visit her in her room."

Aldo chewed on a toothpick he'd made from a broken-off piece of bush.

"And so you want to be like the signora," he said deprecatingly, because giving Andrina any advice was hopeless.

"Yes," Andrina said, with a note of rebellion in her voice. "Just as rich, beautiful, and admired." She gave Nika a challenging look. "If men who are respected in the village pay court to the *straniera*, it shouldn't be so hard for me."

Nika blushed. Benedetta interrupted Andrina with an emphatic gesture of her hand.

"What are these stupid things you're saying?"

But Andrina wasn't finished yet.

"I know everything. Old Gaetano told me. Signor Segantini comes by to see her any opportunity he gets. And not because he's longing to see the old man." She looked coolly at Nika. "You can be glad that Gaetano talks almost as little as you. And besides, nobody in the village thinks he has any stories to tell anyway."

"Now, that's enough," Aldo said, getting up from the table. "All this nonsense is just unbelievable."

But Andrina knew better; she wasn't stupid.

"Of course you'll go to the dinner," Mathilde said. "In any case, whether you eat in the hotel or at this Segantini's, I have to stay here in the clinic. Who's going with you?"

Betsy hesitated about giving her an answer, but then decided to be honest with Mathilde. "Edward is going. And James too. He's supposed to write a story about Segantini for a newspaper . . ."

Mathilde held her handkerchief to her lips. Her cough sounded awful. "Do you think James will come here to see me sometime?"

"Of course he will, Tilda. He just found out that you're here. You have to give him a little time." Betsy tried to sound cheerful. "I'm sure he's going to ask about you tonight, and then I'll tell him that you're eagerly awaiting a visit from him . . ." She hoped Mathilde would protest, and she did.

"Aunt Betsy! Please! Don't say a word. Not a word! If he doesn't come of his own free will, I don't want to see him anymore." The girl looked so unhappy as she said this that Betsy reached for her hand.

"My God, Tilda. You have a fever again, child. You have to think about something else right away. You're not supposed to get upset. You hear? And you can be sure, James is going to come to see you soon. Even if I don't tell him how much you're hoping that he will." She gently stroked Mathilde's forehead and got up.

She didn't say anything about Adrian. She had decided that she wouldn't show Mathilde his latest telegram, at least for the moment.

Problems and Temporary Solutions

"Well, I certainly can't use you as an interpreter," James said as he and Edward were driving back to St. Moritz after the dinner at Segantini's.

"I never claimed I could be of use," Edward answered curtly.

The evening hadn't exactly been a success. The conversation had never really gotten under way, and then Betsy had mentioned the girl with the reddish hair whom she'd seen in the hotel garden several times with Segantini. Her harmless remark had distinctly embarrassed Segantini, and obviously caught Bice by surprise.

"Betsy won't do as an interpreter either," James continued brusquely. "She didn't exactly score any points with Segantini." He sighed. "I'll have to take up the offer from the man at the hotel to find someone for me. I'll call him tomorrow. It's urgent."

They fell silent.

After a while Edward said, "Poor Mathilde. What a shock! Tuberculosis. That's almost a death sentence! You were with her while I went on the mountain trek with Betsy, weren't you? Did you notice anything then? Fever? Weakness?"

James shook his head.

Edward didn't know what had happened between Mathilde and James that day. James had been suspiciously vague about it, although in general, he loved to boast about his conquests. One thing was certain, the young woman had fallen seriously in love with James, and Edward thought that as the older of the two, James had to accept the responsibility and be kind about it at the very least. In any case, he expected some gallantry from his friend, just as Edward would have expected it of himself.

"Do you love her then?" he asked. At least James was unattached and could possibly court her, although Edward knew the prospect of getting her family's approval was not exactly great. James wasn't wealthy, but if his happiness depended on it, Edward would vouch for him any time.

"The things you want to know, Eddie! You know me better than I know myself, after all. You tell me whether I love her. Have I ever loved anyone the way you define love? The way you loved Emily?"

Edward didn't answer him because he didn't like being asked about Emily. No sooner would someone mention her name than he would see the gentle oval of her face before him, with those always-ready-to-contradict brown eyes that didn't quite seem to fit in it. She was more spirited and passionate than her outward appearance might lead you to think—and it was precisely that which he so loved about her, and which made him so unhappy. He was not as carefree as Jamie. His wit rarely drew admiration in large groups of people. You discovered Edward's charms only if you allowed yourself the time, and James, who had been in school with him for many years, had taken the time. Emily, who let herself be easily captivated by other people, hadn't been captivated enough by Edward, even with all his good looks. His gentleness, his humor, and his depth were hidden under a layer of politeness. Few made the effort to imagine that behind his show of conventionality and slightly boring uprightness there might be a surprising degree of emotion and passion to be discovered. Emily in any case hadn't made the effort to discover the deeper Edward, and he himself had to admit that he had hidden it quite skillfully.

"Mathilde's situation is difficult," James finally admitted. "Tuberculosis. Not exactly what you would wish for." He made a gesture as if to shake off the unpleasant business.

"I mean, from her point of view," he quickly added. Despite the comment, Edward suspected that James was primarily speaking of himself. A sick lover—that just wasn't his dream.

"Have you gone to see her yet? Or written to her?" Edward asked. But James again shook his head.

"I just now found out about it. At the same time you did."

Well, that much was true. But he didn't seem to be terribly interested in the sick Mathilde.

"I hate hospitals," James said instead. "There's something contagious about them. The more septic they smell, the more afraid I am of what awful things could happen to me. Sickness is so ugly." And when Edward didn't say anything, he continued, "Do you like making hospital visits?"

"I don't mind," Edward said.

"I hope I can be of help to you, Mr. Danby," Achille Robustelli said. "There's not much time left to find an interpreter if your meeting with Signor Segantini is scheduled for tomorrow. But I'll do my best to reach Signor Bonin. He just happens to be staying here in the hotel, a charming young man who is acting as Count Primoli's secretary for the summer. The count thinks highly of our hotel . . ." Robustelli interrupted himself briefly to hand a letter to the director of the hotel, who had just put his head inside the door. Then he continued, "Bonin is Italian but speaks fluent English and is familiar with the field of fine arts. And of course also photography, otherwise he wouldn't be working for the count who, as you may know, is one of the most famous photographers of our time."

There was no denying that Robustelli looked especially favorably on guests from Italy, perhaps a sign of a secret homesickness he didn't even admit to himself.

"So if you would, please give me a call this afternoon. As far as I know, the Pension Veraguth has no telephone connection, otherwise I could call you once I have more information."

Robustelli was in fact able to persuade Fabrizio Bonin, a young Venetian, to act as interpreter for Mr. Danby's interview with Signor Segantini. Robustelli felt proud to have been able to solve this problem so well and in so short a time. But being a modest man, he didn't credit Bonin's acquiescence to his skillful approach, but rather to the fact that it wasn't a difficult assignment and that any of his guests would have found a meeting with the well-known painter interesting.

Meanwhile, a much greater challenge was awaiting Robustelli. Without much advance notice, Signora Bice had announced she was coming to see him. He sighed.

"Forgive me, Signor Robustelli, for disturbing you at work. I won't stay long."

He courteously offered the signora a seat in order to gain some time to reflect on just what his obligations and responsibilities were in the situation; he already had an inkling of what it was all about.

"We had visitors yesterday, among them a signora who lives here as a guest in your hotel," Bice Bugatti said. She was called Signora Bice because she wasn't married to Segantini. "She said that she had seen Giovanni several times already with the *straniera* in the hotel gardens. Giovanni says you hired her to work in the garden. Is that so, Signor Robustelli? Have you noticed that my husband comes here frequently to see the young woman? He says that he knows her and wants to get her to talk again . . ."

Robustelli nodded.

"Yes. Andrina Biancotti asked whether I had work for the young woman, and I hired her. Signor Segantini told me that he knew the young woman from Mulegns, where they told him that she had been abandoned as an infant and subsequently entrusted to a farmer as a contract child. He thinks she isn't dumb, that she can speak, and he wants to get her to speak again."

His voice was firm and calm, and the fact that the information tallied with what she had been told by her husband reassured Bice Bugatti.

Robustelli continued. "I can't say that your husband comes here any more often than before. He thinks well of the hotel and has for a long time been coming to see me now and then. He asks when the next concert will be, exchanges a few words with the people . . . He has always done that."

Bice was relieved by this thoughtful reply, which saved her further worries. She gave Robustelli—who wasn't quite free of guilty feelings—a grateful look.

"Thank you, Signor Robustelli. You meet people in the village of course, but the *straniera* is shy. We have little to do with the Biancottis with whom she lives. And from what I hear, it seems the only person she likes is Giuseppina from the laundry. It's as if she just flits by all the others. Still, she attracts the eyes of other people. And their thoughts. The hotel is closed during the winter, isn't it? Where will she go then?"

"I don't know," Robustelli said. He escorted Bice out of the hotel.

Why was he protecting Segantini? Achille didn't know. Bice loved Segantini and was worried that someone could break apart her sheltered home, he understood that. But no one could keep love from taking what it wanted. Segantini was clearly drawn to Nika. The attraction was so great that he was getting careless and not thinking about the consequences of his actions. Robustelli sensed that the girl loved him with a passion that would remain unfulfilled and could not but end unhappily. And yet, Achille had done nothing to make these people come to their senses. Nor had he told Segantini that other people might have seen Nika pressing his hand to her face . . . So far, he had not asked Nika to come to see him or forbidden her to have private conversations during working hours. These were all things he had failed to do, and instead he had dispelled Bice's doubts. Why? Why was he so fascinated by what he saw? It wasn't only his discretion that kept him from doing something, or standing by a fellow man. No. It was more than that. He saw in them a feeling that was beyond all common sense, one that he longed for. He longed for love.

ᘓᘌ

Nika sketched. She made drawings in her notebook and on any piece of paper she could find. Segantini had brought her a new book when the old one was full, and then another one. Nika also practiced writing. Next to the drawings she made, she carefully wrote the names of the things she had drawn: lake, boat, hotel, tree, Gaetano. Segantini showed her how to hold the pencil when she was drawing, his hand guiding her hand. She began to tremble when she felt the warmth of his skin. She wasn't used to being touched by other people. To be touched gently especially was something new. He looked at her briefly, but said nothing.

"Try to draw a self-portrait," he said to her one day. "Doesn't matter if it's not successful. It's very hard to draw yourself. After all, can anyone really see himself or herself?"

"I'll try," Nika said.

She went back to the hotel and sneaked into one of the guest toilets that members of the staff were not allowed to use. Those were the only places where there were mirrors, and it was the only place where she could lock herself in and be unobserved. With one blow from a sharp-edged stone, she shattered the mirror hanging over the sink. She selected a fragment from among the many that had clattered to the floor and hid it in her garden apron. Then she waited until she couldn't hear anyone moving outside and darted out again like a shadow.

Before she fell asleep at night, she would slowly write the letters of the alphabet and form them into words. Early in the morning, before going to work, she would sketch herself. It was hard to draw her face from the little of it she could see in the small mirror fragment. It drove her to despair. The mirror fragmented her face—the hairline, a section of forehead, an eye, her nose—and in

162

the end she mimicked the images on paper. She created a separate drawing for each feature—the nose, the mouth and chin, the ear, and cheek.

She gave the drawings to Segantini. He made no comment, just passed a finger across her forehead to compare the actual hairline with her drawing of it. She reached for his finger and held it. He pulled his hand away.

The next time he came, he brought her a bouquet of alpine roses.

He still didn't comment on her sketches.

She drew her upper body, with the flowers lying between her naked breasts; you could see the crumpled edge of her pushed-up shirt. She liked the drawing. She rolled it up and tied a red velvet ribbon around it that she once found outside the hotel and carefully saved. Segantini took the rolled-up drawing but didn't untie the ribbon.

"It's a present for you," Nika said. "I would like you to look at it and tell me if you like it."

"I'll look at it later," he said, "when I'm by myself."

He could see that her feelings were hurt.

"You're afraid," she said, and there was annoyance and disappointment in her voice. "I wouldn't have thought you'd be afraid."

He wanted to answer her, but she angrily pulled the roll out of his hand, took off the ribbon, and tore up the sheet of paper. The scraps fluttered to the ground.

Then she left without even turning around.

She was right. He was afraid. For some time already he had not been sleeping well, which put him in a bad mood, since in the morning and for the rest of the day he needed all his senses to paint. He thought about Nika too often, and that turned

163

everything topsy-turvy—his daily routine and his body and mind. In his thoughts, he apologized to Bice, and yet he couldn't rein in his fantasies. Bice didn't mention Betsy's remarks, but he knew that she had pricked up her ears. He didn't bring up the subject either. There was almost a sort of rebelliousness in it, stubbornly ignoring the topic because it gave him the sense of retaining a degree of freedom. So what if he wanted to keep a part of his life entirely for himself? He hadn't done anything wrong, and no one could reproach him for helping a young person. He had helped others, too, Giovanni Giacometti, for instance, a friend from Stampa and a talented painter. In spite of all this, he had a guilty conscience. If he spoke to Bice about it, he might have had to suspend his visits to Nika for Bice's sake, because he loved Bice and needed her more than anyone else. But to never return to the hotel garden was impossible.

Whenever he went to see Nika, the first thing he saw was her hair glowing from afar, like a temptation. The "bad mothers," the "lustful women" in his paintings all had Nika's hair; they were like her. The comforting thoughtfulness and motherliness that Bice possessed in spite of her youth were missing in Nika. Nika challenged him as if she were his equal, and she was turning the order of his daily life—which he had so carefully constructed—upside down.

After she had ripped apart her drawing and walked away from him, he'd pieced the scraps together and glued them with great care. It was shameless of her to have placed his roses between her breasts. The bristly green leaves in the drawing made her flesh look even softer. There was a brazen cry in the picture, a passionate longing.

She was as rebellious, as excitable as he was, eager to learn, filled with a hunger and thirst for life.

It was not proper for a woman to show her breasts so shamelessly to a stranger like him, even if it was only a drawing. It was as if she were offering herself to him. Yes, that was exactly what she'd intended; that he would now have to see her body whenever he closed his eyes.

And that's how it was. He wanted to know what her skin felt like; it was why he had guided her hand when she was drawing.

And by God, he didn't know what he was supposed to think about the fact that she was so very much like him.

Nika, on the other hand, felt a vague fury growing inside her that threatened to overpower all other emotions. She no longer knew what she wanted.

The locket had given her a task. It had challenged her to find her mother. And then there was the piece of paper inside the locket that had to be deciphered. You don't write something on a piece of paper, fold it up, and then put it inside a valuable locket if you don't want it to be read and understood. But the writing could not be deciphered using the alphabet Nika had learned. These were different, foreign characters that her mother had used.

Nika was angry with her mother for abandoning her to such a miserable fate yet forcing upon her this mysterious reminder. She felt forced to keep thinking of her, to rack her brain about her whereabouts, to long for her.

Nika was also angry with Segantini and for similar reasons. He was the first person in her life who had really showed any affectionate concern for her, who'd understood her, who'd given her what she needed. And despite that, he pushed her away, didn't want the love that he himself had engendered in her.

And Nika was angry with herself. Once again, she was left with a passion that had no hope of fulfillment.

She would tear up all her drawings, all her notebooks. She would focus on her work at the hotel. Signor Robustelli was a nice man and perhaps he could find somewhere else for her to live during the winter and hire her again next summer. She earned a little money, had enough to eat, and was no longer beaten the way she had been by the farmer, who had begrudged her every single piece of bread. It was enough to be happy.

When she got ready for bed that night, she opened the collar of her blouse and took off the chain with the locket. She wouldn't wear it anymore. And she wouldn't look for her mother anymore, either. After all, where could she search? She had run away from Mulegns because she hoped by some miracle to find her family. But there were no miracles.

And Segantini could go to hell.

She would work, would forget about her desire to learn to read, to write, and to draw. When the season came to an end, she would speak with Signor Robustelli. She'd bury all her stupid dreams along with her locket.

Gaetano would be glad to see her working without interruptions. For some time already, he hadn't been happy about the visits she was getting, and it wouldn't be long before he'd complain to Signor Robustelli.

The only thing she planned to keep was the fragment of mirror in her apron pocket, even though she'd once cut herself on its sharp edge.

That night, Nika dreamed about her escape from Mulegns. The dream was so real and detailed that she didn't know where she was when she woke up.

Oh God, yes. Her flight from the farm.

One morning toward the end of May, the farmer's wife had started turning the house upside down; had ordered Nika to scrub the floors, to clean the windows. Suddenly she decided to haul the big wooden chest in which the family's clothes were stored, outside. "Grab hold!" she called to Nika. "I want to take a look at these clothes. We're getting visitors from Chur tomorrow." That didn't sound like good news, but Nika couldn't figure out what was going on. Nobody had ever come there from Chur before. "Make sure you look neat and clean tomorrow," she said. And Nika watched in horror as the woman opened the chest and began pulling everything out of it, all the things that she had hurriedly stuffed back in disorder. If the farmer's wife really took everything out now and looked through it all to put it back in order, she'd notice that the locket was missing.

"But years ago I . . ." the woman mumbled to herself.

Suddenly, Nika couldn't think clearly. She realized that in only a few minutes the woman would discover that the locket was missing. It didn't occur to her that she could just pretend she didn't know what it was all about. She knew only that in her desperation she'd give herself away and that the farmer would beat the living daylights out of her.

Then, as if an angel was helping her, something made the woman pause in her work and go inside. Nika used that moment to go behind the stable, shove aside the stone that marked her hiding place, dig in the soil with her bare hands, take out the necklace with the locket, and start running. The dog began to bark. Nika could hear the farmer's wife, who hadn't yet noticed anything amiss, scolding him. She ran and ran, leaving the village behind her. Then she was on the road that led to Marmorera and Bivio. It forked there, one road leading over the Septimer and the other, the Julier Pass.

Luckily, it was the end of May. Had it been just two or three weeks earlier, there would have been no getting through without sturdy boots and warm winter clothes. The snow would have forced her to give up in the next village. Yet if she didn't get far enough away from Mulegns, she would be in danger of being recognized and sent back. She had to get over the mountain pass.

She knew that the Septimer Pass led directly into the Bregaglia Valley and toward Italy. But it was isolated and was seldom used. The road over the Julier, because it was the postal route, was in much better shape and more developed. She had no money for the post coach, but she had hopes that a carriage would take her part of the way once she was far enough away from Mulegns to avoid raising any suspicions.

As it got dark, she crept into a stable near Bivio for the night and started out again early the next morning. She was able to slake her thirst with snow; there was enough of it as she got higher up. But she was tormented by hunger.

The road snaked toward Silvaplana, and she had reached the top of the pass when a carriage actually stopped. A man looked out of the window and told her that if she would like to sit up front next to the driver, they could take her as far as Silvaplana. Nika, frozen through and through, with her woolen shawl wrapped tightly about her shoulders, gratefully climbed up. The driver, a pleasant man, lifted the heavy blanket that covered his knees so that Nika could warm her legs under it too. He drove off with a flick of his whip. He said nothing but held out a canteen with hot tea to her.

The warm tea ran down Nika's throat, and she couldn't tell what burned more, the tea or her tears of relief, as sensation slowly and with a painful tingle returned to her frozen feet.

When they arrived in Silvaplana, she was lucky again. The driver said, "We're staying here, but if you want to go to Maloja and Italy," he pointed out the direction with his arm, "you have to go this way."

And so Nika now knew which way she had to go. She took the high road to Maloja.

New Experiences

Nika wasn't the only one tormented by memories. Mathilde also was haunted, even in her sleep, by the afternoon she had spent in secret with James at the Pension Veraguth. How easily she had given in to him—and to herself!

James had slowly pulled the gloves off Mathilde's fingers, had kissed her palms, had only let go of her hands once he was certain that she would fling them around his neck. And that is just what she'd done. Closing her eyes, she'd held her face toward him full of expectation, as if the sun were shining on her. But he hadn't kissed her. He'd taken the comb decorated with a glowing blue butterfly out of her hair, and as she'd held her breath, he'd run his hands through the blonde curls. Then gathering the rebellious hair at the back of her neck, he pulled her head gently backward. She yielded easily, her eyes still closed. And now he kissed her, first on her arched throat, then her small well-formed ear, her cheek reddened by excitement, and her temple on which there was a tiny mole. Mathilde opened her lips, and he traced the soft contours of her lips with his finger. How young her lips were.

"Mathilde," he said softly, "have you ever kissed a man before?"

She nodded with closed eyes. "Not properly," she murmured.

"Open your eyes," James said, "and look at me."

Mathilde felt his hands on her throat. They slid downward over her breasts, and then began slowly, braced for protest, to undo one button after the other. Next, they slid under the white summertime muslin of her dress, pushed their way under her shirt, and cupped her naked breasts. She didn't want to open her eyes and look at him, better not to, it wasn't right what she was allowing him to do. And it wasn't just that, she wanted only to feel his hand exploring her skin. He was doing it for her, allowing her at last to explore herself, her own body, along with his desires. She thought of Adrian, her fiancé, who didn't permit himself to do more than kiss her closed lips, gently and lovingly but without passion. Those were the rules. After all, he had a whole lifetime to make love to her and could gather the necessary knowledge for that elsewhere. Yet she . . . The hands, not stopping, moved on, began touching her hips, easily loosened the waistband of her underpants, which were open at the bottom. She would be totally unprotected if he were to push her skirt up . . .

Suddenly she was scared to death. What was she doing? Where were her shoes? All she had on were her white stockings. Where in the world were her shoes? She had desired James so very much, and now she was afraid. Not because she was thinking of Adrian, but because she herself had gone so far. James pulled away, poured her another glass of champagne, and handed it to her. She was glad he had stopped. The champagne was refreshing and cold, oh, that was good. James smiled at her and poured some more into his own glass.

What was she afraid of? He wouldn't harm her. After all, he had stopped as soon as he sensed that she no longer felt comfortable with what he was doing. What a wonderful adventure she was having! No one would ever find out. James knew exactly how to treat her, and he had so much more experience than she did. That he was even interested in her . . . Her mother, she was sure, had never had such an experience, maybe not even Aunt Betsy. Mathilde held her now-empty glass out to James, suddenly proud of her recklessness. James shook his head.

"No, no, Mathilde, the champagne will go to your head, and it will be my fault if you have a headache afterward. I won't let you have any more. Not another drop!"

"Hold me in your arms," she whispered, but again he shook his head.

"No. We have to go now. Kate is waiting for us, and we don't want to have to answer too many questions, do we?"

Mathilde was disappointed. He was too sensible, she thought now. He didn't love her after all. Not really. Not the way she wanted it. He was supposed to press her, and she would then say no. He was supposed to desire her passionately and only rein himself in at the end because she asked him to. And then he would realize that he loved her so very much, that . . .

"Mathilde," he said, interrupting her thoughts. "Mathilde, will you allow me to take a picture of you? A photograph? Your Aunt Kate emphasized that you are engaged. That means that I shall lose you. Please allow me to take a memento of you home with me, something that I can always look at. It will be as if you were physically there. I will smell your perfume, hear your laughter . . ."

Mathilde was confused. A photograph! As a memento! So he didn't want to fight for her and eliminate Adrian. It made her all mixed up. She didn't know how to answer him.

James got his camera from the closet. "Please," he said. "Don't act holier than the Pope. The camera won't bite. It won't even come close to you. Nothing will happen to you. And it won't hurt, I promise!"

It made her laugh. He was right.

"Very well, I'll get properly dressed and comb my hair," she said. She actually felt flattered that he wanted to photograph her.

"Oh, no!" he cried, disappointed. "Then I could be snapping just any lady. I want you, Mathilde, you, just as beautiful as you are at this instant."

He thought she was beautiful. "All right then. But hurry before I change my mind," she said with a trace of the doubt that was on the point of penetrating the champagne fog.

He kissed her hand.

"Miss Schobinger . . . Miss Schobinger!" The nurse in a white apron and a little white cap bent over Mathilde, brushing the damp hair from her forehead. "Wake up, Mathilde. What's wrong? What were you dreaming? Come, come. Look at me!"

The sun was shining into the room, its rays falling on the feather quilt that the nurse had carefully fluffed up. Through the open window came the scent of the summer meadows.

"Yes," Mathilde said. She looked around the room still dazed with sleep and the dream she had dreamed. Oh yes, she was in Dr. Bernhard's clinic under the care of the nurses. That was good. "Yes," she said again, trying to smile, "it was only a dream that confused me."

The nurse brought Mathilde out onto the balcony and wrapped her in blankets and disappeared again. Then, moments later, she returned with a visitor.

"Good morning, Mathilde. I hope you don't mind this inter-ruption?" Departing, the nurse silently closed the door behind James. "You look frightened," James said, embarrassed. "Would you rather I hadn't come? I brought you some flowers." He held out a colorful bouquet of roses.

Mathilde was still silent. Tears came to her eyes.

"Please, Mathilde, don't cry," he begged her. "Should I have come sooner? Or not come at all? Should I leave now?" He took her hand and kissed it. Then he turned it palm up and placed a luminous blue butterfly in it. "You left this in my room," he said, and folded her fingers around the butterfly. Then Mathilde really began to cry.

"None of it should have happened," she managed to say between sobs.

"But you were so lovely," he said, "and you wanted to be kissed."

"No, don't! Don't say anything. I know. You don't have to explain. And in the end, it's even my fault. But you realize that I cannot see you anymore. That's clear, I hope."

"But I wanted to tell you . . ." he said, trailing off hesitantly.

"There's nothing you should tell me. You should simply go and leave me in peace. And not a word to anyone, ever. Do you understand?"

As James walked down the hallway of the clinic, he no longer noticed the septic odor given off by the freshly scrubbed floors. For once, he felt—and it was an unfamiliar feeling for him—that he had done something he shouldn't have done.

❧❧

"Come in!" Achille Robustelli called out. He was in a good mood. Business this summer was flourishing. The season would probably turn a profit, and the usual complaints about the personnel and illness had remained within reasonable bounds. Everything was functioning smoothly. Only the emptiness in his heart remained; the feeling of satisfaction he got from his work did not make up for it. This was a good moment to devote some attention to Andrina. She was the one who had just knocked and stuck her head inside the door inquiringly.

"So, how does your brother like working for the railroad?" he asked and indicated that she should sit down on the other side of his broad desk.

"Luca? He's doing well. He sent us a postcard and asked me to give you his regards. The entire family is grateful to you," Andrina lied.

"You don't have to say that," Achille said, for he was not as vain as Andrina thought. "From what I hear, your mother isn't exactly happy about it and doesn't have anything good to say about me. But I was glad that I was able to do you and Luca a favor, because," he turned his ring once or twice, "you've surely noticed that I care for you, that you're important to me."

He had spent a long time thinking about whether he should invite Andrina to go with him to the dance on Saturday in St. Moritz. He was sure the head housekeeper would give her a few hours off; after all, he did favors for Signora Capadrutt now and then too.

Moreover, he had decided not to tell his mother about Andrina for as long as possible, because she would probably find just as much to criticize about her as she had about all the other women he had liked in the past. Why hadn't he thought before of keeping from her any information having to do with women, marriage plans, and his ideas for the future? His sudden realization—that he didn't have to tell his mother everything, and nothing at all about Andrina—seemed to him like proof that Andrina was the right one. All these years he had been fully aware of her critical nature, yet he had subjected the other girls to his mother's pitiless gaze. This time, though, he would guard his treasure more carefully—because he wanted to keep it.

Andrina, contrary to her usual style, waited patiently for him to emerge from his reflections and look at her directly. Then she said, cautiously, "Yes, Signor Robustelli, I noticed that you like me. And that is why I took a chance and turned to you about Luca. And I knocked on your door just now because I was hoping you'd be happy to see me . . ."

"I am," Achille said, a bit stiffly and went on, "and I would like to invite you to come dancing with me in St. Moritz this Saturday."

He laughed, because it was clear that he had actually succeeded in surprising her. "You're not saying anything. Surely you have gone dancing before?"

"Yes," Andrina said, "but not with a gentleman like you."

"And that makes you speechless?" Signor Robustelli asked, less inhibited than before.

Andrina shook her head.

"Well?"

Achille watched, fascinated, as Andrina's full lips pursed to form an answer. A flood of wild desires surged up inside him with a vehemence that surprised him, but he controlled them, realizing that he'd probably have to rein them in for a while.

"I'd like to come," she said hesitantly, "but I don't know what the head housekeeper . . ." She looked questioningly at him with her chestnut-brown eyes.

"I'll worry about that," he replied. "But now, go back to work." He returned energetically to the papers on his desk.

"Signor Robustelli?"

"Yes, what?"

"I don't have a dress in which I can be seen with you."

Andrina had gotten up, and Robustelli smiled as he allowed his eyes to glide over her breasts and hips.

"You don't need a dress to please me," he replied.

Kate considered her night with James only half a success. He hadn't stayed until morning nor had he been a particularly tender lover. At breakfast, she felt so unloved that she almost longed for the return of her husband just to avoid the thought that she might actually have suffered a defeat. But not only would it take Robert thirteen hours to get down to Chur, he'd need another thirteen to come back up to St. Moritz, and so she would have to try, without him, to give this day a more pleasant aspect than her dark mood and the hazy clouds outside promised.

The waiters were anxious to remove the breakfast dishes because it was time to set the tables for lunch, but Kate, who had dithered for a long time between going downstairs or ordering something to be brought up to the room, had appeared late for breakfast. She had decided to leave the site of her partial humiliation.

"Oh," she said as the waiter discreetly approached her table in the hope she would get up, "now I know what I really want! Please be so kind as to bring me a fresh fruit salad. That's exactly what I feel like having now." She smiled graciously up into the waiter's face, which was not exactly delighted. "And please tell them in the kitchen that I'd like it with a fresh peach and . . ." she called after the young man who had without a reply already turned to go, "a little fresh toast. This bread here is too soft and chewy, as if it were two days old."

The waiter neither turned around nor answered her. He just nodded silently. Kate felt a trace better.

That changed when they handed her a telegram at the reception desk in which Robert informed her that he would be staying in Chur a day longer than originally planned.

"Is everything all right, Madam?" the man at the desk asked.

"Yes, yes. Of course," she replied and stepped outside. After a moment's hesitation, she went down the avenue that led to the lakeshore. About halfway there, she stopped by some benches near a beautifully laid out circular flowerbed. The flowerbed was deserted around this time of day. Only the birds chirped and flew busily back and forth in the trees. With a relieved sigh, she sank down on a bench. Here, there was no one to notice the gloomy mood so uncharacteristic of her.

James had not said a word to her about getting together again in the next few days. On the contrary, he had mentioned that he would be spending a day with Edward. Why was he arming himself so carefully with excuses? He needn't fear that she planned to chase after him!

The sky was covered by a thin whitish veil, and a diffuse light lay over the landscape. A remarkable emptiness spread out before Kate, even though she tried to pull herself together, to become her usual self, the alert, witty Kate, the one she preferred to show to the world. Oh, yes, she had an iron will, and that had often come to her aid. But today, life seemed oddly burdensome. She stretched out her right arm and held her palm into the air. Sparrows hopped toward her and a few tufted titmice on the lowest branches of the trees turned their heads sideways, rubbing their beaks on the branches, unsure whether to come nearer. But Kate had neither breadcrumbs nor birdseed to offer, and so no bird came to perch on her empty hand. Unexpectedly, tears came to her eyes and she quickly got up.

Since they had been staying at the hotel, no one had asked why she and Robert had actually come here, and she had liked it that way. Only now, at this moment, it upset her, just as she felt hurt that she had no children, although she actually didn't want any. She had the curative water brought to her room in bottles so that she could do a *Trinkkur*, a mineral water drinking cure, but she didn't want to take the baths, even though Robert had urged her to do it. Robert was so simple. "If you can't have children, let's try the baths. Maybe they will help," he said. That was all that had occurred to him.

Sullenly, she dispersed the complaining sparrows with her parasol and resolved to take the horse-drawn omnibus to visit the shopping gallery in St. Moritz. Somebody had claimed that Swiss clocks were terrific and very much in vogue. And she could also take a look at the Palace Hotel, which was supposed to reopen very soon with a festive celebration.

"Have you ever been to St. Moritz?" Segantini asked. Nika shook her head. She had decided that she didn't want to see him again, but since she hadn't yet told him, he continued to come by freely.

"I have to buy some things there, and if you'd like to, you can come along. I've asked for a carriage. Wait by the side of the road at three o'clock, and I'll ask the driver to stop for you."

Nika averted her eyes. She didn't like the way he spoke to her.

179

"I have to work," she said. "You know that."

"Gaetano!" he called, and when the old man shuffled up, he said, "Nika is going with me this afternoon to St. Moritz. She'll make up for the time she missed."

"I quite understand," Gaetano replied.

"You don't understand anything," Segantini said angrily.

The gardener made no reply and left.

Nika shook her head; she didn't understand either.

Segantini looked at her in surprise.

"Then think about it for a while," he said. His voice had turned gentle again.

Nika looked down and said, "Maybe it's you who should be doing that."

The driver stopped but didn't get down from the carriage. Segantini leaned forward, holding a hand out to Nika, and pulled her up into the open carriage. Dust whirled up behind them as the horses trotted off. Segantini laughed when he saw Nika's reserved expression.

"Haven't you ever sat in a carriage?"

Nika shook her head.

"Farm wagons don't go as fast as this lovely victoria, eh?"

She said nothing. It wasn't the speed. She was reproaching herself for even having climbed up. Why had she gone to wait by the side of the road in the first place? She should simply have gone on with her work. Gaetano was angry about this escapade and had threatened to speak to Robustelli. Under no circumstances must he do that. She needed Signor Robustelli's help to find work and new lodgings for the winter. And yet, whenever Segantini came near her, she again felt good about things and wanted to sing and chirp like a bird in the spring. Yet he was an old man, and he had a wife. Couldn't she get that through her thick skull? And he ordered her around like the farmer had.

The carriage was a two-seater. An elegant folding roof arched overhead. Segantini didn't want to have it lowered. They sat close together. Ahead to the right, the lakes glittered in the sun, but their faces were in the shade. Nika had rolled up the sleeves of her blouse, baring her slender brown arms. Now and then, his jacket touched her skin, but that was because of the slight rocking motion of the carriage, which flew along, much too fast.

"I love you," Nika suddenly said, without looking at Segantini.

It was as if the words had dropped on the floor of the carriage and from there onto the road, had simply rolled out of her mouth and disappeared into the gravel. And now they were lying somewhere, unnoticed behind them on the road, because nobody had caught them, had stretched a hand out for them.

"What did you say?" Segantini turned to her and looked at her face.

"Nothing," she said.

"Yes, you said something."

"I don't want to repeat it."

He was silent. Finally he said, "I say what is important to me, over and over again. I keep painting this landscape, these mountains, the sheep, the cows, the people, whether they are at work or at rest. Again and again, I paint the light after the sunset. The stillness. Death. Love."

Nika did not reply. She saw the words she had spoken lying in the road like little gray marbles, somewhere between Maloja and St. Moritz, totally meaningless, worthless.

"I paint the love that is in everything," he continued, "that is the mission, the task of art. It is in the beauty of every little flower—the love that surrounds us."

They passed the little, old San Lurench Church; they passed Sils-Baselgia.

"I was orphaned early," he began. "A little boy who could sense that his mother was ill and would soon leave him, no matter how much he loved her. Even while she was alive, she wasn't quite all there. I killed her by being born. She never recovered from my birth. My older brother died in a fire at barely three years old. That also may have contributed to her condition. My father was rarely at home. I scarcely knew him. Only poverty was always present. When my mother died, he took me to Milan, to his daughter, Irene, from an earlier marriage. I not only lost my mother, but I also lost the countryside, the surroundings in which I grew up. The little town of Arco, the river in which I almost drowned once, the sky I still remember. I never liked Milan."

So that's why, Nika thought. That's why he bothers about me, because he knows what I know. Because I know what he feels.

"Irene kept house for her brother Napoleone," Segantini continued, "but his little drugstore was not doing well. They themselves were both strangers in Milan and found no support anywhere. The store closed; the furniture was sold. My father left with Napoleone."

Segantini cleared his throat; he didn't remove his hand when Nika's hand searched it out and held it tight. Her grip was strong and without false consolation. He talked on into the dim light under the carriage roof. Outside, the brightness made the water quiver with gleaming flecks of light.

"I stayed with Irene, whom I hated. And she felt the same way about me. She was a skinny, bitter woman without any understanding for a young child."

Not saying a word, Nika squeezed his hand. It was so large that she could barely get her fingers around it.

Segantini cleared his throat once more. "I never again saw my father."

He felt the strong, almost masculine, pressure of her hand. Then he pulled his hand back and leaned forward to see where they were. They were just then going through Silvaplana. On the left was the road that led up one of the mountains.

"I came from there," Nika said, and pointed. "Over the Julier Pass."

He nodded absently. He at least had known his parents. He didn't want to judge whether that was better or worse. "Was the farmer with whom you grew up in Mulegns good to you? Better than Irene was to me?"

"No," Nika said.

At that point, he didn't know what to say.

They had left Champfer behind and would soon be reaching the first houses of St. Moritz.

"We'll soon be there." Segantini took Nika's arm and pulled her forward. "Look, there are the mineral baths and the big hotels where people enjoy them . . . the Spa, the Kurhaus, the Victoria, the Stahlbad. But we'll drive up to the village first. Look, there's even a streetcar here. Have you ever seen a streetcar?"

"No." Nika smiled. "That's a streetcar? On the tracks? Like a train?"

"And up in the village there's a new grand hotel opening next week called the Palace; it's near my friend Peter Robert Berry's house. We'll be driving past it next." He called out to the driver, asking him to stop and fold down the roof so that they could see better.

Nika was amazed. The Palace Hotel was immense. In contrast to the Spa Hotel Maloja, it looked like a huge fortress with a fortified tower and battlements. All in all, this was a totally incomprehensible world for her: the streetcar, the noble carriages, the many elegant people. Lots of high-class guests came to Maloja too, but the village had remained what it was originally: there were no baths, no fine shops, and no collection of luxury hotels. The guests of the Spa Hotel Maloja went to St. Moritz on the horse-drawn omnibus whenever they had treatments, wanted to dine out, go shopping, or attend soirees.

Segantini asked the driver to stop and jumped down.

"Wait for me here," he said. "It's better if you don't walk around in this place by yourself. Sit up front with the driver. From there you can watch all the goings-on."

Nonplussed, she nodded, watching him hurry off. He was like her. And yet he wasn't.

In a short while, he came back, bringing some cake wrapped in paper.

"From the Hanselmann Bakery," he said. "You'll like it."

"Thanks," she said, totally surprised. It was the first time someone had bought her something sweet.

"To make the waiting seem less long," Segantini explained.

Nika watched him go again. She broke off a piece of cake and put it in her mouth. The unaccustomed sweetness spread through her entire body; she felt as if life had just taken on a new, overpowering taste. She pulled off another piece of cake and wrapped the rest up in the paper it had come in to save for later. But then a moment later she unwrapped it, offered the driver a piece, and put the chunk that was left into her own mouth. The cake would only dry out if she didn't eat it now.

Now is when it tastes best, she thought. Now at this moment, when I can still make out his dark hair in the crowd, and know he'll come back.

"Have you ever dealt with horses?" the driver asked Nika.

"In the village on the farm," she replied.

"Could you stay here by yourself for a while?" the driver was already halfway down from his seat. "I have to go take a leak, and if you don't mind I'd also like to get a quick beer. It's hot and I haven't taken a break yet today."

She nodded.

The horses had their feed bags around their neck and were standing quietly. Now and then, they switched their weight from one leg to another, causing a slight movement of the carriage. Nika watched the people walking by. She bit her lip. Why hadn't she brought her notebook along? The horses from the unusual perspective of the driver's seat, the houses, the strolling people—she could have sketched it all.

But she had sworn to herself she'd never draw again. Then again, she'd also vowed to have nothing more to do with Segantini. And she knew that her hand had become more assured, her perspective more detailed. Segantini was a good teacher.

She wondered whether he felt the same way as she did—did all his loneliness, all his troubles, vanish when he looked at something closely? When he painted or drew? The happiness that flooded her when she was drawing came to her slowly and almost imperceptibly from deep down. Not like the sweetness that exploded on her tongue when she ate the cake. What she saw and then tried to capture with her pencil drove out—more and more, the longer she practiced—everything else she felt: her loneliness, her forlornness in the world, her longing for tenderness and security, and yes, even her thoughts about Segantini who had opened up this new world for her. She forgot everything, even herself, and that gave her relief and liberated her as if she had wings, as if she were a bird who could leave everything behind and let herself be carried off by the wind to new and unfamiliar places.

"You have a beautiful driver there, Segantini," Oscar Bernhard called out to him. "I haven't seen her before!"

Nika looked at Segantini, startled.

He seemed to be in a good mood, and laughed, saying, "That, my dear Bernhard, is the young talent I was telling you about."

"But you didn't tell me that she is such a beauty, my dear man. Or did you, a painter, not notice that?"

Nika blushed in shame and anger. They were talking about her as if she weren't there. And in the midst of all these people.

She climbed down and went to fetch the driver.

Kate was brooding because her husband had not made every effort to come back to St. Moritz as soon as possible. She almost felt that it wasn't she who had been unfaithful to him, but rather that he was the one who had wronged her by leaving her for such an eternity. And she had to wait impatiently for his return. She rather liked seeing herself in the role of the abandoned wife, and would only reluctantly have admitted that she would hardly have missed Robert if James had lifted a finger to make use of the situation. But over the last few days, he had come to Maloja just once, and had merely given her a brief kiss on the cheek when they met by accident in the hotel lobby. He'd said, "Oh, I'm sorry for your sake that Robert isn't back yet. I hope you're not worried that something unpleasant might have happened?"

"What could possibly have happened to Robert in a town like Chur?" she answered, giving him the cold shoulder in return. "Excuse me, I have an appointment . . ." And with that, she had quickly walked off.

When Robert finally arrived, he seemed prepared to ignore her injured expression as he impatiently ripped his carryall out of the porter's hand and sent him off without a tip. And so Kate at once decided to stop acting hurt. It was obvious to her that he had no desire at this point to discuss his delayed return to St. Moritz.

"You look tired," she said instead, as he briefly and reluctantly embraced her. "The trip must have been torture. Why do mountains exist? I certainly don't need them. Shall I have them send up some coffee?"

"No," he said curtly, "but I'm hungry. The trip was horrible. I could have throttled those two ladies sitting in the coach with me, just to make them shut up."

Kate gathered that he wasn't particularly fond of the female sex at the moment, and congratulated herself for having so quickly switched from acting offended to showing concern for him. She wondered whether his remark indicated that he had met a woman in Chur whose behavior had not been what he'd expected. In any case, a visit to a brothel might have calmed him down. But was there even a brothel in Chur? And why should he meet a lover in Chur of all places?

"I can understand that you're hungry. Let's go down for supper right now." She took him gently by the arm, but even that seemed too much.

While she was getting dressed to go down to eat, Kate concluded that what had put Robert into such a bad mood probably had nothing to do with a woman. Unless he'd had a rendezvous with some secret beloved who had just been passing through. At this time of the year, anyone from England who could afford it came to Switzerland. Still, the likelihood of such an encounter was unlikely. Well, whatever, she'd be acquiescent today.

"The Palace is opening next week," Kate said, trying to cheer him up. "There'll be a magnificent gala. I thought I'd wear the cream-colored lace dress you like so much . . ."

She flinched when Robert interrupted her.

"I have to talk to you later," he said brusquely. She wondered what was so important that it had to wait until they were alone, but he clearly didn't want to be pressed. He nervously pushed his plate aside. Even though he'd been hungry, he had eaten less than half of his *brasato alla Valtellina*, not to mention the vegetables, which he'd scarcely touched. That wasn't unusual though, since he considered carrots food for rabbits, and complained that peas always rolled off his fork. But something was amiss. Since he was being so extremely prickly, Kate turned to say a few words to the guests who were sitting next to them at the *table d'hôte*.

Her attempt to draw him into their bedroom that evening failed. That meant the situation was really serious. Robert came to the point in the living room of their hotel suite.

"Stop running around like a nervous hen," he said irritably. "Sit down. There's something I have to tell you."

Kate decided for the moment to suppress any criticism of her husband, in spite of not feeling very fond of him just then. She sat down.

"For heaven's sake, what happened? Tell me."

"We're leaving. Start packing your things immediately. And don't forget the love letters your various lovers may have sent you up here."

My God, Kate thought, he's unbearable. Did he find out somehow that James had come to see her? She got up, but sat right down again.

"I met with an important business associate in Chur," Robert went on. "In short, I found out from him that I have lost a lot of money. You don't need to know the details. From there I went on to Zurich to speak to the bank and to clarify any possibility of getting credit. But the situation looks bad. In any case, we have to leave this place. It's urgent that I go to London to see about what steps to take next."

"But . . ." Kate said.

"No buts. Your fun and games here would certainly be diminished by the thought that your husband has gone bankrupt."

Robert's face had turned so red that his wife suppressed a second *but*. It couldn't possibly be that they suddenly didn't have any money. That was unimaginable. If it was really true, she wanted to go home to her parents in Boston, at once. A bankrupt husband. What a disgrace!

Robert seemed to have guessed what she was thinking.

"And you will stay with me and stand by me. You're still my wife. We'll have to dismiss the help, and you'll probably have to pay more attention to the housekeeping than before." He nervously drummed with his fingers on the arm of the chair. "I'll have to see what I can save. Do you think this is any fun for me?"

His fury slowly gave way to depression. He suddenly seemed small, shrinking in his armchair in front of Kate. He was actually only average in size, but she realized it was really his money and status that made him seem imposing.

Kate sensed a feeling of disgust, almost revulsion, welling up in her. What was he if he wasn't strong enough to protect her and take care of her? He struck her as an unloved nothing of a man— he hadn't even managed to make her pregnant. What a disgrace, leaving in such a rush, even before the big event of the season.

How was she going to explain it to her friends? He looked like a sack of potatoes sitting there in his chair. Tears came to her eyes.

She was crying for several reasons. The news was a shock, of course, and she was only slowly beginning to realize what it would mean. In addition, she despised people who failed, and now here was her husband, standing before the entire world as a loser. And moreover—the realization was only vague and indefinite, but painful enough—so was she. If her husband was nothing anymore, then she herself was nothing too. A failure who couldn't have children and had nothing else to show. A woman who depended on servants to hide the fact that she couldn't do anything, not even brew a cup of coffee or darn a stocking. A person who needed constant admiration so that she could feel like somebody, so that she could think of herself as lovable.

A remarkable sound came from her chest. She was sobbing even as she forbade herself to sob. Oh no, her parents had never wanted to see their little Kate cry.

Going back to America wasn't a good idea. And when she thought that she might have lost James, who seemed such a sure choice as playmate for her, to the naïve and insignificant Mathilde, who was sick into the bargain . . . when she thought of this—as if she wasn't suffering enough already—the tears really started flow.

Robert, who loved his wife, not unconditionally but in his own somewhat devoted sort of way, looked in surprise at this rare picture of Kate, weeping uncontrollably.

"Well," he said helplessly, "not everything is lost yet. Come on, stop crying."

But Kate didn't want to stop crying.

Achille had no choice. He had to do something, even if it was unpleasant for him and went against his usual discreet way of doing things. Gaetano had complained. Segantini had not only kept the *straniera* from working in the garden, he'd said, but had taken her along to St. Moritz in the middle of the day. It didn't matter how far up Segantini's good connections reached—this was really going too far. Robustelli had to agree with the gardener. And the more dramatic this unfortunate affair became, the more bad feelings it would cause. He didn't want to fire Nika, even though that's what he should really do. It was clear that he would have to speak with Segantini, which was exactly what he'd hoped to avoid.

But restraint was a virtue; cowardice wasn't. Achille decided to bring the situation up directly with the painter. Perhaps he didn't realize that his interest in Nika put her in such a risky position. He didn't want to dramatize the thing, but he would take Segantini aside for a moment when he came to the hotel to meet Mr. Danby.

"Hello, Mathilde, may I bother you for a minute? Oh, sorry, I woke you up."

Betsy had taken her for a little walk and then dropped her off in her room. And Mathilde had actually dozed off on the balcony. She opened her eyes—the young, male voice reached her while she was still confused by a fleeting remnant of a dream. For a moment, she thought it was James, and her heart began to pound. But once she sat up in her deck chair and looked around, she saw it was Edward smiling at her in embarrassment.

Mathilde was relieved. She smiled radiantly at him. How nice of him to visit her, and more importantly, her heart calmed down when she saw that it wasn't his friend standing there in the doorway. She asked him to come in and sit down next to her. Somewhat formally, he handed her the bouquet of flowers he had brought, a combination of tiger lilies and Turk's Cap lilies, brilliant orange and purple. To Edward, the colors seemed reflected in her cheeks.

"How beautiful they are," she said in delight.

"There are a few places where they grow in great profusion."

Mathilde smiled. "Would you be so kind as to look for a vase? Either in my room or you can ask the nurse. And then, if you please, come right back. You must tell me what you've been doing the last few days. It's a bit boring here," she wrinkled her nose deprecatingly, "and I'm not allowed to walk a lot yet. But I am supposed to eat a lot."

"It won't do you any harm to gain a little weight. At least, that's what I think." Edward took the flowers and went in search of a vase.

He was scarcely out of the room when Mathilde jumped up, looked critically at herself in the mirror, put on some powder, and tried to put her stubborn curls in order.

"Oh, let the curls do what they will," Edward said. He had come back without her noticing. Mathilde, caught unawares, let her hands sink down and looked a bit abashed. Now he must think that she was trying to look pretty for him. And to her own surprise, it was true. A short silence ensued, but not an unpleasant one.

Then Edward said, "If you will permit me. I've come to see you as James's representative. You know that James is . . ." he laughed, hesitated, for he didn't want to step on her toes or offend her. "In any case, I thought I could pass the time with you now and then when James can't come."

She took a deep breath intending to give him an angry reply, but bit her lip instead and said nothing. He couldn't know what had happened between James and her, and that she had sent James away. Of course, she had waited longingly the next few days, hoping that James would come back in spite of everything. But he had taken her at her word, and that was more proof, she thought, that he didn't care all that much for her. Whatever. The worst was the way that Kate, right after the illicit hour of bliss and disaster, had rubbed James's nose in the fact that she was engaged. Oh well, it was all quite horrible.

Yet, from another viewpoint, it was nice that Edward had come to stand in for James. And she had never before been presented with a bouquet of flowers that glowed with such extraordinary fire.

☙❧

Reluctantly Kate started packing her things. She had asked Andrina to come and help her. But whatever Andrina did seemed to be wrong.

"Good Lord! How stupid can you be!" she said angrily. "Do you think that just because you have a pretty face you don't need to work?" Kate pushed the chambermaid roughly aside. "Don't simply stand there getting in the way!" She dropped the salmon-colored silk coat she had just taken out of the closet. Andrina tried, dutifully, to pick it up but Kate hissed at her, "Leave it alone! That's not for you to touch with your peasant hands. Go away, you're not helping at all!"

Andrina left feeling hurt that the woman she had taken as her example had treated her so contemptuously. She had to do everything, everything possible in her life to rise above this job as a chambermaid. Who wants to let people order them around and humiliate them like this for the rest of their lives?

But just then, she heard Mrs. Simpson, already calling her to come back.

"Go and tell the room service waiter that I'd like some hot chocolate brought up. It will calm my nerves. And then pack the hats in the hatboxes. But be careful."

The hot chocolate actually did seem to soothe Kate.

"By the way, do you know whom I happened to see in St. Moritz?" she asked Andrina. "You'll never guess. That beautiful young girl who works in the hotel garden. And you know with whom? With that man with the dark, curly hair, the painter from Maloja. What was his name again?"

"Segantini?" prompted Andrina.

"Right, Segantini. I think that's his name. How about that? Quite improper, don't you think? That little peasant hick walking around St. Moritz among all the hotel guests, it's quite unthinkable. Well, she's quite pretty and seems to be profiting from it." She turned gloomy again. Looking at Andrina, she said casually, "She's prettier than you. But so what. A painter isn't a particularly special conquest."

The Interview

James had prepared for his conversation with Segantini, which surprised his friend.

"You ought to know by now that I take my work seriously," James told him, "even though not every assignment is fun. I'm going to get that 'painter of the mountains,' the 'athletic Christ,' as someone called him, to reveal some of his secrets. Don't you agree, Eddie, that he envelops himself in a sort of prophet's aura?"

"Don't know." Edward was in a hurry because he was planning to visit Mathilde. "He is an impressive figure, strong, very masculine, I'd describe him more as a patriarch . . ."

He picked up his hat, waved briefly to James, and was out the door.

James, for his part, went to Maloja. He hoped the young man who had volunteered to act as interpreter would do his job well.

Achille Robustelli had already introduced Giovanni Segantini and Fabrizio Bonin to each other and informed the staff to reserve a quiet table in the library for them.

Young Bonin was a nice-looking fellow. An ash-blond Venetian in his midtwenties—not as dark and striking in appearance as Segantini—well dressed but not conspicuously so. His clear, pleasant voice was as unassertive as he was, and still, Robustelli thought, you would not overlook Bonin. He had presence. Robustelli, in any event, had liked him from the outset.

Count Primoli, with whom Bonin was traveling, had agreed to exhibit some of his photographs of Venice at the hotel before he went on to Paris, and Bonin was taking care of the practical aspects of the show.

"Do I have a message?" Segantini said, repeating James's question. "The light. Pure, unmixed color."

James sat quietly, waiting.

"When I was at the academy in Milan," Segantini explained, "I did my first oil painting, *The Chancel of Sant Antonio*." He smiled remembering those days. "The sun was streaming in through an open window and over the carved wooden seats of the chancel, flooding them in light. Even back then, I tried above all to capture the light. But if you mix the colors on your palette, you get neither light nor air. So I sought a way to make the colors look genuine and pure, and I found it by setting them next to each other on the canvas, unmixed, leaving it for the retina of the viewers to meld them as they looked at the painting. In this way I achieved an animation of color, along with a greater degree of light and air in a way that felt faithful to life."

Segantini had an inkling that James Danby would now ask about his training, his models—all the others did that. So he immediately continued, as soon as Bonin had translated his last words. "I registered at the Milan academy for life drawing and was accepted without any difficulties because I had already attended evening courses in decorative art. But only a few months were enough to convince me that academic instruction was useless for anyone born with an artistic soul. I taught myself what I needed to know. The academies train a lot of painters who are not artists," he added in a dismissive tone.

He waited to be contradicted, but James did not contradict him.

"So you haven't modeled yourself on other painters?" he asked instead.

"No," Segantini replied, slightly irritated, "I already said that. Later, my friend Grubicy showed me reproductions of pictures by Millet, and of course I exchanged views with friends and colleagues."

Segantini sank back into his memories, but then took up the conversation where James had interrupted him. "After having arrived at this knowledge by myself, I went to live in Brianza for almost four years. Bice came with me, our children were born . . ."

James sat forward in his chair and interrupted.

"Brianza? What is that? A region?"

"Yes," Bonin said, answering for Segantini. "Brianza is the countryside north of Milan and south of Lake Como."

Segantini nodded, realizing that Bonin was speaking about Brianza.

"I was attracted to nature, the out-of-doors," he went on. "Nature had become for me, as it were, like an instrument that gave off musical sounds that accompanied everything that my heart was saying. Again and again, it is in the calm harmonies of sunsets that I find myself. In outdoor light, I find sweetness in the melancholy that has repeatedly filled my spirit since the days of my childhood."

"You lost your mother very early," James broke in. "Your brother, your father. The German poet Rainer Maria Rilke called you not only the 'Painter of light from Maloja' but also 'a great solitary.'"

Segantini pricked up his ears yet didn't elaborate on this, but rather continued with his account. "I realized that I needed the light of the mountains. I was attracted to the high altitudes, always farther upward. I sought brightness, light. Milan is a swamp . . ."

James, who had collected some information about Segantini in London, added, "Then you moved to Savognin in 1886."

Segantini laughed aloud and helped himself to some of the pastries that the waiter had put on their table. "Yes, my friend Dalbesio had gone on an excursion in the Grison mountains and was so enthusiastic that Bice and I decided to hike on some hair-raisingly dangerous paths across the Bergamasque Alps into the Valtellina," he said, laughing again as he remembered the exertion involved. "We rented a one-horse carriage and had it take us through the Bernina Pass into the Engadine, and then I continued on over the Julier Pass to the north, past Savognin to Tiefencastel. But suddenly I had the driver stop and return to Savognin. I knew instantly: this was the landscape I was seeking, which already had its counterpart within me . . ."

Bonin translated, and James took notes.

Segantini waited politely and ordered a bottle of the local wine and three glasses. Then he went on, "Although I was penniless and unknown in Savognin, the hotel owner, Signor Pianta, had faith in me and helped me with the required security deposit so that I would be permitted to settle in Switzerland. Perhaps you already know this, but due to certain unfortunate circumstances, I am stateless." After the wine arrived and was poured into glasses, he raised his with a nod to James, and took a drink. "In August

1886, I brought my family to our new home in a carriage loaded to the top with our belongings and thirty-five *centesimi* in my pockets."

He made no further mention about how much Pianta had done for him or the debts he had incurred by the time he left Savognin in 1894.

"I was captivated by the strength of the colors, the crystalline clarity of the mountains. I kept going higher and higher up, alone. I immersed myself in nature, the quiet, the stillness."

James interrupted Segantini. "The same basic motifs keep turning up in your pictures: maternal love and the common destiny of men and animals—death."

Segantini nodded. "That's what nature teaches you: the inescapable cycle of birth, life, death. We are part of it, like the plants, and the animals. Nature is not good and it is not evil; nature is. Religion doesn't mean much to me, but my love of nature is boundless. The ultimate aim of my efforts is to achieve an absolute and complete knowledge, an understanding of nature in all its shading and nuance, from sunrise to sunset, in its structure and in all the variety of its beings—people, animals, plants. I want to use all my power to create a work that will be ideal."

James felt uncomfortable whenever the word "absolute" or "ideal" was used, for he found that life in general and he himself were very fallible, and he mistrusted all absolute truths. It pleased him that Segantini was at least partaking freely of the wine.

"But nature is not ideal," James said. "You yourself say she simply exists."

Segantini loved discussions, and wine and ideas warmed him up. "Nature exists, but art shapes, creates. Matter must be worked on by the mind so that it can grow into eternal art. A picture is a thought, an idea that has been flooded with light. Art without an ideal would be like nature without life. After all, what is art if not a true image and a criterion for the perfection of the human soul?"

James poured some more wine into his glass, seeing that soon the bottle would be totally empty. "I have some doubts about the perfection of the human soul," he said, countering the artist's glowing statements, which Bonin had translated faithfully but without much emotion.

Segantini took off his jacket and ran his fingers through his black curls. "But we have to strive for it. Real life is nothing but a dream, a dream to eventually approach an ideal that is as distant and high as possible, so high as to extinguish matter. I pursue this ideal. I search for it up in the mountains, outdoors, where the paint freezes on the canvas in the icy cold . . . Human greatness begins where the mere mechanical work of our hands, the crude action stops, and where love and mental effort begin." He leaned back in his chair, adding, "If you would like to, you can come with me to some of the locations where I'm working just now. I usually work on several paintings at the same time. I leave them outside through all sorts of weather; but they're kept safe in wooden boxes."

James, who preferred the streets of a big city, wasn't sure whether this offer was attractive to him, but he thanked Segantini and said he would think about it. And because he preferred not to discuss the question of whether love began with the intellect, he changed the subject and asked, "What is beauty, Mr. Segantini?"

Bonin looked at James Danby in surprise, and then translated his question.

"Beauty," Segantini replied without hesitating, "Beauty! You need only look at a flower. It tells you better than any definition what beauty is. Art is love enfolded in beauty."

"But is the bellowing cow in the pasture that you painted beautiful?" Danby asked.

"Yes. Because I saw her with love, and because the picture is true. It shows the creature—and we are not very different from her—the way I saw her with my inner heart and the way I understood her with my mind."

James nodded after Bonin had translated Segantini's words. He had actually wanted to direct the conversation to *The Punishment of Lust*, the painting that had caught his eye in Liverpool because of its technique, and whose message he did not approve of at all. Because in addition to the Madonna-like women, there were those "evil mothers" who were hanging in trees, half-naked, their bodies ecstatically curved backward, one of whom had at her breast a nursing child with a face that seemed to be more like that of a man. The expressions of ecstatic pain in the faces of these women with the long reddish hair reminded James more of passion than the punishments of Hell. Was a picture of pure maternal love the only thing that could fill Segantini's soul with peace? Did these sensual figures, surrounded by ice, embody all those strange, menacing feelings he was trying to shut out of his life? Did the women who found grace in Segantini's eyes have to resemble the image of his mother as he wanted to see her?

James suddenly remembered his days in boarding school. He had been furious with his mother, had hated her, because she had sent him to England, abandoning him to loneliness. She wanted only the best for him. He knew that. And for that reason he ought not to be mad at her, ought to avoid letting her see his anger. But this only made him more furious. Perhaps Segantini had a similar experience.

James suddenly knew that he could save himself that question. Segantini had painted an answer, but he had not understood it as such. By painting loving mothers, he painted for himself an ideal of the thoughtful maternal figure that he had lacked as a child. And his paintings of the "evil mothers" reflected his rage against this deprivation. And even though his mother was not to blame for her own early death, he had to punish her, not in a realm where his mind held sway, but where hidden feelings ruled. He would never admit those hidden feelings, not to James nor to himself.

Segantini had escaped the darkness of his childhood by seeking light, and he had found his ideal—although he, like no other painter, gave masterful expression to the transitions between brightness and darkness. He was best at depicting not only that which he loved, but also what he feared: dusk, the twilight hour, which held the sweetness of melancholy but in which also lurked the darkness of being lost.

Segantini sought an ideal without shadows; he painted the idea, the thought. But he was most brilliant in giving form to the broken light that embraced the pain he had tried to get away from all his life long.

James returned to St. Moritz. He was impressed by Segantini, by the battle people fight against the ghosts of their own histories in an attempt to give meaning to the meaningless, to counteract indifference with beauty and love. Or what they thought they were.

Segantini was satisfied with the interview. The older he got, the more he liked to talk about his work and discuss theoretical and artistic questions. He was in a cheerful mood after the interview, and when he met Achille Robustelli, he returned the latter's greeting. "Thanks, Robustelli, for arranging this interview, and even finding an interpreter. I had a pleasant conversation with Mr. Danby."

"I'm glad," Robustelli said. "May I accompany you a few steps? I wanted to talk to you about another matter, just briefly."

"Of course. Go ahead."

"It's a rather delicate matter. I hope you won't take offence. Gaetano, the gardener, has complained to me that Nika is being distracted too much from her work." Achille took a deep breath. "You come by to see her frequently, and evidently you also took her with you, in the middle of her workday, to St. Moritz."

Segantini was about to fly off the handle, but Robustelli placed a hand on his arm to calm him.

"Wait a moment. I don't wish to criticize you. I just wanted to tell you that the girl is going to have difficulties because of this. Actually, I should let her go. She can't simply leave work, even if you," he cleared his throat, "even if you have asked her to. If it gets around, it will stir up bad blood. And the negative effects will hurt Nika, not you."

"Nobody can reproach me with anything," Segantini said angrily.

"But it must matter to you if I can't employ Nika anymore. She will hardly be able to stay in Maloja then. The Biancottis won't just keep on feeding her."

Segantini gestured emphatically with his hand and gave Robustelli a cool look.

"You seem extremely worried about the girl."

Achille said nothing. He found this only normal and wished that Segantini would also take the girl's welfare into consideration.

"I hear what you're saying, Robustelli."

With these words, Segantini turned, waved good-bye, and quickly walked away.

Achille watched him thoughtfully. For the first time since he had known him, he didn't like the man.

He went back to his office, closed the door, and sat down at his desk. He took the silver cigarette case out of the drawer. He didn't look at his reflection in the gleaming surface but absent-mindedly lit a cigarette. He really didn't know anything about Nika even though he saw her every day.

❧❧

Kate had cited her husband's urgent business affairs as the reason for their sudden departure. It was supposed to look as if Robert were about to complete an important transaction which she, as a loving wife, was also anxiously anticipating. So supportive was she that she was willing to break off her vacation prematurely and miss out on the festive opening ceremonies for the Palace Hotel in St. Moritz to be at her husband's side at this important moment.

With her head held high, she rushed down the stairs, bestowing a warm smile on Betsy when she ran into her at the reception desk.

"Betsy, how nice that I get to see you before I leave!" she said. "How lucky you are! Enjoy the opening celebration at the Palace. It's sure to be an unforgettable event." She took Betsy's hand. "I envy you!" She paused briefly so that her regret could be felt, then continued with a happy look on her face. "Just think, my dear Betsy, with your niece in the hospital and me already on the train, you'll be brilliant, the center of attention!"

Betsy, who never ceased to be amazed at Kate's lightning-fast insults, didn't say anything to answer this remark, merely wished

Mrs. Simpson a good trip. Kate nodded. "Yes, it'll be good for dear Robert that I go with him. There's nothing that beats a good marriage, but you know that, after all, you were married once too."

Betsy abruptly let go of Kate's hand, which was still holding on to hers. It was a blessing that this woman, for whatever reason, was vanishing from the stage. But something else had occurred to Kate.

"Oh, just one more thing, Betsy. I think I ought to tell you, otherwise I'll reproach myself later."

Betsy raised her eyebrows.

"Well, what is it you think I absolutely have to know?"

"Oh, it's about your niece. Our dear James—I think you like him too—has not exactly behaved comme il faut toward your young Mathilde, so he confessed to me. I assume Mathilde did not tell you about it, and it's certainly understandable that James won't tell you about it. But I thought you really should know that he more than compromised your niece. You did tell me she was engaged. But now I really must go. Good Lord, Robert has been waiting an eternity in the carriage for me . . ."

With that, she hurried off, before Betsy could say anything.

Nika was having dreams about post coaches. In one dream, the post coach was racing through Mulegns, the wildly galloping horses running away with it. The woman at the post coach stop was watching the lurching coach in horror. Nika, as a grown-up, was standing beside her and pointing at a woman's white arm waving out of the coach window.

In a different dream, she saw Segantini sitting in another coach. He stuck his head out of the window. All she could see were his dark curls, as she had on the day she saw him for the first time. As the coach moved along, he threw the drawings she had given him out of the window. Saddened, she gathered up the scattered sheets of paper.

Another time, it was she who got into a coach. "To Italy," she called out to the driver, but he only shook his head. "I don't have a license for Italy," he said. "You'll have to walk. No one will drive you there."

Nika was not only plagued at nighttime by bad dreams. In the daytime, too, she felt unhappy. She couldn't stop feeling furious with her mother, who had only managed to do things halfway. If only she had simply abandoned Nika without leaving any clues. Then she wouldn't have to worry now about whether her mother perhaps still loved her in some corner of her heart and was calling to her with the message in the locket.

In spite of that, Nika had searched for the locket she had angrily taken off a while back. It was a miracle that she found it again in the hay. Now that she no longer wore it, she hid it under her straw pallet.

Segantini was coming less frequently. Either he was using the days to paint or he had become more cautious. She had sworn to herself not to practice writing anymore and not to draw because it reminded her of Segantini. In spite of that, she did both. She wrote and sketched. Once, when she was daydreaming, she wrote, "I love Segantini."

Gian had made a complete recovery from his illness, and Benedetta gave thanks to the Virgin Mary, something she hadn't done in a long time. She wasn't happy about letting her oldest son leave home again, but Aldo insisted. Gian, he said, would become a laughingstock if he clung to his mother's apron strings, and Benedetta wouldn't like it either.

Still, she was afraid her dreamy son might get lost in solitude up in the mountains and plunge to his death simply because he didn't pay attention. Now, after his illness, he was even less alert and engaged than before. When no one was looking, she would stroke his tousled hair, and he would smile at her in his distracted, lost-in-a-daydream sort of way. He was such a good-looking boy, with his brown eyes and his gentle, boyishly mischievous face. But with a sigh, Benedetta had to admit to herself that he lacked all aggressiveness, something you needed in life.

He didn't object when his father sent him back up to Grevasalvas. Benedetta went with him, loaded down with all sorts of good things she had canned, cooked, cured, and smoked for him. Nika wanted to go with him, but Benedetta didn't want her to, perhaps because she had a maternal inkling that her son was secretly suffering because of this girl.

Gian loved the view of the mighty Piz Lagrev, whose sides were scarred by rockslides and avalanches. He loved the waterfall that roared between the huts and stables of Blaunca, and the smell of its mist and spray. And he loved the four little brown cows that had been entrusted to his care. Yet he felt lonely, a feeling that he had not ever had before. Now there was Nika, and because of her, he knew what loneliness was. When he was near her, he felt different than when he was alone. What he felt when he was next to her was different from anything he had ever felt. Suddenly there were several feelings within him that he could compare, and the contrast was marked enough to make him realize that there were the moments when he was lonely—and other moments when he

DÖRTHE BINKERT

wasn't. Gian had learned what love is. Yet that gift had made him sad. For Nika had told him she could not return his love.

"I don't want you to kiss my lips," she had told him gently and turned her face away from him as they were saying good-bye. "Lovers kiss each other on the lips. I like you very much. But that is something different."

"Why aren't we lovers?" Gian had asked in disappointment.

"Because I love another man," Nika said.

"So what Andrina's been saying is true."

Nika shook her head.

"No. It isn't. I love Segantini. But he doesn't love me."

Achille Robustelli had noticed that Segantini was coming to the hotel less frequently. He was relieved. Yet in spite of that, he wasn't particularly happy about it, because he could see that Nika had started to look like a weeping willow. One day he asked her to come to his office, even though he had no idea why he wanted to see her.

"Sit down," he said, and once she was seated, he went on, "Signor Segantini told me that you've started to speak. At any rate with him. I don't know whether you'd like to talk with me too. I would be happy about that. I have been wondering what you are going to do once the season here is over. I'm sure you know that we close for the winter."

Nika looked at him with her blue-green eyes like the sea. Was that a flash of gratitude? he wondered.

She said nothing, seemed to be debating whether she should say something or not. Then she smiled, and he felt as if an entirely different woman were sitting before him.

"You're very kind," she said. "I've also been wondering what will happen in the winter . . ." Suddenly she even laughed. "And I thought I would ask you for help."

Achille Robustelli, a bit confused by so much unexpected trust, touched his prematurely gray temples and leaned back in his chair.

"Really?" he mumbled.

Nika looked at him calmly.

Robustelli said nothing for a while. Then he said, "And what would you like to do?"

"I'd like to go to Italy, not this winter, but when I have saved enough money for the trip."

"To Italy?" Robustelli repeated.

"Yes," Nika nodded.

"And why to Italy of all places?" Achille asked.

"Because I think my mother lives there," she said. "I don't know my mother, but I will look for her. And eventually I will find her."

"*Bene*," Robustelli said. "Do you know where you should be looking for her?"

"No," Nika said.

"Aha."

"I'd like to stay here for the winter, look for a job, maybe in St. Moritz at one of the hotels that stays open for the winter. I could work in a laundry again."

"You would probably have to, in the winter," Achille Robustelli said, smiling.

Nika smiled too. "I thought you might be able to give me a reference."

Robustelli leaned forward and looked at her. She was no longer as thin as she had been when she first came. Benedetta had obviously taken good care of her. And whatever Segantini had done with her, it had been good for her too. It was as if an ugly duckling had turned into a swan—something within her had unfolded and was now visible. She is beautiful, he thought. He said, "All right, I'll think about it."

A Visit Is Announced

"And with whom are we attending the opening of the Palace Hotel?" James asked, sullenly.

Edward who, in contrast, was in a very good mood, looked up briefly from his newspaper. "Why, what do you mean? I thought we would go there together." He went back to reading.

"Kate and her husband left quite suddenly, did you know?"

"No," Edward replied. "How should I have known? Kate is, after all, your department."

James refused to be deterred.

"It's boring to go there just with you, my dear fellow. And Mathilde is in the hospital. It would have been a very special event for her."

"Oh, you're suddenly worrying about what might make her happy?" Edward let the paper fall to his lap.

"Don't act so sanctimonious," James said. "You don't know anything. She sent me away when I tried to visit her in the hospital."

"Well, and so?" Edward said. "You could have tried to find out why she did that."

"She's engaged. And Kate knew it. That surprises you, eh?"

Upon hearing this, Edward folded up the paper and got up from the flowered easy chair to open the window. He leaned far out. Then he turned back to James.

"And that's why she sent you away?"

"No."

"Well, whatever. I thought I'd ask Betsy whether she'd like to go with me to the opening," Edward said. "She's intelligent, entertaining, and attractive. And since she's been in mourning, she might now feel like participating again in a big social event."

"Good Heavens!" James, who'd stretched out on Edward's bed with his arms crossed under his head, jumped up suddenly. "I don't recognize you! You were already paying her compliments that evening at Segantini's. You don't have designs on her, do you?"

Edward said nothing.

"Eddie?" James said.

"It's my affair." Edward closed the window and leaned with his back against it so that he could face James directly. "If I remember correctly, Jamie, you made more advances to her that evening than I did."

"You remember that?"

"In any case, this time I'm ahead of you. Maybe you spent a bit too much time with Kate."

"Even at school you were a moralizing prig," James said, his tone deprecating. "Why didn't you become a preacher? Or a teacher?"

"Because I didn't want to have anything to do with pupils like you," James said.

On July 29, 1896, before the eyes of countless, elegantly dressed guests, the hotel owner, Caspar Badrutt, danced the opening dance with a genuine English princess. And with that, the fashionable Palace Hotel opened for business, another attraction for the mountain village of St. Moritz, which had succeeded in becoming a sought-after destination for the entire world.

The hotel was extraordinary. Famous Zurich architects had constructed it to resemble an English Tudor-style castle complete with a square corner tower, crenellations, and palatial great halls. Fires crackled in open fireplaces in the wood-paneled rooms, even though the hotel, of course, also had central heating. The elevators had been shipped by sea from New York, the furniture from Berlin. Beautiful, flickering light from innumerable brass candelabras and crystal chandeliers flooded the dining room, the great halls, the parlors, the smoking room, the library, and the billiard room. And, on this ceremonial opening evening, vintage champagne was poured into Bohemian crystal goblets as buffet tables groaned under hot and cold delicacies.

"Doesn't it seem to you that we're a bit like onlookers among all these maharajas, princesses, princes, and steel barons?" Betsy asked. She was wearing a very elegant amethyst-colored evening dress that she had ordered by mail from Zurich. Her necklace, although more modest than many of the diamonds on show, outdid most of those creations because it had been chosen with exquisite taste.

"Not a bit," James replied, not bothered at all. He had the least money of the three in their group, and was skillfully making his way through the crowd carrying his Rhine salmon and a glass of champagne. "Come," he said, "I just discovered Segantini and his wife. Let's say hello to them."

Betsy, who remembered her rash remarks at Segantini's house, didn't think this was such a good idea. On the whole, having been infected with mistrust by Kate, she was keeping her distance from James who, quite unsuspecting, was surprised at her coolness. He tried to push his way through the crush of people to Segantini. Betsy, on the other hand, took Edward's arm and pulled him in another direction.

But before James reached Segantini, he ran into Fabrizio Bonin, who introduced his new acquaintance to Count Primoli. They were soon deeply involved in conversation. Although they had started by talking about Segantini, the subject quickly turned to a discussion of the new art of photography. Both of them knew something about it, although Primoli was much the better informed.

"Tilda," Betsy said, "there's nothing further we can do. Your mother is coming, and she isn't bringing your Aunt Frieda but rather your fiancé, Adrian. I couldn't stop her. After all, she is your mother." Her tone of voice always became harsher than usual whenever she felt helpless.

Mathilde made a face.

"Really, Tilda! Your mother is worried about you and about your engagement. That's easy to understand. So just prepare yourself. They're arriving tomorrow."

From the start, Betsy had thwarted every evasive maneuver on the part of her niece, and she was exhausted from the effort. She reached for Mathilde's wine glass. They had been having lunch together, and a glass of the local wine was part of Mathilde's diet, for they said it had special healing powers. "It's not too strong, not very acidic, and even tolerated in cases of gastroenteritis," Dr. Bernhard had said. "Red wine stimulates the heart and promotes the coughing up of sputum, and for that reason, my dear Miss Schobinger, you not only may but you should have a couple of little glasses every day."

Now Betsy hoped for a supportive effect from the highly praised wine and that it would stave off any despair on Mathilde's part. For the time had come for Betsy to confess to her niece that she had withheld the telegram Adrian had sent her. It had arrived right after Mathilde had been diagnosed, and Betsy had wanted to protect Mathilde, since she was still shocked by her diagnosis and also still in a state of agitation about James.

"But Edward is coming to see me tomorrow!" Mathilde said, her voice almost despairing.

Betsy looked at her nonplussed. "And? If James were coming, I could understand your excitement, but Edward . . . Oh well, so you'll have two visitors tomorrow. I can send a message to Edward asking that he come to see you in the morning. Your mother and Adrian won't arrive till evening. By the way, how are things with James?"

Mathilde made an indefinable sound, something between anger, disappointment, and sadness. "I won't be seeing him anymore."

"Oh. Maybe that will make it easier for me to tell you," Betsy said. "There was a telegram from Adrian that I kept from you. It arrived shortly after you were admitted to the clinic."

"What?" Mathilde cried indignantly. "You simply didn't give it to me? I'm not a little girl anymore!"

"No, but you were all mixed up because of the diagnosis and also because of James. Remember, you told me you loved him?"

Mathilde smoothed the tablecloth to the right and to the left of her plate and fanned her face with her napkin for air.

"But since Adrian is coming tomorrow, you should know what he wrote you, and how he feels about you." Betsy paused and sat down, "Even though you may not yet know how you feel about him."

Betsy's gentian-blue eyes looked questioningly into Mathilde's forget-me-not-blue ones. If she was to believe what Kate had told her, then Mathilde had kept something much more important from her aunt than the aunt had kept from her niece.

Mathilde lowered her eyes and reached for the telegram without further explanations.

DEAR MATHILDE, YOUR ILLNESS SHOULD NOT AND WILL
NOT BE A REASON FOR DISSOLVING OUR RELATIONSHIP
STOP EVEN IF MY PARENTS THINK SO STOP I LOVE YOU
AND AM AT YOUR SIDE STOP ADRIAN.

Mathilde bit her lip. Thanks to all the fresh air, and the plentiful food and wine, her cheeks were usually a rosy pink, but now angry red spots spread over her neck and face.

"That's why I didn't give you the telegram right away."

Mathilde only nodded.

When Betsy could no longer bear the silence, she said cautiously, "His parents own a bank. He is their only son and heir. They want to be certain . . ."

" . . . that I won't die," Mathilde said. "I might of course die."

She was silent again.

"But look, Tilda, Adrian will stand by you. And that's what he wanted to tell you in the telegram. It wasn't very clever of him to let you know right off what his parents were thinking, but he wanted, above all, to tell you that he loves you and will stand by you. That you are more important to him than his parents and the bank." Betsy took a deep breath. It would be good, she thought, if Mathilde turned to Adrian again after all that had, presumably, happened. At least that would be the easiest way out. "You can count on him," she therefore said encouragingly. "And that is really something wonderful. Look at him with fresh eyes after this business with James. Take the time to think it through. Maybe you'll see then that he is the right man for you."

Mathilde looked at her aunt thoughtfully.

"I think I have to lie down," she said. "I'm not feeling well."

Betsy took her upstairs to her room.

"Aunt Betsy?"

Betsy, already at the door, turned around to look at her niece.

"I'd like to see James," Mathilde said.

❧❧

Edward and James had each received a letter from Betsy. Holding the envelopes in wonderment, they waited for the messenger who had brought them their missives to leave.

"And what did she write you?" Edward was the first to ask. He had been disappointed to find she was merely asking him to visit Mathilde in the morning tomorrow because she was expecting company from Zurich in the evening.

James looked up from the note he had received. "I don't quite understand what Betsy is saying here," he said and frowned. "On the one hand, she says Mathilde would like to see me, but then Betsy has also asked me to meet with her separately. Odd. It all seems quite rushed, and I really don't know whether she wants me to visit her first or first go to the hospital." He looked puzzled.

"In any event, she's expecting company from Zurich tomorrow," Edward said.

"Who? Betsy or Mathilde?"

"Mathilde, of course."

"Why *of course*?"

"Because, Jamie, this is all about Mathilde. After all she's the one who is ill and needs to be visited," Edward said, slowly losing patience.

"And does it say in your note who is coming to visit?" James asked with a note of irritability in his voice, for he realized that it could all get very complicated.

"No, it says nothing about that here. Her parents, I assume."

"It might also be her fiancé. What do you think?"

Edward paced back and forth. It was what he did whenever he felt something he didn't want to express. "Yes. Naturally. She's engaged, you said." He kept pacing back and forth.

"I think I'll go see Betsy first," James said.

"I think I'll go see Mathilde first," Edward said at the same instant.

❧

"Edward understands Mathilde much better than I do," James was saying as he and Betsy were drinking tea in the lobby of the Spa Hotel Maloja. There was waltz music in the background.

"The trio that usually entertains here in the afternoons plays abominably," Betsy remarked. "Don't be so sad," she said to him. "It doesn't become you."

"Besides, Betsy, Edward talks about her so enthusiastically that I'm gradually beginning to wonder . . ."

"I feel comfortable with him," Betsy said curtly.

"You realize, don't you, Betsy, that my friend Eddie and I are competitors for your attentions?" James gave her an appealingly boyish smile.

"But I asked you to meet me because of Mathilde," Betsy said. "I'd like to save her any more confusion and unnecessary pain. I don't know what happened between you and her; I know only that it has bothered and tormented her. And guessing from what Kate Simpson told me, whatever happened is not a trifling matter, but something compromising for my niece. I have to assume that you exploited Mathilde's naïveté in a not very nice way. I wanted to see you for two reasons. First, I want to ask you how seriously I should take whatever happened between you and Mathilde, and second, Mathilde wants to see you, and she wants to see you now, right now, before her fiancé arrives. He has assured her of his love, and that he will stand by her even against the objections of his parents, and he knows nothing about your affair. Perhaps that will explain why it was so urgent that I see you. I can't keep Tilda from seeing you, or from loving you. But I appeal to your decency, if you have any. I expect you to support Tilda, and to encourage her to return to her fiancé. I also expect you to tell her that you don't want anything from her, and that she cannot expect anything from you, in spite of all that has happened."

The orchestra had meanwhile broken into a fiery gypsy tune.

How about that, thought James, a good-bye present from Kate. What she can't have no one else should have either. The consequences of his insignificant affair with her were really getting to him. "I can calm her down, Betsy. To be quite frank, I did not deflower your niece. Though I'm not sure that Mathilde would have protested greatly had it come to that. Nevertheless, I can assure you that it never went that far. As for my talking to her, I can't let you dictate exactly what I will say."

"So you don't want to give up Mathilde? You know how much the girl is in love with you and that you won't be able to make her happy," Betsy said. She was very upset.

"Oh, you're sure of that? Mathilde is a young woman who can stand on her own two feet. What she and I have to say to each other we can say without the help of outsiders." James's answer sounded unexpectedly sharp.

And all of this, thought Elizabeth Huber née Wohlwend, because I went hiking in the mountains one day, and left Mathilde alone. She was tired of this substitute motherhood. Thank God she didn't have any children of her own. Now she didn't even like James anymore. James, whom she had even thought of approaching in the fantasies she'd had about her new freedom. Oh well. Common sense had ruled against him from the beginning. Maybe it was time to go back to Zurich at last and devote herself to charity and fighting for widows' and orphans' pensions. But at the moment, that didn't seem too tempting either.

Besides. Betsy sighed. What should she do with her vaunted independence? What, after all, was a woman without a man? The question was harder to answer than she expected. She could expand her intellectual horizons or get absorbed in some specialized field, but those ideas crossed her mind without arousing much enthusiasm. After all, she was already well educated. Well, it was all wide open; there were lots of possibilities.

While Betsy was pondering this, James Danby was looking toward the other end of the lobby. The last sighs of the violin had just faded into a pianissimo. He let her have the last word.

"Too bad," she said, "that we're separating on this note."

The evening with Andrina had been a complete success, even though Achille Robustelli had not bought her a dress for the occasion of the dance. Not because he was stingy, but he thought it would give her the wrong idea. He didn't want to buy Andrina, but to win her—and perhaps, in the not-too-distant future, to ask her to marry him. Andrina herself had hinted that she would be interested in a serious relationship, and she was not only vivacious and pretty, she was also hardworking and strong willed. Achille liked that. It was possible that she would turn out to be a bit too ambitious, but he was not intimidated by a woman who knew what she wanted. On the contrary, his mother had always been a strong woman, even if, while her husband was still alive, she acted as if she were subservient. Achille could simply not imagine that he would be happy with a woman who worshiped him and had no mind of her own. Like Bice, for instance, who enormously admired Segantini and always put her own interests last.

Segantini was pretty overbearing, Achille thought now. That had never occurred to him before, even though some of the people who had been guests at the Segantini home had spoken of it. It was interesting . . . After his short talk with Segantini about Nika, he saw the painter as—well—as somewhat arrogant.

But Achille's thoughts soon returned to Andrina. She was really a talented dancer, a big plus for a woman, he decided with satisfaction. She was musical, had spirit and endurance. And flushed from the exertion of dancing, she had seemed even more sensuous than usual.

Lost in pleasant fantasies about the future, Achille was pulled back to reality by the sound of knocking on his office door. He called out a hearty "Come in" and was surprised to see Fabrizio Bonin, and not Andrina, step into his office. The young man closed the door behind him.

"Good morning," Robustelli said, rising from his chair and walking toward him. "Please take a seat. I hope the interview with Segantini was interesting for you too? In any case, I'd like to thank you again for helping out as interpreter."

Bonin nodded. Yes, he had found the interview most stimulating and from the start had gotten along well with James Danby.

"I have you to thank for letting me make a very pleasant acquaintance, Signor Robustelli," he said. "Mr. Danby and I accidentally met again at the opening of the Palace Hotel. We talked a long time with Count Primoli about photography. James Danby, like me, is a journalist, and we share many points of interest. I have you to thank for a new friend."

Robustelli was pleased. He liked helping people get to know one another. One nice thing about his job at the hotel was that he had the chance to meet so many different individuals. Arranging introductions between them was something he enjoyed.

"I would like to ask you for a favor, Signor Robustelli," Bonin said, with an embarrassed smile. "May I inquire about the young woman who helps the gardener? I've seen her a few times at work. She is rather shy and avoids the hotel guests, but she seems to be quite an unusual person. I have never dared to speak to her, although I've seen her now and then talking with Segantini. She has probably known him for a while."

Achille Robustelli rummaged about in his drawer and finally came up with his silver cigarette case. He offered Bonin a cigarette. A difficult story, with the girl, he thought. Actually, he ought to consider it a good thing for her to finally emerge from her cocoon and come into contact with others besides Segantini. In spite of that, he wasn't particularly pleased by the fact she had drawn Bonin's eye. Would the attention of a hotel guest be helpful for Nika? Robustelli decided, almost grimly, that it would not be. Even if a connection was made, there was no future in it for her.

Strangely, he was suddenly no longer in a good mood, and quite out of character, he answered the man, unwillingly, almost coldly. "I hired the young woman, but we don't know much about her. She isn't from Maloja. Two young fellows from the village found her, injured, up in the mountains and brought her here. She was probably headed elsewhere, but since she obviously had no money and no home, she stayed here. That's all I can tell you."

Robustelli closed his cigarette case emphatically.

Bonin nodded. He was surprised at the harsh tone of the reply. Robustelli was normally such a pleasant man. "Thanks, anyway," he said. "You were able to give me quite a bit of information. And please forgive my curiosity."

Achille Robustelli went back to work. Andrina had promised to come by at the end of the day. He hoped to ask her more about Nika, who was, after all, living with Andrina's parents. And now the young Bonin was interested in her too. Things were getting more and more interesting. Why couldn't Nika make a connection with a normal man, a cook, a coach driver, a waiter—someone who could give her a quiet and safe future?

La Vanità

"I found the place," Segantini said. He sounded elated.

"Which place?" Nika asked.

"The source, the spring. The place. The setting for the picture you've inspired. Come, I'll show you."

"Please come back for me at noon. I'm working now."

He frowned. "At midday I'm at home."

"So don't come," she said.

He had searched for a long time to find a spot that matched what he saw in his mind's eye. Since he had seen Nika looking at her reflection in the waters of the lake in Sils, he had been pursued by this idea of painting a similar image. Now he'd found the backdrop he wanted.

Nika walked silently along beside Segantini as he took the path up to the Belvedere. They were working again on the hill above the pass, where the Count de Renesse had intended to build a medieval-style castle for himself. The tower was now going to be completed, and the annex was to be turned into a hotel.

The path snaked between mountain pines and alpine roses. Nika walked in the shade; Segantini on the sunny side of the path. Then he veered off the path, which wound up to the left of the tower, and walked straight ahead, farther into the woods. Nika followed him over knotted roots, moss, and dead branches. Boulders blocked their way; the scent of pine resin filled the air. In the distance, she could hear the roaring of a waterfall, the sound loud and bright. The alpine roses were almost finished blooming; yet among the dark-green bushes creeping over the ground, a few splendid red blooms still gleamed here and there.

"Where are you going?" Nika asked. "The woods are getting more and more dense and wild."

"Soon," Segantini called back to her, without slowing down, "we'll be there soon."

They weren't far from the Belvedere, and yet it was as if they were diving into a world that no living being had ever set foot in before. Not a single bird could be heard; the humid midday air felt heavy. Segantini stopped abruptly.

"We're here."

He felt hot too. He took off his jacket and vest, and stood facing her in his white shirt, running his fingers through his damp curls. Yet his dark eyes seemed to barely notice her. He was enthusiastic about this unusual place, which had been created, eons ago, by the glaciers of the Bernina mountains, around the time the ice age was coming to an end. The melting masses of ice had worked their way westward, creating the Engadine, pushing scree and rocks before them. The gravel and stones sank into cracks, and with a grinding power, aided by melting snow and ice, they created deep, round pits filled with the water—like this one.

"*Le marmitte dei giganti*, a giant's kettle," he said. "Look at what the glaciers created. Just look at that."

Nika stepped closer; he took her hand, and she bent over the deep pool.

"Come," he said, pulling her onward. "There are more of these; I've picked another one for the picture." He was familiar with every feature of the landscape here, every stone.

He was still holding her hand. His shirt gleamed white, and beneath it, she sensed his body was strong, powerful.

Nika closed her eyes. Why? Why did she love him?

Segantini, joyful at finally having found the spot for his picture, drew her to him. But as soon as he felt her body against his, he let her go again. He showed her the pool that he had chosen.

Nika shuddered as she looked into the cloudy water, which seemed to go deep down into the center of the earth. The pool was surrounded by bushes and overhung with bunches of grass that reminded her of hair. Where the grass extended across the water's surface, it was softened and rotting. At the water's swampy edge, an alpine rose spread a last touch of pink. Trees formed a dark circle around the place. To the left of the pool was a granite boulder, worn by time and weather, with green and brown vines growing on its surface. Moss and ferny weeds forced their way out of all the cracks in the rock.

She leaned over the water. Mosquitoes and water striders flitted soundlessly over the dark surface. The farther forward she leaned, the more like a mirror the water became. And mirrored in the black background was the bright sky, the tree trunks and their leafy crowns—a faithful reflection of the light in the dark. Nika reached out an arm. She saw herself, her hair gleaming in the dark water; her arm and hand reached out, and the deep, calm, and clear surface mimicked her movement, without any distortion.

Nika stood motionless. She grasped Segantini's hand. A small white cloud swam into the picture and sailed out again.

A light breath of wind rippled across the surface of the water. It appeared again on the boulder as a trembling play of shadow and light. In silence, Segantini pointed. Fresh light-green grass was forcing its way up next to dead branches and the corpse of a bird covered with thousands of teeming ants.

"Look over there," Segantini finally said, "at the boulder. There, on the right, it ends in a flat stone step. That's the spot where you'll stand and be reflected for my painting."

She let go of his hand, climbed up over the boulder, and came to the flat step. She was now standing directly across from him. She put her head back, looking up at the sky, into the bright light. She squinted, and looked again at Segantini. Then she slipped out of her long black skirt, took off her blouse, and stood naked on the other side of the water. She raised her hands to loosen the knot of hair at the back of her neck. Bending down, she grabbed the long reddish-blonde hair and held it out of her face so she could see herself, her reflection, better.

There she stood, on a three-hundred-million-year-old rock, looking into the depths of a glacial pool, an opening in the body of the earth.

"Look!" she called over to Segantini. "Just look at all the things crawling around in this marshy hollow!" She shook herself, laughed. "Can you see that creepy thing there? The little monster swimming around—I can't tell if it's a grasshopper with the tail of a fish or a little fish with a grasshopper's head!"

Segantini stood there as if rooted to the spot and looked in disgust at the strange insect. Then he pulled on his vest as if he was suddenly cold, and said hoarsely, "We have to go back."

"But it's beautiful here!" Nika called over to him from the other side.

Segantini said nothing. He was already fleeing.

Male Visitors

"Your friend did a good job of representing you," Mathilde said, when James stepped out onto the balcony and greeted her. She put aside the book she was reading.

"He represented me so well that you even consented to receive me again." James smiled. "I am glad that you asked me to come. But after you sent me away the first time, I didn't want to go against your wishes," he said.

"I wish you had come anyway," she said. "Then I would have known that you really cared for me. When you didn't come anymore, I was left wondering what to think—either you didn't care for me, or you were respecting my wishes." She opened her hand in which she was holding the blue butterfly and breathed on it, as if she were trying to bring it to life.

"But it's not enough for me to be wondering about all sorts of possibilities," she continued. "It gives me no peace of mind. So, please tell me—that's why I asked you to come here—how you feel about me."

She was sitting upright in her chair, a charming figure. She had become more mature and self-assured. James suddenly liked her very much. And she was giving him another chance. He thought of Segantini, who had chosen an entirely different path to escape the feeling of loneliness than the one he was following. He, James, had not created an ideal for himself that he was approaching full of hope and high expectations. He ran away from loneliness by not staying anywhere long enough for it to catch up with him. He hesitated about answering. How did he feel about Mathilde?

"I like you more than you think. And more than Edward or your aunt can imagine. Yes indeed, I flirted with you the way people flirt. I like to flirt. I'm easygoing, I prefer to avoid serious feelings. It was Kate who called my attention to you, she spurred me on. To be frank, without Kate, I probably never would have noticed you. But the more we saw each other, the more I liked you."

He had hesitantly taken her hand, but then she had a coughing fit that shook her so hard that it scared him, and he let go of her hand.

"A glass of water!" she gasped, struggling to breathe. Helplessly, James held out the glass to her, waiting for the coughing to subside.

"I don't like hospitals," he murmured. "They make me feel helpless, incompetent." He got up and walked over to the window. "You're engaged. And you're asking me whether I love you. That is to say, you're actually asking yourself whether it's possible that I am the right man for you. Better than your fiancé. And I cannot answer that question for you." He had avoided answering her question and was ashamed of his cowardice. But he couldn't help himself.

"When you went with me to the Pension Veraguth, I wasn't thinking at all about whether I was right for you or not. I wanted you, and for that reason, I urged you to let me photograph you.

It wasn't the first time I saw a nude female body and not the first time I took a nude photo. I didn't think it was anything so terribly shocking."

Mathilde looked at him.

"But I'm not a model," she said calmly. "I went there with you . . ." she couldn't finish the sentence.

"I should have kept in mind that you're not a model and still very young and that you come from a good family. And I should have resisted Kate's whispered suggestions. In short . . ."

"It doesn't change matters," Mathilde said. "You didn't force me to go with you. And you didn't force me to let you photograph me. Now everything has changed anyway. I'm sick. And I'll probably be sick quite a while longer, although Dr. Bernhard thinks that I'll recover. But who really knows at this point? Usually people die of the disease I have."

James had to admire her. He also felt more ashamed of himself by the minute. She was so much younger than he, and yet so much more mature. The illness had changed her. And he, who avoided sick people whenever possible, felt that he desired her more now than before and that he was less than ever the right man for her.

"I'm only a young fellow," he said, "always searching . . . or running away. Fleeing or flirting. It's all the same. Will you be seeing your fiancé tomorrow?"

"Yes," Mathilde said.

"Mathilde, you're crying!"

Edward didn't have the nerve to sit down, and Mathilde forgot to ask him to.

"Please sit down," said the old nurse who had ushered him in. "I know that she always looks forward to your visit."

He sat down on a chair next to Mathilde's bed but said nothing.

His presence seemed to make her cry even harder. The tears seemed to flow endlessly. Edward wondered where so many tears could come from so quickly. It was probably best to wait until the crying spell subsided. But as her sobbing got more and more violent, sounding as if it could be tearing her throat, he pulled his chair very close to the bed and took her hand.

She held on to his hand, but turned her face to the wall. Gradually the crying stopped and the room became very quiet. And it remained that way until the nurse came into the room and said, "Miss Schobinger. Mathilde, I'm sorry to interrupt, but the doctor will soon be here to see you."

Betsy picked up her sister Emma Schobinger and her niece's fiancé from the post coach stop and took them to the Hotel Victoria, where she'd reserved rooms for them. Emma was still wearing black.

Emma's plan was to freshen up and then hurry off at once to see her daughter. Adrian was supposed to follow a little later.

In the meantime, Betsy didn't mind going for a walk with Adrian in the park of the Kurhaus. That way she could form an impression of the young man, whose star seemed to be on the wane. At first glance, Betsy didn't find much of anything to object to. He actually seemed well suited to Mathilde. It would be best for everyone if his star ascended again and James speedily vanished from Mathilde's life. Betsy imagined that Mathilde might find Adrian to be a loyal, caring husband. Even better, her family would be satisfied, and no one would ever have to know anything about the affair with James. As to what would happen with herself and Edward, that was yet to be seen. The only uncertain factor was James, because men—in Betsy's opinion—had no talent for dealing with women who'd been led astray.

୧୨

Adrian had prepared himself to find a sick, emaciated girl, and was surprised when Mathilde's appearance didn't correspond to his expectations at all. She had gained weight and looked in the pink. Indeed, she was as tan as a peasant girl who's never used a parasol. But it wasn't just her appearance that defied his expectations, for Mathilde accepted his affectionate embrace like a dried codfish. Not that she was unfriendly, but she seemed to have become distant, a stranger, and his embrace seemed to have no effect on her at all, absolutely none.

"Tilda," he said, "you look well, much better than I thought you would. What does the doctor say? He must be very pleased with you. What does he think, how much longer do you have to stay up here? I'm sure I'll be able to take you back to Zurich soon."

He embraced her again, and because he was disconcerted by her reserve, he tried to fill the rift between them with words. "Please don't worry. I already spoke with your mother. We're not going to rush forward with the wedding preparations. First you have to get completely well again. But after you come back, it might be a distraction and fun for you to choose the last few things for your trousseau at your leisure. And we'll take all the time we want to find an apartment . . ."

But what was wrong? She wasn't even really listening.

"Would you like something to drink?" Mathilde asked, and pulled out of his embrace to pour him a cup of tea. But she stopped in the middle. "Or would you prefer water?"

"Thanks, thanks," he mumbled. "It doesn't matter, I really don't care . . ."

He sat down and looked out into the distance. From the balcony, you could see a corner of Lake St. Moritz. Its glittering surface was just turning darker because the sun was beginning to set.

"I like to look out at the lake," Mathilde said. "It's so full of life. Can you see, over there, the little steamboat? Just think, they glide all over the lake. The tourists love going for boat rides!"

She noticed that Adrian was looking at her uncertainly, not knowing what he should say in answer.

"You know, I live here now," she said, by way of apology. "After so much time here, you forget the city and the people who live there, the life you once thought was so important. Here the sun rises, shines down on us, warms the air, descends, casts shadows, sets. I eat six times a day, lie down to rest, take walks, sleep. Fall will soon be here, then winter. Dr. Bernhard thinks that winter will be especially good for me."

"But Tilda!" Adrian cried. "Who's talking about winter? That's still far off, and by then you'll already be back with your parents and with me."

Mathilde shook her head.

Adrian didn't want to believe that she could be so resigned to her fate, so unperturbed. "You're alone up here, my dearest," he said, "terribly alone! It will cause you to turn sad, melancholic. And the boredom. You must be terribly bored. There's nothing stimulating to do, no theater, no concerts, no teas, not even a fair. Nobody except your Aunt Betsy. She's kept us from coming to see you for much too long. I should never have allowed it! She kept saying that you needed time to recover from the diagnosis. But instead you've been isolated and lonely, terribly lonely."

Mathilde shook her head.

"No," she said, "I'm not lonely. Not at all. Every day I have visitors. I'm not bored either. It's just different here. Everything is different now."

Adrian was worried. Mathilde was sick, but in a way different from what he had expected.

"It's nice that your aunt takes such good care of you . . ."

"Oh no," Mathilde contradicted him. "It's not just Betsy who comes to see me. We've met two young Englishmen, and we've done some outings with them. Betsy goes out with them often; they go for mountain hikes and have even gone to see the famous painter Segantini. One of the young men comes to see me. I can set my clock by his visits."

Adrian frowned.

"What did you say?" he said. "You can set your clock by him? He comes that regularly to see you? That's rather compromising for an engaged girl, Tilda."

"The doctors and nurses don't see it that way," she said vehemently. "It's good for me, and stimulating; I can feel that myself. And red wine tastes better with company. Drinking alone makes me sad sometimes and . . ."

"What kind of red wine?" Adrian interrupted, horrified. "You drink wine here with this person, here in your room?"

"No." Mathilde laughed. "No, there's a lovely room downstairs in the clinic. After all, I don't lie in bed all the time. I even take fairly long walks, even up the mountain. And once I'm not such a slowpoke anymore, I can even ask Edward to go with me . . ."

"Edward?" Adrian asked. "Edward?"

"Yes," Mathilde nodded. "He knows where the tiger lilies grow." She was silent for a moment, then she added, "Oh my, by the time I can go that far, they'll have finished blooming." She stopped, seemingly absorbed in thought.

Adrian was shaken. What had happened to Mathilde? He didn't recognize her. "Tilda," he said, "maybe you should take a little rest. I'll come back very soon. We're staying a few days, your mother and I, and we'll have lots of time to get used to each other again."

"But not tomorrow around ten. That's when Edward is coming. Come in the afternoon, all right? In the morning you can explore St. Moritz with Mama."

୧୨

"I'm leaving," James said.

"But Jamie, why now when it's so beautiful here?"

"I don't see that it's all that beautiful here," James said, looking at his friend as if he were suffering from hallucinations.

But Edward continued, "I like it better here every day. The air is so very good for me. And I'm no longer brooding about Emily and the past. I haven't felt this lighthearted in a long time, so alive and so much a part of things. Didn't you want to go with Segantini to see his paintings and take photographs? Your readers, after all, want to see Segantini—the way he looks, the way he lives, and the way he paints!"

"All right. All right," James interrupted. "But I think it's really Mathilde who's making you feel so good. Please, you don't have to say any more about it."

The two were sitting in the *Stüva* of the Pension Veraguth and had already drunk generously of their bottle of wine.

"But why are you suddenly so negative?" Edward asked.

"I'm not. It's just that I miss the city. Besides, at the moment, everything here is too emotionally charged. That's not good for me. You understand?"

"No," Edward said, looking at him blankly.

The First Snow

The days were getting shorter, the evenings cooler. On August 28, 1896, it snowed in Maloja, and a strong wind was blowing. In the evening, Baba lit the stove, and Segantini declared that they would soon move back to their winter quarters in Soglio in the Bregaglia Valley, where the climate was milder and he could paint out of doors longer than up here in Maloja. Mounting debts that were less and less easy to ignore also contributed to the decision.

Nika was freezing in the barn. The room in which Luca and Gian had slept was available for the time being, but Benedetta was hoping that Luca would come home. And if winter were to come early, then Gian would soon be coming down from the mountains with the cows. And so there wouldn't be any room for Nika in the house. When it got really cold, she'd have to move on.

With stiff fingers, Nika took the locket out from under her straw pallet. She opened it and unfolded the piece of paper, staring at the writing, the meaning of which she still could not decipher even though she could now read fluently. She could effortlessly read the words of the hymns in the hymnbook on Sundays in church. She breathed on the golden locket and polished it with her skirt till it shone. Where would the locket lead her?

But right now, there were other things to think about. It was cold, and she had to find a warmer place to spend the nights. She intended to go to see Signor Robustelli again and ask him to help her out now. If it didn't work out with a winter job soon enough, he might think of another possibility of where he could put her up.

Standing outside Signor Robustelli's office, she wondered why she hadn't asked Segantini for help. He knew a lot of people. But the thought hadn't occurred to her before this moment. And now she was standing in front of a different door.

Achille Robustelli wasn't in the best of moods. He had received a letter from his mother telling him she was coming to Maloja for a visit. She finally wanted to see the place where her son had been working all these years. Carefully he folded the letter up again into the same creases his mother had made in the paper. He wasn't pleased to hear a knock on his door.

"Enter," he said in a voice that didn't sound very inviting. Nika was the last person he expected to see standing in his doorway.

"Well, what now?" he asked brusquely.

Nika was perplexed because he was usually so pleasant. Awkwardly she said, "It's snowing."

"I saw that," Robustelli said, not at all graciously.

"Signor Robustelli, please excuse me, but I have a request. I'm staying with the Biancottis in their barn. It's getting too cold there. They have no room in the house, otherwise they would let me sleep there. I need some place to stay until I can find work for the winter."

Robustelli looked at her in surprise. "Come sit down, Nika," he said. After all, she couldn't help it that he was upset.

"All right, tell me slowly. It's too cold in the barn. There's no room in the house at the Biancottis. But the season isn't over yet." He thought it over. "That means," he said, turning his ring, as if it would help him solve this problem, "you'll have to stay in the hotel for the next few weeks. I'll have to work that out first, but I'll let you know when I've found a place for you."

He was a little surprised that she'd come to him. Obviously, she trusted him. He wondered why she didn't ask Segantini for help with such everyday yet essential things. "Why don't you want to go back to Mulegns? You told me that you want to look for your mother. That's all very well, but you don't even know where to start the search. Is there no one in Mulegns who could help you? The minister? Maybe even the farm family with whom you grew up?"

Nika looked at him, taken aback. Amazed at his ideas. "I can't go back. I secretly took a locket out of their chest—it was mine. It was left with me when I was abandoned as a baby. But if they'd discovered it was gone . . . well, I ran away when the farmer's wife was about to discover it missing. I don't ever want to go back there."

"But the locket is yours. You weren't stealing it. You don't have to be afraid of anything."

She was silent. He didn't know anything. Segantini had known without asking.

"So," Robustelli asked again, "there's no one who was good to you there?"

"Yes, there was." Nika nodded and smiled at the memory. "The woman at the post coach inn. She was always kind. She even taught me to read. Sometimes I ran away from the farm to visit her and she never betrayed me."

"And would she help you?"

"I don't want to go back," Nika said, emphatically.

※※

"Listen, Andrina," Robustelli said. "Nika can't go on sleeping in the barn. It's getting too cold. There's no room for her in your parents' house, and I'm going to have to put her up somewhere in the hotel for the rest of the season. I thought that since you know each other, you might be willing to share your room with her, and I'll put the girl with whom you're sharing now somewhere else. If I can't find another solution, all three of you might have to sleep together in the same room for a short time."

"Definitely not," Andrina protested. "I get along very well with Clara. I don't want you to put her somewhere else. And there's not enough space for three people. Not in our room. Impossible. I really don't see why the *straniera* has to sleep in the hotel, and on top of that, in the attic." Andrina still considered it a privilege to live so high up.

Achille Robustelli had suspected that he'd encounter additional difficulties. He longed for his weekly bridge game, but it was still several hours away.

"*Tesoro*, please be reasonable. Where else can she sleep?"

"Maybe in Signor Segantini's bed?" Andrina's tone was quite snippy.

"That's enough!" said Achille, his gentleness exhausted. "What nonsense. So you don't want to have her in your room. Too bad. She hasn't hurt anybody. Just because she's a stranger doesn't mean you have to treat her badly. If you want to stay in the hotel business, then remember this: Each guest is a stranger, a foreigner. And the hotel has to extend a warm welcome and offer him a temporary home away from home."

Andrina looked hurt. But it was smarter not to say anymore and leave the solution of the problem in Achille's hands.

"Then I'll leave now," she said.

"Yes, do," he said, still upset.

"Don't you want a kiss?" She couldn't quite read his mood.

"All right then, come here," he smiled a conciliatory smile. "Of course I want a kiss. But don't think that I'll forget what you said."

☙❧

He couldn't have explained why he did it. When he spoke to the director of the hotel about taking two days off, he used the vague excuse of needing to arrange a personal matter. He knew the director wouldn't argue. Achille was conscientiousness personified, and in all the years he had worked at the Spa Hotel Maloja, he had never taken a day of sick leave.

"Take all the time you need," the director said and shook his hand. "The hotel won't collapse if you're not here for two days."

Achille did not confide his plan to Andrina. He didn't even try to justify it to himself. He was a man who liked to get a situation clear in his mind, and that was that. In the army, he'd often said that the successful solution to a problem depended on having a thorough knowledge of how the problem got started. Wanting to learn more about where Nika had come from was the issue. He would be better able to help her if he could find out more about her past. But he was afraid of admitting to himself that something in his own life was off kilter; nor could he admit that this lack of inner balance had something to do with Nika.

He took the post coach in Silvaplana, crossing over the Julier. In Mulegns he took a room at the Lowen Inn; the woman proprietor herself served him supper. Once the inn began to empty out, he asked her to sit down with him at his table.

"You may be surprised when I tell you why I've come here," he said, finally getting down to the personal part of the conversation. "I came here because of Nika, the infant you found abandoned many years ago."

The innkeeper was surprised. She looked closely at him. How was it that this well-dressed man—she judged him to be in his midthirties—knew Nika? With a certain degree of suspicion she said, "What do you have to do with Nika?"

Achille smiled. "Don't worry. I'm not with the police. And I'm not bringing you bad news. Nika is doing well."

The innkeeper wiped her hands on her apron. She again looked at the stranger searchingly. The gentleman was an imposing man, good-looking, and he seemed trustworthy.

"Where is she?" she asked. "I've worried about her. She simply left a few months ago."

"She wanted to go to Italy," Robustelli nodded.

"The stupid child!" the innkeeper cried. "She's had that idea in her head for years!"

Robustelli laid a hand on her arm to calm her.

"You needn't worry. She is in Maloja. A family there took her in. Nika is working in a hotel, the same hotel where I work."

The woman looked at him, flabbergasted. "She's working in a hotel? Ah well, she was always curious, eager to learn; she asked the most impossible questions and insisted that I teach her to read." The woman smiled as she remembered, but then went on

242

immediately, "Still, she could have sent me a sign of life! After all, one worries."

Achille nodded. "She doesn't know that I came here, Signora. Otherwise she would certainly have asked me to send you her regards. But I have the impression that the family she grew up with did not treat her too well."

The innkeeper gave Robustelli a sharp look. "Why should you care?" she asked, suddenly suspicious again.

"Nika has confided in me a little. I would really like to help her in her search for her real parents."

"Well," the woman said hesitantly. "The farmer's family didn't exactly treat her like a princess. But what do you expect? Nika was a contract child, they're all treated the same. Nobody cares a lot about them, how they're doing. Here nobody can afford to give things away." But then she saw how carefully he was following her words, and she confided in him. "The farmer did beat her a lot. And she didn't get enough to eat. I gave her something to eat now and then, whenever she secretly came here." She leaned closer to Robustelli and lowered her voice. "To be frank, I tried to make things better for her. First, I went to see the minister. But those religious types! The man didn't lift a finger for the girl. Avoid trouble, that was his motto. He wasn't there to defend the weak, this man of God." She made a hasty sign of the cross. "God save his soul. He's dead."

Achille nodded again.

"Then the girl got thinner and thinner and stopped talking. At that point, I reported the matter to the authorities in Chur. They have inspectors who can check on the living conditions of the contract children. And I was amazed—they actually intended to send someone here. But on the very day they were going to come to check on the conditions under which Nika was housed, she ran away."

The innkeeper shook her head. "She would have come of age soon anyway, and would have been free then to go wherever she wanted to . . ."

"But was there no information with the locket about Nika's parents?" Robustelli interrupted.

"No sign of anything," the woman said. "Of course I was curious, as you can imagine one would be when one suddenly finds an infant outside one's door. I opened the locket. And the minister did too. But there was just a scrap of paper with some scrawled writing that I couldn't make out. And the minister couldn't figure it out either."

"And in spite of that you think that the mother was Italian?" Robustelli asked. He was beginning to realize that he wouldn't be getting any new information.

"I'd hold my hand in the fire about that," the innkeeper said.

After his return journey to Maloja, Robustelli felt tired. He hadn't been able to clear up anything. He evaded Andrina's questions about where he had been. And oddly enough, he had a guilty conscience doing so.

James received a message from Segantini via Fabrizio Bonin that the painter wanted to meet him at the hotel in Maloja at two o'clock. James hoped fervently that the trek to see the painting in its outdoor location would not turn into a long excursion. He was looking forward to spending a few hours with his newfound friend Bonin, for he wanted to ask him, as a fellow newspaper man, about the situation of newspapers in Italy. He was also avoiding Edward's company. He hadn't wanted to talk with him ever since his last conversation with Mathilde.

He hadn't gone to see Mathilde again after that, but he certainly hadn't forgotten her. It had been cowardly of him to demand an admission of love from her when she was the one who had asked him for one first. And yet, he simply couldn't bring himself to seriously court her. He had too many doubts—fewer about Mathilde than about himself and his own constancy. And now here was Edward who'd jumped into the breach and seemed to have successfully established himself.

That had hurt James's vanity, even though he wouldn't have admitted it. Between the two of them, hadn't he always been the more successful in conquering ladies' hearts?

"Don't worry," Segantini said, smiling after looking James up and down, and taking note of his not-very-serviceable mountaineering clothes. "The picture I'm going to take you to see is in an easily accessible spot just outside the village. I call it *La Morte* and I visualize it as just one part of a larger project." He set out with a strong stride, going ahead of Bonin and James and heading up toward the pass.

James was startled when Bonin translated the title of the picture: *Death*. Thoughts of death and mourning had never been of particular interest to him. Fabrizio asked him if he knew Segantini's *The Dead Hero*, a painting he had done when he was a young man, in which he gave the dead hero his own features.

James nodded.

"He kept coming back to this same subject," Bonin said thoughtfully. "And again and again he had given the laid-out corpse his own face. Remarkable. As if the image of his own death was always very close to him. Do you also know the painting *Return to the Homeland*? It was shown in Venice in 1895, and I thought it impressive. A dead man is being taken back to his home in a coffin borne on a horse-drawn cart. The mountain landscape in the painting resembles this area. The painting was awarded the Prize of the Italian State."

James shook his head. "No. Don't know it."

Segantini, who had walked on ahead, stopped and was waiting for them. "Come on. We're going to leave the road that leads up to the pass and bear left. It isn't much farther. But if you want to take a beautiful hike one day—then keep on going in this direction and you'll come to Lake Cavloc. A really worthwhile excursion."

He turned and looked back in the direction of the village; he pointed to the small white church a little distance outside the village.

"I painted one of my most recent works there. I called it *The Comfort of Faith*. A father and mother are mourning at the grave of their child whose soul is being carried off to heaven by two angels. Unfortunately, I can't show you the painting; it's in Munich just now at the Exhibition of the Secession. For me, the vast wintry landscape I used as the backdrop is more of a consolation than the religious imagery. In nature we are in good hands, with or without religion."

He walked on ahead of them again, then stopped at a large wooden box. When he opened its double doors, they saw a painting inside the box.

James, who was afraid not only of hospitals but also of dead people, breathed a deep sigh of relief. There in the late-summer countryside where they stood, a wonderful winter landscape was revealed to their eyes.

There was nothing dark or shocking in the painting; quite the opposite. James felt drawn into the picture as if by magic. It seemed as if he were walking on the crunching snow that covered the path toward the mountains over which the sun was just rising. A horse with a sleigh was waiting for a coffin that was being carried out of an alpine hut; mourning figures stood about, looking very small in the magnificent landscape. A cloud, warmly lit by the morning sun, floated above the highest of the mountains, like a messenger bringing redemption. James stepped closer, quite taken, almost against his will, for winter was not his favorite season.

Asking Segantini to stand beside his picture, James photographed the scene. He squeezed his eyes almost shut, concentrating his gaze on the majestic mountain with the luminous cloud which dominated the painting. He said nothing, but as he narrowed his focus even further, he suddenly saw here too, in the mountain, the same face that appeared in *The Dead Hero*.

Shocked, James tried to drive away the monumental face of Segantini that stared back at him from the painting, but couldn't. Was Segantini working here on an apotheosis of himself? Or did he visualize himself humbly being assimilated into an eternal, everlasting nature, into the landscape that he loved?

He gave Segantini a sideways glance. The artist felt called upon to say something about the picture.

"You can see that it's winter; nature is buried under snow; the mountains in the background are lit up by the rising sun. In the alpine hut a young girl has died . . ."

"Why a girl?" James asked.

Segantini did not answer his question.

"The painting is still far from finished. Will I be able to depict the eternal meaning of the spirit in these earthly things? Will I be able to capture the light that gives space to the distance, which makes the sky infinite? Will I be able to show the connection between the idea of nature and the symbols that arise from our soul?"

Symbols, James thought, are always ambiguous. Perhaps even though Segantini elevated himself into immortality, he was still full of humility? Maybe he wanted to make himself eminent and yet cease to exist? It was as if he was certain of salvation and entrusting himself to it.

"You will need the light of winter to complete this painting," Bonin said. "You'll be able to do it. But it isn't there yet."

And with that, Death, which Segantini repeatedly conjured up, was once again warded off.

⁂

"Bye, Aunt Betsy. When will you come again?" Mathilde had tears in her eyes as she embraced her aunt. "I don't like to see you leave. But I can understand that you have to go home again."

"Tilda . . ." Betsy held Mathilde close. "Just look at you! You can ask Dr. Bernhard! You're already doing much better. Up here in the mountains, you'll get to be a strong, healthy young woman, and a very athletic one, with all the walks you take every day! And soon you'll come back to Zurich. Adrian will come to see you here as often as he can. And your parents promised to come for a visit. You won't be alone. And Edward is still here, too, after all."

She didn't mention James. And her niece said nothing about the conversation she had had with him before Adrian's visit. It seemed as if James had withdrawn, either because he'd come to his senses or because he didn't love her.

"I'd like you to come back soon. I'll miss you, Aunt Betsy."

"Shh," Betsy put her finger to her lips. "Don't talk about it. We'll see each other again soon."

Mathilde didn't go with Betsy to the coach station. After these eventful weeks they had experienced together, she preferred a quick good-bye.

Betsy turned to wave several times; then she disappeared around a corner. The wide brim of her hat was the last thing Mathilde saw of her.

Once fall arrived it would get lonely up here, she feared. But Dr. Bernhard had assured Mathilde that October was often the most beautiful month of the year, and that the silent falling of the golden larch needles would conjure up a fairy tale rain of gold right before her eyes, a symphony of gold just as his friend Segantini—like no other—had painted it. She should be patient, he said, and she'd soon be strolling around in this fairy tale.

Mathilde smiled. Everything was still green outside, and in a little while, Edward would come by to pick her up for an afternoon walk. She was going to ask him whether James was leaving too. It would be easier for her if she knew that he wasn't here anymore.

Entire hours had passed in which she hadn't thought of him, sometimes half a day, and when Edward was with her she forgot him entirely, even though the two men were friends and belonged together. A few weeks ago, she could easily have chopped the head off anyone who said that there would come a time when she would no longer think of James every minute of the day. And yet, it had happened. I'm just like all the others, unfaithful, and fickle, she thought, feeling ashamed.

"Thanks, Edward, for being so thoughtful to my niece," Betsy said. "When you leave here, you really must stop off in Zurich. Will you promise me?"

Edward had come to the post coach station to say good-bye to Betsy. James had sent his apologies, saying that he was on an excursion with Segantini and Bonin. Betsy's baggage had been stowed away.

"We're ready to leave," the driver called out.

"Please promise that you'll come by to see me?" Betsy asked again.

Edward nodded and kissed Betsy's hand. "Yes, I promise. Have a good trip, all the best."

Betsy waved once more to him. She hadn't wanted to let on to Mathilde, but it was time for her to think of her own life and future. The summer in St. Moritz had caused quite a stir in her state of mind. She had stopped mourning, and had almost fallen in love with the same man as her young niece, and she actually would have liked it if at least Edward had made more of an effort to win her affections. He was very pleasant company; they had gotten along well, and he had always treated her in a way that made her feel respected and admired as a woman. But Edward, in spite of the lovely evening they'd shared at the Palace Hotel, had made no attempt to get closer to her. Betsy watched the landscape glide past through a kind of haze, for the horses and coach stirred up a lot of dust. Some of it must have gotten inside the carriage too, because moments later Betsy was searching for a handkerchief and dabbing at the corners of her eyes.

She wasn't so very young anymore. But she wasn't old either. She had enjoyed doing things, wearing bright colors, being with men, feeling pretty, and flirting.

Once back in Zurich, she would first work on improving the appearance of her house, her garden, and her wardrobe, and only then would she consider whether she wanted to spend the rest of her life working for charity and the introduction of a pension for widows and orphans. But, she thought, as she left the Engadine behind her, maybe she was really still a bit too young to devote herself completely to charity work.

The air was cool. Although the first early snow had already melted, it was a harbinger of fall, like the meadow saffron whose pale pink now appeared in all the meadows. The sun was still warm, and there were some glorious days, but the weather was no longer dependable. Cool days on which the sky clouded over alternated with the summer brightness.

Emma Schobinger had sent warm underwear and dresses up to the clinic, and Edward, who originally had planned to leave at the end of August, had some warmer clothes sent to him: woolen leggings and heavy tweeds, even a warm coat. He didn't want to leave until he had found out how Mathilde really felt about her engagement to Adrian, and until he, Edward, had told her of his affection for her and found out whether there was any hope that she would one day reciprocate his feelings for her.

James, who had actually planned to be gone long before this, had let himself be persuaded by Fabrizio Bonin to stay for the big Venetian Ball, a grand event the Spa Hotel Maloja held each year to mark the end of the season. Primoli and Bonin planned to leave after that.

James was now spending most of his time in Maloja. In spite of himself, he was impressed by Segantini who was so different than he was, and he wanted to see more of the paintings the artist was working on. Whenever he could, he spent time with Bonin, and he was also spending more time with Primoli, who was not only a master photographer, but also a splendid conversationalist.

James had taken photographs of Segantini with his recently developed and practical handheld camera, but he was also interested in the special techniques used to create the type of art photography that Primoli and Bonin spoke of with great enthusiasm.

Insights and Confessions

"I wanted to tell you something." Segantini, stroking his dark beard, fixed Nika with a penetrating gaze.

She said nothing, her eyes as unfathomable as the sea.

"This year I'm leaving early for Soglio. In the winter, the Bregaglia Valley is a more pleasant place. Milder. Up here you're buried under snow."

Nika was still silent. So he was leaving. And soon. He could also have said tomorrow. Or, this evening.

For weeks I won't be seeing him, she thought. Not all winter long. I won't ever see him again. Once someone leaves, he doesn't come back. That's how things go. Her mother left and never came back. She, Nika, had run away from Mulegns and would never go back.

"When will you be leaving?" she asked.

"Soon. The end of September, I think. It looks as though winter will be early this year. In Soglio I can paint better out-of-doors." For the first time she heard him laugh, a bitter laugh. "I have to be able to paint. You understand, don't you? Without pictures, no money. I've never bowed to a theory, the opinions of the art critics, or academic arrogance. I'd rather live in the solitude of these mountains than in the salons of Milan and Paris. But my family has to eat; they need shoes and clothes, and the children need a good education. Even the stove needs to be fed so that I can gaze into its glowing red embers when I'm cold."

"When will you come back again?" Nika asked.

"That depends entirely on the weather and my work. Maybe after Easter. Or maybe later. But you may have to leave if the Biancottis don't want to feed you. The hotel is closed in the winter."

Nika didn't listen to what he was saying. Why should she listen to him now that he would be going away soon?

"Are you listening to me?" Segantini asked.

She seemed completely indifferent, shook her head.

He looked at her questioningly.

"Will you miss me?"

"No," she said, again shaking her head.

She wanted to run away. But he was standing directly in front of her so that she felt she couldn't get past him. She gathered all her strength as if she were going to jump over him in one powerful leap.

Segantini took Nika in his arms, holding the sobbing girl close.

❦

"The season will be coming to an end soon," Achille Robustelli said.

"I know," Andrina replied. And this was precisely what was worrying her. They'd gone dancing several times already and she'd done her best to encourage his advances, but he still had not proposed. She had managed to get him to make some more intimate overtures, but it had all been somewhat delicate. Now the little plant needed to be nourished so it could grow—he remained too discreet in his courtship. She could not offer herself too openly for that would give her the air of being easy, which might ruin any chance she had of achieving a higher social position at his side. But time was short. He would be going to Italy for the winter, and it was anyone's guess whom he might meet there.

"The hotel closes for the winter, and I'll probably spend the winter months in Bergamo. What will you be doing? Would you like me to help you find a job in St. Moritz for the winter season?"

Exactly. Here they were. They had arrived at the point of danger.

Without a word, Andrina walked over to the door, turned the key in the lock, came back, and sat down on Achille's lap. He was young and in the best of health, and Andrina sensed the desire coursing hotly through his veins. She slid a little higher up on his thighs and affectionately put her arms around his neck.

"I know you would do that for me. And of course I'd like to work here again next summer. With you, at your side. But if you go to Bergamo, Achille, it means that we won't be seeing each other for months!" Her round breasts were so close that his breath came in gasps and he felt hot. "And do you think I could hold out that long?" she whispered close to his ear.

He stayed quite still, thrilled by her proximity, overcome with desire, embarrassed by the obviousness of his arousal.

"Did you hear me?" she whispered, now touching his ear with her lips, brushing against his cheeks with her cherry-red mouth.

"Oh yes," he mumbled, visualizing the seductive Andrina with the chestnut-brown eyes lying in bed, waiting for him as— but, no, he couldn't get carried away. First, he had to propose to her and tell his mother about the seriousness of the matter. He straightened up and gently pushed her back a little.

"I didn't tell you anything about this before, but in a few days my mother is coming for a visit. Not exactly the most opportune moment as it happens—just before the end of the season and the grand ball. But maybe her visit is coming at a good time after all. I would like to introduce you to my mother. Then, perhaps, you could come to visit me in Bergamo . . ."

Andrina beamed. "You will?" She kissed Achille on the lips, utterly delighted. She embraced him as if wanting to choke him rather than marry him. He smiled, half in joy because of his decision and half in doubt.

"And then we'll be engaged," she cried. "And you'll even buy me a real engagement ring with a diamond."

Achille smiled. "That seems to be the most important thing to you. And when the time comes, you will get a ring."

"Then you won't have to find me a job for the winter," she said, decisively, playfully turning the ring on his finger. "And as soon as you let me know, I'll come to Bergamo. As fast as the wind."

Achille was relieved. The side of his life that involved his emotions had lain fallow too long. But they were all still there. Indeed, he felt that it was this very abundance of unexpressed feelings that had led him to hide them over the years, displaying them less and less.

Not that he was inexperienced in sexual matters. In the army, and afterward too, he had occasionally gone with friends to brothels. But he didn't enjoy these visits and always felt slightly out of place. Being good-looking, somewhat shy, and very polite as an officer, he'd effortlessly outrivaled the others. He had never wanted to share in his comrades' coarse jokes, their stable manners, and disrespectful treatment of the women.

But now he sensed quite clearly that it was time to give up his solitary life. Andrina had recognized this, and he was grateful to her. He longed to have a woman's body lying next to him at night, to finally yield to his own desires, to receive the mixture of tenderness, sex, and affection that he craved. To let his feelings, for which there had been no room while he was in the army or pursuing his career, all pour out. This completely different kind of passion and intimacy was what he needed.

Suddenly he saw Nika again, saw the way she had stood before Segantini yesterday, looked at him, before rushing into his arms; or had he been holding on to her because she wanted to run away? Why did this scene come to mind just now? He had felt ashamed watching them, but he hadn't averted his eyes; he always seemed to be there when Segantini came to look for Nika. It struck him how inappropriate it really was.

Achille pushed Andrina off his lap.

"You have to unlock the door now, Andrinetta," he said gently. "And another thing. I've been able to arrange for Nika to stay in the room next to yours. Seraina had to leave before the end of the season. Her mother died, and they needed her at home. There are many little brothers and sisters."

Andrina felt herself getting angry. "So now she'll have a room all to herself while I have to share mine?" she asked, her voice sounding dangerously calm, even as she was getting increasingly angry and her face was turning red.

"Please, Andrina, don't get upset. It's only for a few weeks. I'm glad I was able to solve the problem. I don't understand why you're reacting like this."

"Let me explain," she replied, quite furious, even stamping her foot as she stood in front of him. "This *straniera* that nobody knows anything about, this nothing of a nobody, she simply gets everything. People feel sorry for her. She settles in with us, eats at our table. She's courted by Segantini, whose head she's turned—the witch—just like she did my poor brother Gian's. And you," she took a deep long breath, "you allow her to stop working in the laundry so she can work in the garden and get fresh air, and now she's allowed to lie down to sleep like a princess in a bed of down. And I'm not supposed to get angry? Why don't you simply give her the diamond ring you just promised me!"

Achille looked at her, dumbfounded. "What did you say?"

"I say, why don't you take her!" Andrina yelled, turned on her heel, unlocked the door, and slammed it shut behind her.

⁂

"Edward," cried Mathilde. "I've never seen you dressed this way! Warm cap, woolen leggings. What's the occasion?"

Edward smiled and took off his cap. "I'm preparing for hard times. Today's weather is giving us a foretaste. Have you taken a look outside yet?"

Mathilde laughed. "No, you can't see anything in this fog!"

"You should have seen the primeval soup that I've just traveled through."

"Where are you coming from?" she asked. He always had a story to tell that drove away the boredom of the sanatorium routine.

"I went to meet an old friend from London who was staying in Pontresina," Edward said. "His family is spending the summer there, and he sent me a telegram to say that he'd be visiting them for a couple of days."

London. Mathilde suddenly visualized a salon—yes, she could quite clearly imagine what it must look like in a well-to-do family's home in the West End. She pictured herself as one of the guests, healthy and radiant, although shy, and ashamed of her girls' boarding school English. Edward was asking her to dance, and it seemed not for the first time. No, indeed, they knew each other well, she felt so natural in his arms . . .

"I actually had intended to walk to Pontresina," Edward was saying, "but in this weather I decided to take a carriage instead. Even here, the lake was already rough and gray, but it was still a lake and the clouds were clouds. However, the farther we went, the more everything seemed to flow together. And then it was only clouds," Edward went on. "We were driving directly into nothingness, a void."

Mathilde pulled her chair closer to him.

"Then you really are dressed appropriately," she said. "But what do you mean when you say, you're preparing for hard times?"

Edward hesitated. "I've decided," he continued slowly, "to stay here until you let me know your decision . . . even if that should be for the entire winter."

"My decision?" Mathilde asked. "Decision about what? There's nothing to decide. I'll simply have to stay up here a long time, even if Dr. Bernhard believes that I'll get well again."

"You certainly will get well again. I know that for sure. I am willing it to happen."

She laughed aloud. "But Edward, what do you mean, you're willing it to happen? Whether we live or die isn't in our hands. Certainly not with this disease."

"Perhaps you don't want to understand what I'm saying. You are engaged. Your fiancé was here. He will be visiting you again. And he, too, is hoping that you will get well again and come home soon. Are you going to marry him?"

Mathilde sat up ramrod straight.

Edward wouldn't be put off anymore. "I wouldn't have any doubts about this, of course, if I didn't know that you've fallen in love with James."

Mathilde's expression turned cool. "That's over and done with."

"Then there isn't any uncertainty anymore? No decision to make? Because you are absolutely certain that you've found your way back to the right man?"

Mathilde said nothing. She looked out of the window, but there was nothing to see. Just clouds and fog. "His family no longer wants me. They can't depend on me for the continuation of the Zoller family. Not anymore."

"But your fiancé, what does *he* say . . ."

"He is standing by me. Yes. Adrian wants to marry me. Even against the wishes of his parents."

"But that's nice," Edward said, unhappily. He was thinking of Emily, whom he had loved without a successful outcome, and he thought that there are always other men with more charm, wit, or daring than he had. It was time for him to leave. He got up and reached for his hat.

"But you still haven't told me what hard times you're preparing for!" Mathilde said and drew him back into his chair. "And above all, why you asked me about Adrian and my engagement."

"Right," Edward said and sat down again. "But I don't know if it makes any sense to talk about it."

"But talk about what? Come on, tell me what you want to tell me! And please look at me while you do."

She smiled because suddenly she saw again the image that a moment ago had carried her off for an instant into a London drawing room. The truth was, Edward wouldn't carry her off. Not to his "castle" at Pension Veraguth and not to London. He was no robber baron. But she felt infinitely comfortable with him. Yes, that was it. A deep familiarity, a closeness.

She looked at Edward, and it would have been hard for him to persuade himself that her look was not affectionate and encouraging. And even though he was very adept at choking off things in the early stage of germination, he now threw all care to the wind.

"I wasn't a good substitute for James."

"Oh?"

"I wanted to kill him . . ."

"Really?"

"I saw what he did to you."

"I hope not," Mathilde said, firmly.

"It doesn't matter," Edward said. "Could you imagine . . ." He was suddenly very tired. "Could you see yourself deciding in my favor?"

"And all that without flowers?" Mathilde asked.

"They'll be delivered afterward," he replied with a crooked smile. He felt as if he hadn't eaten anything for days. "Now of course there aren't any tiger lilies anymore," he said.

"Let's see if it won't work just as well with roses," Mathilde said.

Dr. Bernhard was right. The delicate green needles of the larches were just beginning to change color. Edward went on long walks with Mathilde in a landscape of rocks, glittering lakes, clouds, and light.

"The sun is so bright in one's eyes that one can hardly see anything," Edward said, touching Mathilde's arm affectionately. They stopped, and Mathilde actually closed her eyes. She felt the shadow that fell over her cheeks and the warmth of his face as it came closer and their lips met. Have you ever kissed a man? James had asked her, and she had lied. One didn't have to lie to Edward.

"Oh, my God," she said after they'd pulled apart and she'd taken a deep breath. "You're full of surprises!"

She shook her head. No, she thought, she couldn't possibly tell him what she meant by that. Why had she assumed that Edward would kiss her gently and hesitantly? She took a step back and looked at him. James was athletic, energetic, charming, experienced. Edward was tall, calm, and sensitive. How could she not have seen that he was manly and passionate? She took his hand and drew him closer.

"I am glad that this side of you doesn't immediately jump out at everyone." She kissed him again on the mouth.

"Why?" he asked. "What have you discovered?"

"I'm discovering you. And every day I discover something new. One has to be patient with you. It will take me time to discover everything about you. Thank God that not all women can have the opportunity, otherwise . . ."

He opened her coat and put his arms around her waist. "Or otherwise what?"

"Otherwise I'd be jealous . . ."

"You silly girl," he said. "Do you think I waited this long to fall in love again just so I could go look for another object of affection right away?"

She took his hand and pulled him down to the lakeshore. She tossed a pebble into the glittering golden grid the sun was making on the water.

"To fall in love again?" she asked.

"Yes," he said. "Yes. Naturally, I was in love once before. After all, I'm not a little boy anymore, but a grown man. I've met many women, and there was one whom I loved very much."

Mathilde looked at him in disbelief with her blue eyes, as if it was utterly impossible that he had ever . . .

"Loved very much?" she murmured, shaken, "very much?"

Edward laughed out loud. "Yes, very much."

Mathilde was silent. My God, she didn't know anything about him. She'd always taken it as a matter of course that he cared for her, but she had never asked anything about his past. To her he seemed to have had no other life, except for the interests he shared with her, and his friendship with James.

"Aha," she said, both disappointed and ashamed. "Where is she now? Is she dead?" Obviously that's what Mathilde would have preferred.

"No. She's alive and happy. She's married. But it was me she was actually engaged to."

Mathilde sighed.

"The way I'm engaged to Adrian . . ." She gazed over to the opposite shore of the lake, at a loss.

"The way you are engaged to Adrian," he said, slowly. "It took me a long time to get over our splitting up. You can ask James. Years. It took years. But now I am happy, maybe happier now that I've found you than I would have been if I hadn't had that earlier experience."

He leaned against a tree trunk. "How differently things can turn out. Quite different from what we imagine."

Mathilde looked unhappy. The wonderfulness of his kiss had suffered a bit in the face of the knowledge that he had kissed another woman before her. Kissed her the same way. Or, it was to be assumed that he had kissed her in much the same way.

"Mathilde?" he said softly, "Mathilde. You're not going to be jealous of the past? It is over, you know. But it is a part of my history. Emily is a part of my life. I can't simply cut out that chapter. I wouldn't be the man you know if I didn't have my history. And," he went on, taking her in his arms, "you, after all, have scarcely reserved your attentions for only one man . . ."

"I never . . ." she wanted to contradict him, but he didn't let her finish.

"You fell head over heels in love with my best friend . . ."

She nodded sheepishly. She couldn't deny it. On the contrary, she wanted to tell him. That was a dark chapter that she had to get off her chest at some point, not to Adrian, but to Edward.

"Are you all right?" Edward asked and brushed a few blonde curls out of her face.

"Yes, yes. It's just . . . there's . . ." Her voice faded despondently.

"Maybe I don't really have to know what happened?" he said.

She looked at him with gratitude. Then she frowned and said, "Yes. You *do* have to know. I did something terrible. You won't love me anymore once you find out what it was."

"Yes, I will," Edward said.

"But you have no idea what happened," Mathilde said, convinced that after her confession he would never again kiss her as he had kissed her just now. "He took my clothes off," she said softly, not looking at Edward. "He saw me almost naked." She looked into his eyes. But his expression remained unchanged. "Edward, he touched me and looked at me. And he . . . he took photographs of me. Do you understand? He can ruin my life; he has a photograph of me . . . well, almost naked."

"It's all right. It's all right, Mathilde . . ." Edward held her close. "James told me."

"What? How could he tell you!" Mathilde was indignant. "How could he do such a thing!"

Edward held her at arm's length and looked at her in amusement. "Well, now. He *is* my best friend. And he realized that I had feelings for you. I think he felt an obligation to tell me. The way you did just now. That is really good."

How could he say something like that? Mathilde looked at him. She was perplexed.

"You know," Edward whispered in her ear, "I don't hold it against James that he desired you. He realized even before I did just how wonderful you are. He knows what I have in you; he saw it . . ."

Mathilde was speechless. To hear such a sentence come from his lips. There was really no end to the things she had to learn about Edward.

"And," he went on, "after all, times have changed. Women aren't goods that you acquire only if none of the edges have been chipped or damaged. Women are at last starting to decide for themselves what they want to be—and how they want to live. I like that. I also like your Aunt Betsy. She seems to jump right over a lot of hurdles. And she's right. You may well take a page from her book."

My God, Mathilde thought.

"So you like Aunt Betsy too?"

He nodded. "That's what I've been saying. I like Betsy a lot. She's an intelligent, beautiful, unconventional woman who . . ."

Mathilde put a hand over his mouth. "Enough. Please take me home to my sickbed, to Dr. Bernhard, to the nurses." She looked at him dubiously. So this was Edward? And this was life?

"Kiss me," she said.

"Till the end of my days," he said.

The End of the Season

Sometimes, going around a turn, the coffin on the old horse-drawn cart would slide back and forth a bit. It was made of light-weight pine and only sloppily secured to the cart.

They were bringing Luca home.

Aldo was silent. How different he had imagined Luca's home-coming. How proud he had been of his son. Benedetta, instead of an expression of mourning, just wore her perpetually unfriendly look. What did she care about the suffering of others? What good was it to know she'd been right all along? Luca had been torn apart by exploding dynamite when they were blasting a tunnel. Now there would be another gravestone in the cemetery with the name Biancotti, as if there weren't enough already.

Signor Robustelli didn't dirty his fingers. He sat behind his desk and admired the daring stretches of train tracks from afar. She wasn't pleased that he came to the funeral, but Andrina had insisted. She cared for him. And Benedetta didn't like that either. She didn't want a man like that in her family. It just wasn't right. He didn't fit. And if Andrina went on like this, she soon wouldn't fit in to the family either.

Benedetta's legs were tired, and she was having trouble breathing. Nika had noticed, and she'd climbed up to Grevasalvas to tell Gian and to bring him home. Benedetta needed him now more than ever.

They were all afraid that Gian, upset by what had happened, would have an attack and scare everyone to death. But the worst did not happen. Gian was quite calm. He held on to his mother and supported her even as, standing in front of the open grave, she staggered momentarily, as if wanting to throw herself down into the hole on top of the light pine coffin gleaming up from below. He held her tight and whispered calming words as if he were talking to his cows.

Aldo stood by himself, trying to catch Andrina's eyes. But she was with Robustelli and didn't leave his side.

Even if Luca had had bad luck, she, Andrina, was going to look forward to the future, just as her brother had. She enjoyed the way Achille put a protective arm around her, and she knew he was her future. She couldn't rely on her family, who had only managed to make it from Stampa to Maloja, and not a step beyond.

Nika was standing to one side. Luca had found his resting place. She pulled her woolen shawl tightly about her, pressing her hand to her chest. She imagined him lying there in his black suit. Not able to hear or see anything anymore, not even the dull sound of the clods of soil raining down on his coffin now.

The Segantini family had of course come to the funeral too. Bice looked as if she were suffering, but maybe she was only cold. The wind of Maloja blew over them all, whirling past them along with their thoughts of the dead boy. Segantini saw the wind driving the reddish-blonde strands of hair into Nika's face. Whenever a cloud covered the sun, the fiery note in her hair was extinguished, and only her sad face remained. He had been troubled when she'd told him she would not miss him. If she had admitted the opposite, he wouldn't have had to keep thinking of her. And he would have preferred that.

❦

"Be careful," Adrian was going to say, "they can bite." But by then Mathilde had already stuck her finger into the cage. She screamed. Startled, the squirrel hopped back and forth at the end of its chain, its red, bushy tail beating wildly against the bars. The tears that welled up in Mathilde's eyes were not only in response to the shock and pain of the small, deep wound, but also in pity for the caged animal. It was an unfortunate present Adrian had brought her. She didn't know how she should thank him for it, and anyway, she had some unpleasant news for him.

"You can chain it outside the window," Adrian had said as he greeted her and handed her the cage.

"But I wouldn't chain up an animal that wants to run around free in the forest," she had said with passion, and without thinking twice about it, had stuck one of her fingers in between the bars.

"I thought an animal might pass the time a little for you," he said apologetically while she was trying to stop the bleeding. She said nothing, and a long silence ensued between them that he didn't understand.

Finally she said, "Adrian, I am not going to marry you." She could see from his face that he hadn't grasped the meaning of her words. "I don't know how to explain it to you . . . My life has changed since I've been up here. I'm not the same Mathilde you knew and fell in love with."

"But you don't look sick."

269

"I am not talking about external things," she said. "Many things have changed inside me. What I think, how I feel, what I want . . ." It was no use. He simply didn't understand. He was here, just as he always was, no different from a year ago, and he was only waiting to take her home, to marry her, no matter how his parents felt about it. Wasn't that enough? What else could she possibly want?

"I don't understand you," Adrian said. She was glad at least that he didn't bombard her with questions.

"No one can understand it," she said. "I myself don't understand."

"But it's probably just a mood." He tried again, "Emotions . . ."

"Yes. It is only emotions, feelings. And I am going to listen to my feelings."

"But it isn't all that simple, Mathilde. You can't simply break off an engagement with three sentences. Think of all the plans we've made, your parents, the future that we were planning for," Adrian said, completely at a loss.

"Oh yes, it is that simple, no matter how much we talk."

It was futile to try to change her mind right now. But he'd come back, and he'd ask Mathilde's father to accompany him.

Segantini was restlessly walking back and forth. He was searching for one of his paintings. Where was the oil painting that he'd hastily dashed off one or two years ago, the forerunner to *Love at the Springs of Life*? The painting wasn't large, barely half a meter by half a meter (eighteen inches x eighteen inches), and he had never exhibited it. It depicted a nude female, a rare subject for him.

At last he found the picture; it was with his children's things. Ah, he remembered now—in a fit of dissatisfaction, he had let them play with it, and the boys had used it as a target for their air gun. It was lying in the garden, where it had been carelessly thrown. It had been damaged in several places by the feathered arrowheads of the projectiles.

Segantini picked it up, gently wiped it off, and gazed at it.

The main colors were blue and green with some beautiful turquoise notes, as if he had already been thinking of Nika's eyes. In the background, an idealized landscape rather than a faithful representation of nature—mountains and a gleaming blue lake. And closer to the viewer, two tree trunks close together, with leafy crowns growing out of the picture. In the foreground lay a gentle hill. Round and soft and split into two lush rounded halves by a bubbling spring that flowed from deep within the hill. The flowing waters shimmered white against the dark cavity of the pool the spring had created and tumbled downward into a dark-green lake surrounded by grass. Beside the spring, on a light-blue cloth, is a beautiful nude, relaxed and giving herself up to the light of the summer day. One of her arms is pushed under her head as if to better expose it to the sun. Her eyes are closed, her legs crossed—and yet, Segantini thought, it would be easy to spread her legs. But why—the spring, the beginning of the world was already shamelessly open, much enlarged, it was pretty much an innocuous natural depiction of the female sex, what this reclining nude concealed between her legs.

And just then, Segantini felt a tormenting, painful longing that he didn't want to give a name to. He turned the picture over again, face down on the earth, where it had lain. It was a futile, an idle longing.

☙❧

"That isn't me," Nika said when she looked at the painting Segantini had taken her to see. "Only the hair is right, otherwise, nothing."

Segantini smiled. "But then, you didn't pose for me. The painting is an allegory in which I wanted to express an idea. It isn't a portrait of you."

"So what did you need me for?" Nika's feelings were hurt.

"You were the inspiration for the picture. When I was driving past in the coach and saw you at the lake, I suddenly saw the composition for a painting before me—you, standing over the water, gazing at your reflection."

Nika silently gazed at the canvas. It wasn't finished yet; that she could see. Segantini would still be adding many little brush strokes. But that would hardly change the painting as a whole.

Segantini had chosen a broad format. The action took place in the middle of the picture. It was a picture without sky. That bothered Nika. There was no way to avoid looking at what was happening in the picture, no escape for one's eyes. The upper edge of the picture simply cropped out the green tops of the trees, which stood where the meadow ended. The large waves of grass that took up almost all the upper half of the picture lay in bright daylight. Totally unlike the hidden place in the forest where Segantini had taken her.

In the foreground, Nika saw the glacial pool, but even the pool wasn't like the one they had visited. The boulder she had clambered over, and which had bordered the deep pool on one side, was flattened in the picture, a nearly horizontal line in the middle of the picture. And there she stood, naked in the landscape, bathed in relentless light, and at the mercy of all eyes.

"The boulder looks like a bridge," Nika said.

There was the alpine rose near the water, which Nika remembered. But then she noticed a white cloth tossed over the boulder, as if to represent her clothes.

"What is the white cloth?" she asked.

"White is the color of innocence," Segantini replied.

"It looks like a dress that's been taken off," Nika said.

"So there is something that's right," he said. "Back then, at the glacial pool, you undressed."

Nika, feeling uneasy, looked at the girl in the picture. She was supporting herself with her left hand on the boulder. With the right, she was holding her abundant hair out of her face—reddish blonde like hers—and looking down at the water. True, Nika was also tall and slender, but this girl was much younger than she was.

"But this is a young girl in the picture," she said, with disappointment in her voice, "not a woman!"

"She stands at the threshold of becoming a woman," Segantini replied. "Soon she'll cross the bridge."

"Is that why she is looking at herself? To see who she is?"

Nika looked carefully at the water, which reflected the girl. On its surface, the color of the water was a deep blue. Where the boulder cast a shadow, it was a swampy brown. And then Nika noticed something that the girl had apparently not seen yet. There was a monster lying in the water, a water snake with a dragon's head, brown and ugly, its teeth bared. "She doesn't see what's lurking down there!" Nika cried, taken aback.

"Because she's totally absorbed with her own reflection and isn't aware of anything but her own face. Vanity is a source of evil."

Nika felt hurt. So when he thought of her, he thought of vanity and a monster emerging from a deep pit of water.

"And why is it a girl standing there and not a man?"

"Women, it seems, are vain. And besides, it was you who gave me the idea for the picture."

Nika looked at him angrily.

"There are also men," he said to soothe her, "who look at their own reflection. You don't know the myth of Narcissus. Narcissus was a young man."

Nika felt a chill. So he had carried this terrible picture within himself ever since he had first seen her.

Yet, on the other hand, how enchantingly beautiful was the place that Segantini had brought her to. The quiet forest, the path overgrown with moss and tree roots, and the dark, bottomless pool with white clouds reflected in its blackness. What a wonderful smell in the forest, the mysterious interplay of light and shadow, wood cracking under their feet followed by a deep stillness that returned again when they paused. How the buds of the alpine roses had glowed, and she had felt as if she and Segantini were diving together into a profound, unfathomable dream. But no. He was looking at this girl in the picture from a cool distance; the colors were cold and did not radiate even the smallest spark of love.

"I don't like the painting," Nika said.

"I'm quite proud of it," Segantini said. "I consider it my best so far. I think I shall call it *Vanitas*. It's a Latin word; it means 'Vanity.' One could give it other titles too, such as *The Spring of Evil* or *Venus before Her Mirror*."

He looked at the picture. "I like *La Vanità* best. That name also refers to the futility of all our striving. In the end, there is always Death. Death is always there, always more powerful than we are."

He saw her horrified look and laughed. "Don't be afraid for me. A fortune-teller prophesied I would reach the biblical age of ninety-nine. I'm a superstitious person. So I believe it."

"I still don't like the picture," Nika said. "You look into a mirror because you want to know who you are. Is that a bad thing?"

"Too much looking is damaging," he said. "Then you stop seeing others."

"Maybe," Nika said. "But no one ever showed me who I am. Why I'm here. I look in the mirror to find out."

"It's also vanity to believe that you can know yourself," Segantini said.

"But what if you can't see yourself, can't recognize who you are?" Nika said.

"The only salvation is love," he said. "Selfless love for another—a love like a mother's love."

Nika shook her head. "Not all mothers love their children. My mother didn't love me."

"You don't know that."

"I have been looking for my mother because I want to know why she abandoned me. Maybe I'll understand her better then."

"You have to learn to love without understanding. As long as we don't know about death, we won't know anything final about life either. You will never find out everything. It's better for you to believe that she loved you."

Nika looked down at the ground.

"No, I'll never give up my search. And besides," she added angrily, "that dragon that you painted there, that doesn't exist. What took me by surprise at the pool was only a strange insect on the water's surface."

☙❧

275

Nika looked around the attic room. A bed, a table, a chair, a bureau with a water pitcher and bowl on it. There was space in the bureau for her things. My God, she thought, I have a room. A room. With a window through which the sunlight can come in.

She sat down carefully on the bed as if it might collapse with any violent movement. A bed! A pillow! A sheet, cool, fine, smooth. Nika got up again. Walked around. The wooden floorboards creaked under her feet. She sat down again, startled by the noise she was making. She felt she had to be quiet as a mouse so that the dream wouldn't burst like a soap bubble.

Half a year had gone by since she had run away from Mulegns. And nothing was the same as before. She took the locket from the table and concealed it with her few things in the bureau.

When Signor Robustelli had called her to his office and let her know that he had a room for her, she had stared at him as if he were an apparition. If you're treated badly for a long time, you can't believe it when you're suddenly treated well. You have to get used to it gradually.

Nika sat there on her bed, not moving, her knees pressed together, hands in her lap, letting the sun shine on her. She thought about Signor Robustelli who had looked at her, surprised. He must have noticed that she was staring at him as if she'd seen a ghost. Without being aware of it, she had begun to rely on him, to trust him, to ask him for help. But you can see people a thousand times and still not see them. He was just Signor Robustelli. Up to that point, she had only wondered and thought about Segantini. But at that moment when he'd explained about the room, she'd suddenly seen who this man really was, Achille Robustelli. He was younger than Segantini, more slender. He seemed more elegant, more agile. He took up less space than Segantini, and was probably less full of himself as well. Robustelli had dark, slightly wavy hair that was not as conspicuous as Segantini's magnificent curls. At the temples Nika could see the first silvery gray, a contrast to the young smooth face. He didn't have a beard like Segantini, didn't conceal his lips, which were smiling at that moment as if to say: Well? And so? Did you lose your tongue again?

Then she came back from her reverie, smiled, looked at him as if to say, Aha, look at that, there you are.

Well, at last, his look said.

"Nika," Signor Robustelli said, "I need you inside the hotel. You have to help serve. I know you liked working in the garden. But we have to get ready for the Venetian Ball even while the normal hotel service continues. We need every available hand to help now. Go to the *Chef de Service*, report in, and have them give you the appropriate clothes. And," he said after looking at her hands, "scrub your hands first. And your fingernails."

She looked at her hands, and you could tell they'd been doing garden work. Then she looked at Signor Robustelli. He laughed.

"Don't look at me like that. I know this is all new for you. But you'll get used to it."

છ૭

Stepping into the dining room of the Spa Hotel Maloja, Nika entered a new world. What she saw far exceeded what she had been able to imagine up to then. Indeed, with Gaetano she had raked the pebbles of the driveway that led up to the façade of the veritable palace. Hundreds of elegant carriages and coaches drove up that drive. She had seen the entrance hall by way of which one went to Signor Robustelli's office. Gaetano and she had planted the flower borders in the circular flowerbed; she knew the short avenue that led down to the lake where the rowboats and the vaporetto waited. The boat would steam across the water, taking guests for high tea at the Hotel Alpenrose in Sils-Maria or for trapshooting at Isola, where only a few years ago the servants threw live birds up into the air, not clay pigeons. Early in the morning, she and Gaetano had checked to make sure the golf course and the tennis courts were in perfect condition for the hotel guests.

Nika had seen the innards of this grandiose world, where the laundry from hundreds of beds and an endless number of tablecloths, napkins, towels, and aprons were washed and ironed.

But none of that had prepared her for the splendor of the dining room. Silverware from the famous Hepp Brothers of Pforzheim and Baccarat crystal from France gleamed in the huge hall, where five hundred guests could be served a *table d'hote* meal at the long tables. Nika was shocked by the immense size of the room; it was intimidating, and she felt as insignificant as a little black ant. But luckily there was another column of black ants—waiters and waitresses who were passing the silver platters and taking them away and, in a strict, seemingly rehearsed dance, saw to it that all the guests were able to progress through the menu in accordance with established rules of haute cuisine: *potage brunoise, truite de rivière frites, sauce mayonnaise, pommes naturelles, filet de boeuf à la Milanaise, Caneton à la Rouennaise, haricots verts sautés, chapons de Bourg, salade, glace, tutti-frutti, pâtisserie.* Nika was ordered about, here and there, setting tables, refilling water carafes, passing bread baskets.

The ladies, who during the day had played badminton, walked around Lake Cavloc, or let themselves be taken up to Lake Lunghin on a mule, appeared in the dining hall in evening dress, wearing whatever jewelry they possessed. The gentlemen came from the hunt, which although restricted to the local inhabitants, was made available to guests who were willing to grease some palms. Or they had come down from treks in the mountains to the peak of the Margna or to cross the Fedoz Glacier. Now in evening dress, they were escorting their ladies in to dinner. They were hungry as wolves. Some of their hungry looks also took in the prettier among the serving girls.

In addition to the dining room—inarguably one of the world's most fashionable—there were an à la carte restaurant, a ladies' salon, a smoking room, a billiards room, and several reading rooms. Nika would sometimes be sent to one of these with a cup of tea or a cognac. She walked in awe on the carpets and froze once in wonderment, when she passed the open door to the ballroom. It was located in the midsection of the E-shaped building and was directly above the steam boilers that heated the giant hotel.

The ballroom had large windows and at the end of the room was a theater stage, just waiting for the next lavish production. There was no way for Nika to envision all the things that were offered to the guests in this space. *Tableaux vivants* were rehearsed here, and the latest cinematographic works were shown; the La Scala Orchestra of Milan performed, and stars of the Metropolitan Opera from New York sang here; and of course, there was dancing.

"Say it isn't true!" Andrina didn't quite have the nerve to slam the door to Achille Robustelli's office. But her attitude toward him had changed completely. Ever since he had held out the prospect of an engagement, she had made some concessions. Not too many, yet enough to defend her own interests. But the way he was coddling Nika would have sent even more gentle souls around the bend.

Achille looked up startled. "What isn't true, my darling Andrina? What are you talking about?"

Andrina, hands on hips, gasping, seemed to be struggling for words.

"What's the matter? Tell me."

"Nika is working in the dining room, did I hear that right?"

Robustelli nodded. "Yes, that's right. Why does that upset you?"

Andrina dropped into the chair in front of his desk, throwing her arms up theatrically, as if she wanted to ask imaginary bystanders what they thought of such an answer. "What am I upset about? Can't you see? And haven't I said it a thousand times? This girl comes over the mountains, nobody knows from where or why, settles in our house, eats the soup my mother cooks, turns my helpless brother Gian's head, yet aims for higher things. She gets right to work on the famous Segantini, and now she doesn't want to get her hands dirty in the garden anymore. She intends to hobnob instead with the aristocracy at their tables in the dining room under the crystal chandeliers. And Signor Robustelli thinks, why not?"

Andrina had worked herself into such a fury while she was speaking that she jumped up to face him, looking as if she wanted to pounce.

"Sit down!" Achille said. "In the first place, I was only complying with Segantini's wish. After all, he is a friend of the director of this hotel. Segantini wants to help the young woman. The girl is coming along well . . ."

"Exactly. That's it! The witch's eyes make you all dreamy while she coldly pursues her goals. And you? Didn't it occur to you that there might be other people who deserve to be promoted to the dining room?" Andrina raised her head high and looked out the window.

Achille sighed. This would certainly mean suffering through several days of abstinence.

"Andrina, please calm down . . ."

"Yes? But you like her . . ."

"I just made an observation that anyone can confirm. Right now, I need Nika more urgently to serve in the dining room than in the garden. And quite apart from that, I can't simply do as I like or as you like. I'm neither the director nor the owner of this hotel."

"Then become director!" Andrina hissed. "Then you can do as you like."

She hadn't expected that her outburst would make him so angry, for he rarely got angry. But now she cringed as he struck the top of his desk with his hand.

"That's enough! I'd like to see how happy you'd be if I were hotel director in a hotel with a dozen rooms in some little village."

She'd gone too far. This wouldn't get her anywhere.

"I can see that you don't want to understand," she said, feeling insulted. "Tonight, by the way, we can't get together. It's my father's birthday." And with that, she swept out.

Lost in thought, Achille opened his desk drawer. He took out the silver cigarette case and took out a cigarette, tapped it on his desktop, and lit it unhurriedly. Segantini had wanted Nika in the garden so that he could see her whenever he chose to. Why did he bring Nika back to work inside the hotel? So that Segantini could no longer meet with her? So that he, Achille, would have her nearby? Was Andrina right? Couldn't he just as well have assigned her, Andrina, to the service staff preparing for the big ball?

He flipped the cigarette case open and shut, irresolutely. It hadn't been easy to mollify Andrina when she heard that Nika was getting one of the attic rooms. Wasn't it all too understandable that she would feel rejected all over again now? And she happened to fly off the handle easily; that was her temperament, Achille thought, trying to calm his uneasy soul. And from the first moment on, she hadn't been able to stand the *straniera*.

He drew on his cigarette and blew the smoke out in rings. It was better not to think about it too much. The conflict would blow over once he had introduced Andrina to his mother.

"Si, signore?" Nika asked. She was bent over with a dustpan and broom. She straightened up and found herself gazing into the brown eyes of a young man who had addressed her with "scusi, signorina."

"May I?" he asked, smiling, and took the dustpan and broom out of her hand. "I was the one who dropped the glass." He bent down, swept up the fragments, and returned the dustpan to her.

Nika looked at him in confusion.

"Haven't I seen you outside working in the hotel garden?" he continued.

His voice caused her to feel a pleasant, warm thrill, but the waiter who had sent her to clean up the minor accident had emphasized that it was not permitted to speak privately with the guests. Employees of the hotel weren't even allowed to speak to the guests' servants. Still she had to give him an answer. Nika decided she would nod. In this way, she had answered and still not spoken.

Fabrizio Bonin noticed her embarrassment. He stepped back as if to go, but paused and said, "I'm glad that you're now working inside. That way I'll see you more often." He smiled and turned back to his friend. Nika hurried off with the glass shards.

"You have excellent taste," James said. He was amused. He had by now become quite close to Fabrizio, but had never before spoken with him about women.

"Let's say I have my own personal taste. I don't fall in love easily. I hate flirting, and most of the women other men think pretty or desirable, I find neither beautiful nor compelling. You see," Fabrizio laughed and raised his wine glass, which the waiter had hurriedly refilled, "life is hard for me."

James toasted him. "Cheer up. I love flirting and I think many women are pretty, but I'm just as alone as you are!"

Nika threw the shards into the trash bin and slipped into a nearby ladies' room. She locked the door and looked at herself in the mirror. She had gained weight, for Benedetta had served her generously, and her body, even though slender, had assumed a softer outline. She was suntanned from working in the garden, in contrast to the ladies who were guests at the hotel and always carried parasols to keep their skin from darkening. But her hair was beautiful. She examined her facial features. They were unconventional, not quite regular, and her eyes were an unusual color. She moved closer to the reflection in the mirror, noted the little brown spots in the blue-green irises. It looked as if sparks were flying up inside. She felt ashamed remembering what Segantini had said about vanity, and guiltily she closed her eyes.

The young man in the dining room had brown eyes. Everything about him seemed so carefree, so natural. As if life was easy and cheerful. Why had he spoken to her? The hotel, after all, was full of ladies walking around, bored, just waiting for a man to speak to them.

One last time Nika looked deep into her own eyes in the mirror. Yes, she would have liked to talk a little longer to the young man. She felt that in his company time would fly by, for it was almost as if he lent you wings.

⊗⊛

"And does the *straniera* still give you a part of her earnings?" Andrina asked her mother. She had come home on one of her rare visits.

"Why should she?" Benedetta said. "Nika doesn't live here with us anymore. She's sleeping and eating in the hotel now. Under those circumstances, why should I wheedle any money out of her? Would you like a cup of coffee?"

"No," Andrina said curtly. "Your coffee tastes like anything but coffee. Achille has coffee sent from Italy . . ."

"Which Achille?" Benedetta asked; she was hard of hearing in one ear.

"Signor Robustelli, good Lord. Get used to him." Andrina stretched. "We're going to get married. He is going to introduce me to his mother."

Benedetta turned her back to her daughter and poured herself a cup of coffee. "So, you won't have any of my coffee. And I hope you don't expect me to approve of the man who sent my son to his death from his elegant, immaculate desk."

"My God, you are narrow-minded! He's not responsible for Luca's death! He only made the connection for him!"

"He recommended him." Benedetta put a spoonful of sugar into her coffee. Normally she did that only on Sundays, but she needed something sweet now. Her daughter was becoming more of a stranger the longer she worked in the hotel.

Andrina was angry. "But recommending someone doesn't mean that you killed them or are responsible when something bad happens!"

"But it was common knowledge that it was dangerous. I knew it. And you knew it too. There were so many workers who had died already. At the Gotthard Pass alone. That was no secret. My Luca gave his life like those others so that people like Robustelli can travel in comfort across the Alps. Even though it would be better if they didn't bother us and stayed where they belonged."

Andrina jumped up from her chair. "And I'm going to marry him in spite of that! I'll have a great future. In contrast to you. I'm leaving now."

Andrina was furious. Not just with her mother who couldn't see beyond her own front door, beyond Maloja and Stampa, but also with Achille Robustelli whom she'd just defended so passionately. It was incomprehensible, all the things he was doing for Nika. For this girl her brothers had dragged in, and who seemed to be everywhere now, spinning her web. And to think that she, Andrina, was the one who had brought her to the hotel! She could have kicked herself for it. And now on top of everything else, the *straniera* was living in a single room, working among the guests, while she, Andrina, was still cleaning rooms. But she didn't want to talk to Achille again about it, not before he introduced her to his mother. She was determined to make a good impression. But she simply wasn't going to put up with all this.

❧❧

Signora Robustelli was a small, round woman dressed in black. She was impressed by the hotel her son was managing, even though the area, in spite of its fashionable clientele, seemed a bit rough and isolated.

"I am not the hotel director," Achille emphasized. "I'm only the assistant manager and responsible for the personnel."

"But it's the same thing almost," his mother said. Don't you feel lonely here? The village has only a few houses. And it's just a village, not a city like Bergamo."

"This is a grand hotel, Mama—there's nothing like it even in Milan. I employ one hundred and fifty people, and hundreds of people from the best circles of Europe come here. I have an incredible amount of work to do but enjoy it very much. Why should I feel lonely?"

"It isn't Italy. Not your homeland, Achille. Aren't you home-sick for your country and for a wife who will make a home for you there?"

Achille Robustelli was glad that his mother had touched on this sensitive subject of her own accord and immediately took up the point. "Right, Mama. I've met a woman here who will give me this home. I would like to introduce her to you. I'm glad you're here just now. Because the season will be over soon, and then I'd like to bring her to Bergamo with me this winter."

"Up here?" Signora Robustelli was incredulous. "You found someone up here? Is she Italian? Will she go back to Italy with you? After all, you don't want to stay up here forever. One day you'll manage a grand hotel in Italy." She missed seeing him in the rakish uniform he had worn as an officer, which had looked so good on him. But Achille would reach the highest rung possible in his profession.

"She's from Maloja, Mama. But she speaks Italian like most of the people from this region. Her dialect is very close to the Italian language." The most important thing, he told himself, was to keep calm.

"Dialect?" Signora Robustelli asked, as if she had just sat down on a needle. "I hope that the accent isn't strong. You know how important I considered it in bringing you up for you always to speak perfect, elegant Italian. I certainly hope your children will not speak a *dialect*."

Achille took a deep breath. She was here, and he couldn't change that. Unfortunately, she had appeared at the least favorable moment. The smartest thing would be to avoid any arguments and to get rid of her as soon as possible.

"We don't have any children as yet," he said in a calm, clear tone. "I'm sure you wouldn't like it either if we did, right? And if it's all right with you, we'll go now to have a cup of coffee together with Andrina. And then I'll have someone take you to your hotel in Sils-Maria, because I have my hands full. Tomorrow there'll be a Venetian Ball here, and I have to make sure that everything functions properly."

Signora Robustelli nodded, reluctant but resigned. Of course, she'd hoped to have the evening meal with her son, but, well, her Achille was a very busy man. Naturally, you had to take that into consideration.

Andrina had exchanged her day off with Clara, one of the other chambermaids, so that she could prepare for her first meeting with Achille's mother. She intended to wear her Sunday dress, the one she wore when she went dancing with Robustelli. And she had a terrific idea. Luca had mentioned a couple of times that the *straniera* was wearing a golden locket when they found her in the mountains. Andrina had never seen Nika wear it, but she must keep the jewel hidden somewhere in her room. And for this one important day, Andrina thought she would borrow Nika's locket and then immediately put it back in its place without her having noticed anything.

She knew Nika's room was never locked, and when nobody answered her knock, she slipped into the room without being seen by anyone. She lifted the mattress, didn't find it there; opened the top drawer of the bureau, took out the black woolen shawl, discovered the locket, and was out of the room in no time.

Such a valuable piece of jewelry! How did Nika happen to have it? And why did she hide it so carefully? Had she stolen the piece? Maybe it was the real reason for her having run away? No one really knew anything about her.

Andrina passed a finger over the engraved rose, the red jewel in the middle. She couldn't contain her curiosity, opened the locket, but didn't find a picture in it, no jewel, only a small, folded piece of paper. She couldn't make out the words. Disappointed, she put the paper back in the locket, placed the chain around her neck, and opened the uppermost button on her dress so that one could see the locket. She pinched her cheeks to give them a pink blush and waited for Achille to call for her.

Emma Schobinger had rarely felt as certain about a decision as now. She had decided she was going to St. Moritz at the first possible moment. And she was going there without her husband. Instead, she asked her cousin Frieda to accompany her. She had made an appointment on the telephone with Dr. Bernhard. She was beside herself. To dissolve the engagement! Bad enough that Adrian's family had distanced themselves on the grounds of Mathilde's having tuberculosis. What an affront to her and Franz, and of course Mathilde too. But still, Adrian was sticking by his fiancée, and she assumed that his parents would one day become reconciled to his decision. He was, after all, their only son and the inheritor of the bank. And now this had to happen.

Who had put such silly notions into the child's head? Didn't she, Emma, have a bad feeling right from the outset about having Betsy accompany Mathilde? Betsy was absolutely the wrong example for a curious young woman not yet sure of herself. And the mountains. Emma held her forehead as if she had a headache. If you stayed up there too long, you'd probably go mad. But all this was reversible, once she had Mathilde back home with her.

"It's very simple, Mama. I don't love him," Mathilde said.

"Oh, so you don't love him. And when did you discover that?"

"I've felt it for quite a long time, but I wasn't sure enough to talk about it before I came here. Well . . . actually, I never loved him," Mathilde admitted meekly. She had been utterly surprised by her mother's visit, an effect Emma Schobinger had carefully anticipated.

"Well." With an ungracious gesture, Emma Schobinger sent the nurse who had just come in with a thermometer out of the room. "I want to say something to you," she went on. "It's nice to love the man you marry. But after a few years it all takes on a different aspect, and by then you realize that you're still married."

"But Mama," Mathilde said, shocked, "do you mean to say that you don't love Papa anymore?"

"Yes, I do, but in a different way. But we're not talking about your father and me now, we're discussing your behavior. And that, my dear child, is unacceptable." Even though Emma Schobinger wasn't tall, she seemed just then imposing and implacable.

Mathilde wondered whether she should be honest and mention Edward. But then she thought it would be better to go step-by-step and not to mention anything too early. For that might have an even more negative effect on the situation.

"Is there another man involved?" her mother asked as if she had read Mathilde's mind. She wasn't naïve. "Adrian mentioned a certain Edward who comes to visit you. More often, in fact, than is appropriate for an engaged young woman."

"Oh, that's nothing," said Mathilde who had decided to fight for her point as vigorously as her mother. The engagement had to be dissolved first, before Edward became involved. And so she said casually, "I hope I'm permitted to have visitors. The doctors all say that loneliness doesn't help recovery."

"Rubbish," Emma Schobinger said.

The blood rushed to Mathilde's head so that her curls looked as though an electric current had passed through them. She took a deep breath. "Up here, I've come to realize, and it's partly because of my illness, that I don't want to spend my life with Adrian. I know that there's nothing wrong with him, Mother, that he'd be a perfect son-in-law and husband." She drew herself up again and forced herself to look directly at her mother, "But I want to be in love with the man I marry."

Emma Schobinger got up. She knew that Mathilde liked to involve her in long drawn-out discussions. "None of this matters," she said tersely. "You are going to marry Adrian. And leave your illness out of it. No dramatic fever please. Dr. Bernhard told me an hour ago that he is very pleased with your state of health. He sees no reason why you wouldn't be cured and released in a couple of months."

"I won't marry Adrian," Mathilde said in a firm tone of voice. "And certainly not just because *you* want me to."

Emma was shocked. It wasn't possible that her daughter had lost all respect for her mother. Mathilde wasn't doing herself a favor with such impertinences. "Just so you know," she said coolly as she was about to leave, "I have asked Dr. Bernhard to give me some addresses of tuberculosis sanatoriums near Zurich."

Andrina was just what Signora Robustelli had expected: the sort of woman who wasn't at all appropriate for Achille. Pretty, buxom, vain, and with a tendency to recklessness. A woman who would ensnare a responsible man and then ruin him.

It was obvious that the young woman was ambitious. That might have been a positive trait, but certain details bothered the signora. A young woman with good judgment didn't get all dressed up like this for her first meeting with the family of the man she was hoping to marry. The girl was wearing, to put it mildly, a not-very-tasteful Sunday dress on a normal workday, as well as a valuable piece of jewelry that fit neither with the dress nor its wearer. Signora Robustelli didn't want to jump to conclusions, but this just didn't look good.

Surprisingly, the conversation began to falter not because of Signora Robustelli, but because of Achille. All this time Andrina had been polite and attentive, and the signora was even beginning to like her because she didn't talk as much nonsense as the signora had expected. On the other hand, Achille seemed not to be paying attention. The conversation meandered on for a while without any high or low points. Andrina poured Achille and the signora more coffee. Then she suggested that she leave.

"Achille, I'm sure you'd like to stay a while alone with your mother. You haven't seen each other for a long time. If you will excuse me, Signora Robustelli, I was very happy that you were prepared to meet me."

She got up. Achille's mother gave her a point for politeness, but her son, surprisingly, said in an unusually brusque tone, "Wait, Andrina, I'll go outside with my mother and call her a carriage. Stay here till I come back. I won't be long."

Andrina nodded obediently. She was surprised. What was happening? He wasn't himself; he was different. They had drunk coffee in his office, and she now sat down again. It didn't feel right. She didn't sit in his chair behind the desk, which is what she would have liked to do, but she lingered close enough to get a look at the letters that lay there, opened. But like most of the people in the village, she hadn't gotten very far along with reading, and before she could decipher anything, Robustelli had come back into the room.

"So," he said, closing the door behind him. "Now give me the necklace you're wearing and tell me where you got it. I've never seen you wear it, and it would surprise me to know that it belonged to your mother."

Yet that's just what she had almost told him. Instead, she said nothing, just handed him the locket. She had never seen him this stern. She had just wanted to look pretty for his mother. Why was he so upset?

Achille examined the locket carefully. "This is a coat of arms," he said. "A family's coat of arms that I've seen before. If I'm not mistaken, it's the coat of arms of an old established Venetian family. How in heaven's name did you get it?"

Andrina had an uneasy feeling in the pit of her stomach. The *straniera* had landed her in a real fix. She had destroyed everything, Andrina's entire life, her future. It was obvious that Achille was angry. Now he probably wouldn't marry her, and it was Nika's fault. Andrina stubbornly refused to say anything, pursed her lips.

"Come on now, Andrina, tell me where you got it!"

"It belongs to Nika. She hid it among her things. I just intended to borrow it, to look pretty when you introduced me to your mother . . ."

Robustelli, whose reputation and self-respect was based on his correctness, shook his head. "You didn't borrow it, you stole it. Or did you ask Nika for permission?"

Andrina was angry at her fiancé. He was behaving like a teacher or a priest. That was hard to take considering that he himself was obviously in love with the *straniera*, just like Segantini. Go to hell with the bitch, she almost cried out. But then she thought better of it. "I didn't ask her. She hides it from everybody. But Luca told me that she had it. She was wearing it when Gian and Luca found her. I was going to put it right back in her bureau."

"You won't be doing that now." Signor Robustelli was pacing up and down and thinking.

"I'm going to keep the locket here."

Achille Robustelli did not believe in divine Providence. His Christian faith was not strong enough for that. Not did he believe in coincidence. He believed in precision, prudence, clever foresight, sober logic, and above all, the importance of proper and decent behavior. Yet now, he began to feel doubt. For suddenly, unbelievable currents of feeling struggled inside him. He felt pursued by coincidence, and if he had been superstitious—given all these meaningful omens—he wouldn't have known how to save himself.

Here he was now, holding Nika's locket, her one treasure, and the secret of her life's story that she herself couldn't decipher. She needed someone to help her. And of all people, it was Andrina who had put the locket into his hands, forcing him to think about Nika—Nika, whom *she* couldn't stand and considered her rival.

And indeed, as luck would have it, he had recognized the damask rose with the ruby. One of the soldiers from his old unit, a fellow officer, had been a member of an old Venetian family, and this was their coat of arms. They hadn't been close friends, and Achille wasn't sure whether he remembered the name right. If he wasn't mistaken, it was Damaskinos—yes, a Greek name—Damaskinos.

Achille examined the piece of jewelry, but he didn't open the locket. It belonged to Nika, and he had neither the right nor any desire to open it. He was morally upright, even if there was no one present.

But the negative side of holding the locket was that all the feelings he had learned to suppress now swept over him, and put him in turmoil. Now the thought of marrying Andrina made him sad and unhappy. He felt full of inner conflict, consumed by an ill-fated affection for Nika who loved another and would never reciprocate his feelings.

Achille Robustelli, who had been praised in the military for his objectivity, common sense, and strategic perspicacity, was hopelessly caught in the tangle of his own emotions.

"Oh, Baba," Andrina said, stopping Segantini's servant on the village street. "I haven't seen you in ages! I'm just coming from the hotel, and you can imagine how demanding the hotel guests are." Baba was in a hurry and wanted to keep going, but Andrina held on to her arm. "Baba, just one moment. There's something I've wanted to ask you for a long time. Does Signora Bice know that Signor Segantini constantly goes to see the *straniera*?"

Everybody in the village knew who the *straniera* was.

"It's really none of my business," Andrina continued, "but everyone at the hotel knows about it. A guest, a very influential lady, told me the other day, that she had met the two in St. Moritz. Well, I don't think that's right and proper. But no doubt, there was some reason for the outing, and your signora didn't mind."

Baba's face froze. She didn't like Andrina. Everybody said that Andrina wanted to be somebody she wasn't. Poor Benedetta; she really had back luck with her children—Gian, who wasn't all there, Luca, dead, and this girl here, who was never satisfied.

"I'm sure the signora knows about it," Baba answered, dismissively. "I have to go now. The hotel isn't the only place where people have work to do." She released her arm from Andrina's grip and hurried off.

Baba hadn't let on that Andrina's words had left their mark. Wasn't she his faithful confidante? Didn't she carry his paints everywhere for him, wasn't she the one who read aloud to him, and with whom he shared his ideas? Yes, and hadn't she even been the model for many of his pictures and the one who devotedly cared for his family, even if her meager monthly salary was often paid late? Didn't she sacrifice everything for him? What was he looking for from the *straniera*?

She would have preferred not to believe Andrina. But she knew better. She herself had wondered why Signor Segantini sometimes sent her directly home while he made a detour.

❧

Nika stood in front of the enlarged photographs that Fabrizio Bonin had hung in the Spa Hotel Maloja, furtively glancing at them. The photographs fascinated her and she kept secretly going back whenever there were no guests around. They were not color photographs, and yet they captured the light and shadow in many incredible ways. The photos showed scenes from the everyday life of Venice, a city that Nika knew nothing about. The city seemed to be rising out of the water; canals crisscrossed it the way streets did in other cities. And it was the water with its reflections that created the great abundance of light and shadow, movement and stillness. Nika was enraptured. The photographs resembled paintings, but they seemed more alive, more present; it was almost as if at any moment the people in them would move and begin to speak, even step out of the picture.

"Do you like the photographs, Signorina?" a voice behind her asked.

Nika was startled and turned around. The young man with the brown eyes was standing directly behind her. Warily Nika looked everywhere, but the hallway was empty. "Yes, I like them very much!" she said softly, adding even more softly, "I'm not allowed to talk with the guests."

Fabrizio Bonin shook his head. "What peculiar rules," he said, whispering in turn, which made Nika laugh. "But you must be allowed to answer their questions. If not, it would make you a very impolite employee."

The whispering lent their conversation a note of confidentiality, and they both had to laugh.

"I have to get back to work now," Nika said, covering her mouth, "but I like the pictures very much. They are as beautiful as works of art."

"Photography *is* an art," Fabrizio said, "a new art with a great future and unimaginable possibilities. And unlike painting, you can even make a good living with it if you do it right. Look, do you see how wonderfully light and shadow are depicted here?"

He pointed to one of the photographs and was tempted to take her hand, to lead it to the one he meant. But he didn't.

Nika nodded enthusiastically. "And you really think that photographers can make a living with their art?"

"I *know* they can. Venice is a photographer's city. And how about the city?" asked Bonin, still whispering as if he enjoyed the secrecy and confidentiality of their whispered exchange. "Do you like the city too? It's my home. I live there."

"Yes, the city too," Nika said, smiling. "But now I really have to . . ."

"All right, all right, just one more moment," he begged her. "I want to tell you how proud I am of my city. There is no other city that has so much light yet is so full of shadows, or captures the sky in the mirror of its water . . ."

Nika looked at him. "I could listen to you forever," she whispered and hurried off.

"I would like to show you Venice," Fabrizio said softly. But she didn't hear him. He gestured as if to wave to her, and when she turned quickly, she saw the gesture and smiled at him.

Segantini intercepted Nika outside the hotel. He said, "I have to speak with you. Let's go down by the lake."

He went on ahead, not waiting for her answer. Rowboats floated quietly on the water, the first shadows were forming on the plateau.

"I don't have much time," Nika said. "I have to be in the dining room."

She was still angry with Segantini because the painting had been so little about her. But it wasn't just injured vanity that she felt. She didn't understand the idea behind the picture. Segantini's thoughts were foreign to her. "The picture shows a girl standing at the threshold to womanhood," he had said, and then, he had added a monster. In her life, Nika had never had much opportunity for being vain, for self-absorbed gazing into mirrors, and so she didn't understand his loathing of it.

"Come sit down with me on this bench. It's important," Segantini said. He didn't seem to be feeling well, nervously crossing and uncrossing his legs, and fiddling with his vest.

She reluctantly sat down next to him. Why was he always talking to her as if she were a child or as if he had to order her to do something?

"It would be better if you left this place," he said without any transition.

Nika's ears began to ring. It was as if a storm were breaking out, as if a shrill, whistling wind were approaching with such force that she couldn't breathe. Then the present came back into focus. Yes, there was Segantini, but everything was still revolving. It took moments for things to come to a standstill again.

"Aren't you well?" Segantini asked, taking her arm.

"No, I don't feel well," Nika mumbled, getting up. Segantini pulled her back onto the bench.

"Wait, Nika. I want to tell you about what happened. Andrina Biancotti went to Baba and told her you were brazenly flirting with me. And that it had already gone so far that I came to see you whenever possible."

Nika listened apathetically.

"Nika," he shook her. "Baba didn't come to tell me; she went to Bice with the story. And of course, she wasn't happy about that. I love Bice, and I need her. You have to leave. Bice is demanding it, even though I've told her a thousand times that nothing ever happened between us. Nika?"

Nika didn't move.

"It's better if you leave. I do keep thinking of you," he said haltingly. "That much is true, but it isn't good. For none of us. Say something!"

She shook her head.

"I know your story," he went on. "I wanted to do something for you. You have talent; you deserve another life than the one that's become your lot. I know full well what that's like." He tried to look into her eyes. "My life was saved by a man in the reform school in Milan where they sent me after the police picked me up for vagrancy . . . I was saved by a man there who recognized my talent for drawing and painting. They wanted to train me as a shoemaker, except I was no good at putting soles on shoes. But he made it possible for me to draw. And that way, you see, art became my home. I wanted to show you that people like you can find a home in art. You know my story. My brother died the same year I was born; then my chronically ill mother died, and then my father left me in horrible Milan with a bitter stranger who didn't know what to do with me."

Segantini's gaze became unfocused, distant. Shadows gradually fell over the Maloja basin. How well he knew all that; how many thousands of times had he watched it. "Back then, as a child, I ran away over and over again, looking for a place where I could feel good, searching for a homeland. Just like you. And then—of all places, in the reform school, in the Riformatorio Marchiondi—someone realized that I had talent. That in this talent I could find my home. I found the only remedy there is against loneliness; believe me, Nika. Love is good for a lot of things, but it doesn't help against this ultimate, profound loneliness. But every human being has some gift. For people like us, it's especially important to discover it."

Gently he shook her by the shoulders. "Do you see now that I understand you very well? Don't we have to love each other when we share so many painful experiences? Who else knows it: this loneliness that's like a sea without a shore."

Now at last Nika smiled, and Segantini in relief put his arm around her. "I wish you could bloom like an alpine rose. I love that flower. It is strong and tough and full of fire. You're strong. People like you and me are strong. Otherwise we would have died as children when we were left behind and only loneliness remained. Do you hear?"

She nodded and got up. "I have to go to work."

"Wait just a moment, Nika! Our paths crossed here. But they must separate now. Not only because I am begging you to leave. My path led upward from the cities of the plains, away from the noise, into the heights. Into the stillness. I want to paint nature more and more convincingly, more simply, in a more spiritual way. You are young. You must first go down into the world."

"Yes," Nika said. "But I won't allow you to send me away just because it's convenient for you." She didn't notice that she was suddenly speaking to him familiarly, using the informal *tu* rather than the formal *Lei*, as if they were at last so close that they could speak to each other on the same level. Nor did she feel the pain in the hand she had clamped tightly around the mirror shard in her apron pocket while they were talking.

"Give me your hand in good-bye," Segantini said. "Tomorrow I'm going to my winter quarters in Soglio."

She pulled her hand out of her apron pocket and placed it on his chest.

Segantini stood watching her walk along the narrow avenue up toward the hotel. Her hair glowed in the light of the setting sun. Then she disappeared into the shadow and the colors faded.

They changed horses in Promontogno outside the Hotel Bregaglia. The Maloja Pass descended almost a thousand meters vertically, and from the top, it had looked almost as if the post coach were going to plunge down the pass into the valley rather than stay on the road. Once the descent was over, the coachman had carefully guided the coach and horses through the narrow streets of the Bregaglia Valley villages, through Casaccia, Vicosoprano, Borgonovo, and Stampa.

Segantini, who had gone on ahead without his family, leaving behind numerous unpaid bills, got out to stretch his legs. On the mountain slope to his right, high up on a rock terrace, clung the small village. The bell of the old church in Soglio rang the hour.

Segantini smiled. It sounded as if a smith were hammering on his metal anvil. How close his Italy was from here. One day he, Segantini, son of Agostino Segatini, would no longer be stateless, but an Italian citizen with an Italian passport. Some day his efforts at the various government bureaus would be successful.

He would no longer be considered a deserter in Austria and a man without documents in Italy, and he would no longer have to renew every year his permission to live for another twelve months in Italy. One day he would visit the town where he was born, Arco, at the northern end of Lake Garda. Arco, a town he was not allowed to set foot in because it was Austrian, and when he was young he had not served in the Austrian army, had shirked the country's military service.

Bluish smoke rose from the *cascine*, the huts where the chestnuts were dried. It snaked up between the autumn-colored trees toward the sky in thin ribbons. Segantini breathed in the clear, cool fall air and gazed up at the cliff. He knew that there were golden eagles up there. On overcast days, they would plunge down into the villages, killing sheep and capturing chickens faster than the eye could see. When hunting for eagles, you had a royal opponent who with one wing beat could shatter a man's arm as if it were glass.

The horses pulling the coach struggled up the narrow road to Soglio. Now and then, the clouds would part to give a view of the mountaintops. Palazzo Salis, a splendid structure, was an appropriate place to stay. The pension that occupied the structure's second story would be his home until spring.

The rooms for the Segantini family were ready. He climbed up the broad granite stairway of the Palazzo. The pension proprietor unlocked the heavy doors set into stone and stepped aside to let Segantini enter. The old wooden floors creaked under his boots. The tile stove was warm, and the wooden shutters had been opened so that the glowing light of the late afternoon hour could fall into the room and on the baroque gilt of the old furniture. The coffered ceilings, decorated walls, and doors of larch wood were masterworks of carpentry from a bygone time. His brother-in-law Bugatti would have appreciated all this.

Segantini took off his laced boots, opened the windows wide, greeted the bizarre peaks of the Badile and the Sciora on the other side of the valley, and dropped onto the four-poster bed with the elaborate pillars. He looked up at the canopy over his head, where flowers, plants, and birds of paradise were all intertwined. Just before he fell asleep on the bed after the difficult journey, he thought of the alpine panorama that he definitely wanted to tackle next year and of Bice who would soon follow him with the children. Every separation from her was hard for him. But as his eyes closed, his thoughts became interwoven like the patterns on the baldachin; he saw Nika's face turning away from him and the red handprint her bloody hand had left on his white shirt.

Bice presumably knew how to wash out bloodstains. But he'd rather not give her the shirt.

The next morning he wrote to Bice. And to Alberto Grubicy, his dealer, asking him for an urgent transfer of money by return mail.

The Venetian Ball

Nika hardly slept that night. Even before the sun rose she went down to the lake and walked along the shore, shivering. The nights were getting colder; the first hoarfrost blanketed the lawns in the mornings. As she turned to go back to the hotel, she suddenly saw Achille Robustelli walking toward her.

He had slept badly too and needed the fresh air to wake him up.

"Segantini told me to leave," she said when they met on the path. Dawn was slowly breaking, and she could see the surprised expression on his face.

"Why are you telling me this?" Achille asked.

"I don't know," Nika replied.

"And I couldn't sleep," Achille said.

They walked along silently.

"It's important that I talk with you," he finally said.

"Now?"

"Yes, it would be good. After that you'll probably leave even without Segantini's sending you away."

Nika kicked aside a branch the wind had brought down. "I won't let myself be sent away," she answered. "I haven't hurt anyone."

"It's all right. Never mind."

Robustelli unlocked his office and turned on the light. Nika was shaking; she was tired and cold.

"Wait, I have a blanket somewhere here," Achille murmured. He found it and wrapped it around her shoulders. He turned away when she looked at him the way she had once before already—as if she knew him very well. He saw that her right hand was bandaged and said, "That won't be good for the Venetian Ball this evening."

"It'll be all right by then," she said, and again gazed at him in such a way that he had to look away. He went over to his desk drawer.

"Don't be shocked by what I'm going to show you now. It's irrelevant how I got it. Sometimes it's best not to ask too many questions." He took the locket out of the drawer. Nika gave a soft cry, but by then Robustelli had already put it into her hand.

"How did you get it?" Nika had jumped up out of her chair and was going toward the door.

"I already told you, that's not important. It's more important for you to listen to what I'm going to tell you." He gently pushed her back down onto the chair. "Someone took the locket from your room, and by accident, it came into my hands. But there's a good side to it." He didn't know quite how to go on from there so as not to frighten her too much. "Nika, there's a rose engraved on the locket. I am familiar with this rose. It's the floral emblem of a Venetian family."

Nika's face had turned white.

"I'll get you a cup of coffee," Achille said, continuing. "You told me that you want to find your mother. Now at least you know where you should be looking." He had never told her that he had found out more about her, that he had gone to Mulegns, or that Segantini had told him her story.

Nika just nodded, dazed.

If you've been looking all your life for something, then you can't feel glad when you find it. Not right away.

When Achille returned with the coffee, Nika was still sitting there motionless. He held the cup out to her. She took one sip, then another. And then the cup in her hand slowly began to tremble. It seemed to him as if he were watching his news gradually getting through to her. Achille felt at a complete loss. Not because he wasn't able to take a trembling person in his arms and console her, but because it was Nika who was sitting in front of him. He was afraid to touch her, that he might do something stupid.

Nika was still silent, and so he continued, "I told you already that I'm absolutely sure about the coat of arms. But there are two hotel guests staying here just now, Count Primoli and Signor Bonin, to whom, with your permission, I shall show the locket. The count is very familiar with Venice, and Bonin is a Venetian. If one of them can confirm my suspicions, you will know where you should look."

Nika leaned forward, put her hand on the desktop, moved it toward Robustelli's hand, hesitated, and then put her hand on his.

"Why? Why are you doing all this for me?" she asked softly.

"Oh," he said, shrugging.

She smiled that smile which Segantini had helped him understand, squeezed his hand. "Thank you very much."

Nika thought that he blushed a little, but then he drew his hand away, sat up as if at attention, and said formally, "You are welcome."

The moment of intimacy was over. Nika got up, put the blanket on the chair.

"May I ask you something else, Signor Robustelli?"

"Of course." Achille cleared his throat and casually looked for his box of Emser pastilles in his drawer.

"Did you open the locket?"

"No," he answered truthfully.

She opened the locket, took out the scrap of paper, and held it out to Robustelli.

"I can't read what it says there. There are letters that I don't know. But maybe you could . . .?"

He took the piece of paper, unfolded it, and smoothed it out. The writing was already faded, the paper fragile and slightly soiled, but he saw at once that the sentence was written in Greek. "No," he shook his head, "I'm not as smart or well educated as you think. But I can tell that it's Greek. We should ask Count Primoli."

Nika knew that she had to make use of this opportunity. And that there was no one she would more readily give a free hand to than Robustelli. "Yes, please ask him. Show him the piece of paper too." She got up and handed him the locket. "I am truly grateful to you. Thank you."

He had gotten up and taken a step toward her, but then stopped abruptly.

She shook his hand, and for a moment she thought he was about to embrace her. But he just pressed her hand and accompanied her to the door.

✑✑

A large number of workers were transforming the hotel ballroom into a Venetian scene, complete with baldachin-topped gondolas in which the guests would be served by waiters dressed as gondoliers to the strains of music by Venetian masters. Robustelli was hurrying to the ballroom because he hoped to find Signor Bonin or the count there. He was in luck. Bonin was reading the paper and having a cup of coffee. He nodded to Robustelli, who used the opportunity to say, "Signor Bonin, how lucky that I found you here. I know that you're leaving tomorrow."

Bonin lowered the paper. "That's true. I'm going to Paris with the count and then returning to Venice. But I'm already sad to be leaving here. I liked it very much."

Achille smiled. "Signor Bonin, before you leave, I have a favor to ask. May I show you something? It won't take long. You're a Venetian, and I think . . ." He took the golden locket out of his vest pocket and held it toward Fabrizio. "I believe I once saw this rose in a Venetian family's coat of arms."

Fabrizio took the medallion and examined it from all sides. At that moment, Primoli joined them. He had been looking for Bonin. He peered over Bonin's shoulder with curiosity. And it was the count who, without hesitation, said, "But of course, this is a full-blown Damascene rose with a ruby, the coat of arms of the Damaskino family. An old, wealthy family of Greek origin in Venice."

Fabrizio nodded in agreement, and Primoli, who had many connections among the leading families of Venice, went on, "There's a Greek district in the city where many rich merchants and printers live; these Venetian Greeks live in their own quarter near San Marco. They have a *scuola* for charity cases and their own church, the Chiesa dei Greci."

Fabrizio returned the locket to Robustelli.

"The count is right. The Greeks who live in Venice have money and influence. Many of the families have been resident in the city for centuries. I am also familiar with this coat of arms."

Achille Robustelli found himself having two conflicting visions. In the one, he saw himself giving the beautiful Nika Damaskinos a passionate kiss. In the other, he was embracing Andrina, in gratitude for her little theft. "Gentlemen," he said, "thank you. I don't want to trouble you any further. But I do have another question. Does either of you know Greek?"

Primoli nodded.

And now Achille, whose mother was on good terms with the Lord and often sent a quick prayer heavenward, did as she would have done. But unlike her, he did not quickly cross himself. He felt he had to somehow express his thanks and relief.

James had talked Edward into going with him to Maloja for the Venetian Ball, even though his friend had arrived only a few hours before from Zurich. The long journey to St. Moritz had given Edward some perspective on what had happened, but he was still nervous and didn't want to leave Mathilde alone for the evening. But, finally, he did agree because James intended to leave the next day. His suitcases all stood packed and ready at the Pension Veraguth, and this was the last evening the two friends would be spending together in the Engadine.

There was no way he could avoid it. Dr. Bernhard had told Mathilde that Emma Schobinger had indeed asked him for the names of other sanatoriums for diseases of the lungs, and Mathilde realized that her mother would act as quickly as possible. Edward had tried to calm Mathilde. But she had reproached him for not wanting to fight for her. They had had their first argument since they'd met.

"Aren't you getting a little too upset?" Edward asked.

"You're not taking me seriously," Mathilde said.

"What do you mean?" Edward replied. "It's just that panic isn't appropriate right now. We don't even know yet what your father's reaction will be."

"You mean, it will all be much easier once I'm gone from here? When they've moved me elsewhere? And assured Adrian that I'll marry him?"

"I just want us to think about this calmly," he retorted.

That upset her even more, and she said heatedly, "You just don't want to fight for me. Just like back when you didn't fight for your Emily and just played the casual friend." She was profoundly disappointed in him and bit her tongue to keep from accusing him of being a coward.

Edward said nothing. The arrow had hit its mark.

"Let's discuss this further once you've pulled yourself together." It was hard for him not to tell her that she wasn't the Empress of China; she couldn't send her fighters into battle whenever she chose to.

"No!" she cried. "You are going to stay here now and tell me if you want to stand up for us before my parents create a fait accompli, or if you simply want to admit defeat the way you did with Emily!"

He said nothing in answer to that. Just picked up his hat and left.

But she was right. He hadn't fought for Emily. He hadn't even tried to find out the reasons for her dissolving the engagement. Nor did he confront his rival. And he had not confronted him because he thought that sort of cockfighting was silly and unbearable.

However, this time, without even discussing it with Mathilde and trying to settle their differences, he had climbed into the post coach and gone to Zurich. The telephone operator at the post and telegraph office there told him that only one Franz Schobinger was listed. He asked for his office number, called Mathilde's father, and asked for an appointment to meet him in the city. Franz Schobinger agreed without enthusiasm to meet the unknown young man at the Konditorei Sprüngli at the Paradeplatz, since he saw only further trouble ahead.

What Edward had to say was said quickly. He disclosed all the basic information about his background and his financial affairs and asked for Mathilde's hand.

Franz Schobinger wasn't enthusiastic about this new development. "As you know, I already have one prospective son-in-law," he said without emotion. "And that's actually enough. Above all, my wife considers the planned marriage very advantageous."

This statement made a certain hope rise in Edward's heart, for it didn't sound as if there was complete agreement to this on the father's part. Yet common courtesy kept him from asking more questions.

Franz Schobinger didn't dislike this new contender for his daughter's hand. Quite the contrary. True, he was still a bit young and rough at the edges, but so was Adrian. And what Edward had told him about his family spoke well for him. Certainly no worse than Adrian's background. Oh my God, these eternal lovers' squabbles, thought Franz Schobinger. And what for? Did he go through all this in his youth? If so, he didn't remember it now. In any case, a few years ago, he had fallen seriously in love, but that was another story. With a careful twisting motion, he removed the ash from his cigar and said, "You aren't expecting an answer from me right now, my dear Mr. Holbroke. That's the name, right? And not least, and beyond all the other complications, there's the fact that in the event this goes through, we'd probably lose touch with our daughter. That would only add to the other problems. I don't know how happy parents are on the whole at the idea of their daughters living abroad."

And so Edward left again—without an answer, as was to be expected, but also without a final rejection. And that's how things stood as Edward hurried back to Mathilde, even though he hadn't quite forgiven her for the hurtful things she had said.

"I won't stay long," he said by way of greeting. "I'm going with James to the Venetian Ball in Maloja, and I still have to get dressed . . ." But he was glad to see her smiling with relief as he entered her room.

In the hotel lobby, Edward and James met Count Primoli and Fabrizio.

They were clinking champagne glasses, toasting the season just ending, when James suddenly said, "Shall we meet here again for a few days next year?" He had quite forgotten that the mountains made him feel uneasy and, as he had previously kept emphasizing, that they bored him terribly. In fact, the idea began to appeal to him more and more. "We should invite Segantini to join us and Betsy. And you," he looked at Edward, "will of course bring Mathilde. How about it?"

Edward nodded. Why not come back to the place where he found Mathilde?

Nika was now one of the busy black ants helping the waiters who were serving the Venetian Ball dinner. She could see the inside of the festively lit ballroom, but was not allowed to enter. Here was Venice, like a vision before her eyes. The Venice she had admired in Count Primoli's photographs. The city where her mother had been born, and had perhaps returned to after her journey across the Alps. The city that was home to the young man with the brown eyes. Venice, city of light and shadows, and an infinity of reflections.

"Nika, I've got something for you," Achille Robustelli said a few days later. He was standing in the middle of his office and didn't ask Nika to sit down. He seemed in a hurry, which was understandable these last days of the summer season. He took a large envelope and handed it to her.

"Here is some information about the best way for you to get to Venice. I wrote down the directions, starting from Chiavenna. Up to that point you can go by post coach, but then you have to change to a train and continue by boat to Como, where you can get another train connection to Milan and on to Venice."

He dismissed her attempt to thank him, but stopped as if for reflection.

"I also wrote down how you can find the quarter where the Greeks of Venice live. The Damaskinos family probably resides there; you just have to ask for their address. The rose on your locket is indeed part of their heraldic coat of arms: a Damascene rose with a ruby. I wrote a letter that states that you worked here at the hotel and performed your work satisfactorily. It also says that we would hire you again for the coming season. It will help you if they make any difficulties at the border—after all, you have no documents."

He took a deep breath and hurried to finish what he had to say.

"There is also some money in the envelope, both Swiss and Italian. If, at the end of the season, the hotel has done well, everyone receives a bonus in recognition of their services."

Nika looked at him as if she didn't believe him, but he went on, "And the count has translated and written out what's written on the piece of paper inside your locket."

He walked over to the window, looked out as if he were expecting her to leave without saying anything else.

"Signor Robustelli?"

He turned around.

"Signor Robustelli! Aren't you going to look at me and say farewell?"

Nika walked over to stand at his side. The season was over. The guests were leaving—a great chaos of horses, carriages, servants, and luggage.

"What a mess at the end of summer," he murmured.

"What did you say?" Nika said without looking at him.

"I said, what a mess. What a mess people always create."

"But that's normal," Nika said. She laughed and redid her loose knot of hair. Her face and eyes were as clear as the lake. And in the winter, her skin would be light and white again.

"I have to get back to work," Achille said, as if he couldn't stand so close to her any longer.

"Of course, Signor Robustelli, I didn't want to keep you," Nika said. But then she added, "you must be tired. It's high time the hotel closes. I heard that you and Andrina are going to get married?"

"Yes, that's true." The conversation seemed to be getting more and more uncomfortable.

"Then all my best wishes," Nika said. And when he didn't answer, "Good-bye and . . . thank you. Thank you for everything."

"That's all right. You're welcome," he broke in.

They shook hands.

"Oh, Nika," he called as she was opening the door. "Signor Bonin asked about you. He wanted to know how come I had the locket. I told him it belonged to you."

❧❧

Nika felt sad. She couldn't understand why Signor Robustelli was suddenly acting so cool toward her. Only now, as he dismissed her without showing any emotion, did she realize how much affection he had shown her in the last few months. She would not only miss Gian and Benedetta, but also Signor Robustelli. For a moment, she thought of Segantini but immediately suppressed it. She'd better get busy packing her few things. And only then, once she was actually ready to leave, would she read what her mother had written to her years before.

For one more moment she stood, lost in thought, outside the door to Robustelli's office. She started when she felt a light touch on her shoulder.

"So, I did find you after all!"

Fabrizio Bonin was beaming. Nika took a step back as if to run away, but he shook his head and smiled. "Stay! I must ask you to forgive me for an indiscretion I committed. I found out that the locket with the heraldic emblem of the Damaskinos belongs to you—that you have excellent connections with Venice without apparently even knowing it. Signor Robustelli told me . . ." And grinning at a sudden inspiration, he added, "So actually it was Signor Robustelli who was indiscreet, and I was only curious. Which is a minor sin for a journalist, don't you agree?"

Nika couldn't help but smile at him. Only a stone could remain unaffected and refuse to be cheered by him.

"So I'm sure you'll come to Venice some day," he went on. "Will you allow me to show you the city?"

"The city where the water captures the sky?" Nika asked. He nodded seriously.

"Yes. I'll show you the most beautiful places. Spots that would make any good photographer's heart break with delight. And so that you'll be sure to find me, I've written down my address." He gave her a piece of paper and bowed. "I can't wait to see you again," he whispered.

She smiled and said nothing.

Nika put the piece of paper with Fabrizio Bonin's address— Campo San Rocco, Dorsoduro, Venezia—into Signor Robustelli's envelope, but not before gently holding it to her cheek. Then she put the envelope in with the things she would be taking on her journey the following day.

At dawn the next day, she took her bundle, softly closed the door to her room, and left the hotel that had changed her life. She went down to the lake one more time. The water, roughened by the wind, slapped against the shore in waves topped by small crowns of foam as if it was not a lake, but an infinitely wide sea. Nika felt chilled; she kneeled on the boat dock and put her hand in the cold water.

Segantini did not drive by in a four-horse carriage.

Gian no longer waited for her at Benedetta's house. He had driven the cows down from Grevasalvas and was now staying with Benedetta's sister in Soglio; the cows belonged to her. Both Gian and Nika had had tears in their eyes when they had said good-bye.

Benedetta had given her a blouse and a warm skirt of her own as a good-bye present as well as a bag to hold her things. Since Luca had died, she wasn't attached to anything anymore.

Andrina had been avoiding her; so they didn't even say good-bye.

It was time to leave Maloja. Soon the post coach would carry her down to Italy as she had always dreamed. The whistle of the train would slice through the air and the steel rails would dissect the landscape into the world she was leaving behind and the new one she would have to conquer. It was good to know that there was already one person in this new world who looked forward to welcoming her there.

Now was the moment to read the message her mother had put in the locket to accompany her on her journey; the sun was already rising in a milky sky and she had to get to the post coach station if she didn't want to miss the coach.

It was difficult for Nika to make out the count's bold, elegant handwriting, but finally she succeeded and softly read:

You will search for me and find yourself.
With love,
Your mother

"So Nika went to Venice," Achille Robustelli said to the art collector who had been patiently listening to his story. "Perhaps she was lucky there. At any rate, I never heard from her again."

"And you?" the Collector asked. "Signor Robustelli? What did you do?"

"I kept my word and got married."

"And why is this picture hanging here in your office? Does your wife approve?"

"No, she certainly wouldn't. But she is no longer here. She fell in love with one of the guests and went away with him to Milan."

"And you didn't try to get her back?" the art collector asked.

"No," Achille Robustelli replied. "But once Segantini had finished *La Vanità*, I asked him whether he would let the hotel have the picture on loan until it was sold. To be exact, let me . . ."

"And it was only right that he fulfilled your wish! He owes just as much to you as to the girl in this painting."

Achille Robustelli merely smiled.

"And tomorrow, I'll be taking Nika's portrait away from you too. What will you do? Your wife is gone, Nika, now the painting . . ."

Achille shrugged and smoothed the gray hair at his temples.

"I'm getting older. You see, the gray hair is already there. I am homesick more and more often. Maybe I'll simply go back to Italy. Segantini found a home up here. I haven't. Some people are able to find a home for themselves in the gaze of a loving partner, in nature, or in their family history. Or in art. The hotel is probably my home, this place where people meet, find each other, and lose touch again . . . But come, let's go over to the restaurant. You must be hungry and thirsty. It was a long story. Do me the pleasure and have supper with me tonight."

Three Years Later

Maloja, September 1899

In the end, it was James who actually succeeded in bringing about the meeting. Not one year later, as he, Edward, and Fabrizio Bonin had originally agreed, but three years later, in the fall of 1899.

After his stay in St. Moritz, James had finally gone to see his parents again in Berlin, and there, he had suddenly felt the desire to be closer to them once more. And so, when he was offered a very promising position with a Berlin newspaper, he settled in the city. But, although his connection with Edward was no longer as close, it did not break off entirely. Fabrizio he hadn't seen since the summer in Maloja, even though both had firmly vowed to get together.

Achille Robustelli was happy to hear from James that the friends were planning to meet at the Spa Hotel Maloja. He remembered all of them well. The name of the hotel was now Maloja Palace, but Robustelli's position there was still the same. He was touched that James had not only asked him to reserve rooms, but had also insisted, speaking for his friends as well, that Robustelli be a guest at the supper they had planned.

On September 22, 1899, three years after the splendid end-of-season Venetian Ball they'd all attended, the three arrived one by one in Maloja. The ball was still remembered as a glorious social event; for Achille, however, the memory was linked with Nika, the mystery of whose origins were revealed to her that day.

He knew it was futile to keep mulling over why he had been unable to confess his feelings either to himself or to her back then. Because, if he had declared his love for her, he would have violated his own sense of duty, and would, above all, have had to break off his engagement to Andrina, and to break his word of honor. And this would have been impossible for him. From childhood on, he had learned that you have to stand behind the thing you've pledged to do. The example of his father cast a large shadow over his life. And Nika? How would she have reacted? He didn't know what she'd felt for him then, or would have felt for him under different circumstances. And had he been in her position, wouldn't he have wanted to move toward the future, free of any attachments or ties?

Autumn was cool in the year 1899. Hoarfrost covered the large, soft cushions of grass surrounding the hotel, and they glittered in the morning sun like silvery brushes. It had already snowed heavily a few times, even down in the valley.

Achille stood at the entrance to the hotel. Shivering in his elegant dark suit, he turned up the collar, but that didn't help much; he blew on his hands, rubbed them together, and crossed them behind his back. You might have thought he was one of the handsome Italian guests just leaving—the end of another season was at hand.

One of the group who'd planned to meet that day had cancelled: Segantini. He had gone up to the Schafberg, intending to make use of the last days of fall to work on his painting, *La Natura*. It was the central piece of a planned triptych called *La Vita—La Natura—La Morte* that he hoped to show at the 1900 Paris World's Fair. His bold, ambitious idea to create an alpine panorama had failed for financial reasons. The committee of hoteliers, bankers, politicians, and journalists that had been formed for the realization of the project had sent him a letter on January 28, 1898, informing him that the proposal had been turned down. Segantini in turn rejected the committee's suggestions for a change in the size of the project and decided instead— since Grubicy was delighted by the idea—to exhibit the paintings in the form of a triptych at the Italian pavilion. There was scarcely enough time to complete the ambitious project.

He'd begun painting the left part of the triptych, *La Vita*, in 1897 in Soglio, and gotten quite far along. The picture showed the peak of the Sciora group above the Bodasca Valley as seen from Soglio. He had begun the right part of the triptych, *La Morte*, even before *La Vita*, and put it aside since it was practically finished.

The center part of the triptych, *La Natura*, was going to show the view from the Schafberg across the Upper Engadine Lakes to the Bregaglia Valley. Segantini had conceived the painting on the basis of what he remembered from an earlier climb as well as various photographs; he had painted the foreground in the vicinity of Maloja. Now he wanted to complete the painting on-site.

Robustelli was just about to go back inside the hotel when a carriage drove up. He turned around at the sound of carriage doors being opened. Fabrizio Bonin got out and immediately turned to help a lady down; Achille recognized Bonin immediately. The young lady, in a softly flowing bottle-green velvet dress, took Bonin's arm affectionately. Her hair, pinned up, glowed red from under her hat.

It was Nika. Achille fled inside, hurried into his office, and locked the door.

Fabrizio Bonin was looking forward to the evening with fewer reservations than the other men in attendance. He was anxious to meet Mathilde, whom he knew only from hearsay. Her tuberculosis had been cured, and—as he knew from James's letters—she had married Edward more than a year ago. But above all, he was looking forward to seeing James again.

By accident, James had run into Betsy in Chur, and the two had continued on to Maloja together. Betsy was relieved that she wouldn't have to meet James in the presence of Mathilde. She still bore a grudge against him as a result of the seed Kate had planted in Betsy's mind by telling her that James's behavior toward Mathilde had not been gentlemanly.

"My God, Betsy, please believe me, it really wasn't as bad as all that!" James had said when she mentioned it to him. "You seem to have remembered only the malicious gossip, whereas I always remembered your incredibly blue eyes. Aren't you being unfair? And besides, how would Mathilde and Edward ever have gotten to know each other without me?" He kissed Betsy's hand, and she sighed softly. In Zurich, several admirers had vied for her attention, but she couldn't bring herself to form a closer liaison with any of them. Since she could afford to remain undecided, she continued to enjoy her freedom. After all, she thought from time to time, you never know where indecision may lead. The thought occurred to her once again now, as she looked at James—he was still very attractive and not wearing a ring on his finger.

When the majestic façade of the grand hotel came into view along with the sparkling surface of Lake Sils on their left, Mathilde reached for Edward's hand. How many memories and emotions this landscape stirred in her! She was happy with Edward—and yet, what would it feel like to meet James again after all this time? She was a little uneasy; after all, they'd never really said good-bye to each other.

Achille Robustelli was the one who was most afraid of the get-together. How could he possibly have imagined that Nika would be returning to Maloja today on Bonin's arm? Back then Bonin had asked about her, had wanted to give her his address in Venice. Oh yes, he did remember that. Shouldn't he be happy for them? He had a strange feeling in the pit of his stomach.

Achille took his cigarette case out of the desk drawer and lit a cigarette. Closing the case, he looked at the clear reflection of his face in the silver surface. "It's your own fault, Achille," he thought. It felt good to blame himself. He would have given a lot to be able to avoid showing up at the planned supper. But that was impossible. He closed his eyes; tried to regain his accustomed equilibrium. Absentmindedly he felt for the signet ring that he no longer wore. Andrina had broken him of the habit of constantly turning it on his finger. She said it made him look silly and insecure, and that wasn't appropriate to a man in his position. And so, tired of her criticism, he'd simply taken the ring off one day. Feeling unhappy, he went over to the window. At least Segantini hadn't come, although Nika was probably hoping to see him. Achille's troubled heart felt some satisfaction at the thought that at least Segantini wouldn't get to see her.

He gazed toward the wall where Segantini's painting *La Vanità* used to hang. Even though it had hung there only a few months, it had left behind a lighter square on the wallpaper.

He was relieved when there was a knock on the door, and he was ripped from his melancholy thoughts. He went to open it.

"Signor Robustelli! How wonderful that you're still here in the same place!" Nika cried. She was no longer an employee who would stand in the doorway waiting to be asked to approach. She stepped into the room and with a bright smile extended her hand to him.

Achille's heart was pounding. His voice, usually clear and calm, failed him.

Nika looked at him, beaming. Her hair was as glorious as ever; the color of her dress flattered her light skin and brought out the blue-green of her eyes. "I'm *so* glad to see you!" she said again. He at last took her hand with that somewhat shy smile of his that had always surprised her—a man who dealt with so many people, it was surprising how shy he could be.

"Signora . . ."

"Damaskinos?" she continued for him. "Yes, that's what I call myself, even though . . ." she stopped.

Achille offered her a chair and sat down also. Then he got up again and asked if she'd like something to drink. But she shook her head. "You're all flustered," she said. "What's the matter?"

He cleared his throat. "You know, don't you, there's always this turmoil at the end of the season. Tell me, Signora . . ."

"Would you call me Nika? I would like that." For a moment, Nika felt as if tears might spring into her eyes. "But first tell me," she continued, "where is Andrina? Did you marry her? But of course. You're wearing a wedding ring."

"She is in Milan," he said, almost brusquely. "I'd rather you tell me your story. Did you find your mother? Your family?"

How concerned he is about others, Nika thought, feeling ashamed. Why had she never written to him? "I don't know why I didn't get in touch with you sooner," she said. "Maybe it was because I didn't want Andrina to find out more about me. If my story were a happy one, a triumphant one, I wouldn't have minded talking about it. But it's a sad story."

She gazed at the light square on the wall as if looking back at the last few years through a window.

"My mother died a long time ago. She died of cholera in 1884. She was still very young back then . . ." Nika faltered a moment. "She got married in Venice after she came back from a long trip through Europe. Her husband was a young business acquaintance of her father's, my grandfather. She had two sons in quick succession. The children were still little when cholera took her life. I have only one photograph of her."

Nika opened her velvet muff, took out the photo, and held it out to Achille. It showed a serious young woman leaning with her right hip against a chair back, looking directly at the viewer. Her children weren't in the picture. One couldn't tell whether she was happy or unhappy, sad or contented. Thick, dark hair emerged from under her hat. From the black-and-white photograph you couldn't tell the color of her eyes, but they were lighter than her hair.

"She was beautiful," Achille said. "You might have inherited her eye color. And her mouth, it's similar to yours." The photograph had been taken by a certain Antonio Sorgato in 1882.

"That store is still there," Nika said, pointing at the photographer's signature. "But I couldn't ask Signor Sorgato about my mother because he was dead . . ." She gently brushed her finger over the sepia-colored photo.

"How were you able to get all this information? Whom did you find there? How did your family receive you?"

Nika leaned back wearily as though she felt again the exhaustion, the pain, and the disappointment from that time.

Oh, Lord, what an adventure that journey turned out to be! Following the instructions Signor Robustelli had written down for her, she'd gotten off the post coach in Chiavenna, at the Hotel Conradi. Then she'd purchased the first train ticket she had ever bought and taken the train to Colico. The train had started with a hiss. Nika was almost paralyzed with terror. Then telegraph poles started flashing past and she felt dizzy. The speed! She felt nauseous. She hadn't eaten or drunk anything since she had started out. But she didn't dare unpack her bread there on the train, not to mention the piece of cheese Benedetta had wrapped up in a cloth for her.

After an hour, they arrived at their goal. A horse-drawn omnibus was waiting at the Colico station to take those passengers who were continuing their travels to the dock where the ship was anchored.

Nika's heart was in her throat. Before her was Lake Como with its steamboat, the engine already running. The travelers hurried across the landing stage, Nika among them, her bundle pressed to her chest, in one hand her ticket, a ticket to an unknown future.

And then finally, after she had found a seat on deck, spread the cloth in her lap, and put a piece of cheese into her mouth, the tears began to stream down her cheeks, unstoppable. The tailwind cooled her face, but more tears kept coming. They ran down her throat and dampened the locket with the emblem of the Damaskinos family; a few teardrops fell on the bread and cheese. And Nika, who kept wiping her wet face, couldn't say what it was she was crying about most: the accident that had revealed the secret of her origins, her happiness at being on her way to find her family, or her unhappiness at having lost Segantini. She cried, remembering how Benedetta had taken care of her like a mother, she cried about everything, even about the farmer who'd taken her into service, and for Mulegns. She wept because she would be homesick for the Engadine and because she was afraid of the strange land she was about to set foot in.

Achille Robustelli's dependable directions had taken Nika to the place where the Milano–Venezia train, on its narrow embankment, dove into the sparkling lagoon approaching the city of Venice. Nika was overwhelmed by her first view of the city.

Although they had been going across the water, the train station itself was on terra firma. Nika, bewildered, had taken a few steps as if to make sure that the ground would not give way. Ahead of her, there was more water. On the Grand Canal there were rowboats loaded with vegetables and potatoes. And all around her, people—old ones, young ones, women, children, elegant lady tourists with parasols accompanied by men in black suits—no different than in St. Moritz or at the Spa Hotel Maloja.

In a sudden panic, Nika clapped her hands over her ears. The place was noisy, crowded; the narrow streets lay in the shadows cast by the tall houses lining them—they would have resembled canyons in the mountains, if clotheslines had not been strung across them from one side to the other. There were tables set up outside the houses, loaded with food; the people seemed to live in the streets. Cats ran underfoot, dogs lifted their tired heads from their paws. Nika kept her hands over her ears because she didn't want to close her eyes, so afraid was she of getting lost in this strange bustling activity. The warm, humid air smelled foul and sat heavily on her anxious heart.

"Signorina, watch your baggage!" an older woman called out to her as she walked by. "Don't daydream, or you'll get the shock of your life!" The woman laughed and already she was gone. Nika had scarcely understood the woman because her Italian was so different from Nika's Bregaglia dialect and the Italian spoken by Segantini or Count Primoli.

Evening was falling over Venice. But it didn't get quiet and the streets didn't empty of people as would have been the case in the mountains. All Nika wanted to do was go and hide. A gaunt cat, with a fish head between its teeth, disappeared into a building entrance. Nika watched the cat. There was a pension in the building, and so she followed the cat and asked if they had a room available. They gave her a key and sent her up a dark, narrow staircase. The musty smell from the mildewed walls mixed with the smell of minestrone. "*Numero due*," the man called after her.

The following day, still confused and tired, she tried to find the Chiesa dei Greci. She kept having to ask for directions. She crossed countless canals, then got lost in the narrow alleys of the Ghetto, but finally found her way back to Strada Nuova. She felt as if she'd been walking for hours. The heavy air made it hard to breathe, as did the barrage of sights. Live eels writhed in a vat on a flat barge gliding past. Children jumped into the opaque green canals to cool off. There was no way of knowing how deep the canals were; you could only guess. The light captured by the water was reflected on the flaking walls of the narrow houses. Exhausted,

Nika sat down on the edge of a fountain in the middle of a small square. From a church façade, saints and angels looked down on her, white with golden halos. A young woman stopped in front of her and asked if she needed help.

"Yes," Nika said weakly. "I was looking for the Piazza San Marco."

"But that's right around the corner there," the young woman said, pointing. "You'll be there in ten paces."

And it was true. Nika stepped out of a narrow street into the light and found herself standing in the Piazza San Marco.

Finding the house itself had been easy. Everyone in the Calle Magazzin knew the palazzo of the Damaskinos family.

Nika lifted the door knocker to knock on the door. It was a heavy brass lion's paw. She knocked once more, harder.

An elderly woman opened the door.

"Good day," Nika said, "I'd like to speak with Signor Damaskinos or the signora."

The woman asked, "Who may I say is calling?"

"Nika Damaskinos," Nika said boldly.

The woman, whose face was not discernible in the dark of the hallway, was silent for a moment. Then she said, "Wait here, please," in a voice that was as inscrutable as her face. "I'll ask whether someone here will see you." She closed the large door, and one could hear her steps receding.

Nika stood there in the afternoon heat. She touched the locket at her throat. So this was her family's house, and this the city of her origin, her country.

The tall door had iron fittings; it opened again. "Come in," the woman said, "I'll take you to the master of the house. Signor Damaskinos doesn't have much time and says he has never heard of you." The servant, bent with age, led Nika up to the second floor.

A large room opened up before her. A splendid chandelier made of milky glass hung from the high wooden ceiling. Carpets covered the marble floor. The woman pointed to a sofa standing against the wall directly by the stairway. Then she disappeared through one of the doors leading to various other rooms. Nika sat there, a petitioner, a beggar in the house of her parents and grandparents. The coolness enveloped her.

An old man came through one of the doors, approached Nika, and looked her up and down with keen, penetrating eyes. She rose, but he had his arms crossed at his back and did not extend his hand to her.

"What can I do for you?" he asked icily and took a step back as if to observe her better that way.

"Good afternoon," Nika said, and when he didn't return her greeting, she continued. "My name is Nika. Twenty years ago, I was abandoned with this locket by a young woman and her companion—at a post coach station in the mountains in Switzerland. No one could tell me who my mother was or what family I belonged to. But Count Primoli recognized the heraldic emblem on this locket." She gathered all her courage, looked straight at the man's expressionless face, and said, "That's why I'm here. My name is Nika Damaskinos."

The man laughed out loud. "A lot of people would like to claim the name Damaskinos. It is an old and venerable name and smells of money." The man laughed again, but by now his face had assumed a menacing expression. "My daughter is dead, and she had only two sons. Show me your locket!" He gestured for her to take off the piece of jewelry. But Nika only held the locket, still on its chain around her neck, out to him. The man bent down; the corners of his mouth twitched. Nika took heart. Yes, he did recognize the coat of arms; she was quite sure of that. Now the ghastly business would end, and he would look at her in a friendlier way.

But instead, he grabbed the chain as if he wanted to tear it off her neck. Instinctively Nika took a step backward.

"You little thief!" the man cried. "What an outrage! Back then, my daughter said that the locket had been stolen on the trip. And now, after all these years you want to profit from the theft—whoever may have been the actual thief at the time . . ." He reached for the bell to call the servants. But before he could grab Nika with his other hand, she ran down the palazzo stairway and out into the street. Turning into Calle Moruzzi, she disappeared into the crowd.

In no time, she had lost her sense of direction. She seemed to be going in circles, seemed to keep turning into the same campo, each time closer to exhaustion. When a little barking dog jumped toward her, Nika, already perplexed and confused, was scared out of her wits and began to tremble. She started to run, panic-stricken. Crossing the Grand Canal, she realized she had never been in this part of the city. But here, too, the labyrinth was endless, the light shimmered on the canals, one bridge followed another.

At last, she was in a square dominated by the brick façade of an enormous church. The wings of the church door were open. She entered the gentle dusk of the nave and sank down in one of the pews. At the front, at the altar, a priest was reading the evening Mass. Enveloped by the murmuring of the faithful, Nika's head dropped forward in weariness.

The church eventually emptied; the last white-robed altar boy disappeared into the sacristy; only the faint aroma of incense wafted like a soft evening mist through the nave.

Nika dragged herself to one of the side chapels. Candles intended to carry the prayers of the faithful up to heaven threw their flickering light on a young Madonna looking down on her from the altarpiece. She had reddish-blonde hair, just like Nika.

The next morning Nika awoke with a start and jumped out of the pew when the sacristan opened the door of the Basilica dei Frari to let in the old, insomnia-plagued men and women for early Mass. It took her a while to realize where she was. The picture she had looked at the night before was now deep in the shadows.

Nika's face glowed with fever, and she was tortured by thirst. She needed help, a doctor. She had to find Fabrizio . . . Yes, she wanted to go to Fabrizio. When she left the pension that morning, she had taken his address along, as if to protect her in this strange city. Nika staggered toward the door. The daylight was dazzling; she closed her eyes and walked blindly a few steps onto the campo. Then she saw a young man coming toward her from the café across the way. She had seen that face before. It was a pleasant face, but now it looked surprised, shocked.

"Signorina," the young man with the brown eyes called out, "what a surprise to see you again so soon!"

But Nika did not hear what he said. She had fainted.

Later, Nika remembered hardly anything of the two weeks that followed that morning. Only scraps of recognition penetrated her fever, a cup being held to her lips, cool sheets whenever the bed linens were changed. Again and again, she saw the face with the brown eyes, bending over her with concern. At some point, some words did get through to her: "I'm Fabrizio . . . Fabrizio . . . Do you remember me?"

It was many days before she nodded in answer to his question. "We met at the Spa Hotel Maloja," he said. "I was there with Count Primoli . . ."

Then her mind cleared, and after a long time of accepting only fluids, she began to eat solid food again.

She didn't see Fabrizio in the daytime. A servant named Paolina cared for her during those hours. But mostly Nika just lay there, her eyes closed.

Fabrizio came and went. And came again. That was good. She would smile when he sat down next to her bed, then close her eyes again. He read, filed papers, corrected texts, and would leave her bedside to sleep. Once she stretched her hand out for him just as he was about to quietly leave the room. He saw her gesture, came back, took the outstretched hand in his, and stroked her forehead with his other hand. She drew him closer, whispered, "Fabrizio?"

"Yes," he said.

"It's a beautiful name," she murmured and contentedly turned her face away.

Another time she woke up and wished he were lying next to her. But how was she to tell him?

She didn't even ask him about the pension where she had stayed. Only when she saw the bundle with her few things in a corner of the room did she remember that she had even been there. Now, gradually, she began to ask questions.

"The pension . . ."

"You had the address in your pocket. Probably because you were afraid of not finding it again. We had your things picked up from there."

"We . . . ?"

Fabrizio laughed. "We, my parents and myself. You are in my home. You also had my address in your pocket, but I found you before you could come here."

Nika shook her head, incredulous. "But I was in a church . . ."

He laughed again.

"The Chiesa dei Frari is just around the corner from here. I usually have breakfast at the bar across the way. And as I was leaving the bar that morning to go to work at the newspaper, you fell into my arms without even saying good morning."

Nika did not remember.

Fabrizio was so glad she was feeling better that he couldn't suppress teasing her gently. "Yes, that's the way it goes. As soon as you see me, you simply fall into my arms. But from now on you won't need to faint when you do it."

"And so you ran out of the Palazzo Damaskinos?" Fabrizio asked. He'd looked at her with concern for the entire time she'd been recounting her story.

"Yes," Nika replied.

"Your grandfather accused you of being a thief?"

Nika nodded.

"And that's when you ran away." She nodded again.

"You probably run away quite a lot. You also ran away from Mulegns."

She tried to interrupt him.

"It's all right. Don't get upset." He was gradually beginning make sense of Nika's story.

"But now," he said, "now you don't need to run away anymore."

"Oh yes!" she cried. "I told you what happened. They don't want me here in this city."

She was really from another world. "Venice isn't Maloja, where one man believes he can decide whether you may stay there or not." He didn't mention Segantini by name, but added with satisfaction, "And even there he couldn't have. Venice is a big city. The Damaskinos family doesn't have the right to decide who may enter the city and who must leave."

"But they can have me arrested as a thief!"

"Nonsense." Fabrizio shook his head. "They have no proof that the locket was stolen. But *you* can prove that you were abandoned in Mulegns—with the locket. Because you have witnesses you can call on."

Nika said nothing.

"And in spite of that, you'd still like to run away?"

She nodded.

"Why?"

"Because I don't belong anywhere. Not even in my parents' home."

Fabrizio got angry. "But you don't stay a child your whole life long. At some point every human being has to grow up and take responsibility for his or her own life."

"I've waited so many years for this moment," she said, "for the time when I would belong somewhere. To have a family like other people. You don't seem to understand."

"*Buon giorno*," Nika said, as the bent-over woman opened the tall portal of the palazzo. "You probably don't recognize me. A few weeks ago I knocked on the door and asked to speak with Signor Damaskinos."

The woman nodded hesitantly.

"Today, I don't want to speak to him, but to you."

The woman, uneasy and anxious, stepped out into the street. "Come," she said, taking Nika's arm. "Let's go a few steps away from the house."

She led Nika to the Campo San Zaccaria, where they could sit down.

"Now you can ask me what you want to ask."

"Perhaps you already know the question I want to ask."

Nika showed her the locket. "They found me in the Swiss Alps, along with this and a sum of money. I was a baby. Abandoned by a young woman and her companion; they were going to Silvaplana in the Engadine on the post coach."

The woman still didn't say anything, even though Nika paused at the end of each sentence. "I grew up in that village. In the house of a farmer, who took the money and made me work on his farm."

"I was your mother's companion," the women now said, haltingly. "I was her servant from the time she was a young girl. I spent two years traveling with her on an educational trip through Europe. The Damaskinos family is an old merchant family. And we were welcomed everywhere, in the best houses, by her father's respected business associates. Xenia was beautiful and kind. Her father probably hoped that she would marry one of the sons of his foreign business partners. But your mother got pregnant and never revealed the man's name."

People were walking across the square; a cat chased some sparrows; a dog, lying in the shade outside a shop, yawned. Nika sat still, not moving. Suddenly she felt wonderfully relieved. Whatever her mother had done, she had existed. Like everyone else, Nika had a mother whom someone could tell her about.

"Xenia's father is . . ." the woman broke off. "In any case, Xenia was terribly afraid to have him discover the truth. We decided that she would have the child . . ."

" . . . and then abandon it," Nika completed the sentence.

The woman nodded. "It was the only solution."

"Maybe. How did my mother die?"

"Soon after her return, Xenia married a Venetian, a younger friend of her grandfather's. She bore two sons in quick succession. She never spoke about you with anyone. I don't know how happy or unhappy she was. She didn't talk about that either. In 1884, there was a cholera epidemic in Naples. The plague spread quickly, to Venice too. The sirocco, the many travelers. Your mother died of cholera in 1884. Both the boys were still very small. They grew up with Signor Damaskinos, their grandfather."

Now Nika and the old woman were both silent.

"It's a sad story," Nika said finally. "But I am glad that I heard it."

The woman got up from the bench. "I have to go back inside now," she said, and then, uncertain, "would you like a photograph of your mother?"

Nika looked at her in surprise. Of course there were photographs! She nodded, "Yes, I would like that."

"Then wait here. I'll be right back."

And with her bent back, the servant hurried off.

Nika was still holding the sepia-colored photo of her mother. Achille Robustelli saw she was struggling to hold back her tears.

"No," Nika said. "My family did not accept me. It was stupid of me to think that they would be happy about my turning up. It wasn't a nice moment; believe me, it was horrible . . ."

At this point Achille Robustelli got up, drew Nika from her chair, and took her in his arms. It was the most natural thing in the world for him to do. "You're alive. You're here. You're beautiful. Segantini always admired your beauty. And Signor Bonin is probably waiting for you."

Nika smiled, "How did you know . . .?"

"You came into the hotel on his arm. I saw the carriage arrive." He didn't look happy as he said this, and that's why she interrupted him.

"And how are things with Andrina?"

"Nothing's going on with Andrina," he said. "At the moment, she's in Milan. Moreover, Segantini no longer comes here for supper. He's been up on the Schafberg for several days already, painting."

Nika turned her head away. "I have to leave now and freshen up for the evening," she said simply. "And from now on I'm going to call you Achille. Now that I finally saw you again after all this time."

⸘⸙

Carefully, Benedetta put aside the scarf Nika had brought her from Venice. "You can stay in the house overnight, if you like," she said. "Gian is at my sister's in Soglio."

"What is he doing? How is he?" Nika asked.

Benedetta shook her head. "We don't know if it's going well, but he has a girl. Flurina, from the laundry. You don't know her. She wasn't there yet when you worked at the hotel."

"But that's wonderful!" Nika cried.

"We'll see," Benedetta said. "If the same thing happens as with Andrina, then it isn't so wonderful."

"Signor Robustelli told me that Andrina is in Milan."

"You might say it that way. He married her. Not that I was ever for that. But no sooner was she married than she ran away from him. It's a shame! She used him, that's all. She ran away with a rich hotel guest." Benedetta drank her coffee and pushed the

338

cup away. "How the world has changed. I should have said, I don't want Aldo anymore."

"But you do want him," Nika said soothingly.

"Easy to say that, hard to live it," Benedetta said, and crossed herself.

Nika looked around the kitchen wistfully. "Do you still remember, Benedetta, when you bandaged my ankle? At first you didn't want to have me around, and then you took care of me like a mother."

"Never mind, you paid for your meals, after all," Benedetta growled. "And what are you living on in Venice? Roast pigeons don't exactly fly into your mouth there."

This was something Nika knew very well. After her arrival in Venice and as soon as she was feeling a little better, she had begun to wonder what to do next. She needed work. Venice was a favorite tourist destination; there were many hotels and pensions, and Nika had a good reference from Signor Robustelli. The simplest thing would be to ask around for work in the hotels and pensions. But Nika wondered whether there wasn't another way to approach it. She missed drawing, and yet she knew that without some instruction she wouldn't get any further. And it was expensive to buy drawing paper, canvas, and paints. There were several art academies in Venice. But how was she to pay for her education?

Ever since the old servant had given her the photo of her mother, a new idea had been taking shape in her mind. She remembered Count Primoli's photographs, and how enthusiastic she had been about them, along with her conversation with Fabrizio about the modern trendsetting art of photography. She recalled his saying that in Venice, a photographer could earn a decent living. And she thought how happy she herself was that photographs existed. In his photograph of her mother, Antonio Sorgato's art had given her an invaluable gift.

And so, one day she went to the Campiello del Vin, the address of the photography studio that was on the back of the picture she'd been given of her mother.

The shop was still there, but they told her that Antonio Sorgato had died years ago. She left the store in disappointment and walked slowly across the Riva degli Schiavoni toward the Piazza San Marco. And suddenly—because you're more likely to find something that you're already looking for—she noticed that the street was lined by photo studios, one next to the other. Photography was apparently a lucrative art. Especially here, in this place that everyone wanted to remember.

She plucked up her courage, turned around, and walked back to the studio. She asked to see the new owner of the Sorgato Photography Studio. It was the owner himself behind the counter, Signor Filippi. Business was so good that he had to help out in the shop, even though he should have been working in the studio. Consequently, he wasn't averse to hiring an assistant, even if it should happen to be a female one. And since Nika would present a pleasant personality and perhaps even promote sales in his store, he agreed to employ her beginning the following week. When Nika asked whether he would be willing to train her as a photographer, he said, if she showed talent, then there was nothing to stand in the way. In that early period of enthusiastic intoxication with the technique of reproduction, the world could use a lot of photographers—why not female ones too?

Nika left Signor Filippi's store with a feeling of elation such as she'd had only once before—back when she first learned to read and write.

Ecstatic with joy, she bought a bag of bird food and fed the pigeons on the Piazza San Marco. And for the first time in her life, she went to a bar and ordered a glass of Spumante. The cannons sounded from San Giorgio Maggiore, the signal that it was noon, and Nika suddenly felt a great longing for Fabrizio Bonin. She swept all hesitation aside and looked him up. She found him in a small trattoria right near the newspaper building. She stepped up to him with a happy smile and said, "You can send me away too . . ."

He got up in surprise, but she had already kissed him on the lips. They tasted of sea and the spicy peperoncini that the cook in this restaurant favored.

"Why should I send you away?" Fabrizio asked and kissed her in turn.

"I don't know," Nika said. "I'm used to it."

A few weeks later, she found a modest room she could afford. She was self-supporting.

"I've become a photographer," Nika said, and Benedetta looked at her as if she didn't know what to say to that.

"Are you staying for dinner?" she asked, quickly returning to familiar ground.

Nika shook her head. "No. I'm sleeping in the hotel. I didn't know that you had room here. But couldn't we go to visit Gian together before I leave?"

Benedetta put on her skeptical expression. "Now that he finally has a girl? He'll get all mixed up."

Mathilde was blushing as she held out her hand to James, but instead of taking it, he drew her to him and kissed her on both cheeks.

"I brought you something," he whispered in her ear. "I thought you might like to have the photos I took of you . . ."

"But you have to destroy the negatives," she hissed back softly. Sometimes, with a certain sadness, she still remembered that hot summer afternoon in St. Moritz.

Edward turned his gaze discreetly aside, busying himself with Betsy as he had done back then at their picnic on Lake Staz, so that James and Mathilde could have an undisturbed moment. He trusted Mathilde, and to a certain extent, he trusted his friend too.

Betsy wanted to take a walk with Mathilde before supper. "Tilda, come on," she called to her impatiently. "Who knows when you'll be in Switzerland again. I have so many questions to ask you!"

Betsy was incredibly anxious to find out if Mathilde was pregnant. Her sister Emma had hinted at something of that nature.

Edward, on the other hand, knew that James would applaud enthusiastically once he found out that his old schoolmate had pruned back his obsession with plants—it was now just a hobby. After all, Edward had Mathilde to take care of and look after and had therefore returned to his work at the Art Institute.

His father and his father-in-law, moreover, were both very happy about Edward and Mathilde's marriage. Ever since the wedding, Schobinger, the contractor, had been furnishing his buildings exclusively with bathroom appliances produced by Edward's father. The English baths, it was said, were the best of their time. Edward's relationship with his mother-in-law, however, had remained somewhat cool. Emma Schobinger clearly would have preferred an elevation into the banking circles of Zurich. England, after all, was a very unfamiliar land.

Nika also took a walk. She went down to the lake, to the place Gian had first taken her and where Segantini had first seen her. But the lake was not a mirror today; the surface was choppy; you could still see down to the bottom, but you couldn't see the reflection of your own face.

Segantini wasn't coming to the friends' get-together. His staying away had nothing to do with her; he couldn't have known that Nika would be there too. Nika sat down on the bench she had sat on when he sent her away. He had been quite cruel in pushing her to follow her own path. She had gone her own way, just as he had, but she had done it in her own fashion.

Suddenly she felt as if Segantini were standing at the shore of the lake. There were rings in the water, just like the time he'd picked up a flat pebble and thrown it so skillfully that it hopped across the water with several jumps.

"You were right," she whispered, hardly caring that she was speaking to nothing more than the wind. "Although I didn't forgive you for a long time. The locket led me to my family, but they didn't want me. The hope of finding my family was what had helped me survive for so many years! What happens when you realize that your hope will never be fulfilled?"

She thought she heard Segantini laugh, "That's life."

Nika was lost in thought.

"I have to go," she seemed to hear him say.

"Wait!" she cried. "Only a minute more!" But it was as if Segantini was no longer listening.

The ghostly image she had seen so clearly faded. "Stick to art, Nika." His words floated across to her. "It consoles the one who creates it as well as those who look at it."

Nika sobbed.

"Signor Segantini, I wanted so much to tell you that I'm happy. You climbed up into the light. But I long for the darkroom where my pictures are created, pictures that capture the face of the world in my way."

She got up and walked slowly back to the hotel. "I look for the darkness in the light, and in the darkness, I look for the light," she said. She hoped he could hear her.

Even as Nika thought she saw him once more clearly before her, Giovanni Segantini lay dying in an alpine hut up on the Schafberg above Pontresina.

Before he'd left for the Schafberg on September 18, he'd had a strange dream. With his senses alert, he had dreamed that he had died and that he was being carried out of his house on a bier just as he had painted it in his picture *La Morte*.

His son Mario and Baba had accompanied him to the Schafberg. The painting, *La Natura*, on which he wanted to work, was brought up in a wooden crate. The day after his arrival, Segantini immediately set to work on it at a spot not far from the hut in which they were staying.

On Thursday of that week, he complained of severe abdominal pains. By Friday, he felt no better. But he did not want Baba to send for the doctor. On Saturday, his condition was so much worse, however, that Mario rushed down to Pontresina to tell Dr.

Bernhard. The doctor set off immediately, but a snowstorm made the climb in the dark even more difficult.

Dr. Bernhard reached the hut after midnight, around one o'clock. He saw at once that the situation was hopeless. An operation up there was out of the question, and transporting the patient down to the valley was impossible. They had to give up.

Segantini died of peritonitis on September 28, 1899, in the presence of his family.

He was only forty-one years old.

&⟨⟩

"What is that light spot there on the wall?" Nika asked when she came to pick up Achille Robustelli from his office.

"I'll tell you at supper," Achille said.

"I could send you a beautiful photograph to hang there to cover the spot."

"What kind of photograph?"

"Well, any photograph you would like. Perhaps a picture of Venice so that you won't forget your old Italian homeland. I'm a professional photographer." She laughed. "Don't look at me like that. I'll tell you at supper how that came to be."

Afterword

The events and characters in this novel have been freely invented. However, several of the characters are based on actual people: the painter, Giovanni Segantini, and his family; Baba; Dr. Bernhard; Count Primoli; and the hotelier family Badrutt. These individuals really existed. But in the novel, their actions, their words, thoughts, and fantasies are my invention. Nevertheless, I have tried to adapt the fictional actions of these personalities to the historical facts.

The character Nika and her story are completely fictitious, as well as the idea that she was the inspiration for Segantini's painting, *La Vanità*. There were many *Verdingkinder*, contract children, in Switzerland during the period in which the novel is set—and long thereafter. I chose the village Mulegns because the post coach made its noonday stop there. I don't know whether there actually were any *Verdingkinder* in Mulegns or how they were treated.

Occasionally, for dramatic purposes, I have compressed time and made place changes. The representation of historical events, therefore, might sometimes differ slightly from the facts, to conform to the novel's inner logic. However, it would make me happy if my book were to help keep alive the memory of the historical figures who appear in it.

In my work, I have drawn upon many sources, not just the paintings of Giovanni Segantini and their documentation, his writings, letters, and (unfinished) autobiography. Some of the other sources that were especially important for me are listed below.

Karl Abraham, *Giovanni Segantini: Ein psychoanalytischer Versuch* (Leipzig and Vienna, 1911); Peter Böckli, *Bis zum Tod der Gräfin: Das Drama um den Hotelpalast des Grafen de Renesse in Maloja* (Zurich, 2000); and Claudia Hagmayer's dissertation, *Bis dass der Tod euch scheided: Witwen in der Schweiz um 1900* (Zurich, 1994). Of particular importance for me was the article by Tina Grütter, "Selbstbildnis eines radikalen Pantheisten: Das Gemälde *La morte* von Giovanni Segantini," which appeared in the *Neue Zürcher Zeitung* of May 8/9, 2004. Tina Grütter's interpretation and discovery that Segantini's self-portrait in *L'Eroe Morto* also appears in *La Morte* decisively altered my perception of that painting—and so I would like to express my gratitude to Tina Grütter for this far-reaching observation.

In conclusion, many friends contributed to the successful completion of my book by their critical and repeated readings of the manuscript: Lia Franken, Katrin Eckert, Ursula Hasler, Katrin Wiederkehr, Vera Wäckerlig, and Peter Lohmann, to name only a few.

I have only praise for the commitment, the care, and the patience of my publisher and my editor, Hannelore Harmann. To them, too, I extend my warmest gratitude.

About the Author

© Matthias Mettner 2012

German author Dörthe Binkert's acclaimed first novel, *She Wore Only White*, merged history and fiction in the resplendent tale of a young woman fleeing her past on a transatlantic voyage to America. Binkert, who has published nonfiction as well as fiction, has a PhD in literature, and spent decades working as an editor and editor in chief for several major German publishing houses. Now a freelance writer, she lives in Zurich, Switzerland.

About the Translator

Margot Bettauer Dembo is a German-to-English translator. She has translated the work of Judith Hermann, Zsuzsa Bank, and Joachim Fest, among others. She was awarded the Goethe-Institut/Berlin Translator's Prize in 1994 and the Helen and Kurt Wolff Translator's Prize in 2003. Dembo also worked as a translator for two feature documentary films, *The Restless Conscience*, nominated for an Academy Award, and *The Burning Wall*.